SHARK'S
Pride

SHARK'S EDGE: BOOK TWO

ANGEL PAYNE & VICTORIA BLUE

SHARK'S
Pride

SHARK'S EDGE: BOOK TWO

ANGEL PAYNE & VICTORIA BLUE

WATERHOUSE PRESS

For David, Ivy & Kadin.

The original pride of my existence.
My support team, sounding board, laughter,
strength, and light in all things—I love you dearly.

—Victoria

For Tom and Jess.

You are always and forever my pride, my joy, my life.

—Angel

CHAPTER ONE

SEBASTIAN

"There's no place like home" had never rung truer than that moment. I was back in my private plane, among my personal belongings, with familiar comforts at my fingertips.

If only my nerves would settle into a calm state. We'd be taking off from Hong Kong within the hour, and I'd be back at home soon enough. So many balls in the air—always so many balls.

But it wasn't a new situation I found myself in. Not by any stretch of the imagination. So why was I so agitated?

I already knew the answer.

The X factor jacking my system to red alert was Abbigail Gibson.

More alarms blared through my brain. This—whatever it was with her—shouldn't be this way already, should it? I had no actual frame of reference. Ridiculous but true. Outside of the few internet sites I'd researched regarding the art of dating, I had no concrete facts to go on.

Yes, I was doing research.

About how to date a woman.

What other choice did I have? My father was a deadbeat long before he was actually dead. From that point, I was on my own. The only adults who took an interest in my well-being in my formative years were women. Not exactly the mentors a teen boy could ask for advice on how to get laid.

And not that I ever had to worry about that specific topic. Until, once again, enter the X factor. She was getting good at this role, my sweet Abbigail Gibson. Upending all the usual apple carts in my life. But I had this particular topic nailed down. Ironic choice of words, considering I'd enthusiastically nailed Abbi to her virginal bed the night before I left for Malaysia on an unscheduled ten-day trip.

Unscheduled—and terribly inconvenient.

No. What was the word past that? Way past?

Torture? Persecution?

But at the risk of pathetic redundancy, I'd had no choice. Dire problems with import and export embargos needed to be addressed. Issues had arisen that could delay freight movement in a profitable shipping lane for the Shark Enterprises' foreign cargo transport arm. Because when it came to the maritime logistics industry, I wanted to be king. Kings didn't sit by and watch their kingdom crumble. That meant getting in the trenches where and when it was necessary. And because we were meeting in some very remote locales in this case, the exact *where* was an undeveloped area in Malaysia. Sweaty, grimy, no-Wi-Fi-signal-to-be-found Malaysia.

The timing couldn't have been worse. I'd gotten the call within hours after Abbigail and I spent our first night together. Yeah, that night. The incredible hours in which I'd stripped her of her innocence.

No, fuck that.

I took her virginity. Popped her cherry. Shredded her V-card. I needed to man up and call the act what it was. All my desperate romanticizing since wasn't getting me anywhere.

I had no damn idea why I was still trying to keep up such a ridiculous charade. The well-intended gentleman act hadn't worked over the last ten days either. I thought I'd try the standard boyfriend approach for the first time in my life. On one of the few occasions I had cell phone service, I contacted the florist back in LA with specific instructions to have flowers sent to Abbigail's condo every day around five p.m. so she would be home to receive them. I scheduled one bouquet for each day until I was due to return—ensuring I'd be on her mind even in a small, manipulated way. And yes, she'd be fuming and lecturing about that grandiosity, but I didn't care.

Because God certainly knew, she was all I could think about.

The way she tasted, sweet and creamy. The way she smelled, sugary and spicy. How her body undulated beneath my thrusting one, and the way her pussy clutched around me when she came. Every moment of my time with her burned with dazzling brightness in my senses—and thank Christ, because the woman definitely didn't seem interested in strolling down memory lane herself. Whenever she did finally return any of my text messages, it was a short one- or two-word reply. And when I prompted her to elaborate, she'd beg off with some lame-ass excuse. She was busy with supplier issues. Or equipment repairs. Or website glitches. Or needing to go to bed early because she hadn't slept well the night before. If it wasn't one thing, it was another.

But I already knew the score.

Could read, even from this hellhole on the other side of the earth, exactly what was going on in that busy, beautiful mind of hers.

She'd already invented at least twenty different scenarios

of why I hadn't been in contact. I was sure of it. If I had to guess, much like with a missing person search or a crime scene investigation, the first forty-eight hours were crucial. That was when it had all gone to hell for her. I had been entirely out of pocket, and it doomed me to "just like every other guy" territory. The Siberia of partner candidates. The place where otherwise quality men were hung out to dry, unfairly judged for relationship crimes they didn't commit but never had a chance to explain.

Sultry, steamy Malaysia to desolate, barren Siberia in the blink of an eye.

The worst part of it all? My helplessness to do a thing about it. Not from here. If I pushed and called her out on it, she'd deny, deny, deny. If I made any more gestures besides the flowers, she'd evade, evade, evade.

Right now, I wasn't just stuck on an airport tarmac. I was bogged in geographical limbo.

Fuck this.

The refrain steeled a new resolve in me.

But I refocused. Enough to ditch what little was left of my ego and stab at the icon for her number. As the number rang through, I grimaced. The sixteen-hour time difference made it difficult to plan for reaching her at an opportune time, but I'd take thirty seconds if I could get it.

"Hello?"

She answered as if she didn't recognize the caller. I tightened my scowl. "Hi." Not that my stupid stammer reflected that. "It's . . . me."

"Oh." Her breathless spurt vibrated the line—and stirred my cock even more. "Sebastian. Hey."

Hey?

"Hey yourself. What are you doing?"

"Working. It's the start of my route. I'm on limited time. The BI security guys don't like me to stay for too long."

At once, my chest compressed and my blood boiled. "The BI Building?" I gritted. "You're at Viktor Blake's?"

I wasn't expecting her light exasperated huff. I was still dealing with the surprise from that, instead of the fire and fury for which I was braced, when she chided, "You remember that Blake Industries is also my client, right?"

"Just not your most important client."

"Bas."

And just like that, her sigh was inflating my cock. "What?"

"I'm glad you called."

I blew out rough air for myself. "Me too, beautiful."

"But I really do need to go."

"Okay."

I issued the concession without much fight. She was telling the truth; the same limited-curb situation existed in front of my building. But after hanging up and looking at our call time in my log—only twenty-seven seconds—I gave in to my rising frustration and threw my cell phone across the small jet's cabin. The device bounced off the interior fuselage wall and landed in the center aisle, face up.

Vela's big toothless baby grin stared up at me, where she held the prized position of wallpaper on my lock screen. "Hell," I uttered. Between the balls-deep longing for Abbi and the heart-deep craving for my family, my logic was lost.

Without overthinking the consequences, I grabbed the device and dialed my sister.

One ring. Two rings. Three.

"Hey, big brother." Pia's confident voice came over the

line. "*Apa khabar?*"

"Such an overachiever, Dub. I'm fine, thank you for asking. But if I don't hear another word of Malay ever again, I'll be just fine with that, too."

"Ah, well. When in Rome . . . or so the saying goes."

"So it does."

"Shouldn't you be in the air by now?"

"On the ground in Hong Kong at the moment."

"Delayed?"

"Just for a bit. We had to refuel, and Shane said he needed to file a new flight plan. I didn't get into the details of why." I raised the window shade and looked out. It was two forty-five in the morning local time, and the busy airport hummed with activity regardless.

"Did you call just to hear my voice, Bas? You miss your sister that much?" Her soft chuckle was her way of calling me out. I never called just to shoot the shit, and she knew it.

"Fine. I'll just get to it, then. I— Well, I need some advice."

"From me?"

I was grateful she let me sit for a second, reorganizing my thoughts—and getting used to my humility. At last I muttered, "It's about—" But I paused, not really knowing what to call Abbigail. She was more than a friend, but calling her my girlfriend seemed ridiculous too.

Why is this so difficult?

"Is it the caterer?" Pia cut in. "What is her name again? Abbigail something? Gibbons?"

"Gibson. Yes." Thank God for sisters with quick brains as well as razor-sharp instincts. "Abbigail Gibson. It—this—regards her."

"Ahhh, I knew it."

"Stop."

"I just had a feeling, that's all."

"I said *stop*. I'm serious, Pia. I need to talk to someone about this, and you're literally the only person I can think of. The only person I have."

"Oh, gee. You really know how to make a girl feel special. Are you laying it on this smooth with Ms. Gibson too? Lucky girl."

"You know what I mean." I paused a beat. "You do, right?" The last thing I wanted to do was hurt her feelings.

"Okay, tell me what's going on. What has you so tied up in knots? I can probably count on one hand the times I've heard you sound like this—and never over a woman. She must be special."

During the assertion, her voice had gentled, inflating my lungs with a calming breath.

But Christ, where do I even begin?

"I fucked her before I left on this trip."

Guess that was as good a place as any—though Pia's spurt might have been a protest otherwise. "Okay, Bas. You ever heard of TMI?"

"There's an actual reason I'm telling you that—if you'd just let me finish." I waved my hand through the air as if she could see my gesticulations. "Maybe this was a mistake, talking to you about this."

"No, keep going. I'll be quiet until you say you're through." There was a prolonged silence before she finally coaxed, "Bas, I promise. Continue with the story."

I exhaled long and loud before proceeding. "Well, Abbigail and I have been dancing around our obvious attraction to each other for a while. It's been building and building."

"Says the man named the Lothario of LA four years running?"

I ignored that. "It just happened, okay? A little bit each day, when she would come into my office with lunch. And then there was that day I saw her at Vela's game— Well, shit, you were there . . ." I trailed off without thinking about it, lost in a few seconds of memory about my sister's censuring gaze while Abbi and I eye-fucked each other across the soccer field.

"So what happened?" Pia prompted.

"I finally made a move," I filled in. "That day at the game, as a matter of fact." And yes, deliberately omitted the details about damn near having to blackmail Abbi into our first date. That was the real TMI here.

"Okaaayy . . ." she said in a way that urged me to continue.

"Then she shocked the living hell out of me by telling me she was a virgin."

Pia's gasp could've been heard across the ocean without the phone's aid. "Oh, shit. Sorry. I'm sorry. That slipped out. But dude, that's huge."

"That's what she said too."

I chuckled under my breath. She gasped again.

"Oh my God. You did not just go there with me."

"You lobbed it over the plate, Dub. All I had to do was swing."

Smack. That was probably her palm against her forehead, adding volume to my chuckle. "Continue with the actual facts of the story, please," she ordered.

"At first, I told her to go take care of the problem. I was also clear that if she still wanted to see if something could happen between us, great. But I was in no way equipped to deal with a virgin."

Yet another gasp from her. No, this was a full huff. "Sebastian. Albert."

"Cassiopeia. Artemis." I mimicked her serious tone—for all of two seconds. It was impossible not to laugh when I let her full name fly. "Boy, our parents fucked you good with that name."

"Yeah, yeah," she groused as I let the laugh burst out in full. But honestly, the opportunity would never get old. Poor Pia had to wear our parents' badge of irresponsibility from their hippy phase in the shape of her damn name—yet she'd always just used it to gain strength and courage. My sister was the poster child for making lemonade out of lemons. Young women of the world could take a few lessons from the incredible lady on the other end of this phone line.

"Are you done?" she snipped. I could picture her inspecting her manicure or doodling idly in the margin of the papers on her office desk.

"Yes, mother dearest," I voiced like a bratty child, then added in my normal voice, "Lighten up, Dub."

"Now that's funny," she snickered. "Seriously. That, coming from you, the man who usually has a stick rammed so far up his—"

"I get the imagery, Pia." I cut her off easily, relaxing with our tried-and-true volleys instead of tackling the real problem at hand. Not that she'd let me get away with it for much longer.

"Enough stalling, big brother." Yep, right on time for calling me on my shit again. "What's the actual problem here? Out with it, Bas."

Just rip the fucking bandage off, man.

"All right." Deep inhale. "I had to leave." I stuttered for a second. "I mean, right after." Paused for two more beats. "Right after we ... uhh ... finished."

"Finished?"

"Fucking. Right after I took her virginity."

"Ohhh."

That definitely wasn't a good *oh*.

"Nooo."

And I didn't dare consider where she was going with that response either.

"It wasn't good, Pia."

"You think?"

I ignored her comment. "I mean, it wasn't bad. The sex was outstanding, in fact. Leaving was bad. I didn't want to leave. And I wasn't a dick about it, I swear! I had no choice! I explained why I had to leave. She understood. She said she understood ..." My voice trailed off as I heard my own absurdity.

"Okay, let me see if I understand this," Pia stated, sounding like a damn schoolmarm now. "You took a thirty-year-old woman's virginity and then left immediately after? And now you haven't seen her for two weeks? Is that what you're saying right now?"

"For Christ's sake. It wasn't like that. Not at all!" The words rushed from my lips, fast and frantic. Defending myself wasn't familiar territory. I always did what I did with little to no apology—at least to this point in my life.

Was that what I was doing here? Apologizing?

Was this what some people called *regret*?

No wonder I'd avoided this feeling like the plague.

"Well, by all means, Sebastian, explain to me what it *was* like, then."

"For starters, she's not thirty."

"You know what I mean. Thirty-ish. Whatever."

This was going to be a real mic drop.

"She's twenty-two."

She whimpered, and I could picture her face falling into the cradle of her hands. "Oh Baaaassss . . ."

"That's well within legal boundaries." I forced the nonchalance, knowing her reaction was only the first of this kind that I'd field. Hell, it'd be the same no matter who I spoke to. Although I was also sure most men would give me conspiratorial nods, maybe even slipping in high fives when their significant other wasn't watching.

"Barely," Pia finally bit out. She took a deep breath, likely centering herself. "Okay, go on. God, I'm going to regret saying that, aren't I?"

"You're making a bigger deal out of it than needs to be. It may be a moot point, anyway, given the way she's treating me now."

I cringed at the petulance in my voice. Apparently feeling regret wasn't enough? Now I was discovering the glories of being pussy whipped after one fuck?

Jesus Christ.

"Well, you had sex with the girl—her first intercourse ever—and then skipped town."

"I did not skip town." I gritted my teeth to rein in my frustration. "That's not how it was, Pia."

My sister let out one of her finest, longest sighs this time. "Well, regardless of how you've mentally rewritten history, it's not the most reassuring chain of events—especially to an inexperienced young woman."

"I explained why I had to go out of town. She said she understood." She had said that, hadn't she? "She owns a business, for Christ's sake! She knows how business keeps pushing and pulling, no matter what you have going on in your personal life. The woman is mature beyond her years." A warm smile spread across my lips as I thought about some marketing ideas I'd been brainstorming with Abbi while she set up my lunch one day. I had to shake my head a bit to remind myself of the mess I was actually wading through at the moment.

"She wouldn't have said she understood if she was going to act juvenile about everything afterward," I insisted one last time.

Pia didn't respond for a long moment. When she did, it was with another turn toward tenderness. And damn it, I instantly longed for her fury again. "Maybe she's acting that way because she's exactly that." Yeah, definitely the fire and brimstone instead. "Have you considered the possibility, Bas?"

I fumed. "She doesn't act immature about anything else. Ever. It's so out of character." I drove my free hand through my hair. "Damn it, Pia. I think that's why I'm so confused. I wouldn't have predicted this in a hundred years. It's a total bait and switch."

"A bait and—" She interrupted herself with a choke. Dread invaded my chest. Uh-oh. I'd crossed the battle lines and was now into the realm of the unspoken, invisible sisterhood bond that existed between women. "This is all her fault, then?" And yes, my sister was ever the enforcer of that realm.

"No, that's not what I'm saying." I sighed, already knowing I was defeated in this imaginary battle. That, joined with my exhaustion from the travel, was wrecking my guts, cell by painful cell.

"Good. I was just making sure. Because whatever point you are trying to make here, Bas? It sounds a lot like you're just assigning blame. Tread carefully. And I don't mean with me. I mean with Abbigail."

"But—"

"Carefully."

"Christ. I've even sent flowers!" I offered, despite her scoff coming loud and clear across the miles. "Every day!"

Pia huffed again. No way could I mistake the reaction for anything other than what it was. Disapproval for a ridiculous, over-the-top—not to mention cliché—gesture that Abbi would undoubtedly see right through as well.

"Things are really screwed up, Dub."

"Hold on; I've got to alert the press." But the gibe was given with underlines of love, along with sincere sympathy. My sister, the honest and brave badass that she was, didn't know how to give comfort in any other way.

"The phone service was abysmal where we were in Malaysia," I told her. "Believe me, I tried to get a line out—more than once."

"I believe you."

"But will she?" I countered. "If I know her at all, I'm sure she's convinced I've completely ghosted her. I talked to her so infrequently, and the few texts she actually sent back were so detached . . ." My words drifted off as her text messages flashed through my memory, making me cringe with dread.

"Okay, so it's time to stop wallowing here. It's really not a good look on you. But the Sebastian Shark I know certainly doesn't wallow." Her voice was stamped with confidence.

"No. He sure as hell doesn't." Still, I kneaded my furrowed brow in an attempt to banish the stress.

"He makes plans. He fixes things. And he goes after what he wants."

"But he needs to stop talking about himself in the third person, Dub, because it's super narcissistic and a touch creepy. But you're right about everything else."

"Fine. Point taken." She let a comfortable silence settle between us for a few beats until I looked at my phone screen to see if I'd dropped the call. Her voice came back on the line just before I was going to ask her why she'd gotten so quiet. "So what are you going to do about this?"

Isn't that the million-dollar question?

"I was . . . kind of hoping you had that answer," I confessed. "Admittedly, I'm way outside my wheelhouse here."

Her new pause was like a long-distance hug. "You just need to sit down and talk to her, Bas. Tell her how you feel— and I'm talking about the feelings above your waistline. It's the only way to make sure signals don't get crossed and messages aren't misunderstood in a new relationship. And we both know how equally uncomfortable we are talking about our feelings."

I gave her a token grumble of agreement.

"I love you, Cassiopeia. You know that I do, right?"

"I most definitely do. I'll talk to you when you get home?"

"You will. Bye, Dub."

"Bye, Bas. Have a safe flight home."

My sister disconnected. For several minutes after, I sat staring at my phone's dark screen, letting her final word roll through my mind.

Home.

Twelve more hours and I'd be back on American soil. Another two and I'd be walking into my own house.

All of that felt damn good right now. But not completely fulfilling. To accomplish that, I had to track down the redhead who'd made an Olympic sport out of evading me. The second I did, I'd set her back on track.

Only then would everything be right in my world again.

CHAPTER TWO

SEBASTIAN

First days back at work after being away always reminded me of what it must be like to work in a trauma emergency room. From the moment I walked in, every person with a problem thought theirs was the most important and in the direst need of my attention.

I spent the first two hours triaging the perceived emergencies and then handling the only two that actually were. Once those situations were dealt with, the smaller fires were either passed on to the department heads that should've handled them in the first place or scheduled through Terryn to return when they could present viable solutions along with the dilemma. Which was something I preached to my staff over and over. I didn't want a line of whiners at my door every morning. I needed a team of problem solvers. If someone couldn't be one of those types of thinkers, Shark Enterprises wasn't the place for them.

The morning hours went fast—to the point that when Grant stuck his head in, I had daunting stacks of things to run through with him. Even more alarming: I wasn't sure we'd be finished by lunch. But damn it, I'd be free when Abbigail arrived if it killed me. She'd been judiciously ignoring me since I'd gotten back from my trip, and that point alone kept working its way back to the top of my personal priority list.

Since my goal wasn't to be dead when she arrived, I dug in on business priorities. First things first. I committed my whole attention as Grant filled me in on the progress he was making with the city regarding the plans for the Edge. After all, this was the original problem that had taken me from Abbi our first night together, and I needed to feel like at least some part of that debacle was cleared up. Our planning commission liaison was already showing his worth by helping navigate through some early red tape with the permit rejections we'd encountered two weeks prior.

After that was handled, we discussed my trip. Our specific topic was how the new Malaysian Ministry of Transport's planned changes could affect the way we moved cargo in and out of that area of the world. Malaysia was one of the most significant shipping lanes for our company. If we started having trouble with new embargos or restrictions, we might need to consider alternate routes for our shipments.

"That's ridiculous." Grant stood and paced along the windows. "We will add not just days but weeks to our transport times. We can't bring changes like that to our brokers. We will lose business faster than we can imagine." Though I held my hand up to calm him, he wasn't having it. "Seriously, Bas. This is huge. And I mean huge in a bad way. Not huge in a good, nine-inch cock way."

"How did you turn this into a dick reference?"

He shrugged and grinned. "It's a gift; I don't know. Why aren't you freaking out, though? This will cost us millions in business. You understand that, right?" His smile dropped as he rubbed the back of his neck.

"I understand completely. But you haven't let me finish." I

steepled my fingers. "I've already worked out a solution."

"Why didn't you say that?" he snapped. "Why let me dangle on the end of the line over here?"

"Well, for one thing, it's kind of fun." I added a smirk, making him scowl harder. "Watching you get all worked up, knowing it's for no good reason. And honestly, let it be a lesson to you for interrupting someone before he's finished making his point."

"God." He shook his head. "You can be such a bastard."

I shrugged. "True. Should we call the press?"

He kept up his glare but recovered quicker than most, having dealt with my shit for so many years. "What's the solution, then? Spit it out, man."

I rested my chin atop my fingers. "My mind went to the same place yours did, of course. And there were two solutions. Number one: come up with an alternate shipping lane, which we naturally already have in that area, right? We already explored all of this when strategizing for other unforeseen problems. Weather, pirates...whatever."

Grant nodded the whole time I spoke. Everything I'd mentioned were situations for which we had to prepare daily. Nothing here was breaking news, reflected in the focused calm of his interjection. "What's the second solution?"

"We need to work out a deal with the Malaysian Transportation Minister."

"So...in through the back door." Grant nodded while he absorbed the concept.

"Exactly. We give them what they want. Which of course, ultimately, is more money."

Grant grunted, putting the pieces together. "One way or another."

"For them, the public sees embargos. But if we could work some sort of deal behind the scene ..." I tipped my head and arched my brows. "As long as they get paid, what does it matter, right?"

"Following you so far." Grant perched on the back of the sofa while I settled back behind my desk. "Is there a deal on the table? What did you offer them?"

"It's practically a no-brainer," I asserted. "We route as many of our shipments through that lane as possible, with a quarter percent off the top to the ministry. We may even look at funneling most of our shipments in the area through that lane, if it proves to be easier and faster. If we can get a guarantee that shipments won't be held up in customs like they are in the other ports and we can also avoid routinely striking ports, it's a win-win."

I watched Grant's scowl transform as he weighed the possibilities of my statement. At last, he offered, "So really, what's it going to matter if a few extra miles are tacked on to each trip, if customs and duties are cheaper?"

"Or nonexistent."

"Not to mention demurrage while docks have workers on strike or limited staff to load and unload because of union bullshit. If we look at that line item alone on the last fiscal year's purchase and loss? It's staggering, Bas."

"Trust me, I know. That's what made this seem like a perfect marriage. The government is as crooked as they come. They don't care how the money comes in, just that it does. If we are paying them at the back door, they can work their books however they see fit. If we pay at the front door, it all has to be aboveboard and not as lucrative for the individuals involved."

"Good deal, man. Good deal."

I jacked my brows a little higher. "What's up?" And then pointed to the phone in his hand with a quick nod. "That's the fifth time you've checked your phone, Twombley. And the sixth."

Grant grunted again, though with half the force of the first time. "Sorry, man—but I need to get out of here. Lunch meeting across town. If I leave now, I should get there just in time."

"Understood. Off you go, then." I tried to infuse it with more sincerity than my own restlessness. All in all, I was just as glad he'd be gone by the time Abbigail arrived. The more of the woman I could have to myself, the better. I handled my eagerness by turning my attention back to the paperwork mountain on my desk. Though so many things could be handled electronically in a modern business world, a surprising number of things still weren't. Terryn had several piles neatly separated and labeled for me, coded in order of how they needed to be handled. One pile needed signatures. The next needed to be reviewed and returned to her for corrections. A third stack was all new items, or so the label told me. I knew better. They were problems in disguise.

I moved that last pile off to the side of my desk. Way off. I'd tackle that mess after lunch. At the moment, my brain was only good for blindly scrawling my name on the indicated blank and moving on to the next.

I moved through the stack efficiently until the familiar knock came on my door.

She wasn't a moment too soon. My nerves and my stomach were throwing in the towel, and if Abbigail hadn't shown up when she did, it would've taken three men and a boy to stop me from texting her again.

"In!" I called while resuming my mindless task. No sense changing my habits completely for the woman—or so I kept trying to fool myself. But a man had to keep his balance somewhere, and the woman had already upended me in so many other ways.

"Hey there."

Abbigail said it quietly while scooting her head and shoulders beyond the edge of the door. She gripped the wood like it was a floating panel from the sinking Titanic. I'd never seen anything more adorable.

"Sebastian?"

"Yes?"

"I asked if this was a good time," she prompted. "Are you ready for lunch?"

I swore to God, every answer in my mind sounded over-the-top. Maybe beyond that. But I was helpless to verbalize any of them as I looked all the way up, into her eyes. The world fell away. The minutes stopped mattering. And as soon as she walked over to stand in front of my desk, my balance went to hell too.

God, I'd missed her.

I stood abruptly, knocking my chair back into the now-worn dent in the bookcase.

Abbigail's sharp inhale at my sudden movements just spurred me on more. I rounded my desk to stand directly in front of her, so close that my slacks rustled in the thick canvas of her apron. Her chest dipped with stuttering breaths as she tried to feign calm control.

I slid my index finger beneath her chin and tilted her face up until our eyes locked.

"Hi," I barely whispered.

"Hi."

"You're stunning."

She reached up to nervously toy with her ponytail. I stopped her by cuffing her wrist and directing it back down to her side. "Now you say, 'thank you.'"

A small grin quirked at the corner of her mouth before she said, almost too quietly, "Thank you."

"I'm going to kiss you," I told her, much like I did the first time our mouths met in the park after Vela's soccer game.

"Okay." Her whisper was even softer than before. And a thousand times sexier, if my cock was a correct barometer.

"I'm still not asking, Abbigail." I squinted my eyes playfully—yes, playfully—as I pressed in for a proper hello. Her warm lips welcomed me, yielding beneath mine. I stayed there for a few moments before pulling back, not allowing myself to deepen the kiss . . . waiting on her to either demand or deny me at this point.

As right as her gorgeous little mewl was, I hesitated to take her mouth again. If I started more, I'd never be able to stop. My cock spoke up loud and clear about that point, as well. I was damn sure if—no, when—I got inside her pussy again, I'd want to spend hours showing her all the ways I had missed what was mine.

Mine.

Christ, how right that sounded too.

After stepping back to put even more space between us, I waited for Abbi to look at me again. Instead, she jerked around and started busying herself with my lunch. I cleared my throat in objection—not that she heeded the glaring hint. I got a fast, furtive glance before she continued bustling about.

"Over here?" she asked, all business in her tone. "The

usual spot?"

"That's fine."

I waved my hand, not caring if she left the food in her van for the afternoon. I wanted her attention, not her damn sandwich.

And I was damn determined to get it. No matter what that entailed.

As the resolve firmed in my mind, I walked over to the sofa, positioning myself behind her as she bent over the coffee table. The room was quiet except for the distinct clanks of silverware as she carefully laid out my setting. No matter. The sound was as erotic as a jazz tune, especially with this incredible view. Her tight ass was right in front of me, begging me to grip her by both hips and grind my desperate hard-on into the seam of her ass.

"Fuck. Girl."

The temptation was too damn great, and by now I was too damn weak. With a low hum, I surrendered. With ruthless purpose, I dug my fingers into her flesh through her black pants. Not denim today, thank God. They were made of some sort of stretchy cotton—lightweight with an elastic waistband. One sharp tug and they'd be out of my way. Within seconds, I could be balls-deep in her heat. The heat I could actually feel against my cock as I ground harder into her.

"Oh!" Thankfully, Abbigail said nothing else. Just braced her hands on the coffee table, dropped her head between her outstretched arms, and allowed me to rut against her.

"Such a good girl. Dirty girl," I choked out. "I could come like this, just rubbing myself against you. Imagining I'm inside you again. Would you like that, baby?"

"Goooddd, yes." Once more, she gave up on words, though

her finishing moan was pure music to my ears. And every blazing, burgeoning inch of my body.

"Do you want me to make a mess on your back?" The words tumbled from the darkest places of my libido...the raunchiest corners of my mind. "To come all over your work clothes, Abbigail? Then every other customer, every man, would smell me while you serve them their lunch. Would you like that, my gorgeous girl? To be marked by me like that?"

I wrapped my fist in her ponytail and swiftly yanked her up to stand. She cried out as her back slammed against my front. Her breathing was a ragged match to my own, and I sank my teeth into the side of her neck, right over her throbbing pulse point.

The door to my office swung open.

Seriously?

Terryn was the barging intruder. Oh, she knocked, of course—but did it as she opened the door.

And then gasped in raw shock.

Well, she deserved the eyeful she got. Nosy wench.

"Oh! Excuse me!" My assistant was unable to tear her eyes from what she'd walked in on. There was no possible way to hide the erection I was sporting either.

"Shit. Shit. Shit." Abbi scurried from my grip, smoothing her apron and rushing to the far side of the penthouse. She stopped and flattened herself in front of the refrigerator.

"Terryn." My voice was beyond lethal, evidenced by the steadiness in my tone. "If you ever, and I do mean ev-er, walk in that door"—I stabbed my index finger in the direction of said door—"without clear verbal permission to do so, your employment here will be terminated on the spot."

I finally paused, waiting to see or hear some sort of

acknowledgment of what I had said. Terryn darted her eyes from my crotch to my face, swooping down for another visual loop, before she nodded. Honestly, if I weren't so fucking pissed off, her gawk would've been funny.

When she didn't respond, I finally seethed through clenched teeth, "Have I made myself completely clear?"

She visibly jumped. In my peripheral, I saw Abbigail jerk too.

"Y-Y-Yes, Mr. Shark. I'm so sorry. I didn't realize she was still here."

"She?" I tilted my head to the side, trying the word on for size. Not a great fit. At all. "She?" And that made it official. The woman was really determined to piss me off with her antics. "She has a name, and you damn well know what it is."

"Y-Y-Yes, sir."

"Then show some respect—and you can start with an apology to her!"

"Bas..." After grabbing a pair of bottled waters from the fridge, Abbigail had been making her way back over to the discipline zone in front of the couches. She pushed the water into my hand while muttering, "Don't make this more uncomfortable than—"

"No." The cutoff came from a surprisingly resolved Terryn, who stepped forward like a castigated colt ready to make amends and accept its bridle. "He's...he's right, Ms. Gibson," she mumbled. "And I'm very sorry I interrupted you and Mr. Shark. It was inconsiderate of me." The girl focused on Abbi's kneecaps the entire time she groveled. She seemed stunned when Abbi stretched her hand forward, palm up and fingers open.

"Hey, no worries, okay?" My girl extended a verbal olive

branch along with her gesture, which might as well have been a shovel into my chest. She kept finding new ways to utterly astound my cynical soul.

And Terryn was unearthing new ways to make sure I lost none of that pessimism.

My rude—make that very rude—assistant repaid Abbi's kindness by just looking long and hard at the offered hand. The second I was tempted to bark at her, she turned on her heel and hurried out of the office. Abbigail was left standing with her hand outstretched and a bemused quirk on her kiss-stung lips.

"I...uhhh...think I'd better go too. Your lunch is all set up, and I'm sure you have a ton of work to catch up on."

She hurriedly set the bottle of water on the table by my lunch and then beelined toward the door. Well, tried to. I was quicker though, so I blocked her path by coming around the other side of the sofa and stepping in front of the large portal.

Abbi thrust out a hip in frustration. "I think I've done enough damage here for one day, don't you?"

I stretched a hand out, reaching for her hip that she had conveniently accentuated for me.

"Seriously." She tried batting my hands away, but I didn't budge. "You can stop all the chivalry now, Bas."

"Oh, dear girl. I am feeling anything but chivalrous."

"Is that so?" She canted a brow.

"When can I see you?" I demanded in a growl. "For a longer period than..." I waved my hand randomly around the room. "This."

"Really, Bas, you can stop all of this." She mimicked my gesture, and I scowled.

"What are you talking about?" I was fast on the way to genuine frustration.

"The doting boyfriend bit you're playing at. It's unnecessary. And I certainly don't expect it."

"Doting?" I all but laughed the word but quickly firmed my tone. "What did I miss? I've been gone for ten days and missed you. I couldn't keep my hands to myself before I left, and that problem seems to have grown exponentially while I was gone." I tried to drive in the truth of all that by pulling her against me again, but she resisted.

Again.

"Look, my ego can only take so many rejections in one afternoon, Abbigail." When she went for a wide-eyed gape, I dipped my head in and persisted. "What the hell's really going on here?"

She opened her mouth, but only a rough huff emerged. After resetting her lips to a tighter line, she finally said, "I'm not an obligation, Sebastian. Certainly not yours."

Though she added the last beneath her breath, every cell in my body protested its implication. She'd be mine in whatever way I declared it, damn it!

"Explain."

She raised a brow, maybe not appreciating the clipped tone I used, but I refused to budge. This was odd behavior, pretty clearly tied into our reunion—such as it had been—and she owed me more than ten nebulous mumbles about it.

"Listen." Her shoulders sagged, and she rubbed at her temples. "I don't want to be the proverbial anchor weighing you down. I know you're used to just being with a woman and then leaving and not having to look back. You don't normally have this extra stress the day after." She dropped her hand with a resigned sigh. "The fortnight after. *Whatever.*"

"I told you this was going to be different. You're different.

Have you forgotten already?" I caught her off guard at last, making it possible to drag her to me, ruthlessly *whumping* our bodies together. "Maybe a reminder is in order, Red?"

I didn't let her get a word in on me. I tucked in with focused intent, running my nose along her jaw to her ear and inhaling her tantalizing fragrance. The smell had haunted me every second we were apart. Even my dreams were filled with the sugar-and-spice aroma that clung to her skin. The woman was invading every aspect of my existence, yet she stood in front of me with that same unnerved look on her face.

Shit. Where was the disconnect?

Something told me it ran deeper than the ten days I had been out of the country.

Much deeper.

"I'm serious, girl." As I prompted it against the soft curve of her ear, I slid a hand to the front of her throat. I just rested it there, feeling the throbs of her pulse and the anxious undulations of her gulps. My God, how they both turned me on.

"I—I know," she rasped.

"Then why are we back here?" I charged. "I thought you understood. I'm not fucking around, Abbigail. I want to do this with you." Maybe a little more than wanted, if I was being honest. "I want to see you. Be with you." The new resonance in my voice caused her to shiver in my arms. Despite that blatant abetment, I had no idea what else to say from here. I really didn't know the words that would make her believe I was all-in.

There. I'd said it. Okay, not out loud, but even that silent musing was a bigger step than I'd ever taken with a woman before.

So what now?

Thank God for Pia. At once, the conversation with my sister played back in my mind.

Talk to her, Bas. Be honest with her.

With considerable effort, I raised my head up and away from her skin. "Look at me," I said quietly but firmly, patiently waiting the few moments it took her to raise her gaze to mine.

The sadness in her stunning greens all but knocked me on my ass.

But before I could put it into words, she was ready with hers. "Damn it, Bas," she gritted out. "You don't have to keep doing this, all right?"

She tugged against me now, clearly aiming to free herself from my embrace. I retaliated by tightening my hold. "No, it's not all right. What the hell? I thought you'd be happy to see me today, like I was to see you. Instead, you look like your puppy got hit by a semi."

She choked, finally giving in to the eye roll.

"Calling it like I see it," I countered. "Look, I know the past ten days were shitty, but it wasn't a situation I could control. You get this, right? You have to do this all the time with your own business. I simply had to handle mine halfway across the world. The phone service in the remote parts of Malaysia we were in was so bad—which I tried explaining to you repeatedly."

"I know," she interjected. "I know, Bas. But—"

"I even asked Grant to get in touch with you on my behalf. And trust me, giving that bastard your number all but killed me."

She grinned at that. While her mirth should've lightened my heart, my jealousy only stabbed deeper.

A low growl rolled up from the back of my throat. "Was he

inappropriate with you?"

"No. Don't be ridiculous. It's just that . . ."

I pushed in close to her again. "Just that what?"

"It's kind of endearing when you get all worked up like this." She shrugged coyly. "It's nice, I guess? That you would be jealous."

She drifted off as if she caught herself saying something she shouldn't—leaving me in a huger heap of bewilderment. Christ, I felt like a yo-yo. She wasn't an obligation, but she liked that I was jealous. *Up. Down.* She wasn't an anchor, but she loved the way I was feeling possessive and touching her. *Up. Down.*

Maybe it was time to change the subject. "Did you get the flowers?" As I asked it, I finally let her free from my grip.

I got a new eye roll for my trouble. Not exactly the reaction I was going for, but she rarely reacted the way I would think she would to anything. Why would this be any different? And why would I want that to change?

"Oh, yes. I got the flowers."

"So that's why you still look like your dog got run over?"

A new huff. "Fine, I'll just spit it out." She was too busy fuming to notice me studying her. "It was all a little over-the-top, no? I mean, a bouquet every day? My condo looks like a funeral home, Bas."

Bas. The single syllable had me forgiving her for the griping. "Nothing is over-the-top where you're concerned. You'll get used to that."

A new, intriguing sparkle in her gorgeous greens. "That so?"

"Sooner rather than later." I copied her smirk. "I think I'll enjoy buying things for you."

How's that for a heaping helping of honesty, woman?

"And I'll be sure to thank Terryn on my way out." She pushed back before fussing around the room again, gathering up her catering things.

"Terryn?" My smile fell. I tilted my head in confusion. "What does she have to do with anything?"

"Isn't she the one who sent the flowers? I mean, really sent them?"

"Excuse me?" I gave in to a full glower. I was about three seconds from dragging her over my knee, not caring if she protested or not. The look on my face must have warned her plenty though, because she backed even farther away.

"I—I just figured she does the day-after tasks like that for you." Though she didn't wobble on the assertion, she exposed more of her nerves by wringing her hands into her apron.

"Day. After. Tasks?" I spat each word like the bitter pills they were.

"Well, you know what I mean." She waved her free hand. The move reeked of dismissiveness, as if she hadn't just dealt one of the most significant blows to my fucking gut that I'd had in memory. No, not my stomach. That pain was . . . higher.

"You are walking a very thin line right now, Ms. Gibson." My voice dropped to the lowest register I was capable of, and she visibly swallowed while taking another step back.

"You can't blame me for thinking that, Mr. Shark."

And now it was *Mr. Shark* again.

Fuck.

"You have no basis to say something so hurtful." Step forward. She wasn't going to win this one. "I sent those flowers to you." I proved the point by wrapping a hand around her wrist. When she turned, trying to wrench free, I used the moment to my advantage. Within seconds, I'd bent her arm around to the small of her back. Her back was flush against my front once more, with her forearm between us.

When I stepped in again, closing the last bit of space between us, it brought her hand against my erection. Like the good girl she instinctually was, she wrapped her fingers around the outline of my cock.

Damn, this feels good. So fucking good.

"You're playing with fire right now, girl." I dipped the fingers of my free hand beneath the elastic band of her pants and ran them around to the front, hovering inches above her pussy. "All I can think of is pulling these pants down and spanking your ass until it's as red as your hair. Until I can watch those tears I love so much run down your cheeks and over your lips. Mmmm." I skated my fingers over her mound but didn't pleasure her, just teased. "Your tears could bathe my dick while I fuck this insolent mouth of yours until you apologize"—I sank my teeth roughly into her ear lobe, and she moaned—"and swallow everything I give you. Maybe, in the future, you'd think twice about being so rude when I do something nice for you."

"Baaasss," she whispered, dropping her head onto my shoulder. "Stop this. We—we have to stop this."

I dropped my hands from her suddenly, shocking her as much as myself.

Jesus.

Maybe she was right.

Or not.

Either way, the decision was made.

I wouldn't push her anymore. I wouldn't coerce her into doing something she was so determined to deny herself.

I was a bastard. But I wasn't an assailant. That would make me no different than Viktor Blake, and I'd be damned if I'd be lumped in that asshole's category.

"All right. Fine." I took a step away, my motion as quiet as my voice. A blast of cool air washed over me, chilling my skin instantly.

She spun and glared at me. I returned the look without a flinch. Now was that disappointment crinkling her forehead and plummeting her jaw? I was probably just telling myself that to ease my pride a bit.

"Fine," I repeated, dropping my chin to my chest. "You said stop, Abbigail, so I'll stop. I don't understand what's going on with you, but I'm not going to force you into something you don't want to do." I leveled my gaze, compelling hers to meet mine straight on. She needed to hear my words clearly now. "I couldn't live with myself if that's how you saw me, Abbigail. If it's time you need or space, I can do that. Maybe this—us—is all too much, too soon. Maybe it's because of the virginity thing, or your fears about loved ones going away, or crap about men in general that your brothers instilled in you . . ." I shrugged, but the motion was tight, aptly reflecting my mind-set. "I don't know. I'm in uncharted waters with you, woman. I've said that before. But I can give this time if that's what you need."

I ambled toward the door, trying to track her movements behind me by just listening. I detected none, though could hear her extended whoosh of breath.

"Oh. Uhh, oohh-kay," she finally uttered. "I . . . umm . . . appreciate that. I really do." Shuffling sounds now. Maybe she was righting her clothes? Her hair?

Against every command in my head, I pivoted back to look at her. "But I do have to ask one thing of you."

"What is it?" Her green eyes widened with concern.

"If you decide this isn't what you want..." I motioned between the two of us, waiting a few beats before continuing, but this time, it wasn't for her. Damn. This was more difficult than I thought it would be. I'd let myself get invested in the notion of "us" already. When had that happened? I forced myself to go on. "If you decide that, then you need to tell me. I can only pine after someone who doesn't really want me for so long. It's only right."

She swallowed hard before answering. "Fair enough."

"Thank you." My voice sounded strangled. This was completely surreal.

And so damn pitiful.

"Hopefully I'll hear from you soon, then." The false crispness in my tone at least helped me stride over and open the door of my office for her. "Have a nice day, Ms. Gibson."

Abbi didn't move. Just stared at me for a few moments, as if she didn't understand she was being excused. After slightly shaking her head, she pushed her cart out the door—but at the last minute, she looked back at me.

"So... I'll see you tomorrow for lunch?"

"Terryn will email my schedule like always."

I managed to drench the words in matter-of-fact precision before closing the door. After it was closed, my struggle for composure was no less a torment. I knocked my head back against the door, wondering if I'd transformed into a mooning teenager. But I didn't care. I couldn't stop myself. I couldn't begin to imagine how I'd handle seeing her every day without touching her. Pressing my body against hers... and more. So much more.

But I had no fucking choice. I had to give her the time and

space she needed to figure her shit out, or we'd never stand a chance. Despite my abysmal lack of relationship experience, I knew that much. I was in a way different head space than she was, and things would never work out for us until we both got on the same page—the same chapter, even.

Shit.

Right now, I'd be happy if we were reading from the same damn book.

★ ★ ★

Luckily my week was swamped with work. Plans for the Edge consumed every free minute that the Malaysia deal wasn't. But both were chugging along with no hitches, so they only accounted for the hours at the office. When I finally stumbled home after eight every night, I had nothing but time on my hands.

When Pia suggested she and Vela come over with pizza and a movie, I readily agreed. Unfortunately, they couldn't stay too long because it was a school night. Oh, and by the way, my sister inserted several times, I was shit for company.

I finally caved and spilled the truth to her. With a rueful smile, I relayed the bare minimum details about what had transpired in my office at the beginning of the week. In the end, I gave her enough to render at least a little feedback. Words I didn't know I'd desperately needed until she offered them to me.

"Hey. You've done the right thing, brother."

I thanked her with a rib-crushing hug. "You really think so?"

"I know so—unless you succeed in squeezing me into

unconsciousness." She laughed, goading me into doing the same, as soon as I relented my hold. "Just try to relax, okay?" she exhorted. "I know it's difficult right now, but if she's truly into you, she'll come around. Let her figure it out in her own way."

I tossed a mock grimace. "You know that's easier said than done, right?"

"Oh, not for you, big guy." She mocked as I peeled a pepperoni free and stuffed it into my mouth. "Not at all!"

"Get out of here," I growled, adding a nod across the living room. "Your morning will be hell tomorrow if a certain someone doesn't get her sleep."

She popped up on tiptoe to kiss my cheek. "Love you."

"Mooommm! Come on!" Vela's shout had us both rushing to follow her down the driveway. Our ever-full-of-energy light beam was back to fulfilling both our lives. At least I had a genuine reason to smile as I trudged back inside the big, lonely house.

As I went to shut down the laptop Vela had been playing on during the show, I hesitated—for the better part of a minute. And then another.

Finally, decision made, I sat and pushed open the monitor all the way. "Well, here's to things you never thought you'd do, man," I muttered.

But I didn't waver while typing Abbi's name into the search engine.

All right, maybe I wavered for half a second. Being all too familiar with people invading my privacy, I'd never even considered being the perpetrator of such a gesture. Nervous energy bubbled in my gut as I waited for the screen to populate. What if I saw a bunch of facts and pictures I didn't like or expect? Although it was unlikely, I was braced for anything. I hoped.

The first story was a recent entry from a tabloid newspaper. It was dominated by a picture of the two of us from Vela's soccer game. How the hell hadn't I seen it before that moment? And why hadn't Grant or Elijah told me about it? Not that anything could be done about it now. A quick scan of the short write-up revealed no misconstrued facts.

I voiced my final conclusion in a new mumble. "Water under the bridge." Quickly, I scrolled on to the next hit.

After two full pages of entries, I learned my beautiful redheaded obsession led a pretty dull, law-abiding life. She worked hard to get her catering business on the map in Los Angeles, gave a lot of her free time to the Intrepid Entrepreneurs mentorship program, and spent very little time on social media.

Because I didn't have social media profiles of my own, I couldn't snoop around those very far. Most access required being "friends" or "followers" of the person one was trying to spy on. After cruising the usual suspects in that realm, I stumbled onto a colorful website called Pinterest, where Abbigail apparently had an account too. She had pages that were called "boards," filled with all sorts of ideas, recipes, and pictures others had also liked and then added to their boards.

"Jesus Christ." I scowled, despite a bizarre inclination to keep scrolling. "Is this really how people really spend their free time?"

But I clicked on, fascinated by the things Abbi found fascinating. It was like rummaging through someone's desk drawer while they were out to lunch. I probably shouldn't be doing it but couldn't stop myself. Every new gem was like finding more hidden treasure.

Then, I hit the mother lode.

A board titled "#Goals"—filled with picture after picture of everything from cookware that was astronomically overpriced to exotic vacation destinations. Handbags, shoes, sparkly baubles, slinky dresses—which honestly, I'd kill to see the woman wear—and even a little kitten with huge blue eyes.

"Jack. Pot." I punctuated it with a face-splitting grin. Ideas were now like fireworks in my mind. It was all right there in 4K glory. I could give her every single thing on that board and not blink an eye. If the sassy little spitfire never wanted to receive roses from me again, she'd just given me all the ammunition to make that happen.

And damn, did I like surefire ammunition.

"Oh, yeah," I drawled.

The opportunity was too good to pass up. It was a fucking gold mine of information, and I couldn't let it go unexcavated.

I promised myself I'd pick just a few items. Five at most. I would send them to her with meaningful notes so she would know without a doubt that I'd picked them out myself. Fine, so the woman herself had helped—but this had to count for something! Best of all, this violated nothing about our new agreement. I was giving her the time and space she needed, but I'd also show her I was a persistent motherfucker when I wanted something. When I believed there was something worth fighting for.

And that was what we were. What she was.

This was a no-fail plan.

Still, I thought about double-checking the idea with Pia. I had to be sure.

No. I already was sure. I didn't want to run the risk of Dub being a killjoy, like she had the tendency to be.

No. Fail. Plan.

I knew it in my gut. There wasn't a woman on the planet who didn't love gifts. I would forge ahead. Abbi would love this. And soon, she would love me too.

Whoa there, Captain.

What the fuck? Was that really what I wanted? For her to love me? And what was with the "too" bullshit?

Was I falling in love with Abbigail Gibson?

Fuck me.

Which was what I *really* craved from the woman right now—only first things first here. I had to raise my game on this courtship. The "love talk" would come again soon enough, and I'd truly discover the answer to my inner questions.

Or have my heart destroyed once and for all in the process.

CHAPTER THREE

ABBIGAIL

As I accomplished a strong finish for the final two blocks of my Saturday twilight run, I listened to an old favorite playlist for motivation. Pop princesses warbled about strength and girl power, giving me a needed surge of encouragement.

Since I'd been at the kitchen all afternoon testing out new cookie recipes, there hadn't been any time to head for a more glamorous route than the typical neighborhood loop. It was likely for the best. There was a certain comfort to familiar things—and right now, I'd take the little reassurances where I could get them.

It was the first week of August. The air was warm, the breezes were balmy, and everyone on the planet was likely spending time near the ocean as the waning sun turned the sky into an orange-and-purple light show. As I turned up my final block, I fought to take inspiration from the sky's brilliance as well as the song playing in my ears. The artist was crooning about taking chances and facing life's struggles. The song intensified, as did my gait. I envisioned words on a motivational banner—as if Sebastian Shark were waving it at the finish line.

Because all week long, he'd been the one heeding the song. Making mountains move. Pushing on and refusing to break.

Refusing to give up on me. On us.

With my lungs heaving and my legs burning, I stopped in front of my building. I bent over and planted my hands on my knees. I hissed between my teeth, fighting that truth. Useless battle. This was no half-asleep dream or vague fantasy to indulge while sitting in traffic. This was a leap Bas was ready and willing to take—and had shown, over and over again, since our first heart-halting reunion in his office. And every confusing day since. He definitely had tenacious down to the letter.

And worse: I couldn't resolve what to do about any of it. Did I escape or swim with the shark? Did I heed the screams of my logic and keep my heart intact or surrender to the magical, passionate flood of Sebastian once more and risk becoming the next notch on his bedpost?

"Why thank you very much, universe," I grumbled between deeper breaths. "That was exactly the dilemma I needed in my simple existence right now."

"Uhhh . . . please tell me you're on your Bluetooth."

The source of the callout pushed off from where she'd been leaning against the far corner of my condo complex's first building. For a second, my gaze bugged. Rio looked ready to slay in a sexy black dress, sky-high ankle boots, and sparkly accessories. Her inky hair was slicked back from one side of her face and then artfully curled against the other. She reminded me of Louise Brooks, the original "it" girl of Hollywood's silent films, circa 1920.

"If I was, I'd be getting off the call to snap a selfie with the movie star waiting outside my building." I made the assertion between my lingering huffs from the run.

"Oooo." She teased a couple of glances over her shoulders.

"Who? Where?"

"You, sexy little kitten. Who else?" I came by my golden Hollywood knowledge from my mom. I'd kept all her beloved scrapbooks, filled with pictures of the silent and classic movie actresses she'd idolized as a little girl. She'd seen all the old black-and-white films since there wasn't much else to do during rainy days on a Rhode Island dairy farm.

Her face tightened. "Abs. I think we need to talk for a minute."

I replied with a fast, tight nod. Better that than bursting into tears, even though seven full days had passed since our argument. And we did need to talk. I wanted to make things right with my sister-in-law. I did. But I wasn't in a hurry to repeat the tear festival I'd been having since that night, either. It hurt my heart to be at odds with Rio. She was the only womanly sounding board I had in my life, and I'd been missing her dearly. With all the confusing, confounding, amazing, and exciting changes that had been taking place in my world since Sebastian had so possessively strode into its core, I'd really been needing someone to talk to. Someone to curl up on my bed with and giggle about the parts that were making my stomach do crazy things. Someone to clutch hands with and ask the blunt questions that terrified me to think about while sitting alone.

But that meant getting through this part. My apology would be difficult. I also knew it would ultimately circle back to Bas, and Rio had been many things over the past few weeks, but part of the Sebastian Shark fan club wasn't one of them.

I gathered my courage, yanked on the big-girl panties, and squared my shoulders. "Rio . . ."

"No, Abbi." She shot up a hand. "It's okay."

"It's not okay. I owe you an apology. I was a bitch, and I was wrong for that."

Her huff was nearly a growl. "Stop."

"You have to let me say it."

"I shouldn't have pushed the way I did. That was on me. I'm sorry too."

Her sienna eyes seemed even bigger as they shone with tears. I pushed off the wall and all but forced her into my embrace.

"Don't cry. You're going to smudge your makeup."

"That's what compact mirrors are for."

"But this mess isn't worth it," I protested. "I had no right to behave the way I did last weekend. I was a first-rate brat." I pulled back from our hug, shaking my head, still so disappointed with my own behavior.

The laugh I expected from that was a no-show. Instead, there was quiet affection in the form of her soft stroke along the side of my head. "Maybe you deserve that every once in a while," she murmured. "Christ, Abbi. You're still so young. So many times, we all forget that—but the person leading the pack on that pressure is often you."

I gulped hard. "Maybe that's on purpose."

"It shouldn't be."

"You don't really have a say about it." I stepped back, jamming my hands into my hoodie pockets. And yes, it seemed like the exact same defensiveness from last Saturday, but it wasn't. "Sorry," I mumbled. "But this is all I know how to be." *All I can be.* Because letting my defenses fall for her—or anyone, for that matter—meant everything fell.

I let out a long groan and then dropped my face into my hands. Not even a minute ago, I'd sworn I wouldn't fall apart. Guess I wouldn't be getting a commendation from the composure police today.

Rio climbed a few steps until she was higher than me. I expected to find a preen planted on her face when I turned to face her, but the woman only radiated focus and calm. "Are you ready to tell me about things with Sebastian Shark yet?" she asked.

I turned and leaned my elbows against the railing. "Things," I echoed softly, "are . . . complicated."

She emulated my pose. "I imagine with a man like him, they would be." She tapped my tennis shoe with her shiny black boot toe. "And pardon the distraction for one second, young lady. Aren't these the new sneakers you've been lusting after? From your Pinterest board?"

Ahh! At least we could do the fun part of all this madness! After all, it was still under the heading of "telling her about things." As good of a jumping-off point as any, really.

I hadn't counted on getting into this tonight, but I also hadn't planned on coming home to a sees-all-knows-all sister-in-law on my front step. Perhaps it was the universe's way of giving me a nudge. Rio was going to pry the scoop out of me, one way or another. Why not enjoy the excavation?

"Why yes, yes, they are," I said as noncommittally as possible. Although my face-splitting grin sold me out.

"But they can't be discounted already."

"Not likely."

"So how . . ." Her gasp burst out with shocked realization. "Ohh . . . Did Shark buy these for you?"

I quirked my lips. "Umm . . ."

"Just out of the blue? They're over two hundred dollars!"

I finally gave into a giggle. Just a little one. Along with it, I reached out and hoisted her lower jaw back into place. "Sister, you don't even know..." I trailed off.

Her gaze bugged. "Even know what?"

"It's probably just best to show you. Do you have a couple minutes? Looks like you might be headed out." I gave her outfit another head-to-toe once-over.

"Sean can wait a few minutes," she riposted. "No way can you dangle bait like that and not follow through, Abbigail."

After motioning her to follow me up to the condo, I ducked into my bedroom to pull out the iconic shoe box. When I walked back out with it, Rio collapsed onto my couch.

"What is this?" She gasped, wide-eyed, like I'd placed the Baby Jesus in her lap. "Really? Are these the— Oh, Abbi. The sparkly silver ones you spotted last month?"

I nodded. "And in my size."

"How the hell did he know you were swooning over these?"

"At first, I wasn't sure. I finally figured it out, though." But rather than take the time to explain, I dived right to the more pressing subject. "But honestly, Rio—where in the world will I ever wear these?"

"I'll bet Mr. Shark already has a few ideas." Her saucy drawl took over as she fished out the hand-signed gift card I'd tucked into the box. "'Treasures for the legs I treasure,'" she read. "Yep, he definitely has a few ideas!"

"All right, enough."

"And who cares if you never wear them outside of the house? Points to Shark right here." She pulled out one of the shoes as if it were a rare artifact. "They're works of art," she whispered, turning the shoe from side to side.

"But if my goal here is to be clearer about him..."

She followed the direction of my gesturing hand, over to my condo's dining room area. A wide archway separated the room from the main space of the kitchen and living room, meaning one's gaze didn't naturally trail there first. Rio's definitely did now—right before her eyeballs nearly exploded out of her head.

"Jesus opened a flower store."

"Or a schmaltzy rom-com film set," I groused.

"How many roses is that?"

I joined her on the threshold of the room. "I stopped counting when the peonies arrived too."

"Oh shit."

Her reactions bounced from sarcastic to stunned in three seconds, and I was already wise to the reason why. She'd finally looked up to the new artwork mounted on the far wall of the room. One large painting depicted a majestic shark in a cobalt sea. Its companion featured a dolphin in a mirror image pose. The works were a combination of realism and escapism, with the pair seeming to swim toward each other through sunlight-streamed oceans.

"Holy shit," Rio rasped. "They look like Wylands."

"Because they are." Robert Wyland, my favorite artist, was known for his stunning depictions of ocean life. My bucket list was heavy with visiting parts of the world where his famous sea life murals were featured.

"Incredible."

For a moment, I freed my mind to agree with her. Just for a few seconds, I was drenched in pure giddiness. The flowers hadn't done it. Both pairs of shoes came close. But every time I looked at those paintings ...

Sebastian freaking Shark had really done this for me. Had

sat down and paid attention to what was truly me. I already knew he had no time for his own social media, but he'd taken time out of his insanely hectic life to really learn about me—through mine.

And then had done something about it.

"So . . . these came with the shoes?" Rio asked at last.

"Oh, no. The shoes and flowers came on Monday. The prints on Wednesday."

"And Tuesday and Thursday were for catching your breath?" As soon as I shook my head, she drawled, "Well, of course not. What came on those days?"

Half a laugh spurted from me. "Tuesday was an entire case of Thin Mints, and Thursday was a gift certificate to the Golden Door."

"Thin Mints?" Rio rocked her head back. "Isn't cookie season in February?"

"Don't try to figure it out." I shrugged. "I gave up two days ago."

"Wait. Hold up." She rolled her head in a bewildered figure-eight. "Did you say the Golden Door? You mean the high-end spa down in San Marcos?"

This time, it felt right to let a grin escape. "Yep. And the certificate is for two people. So, if you have some free time and you waaa—"

I'd barely gotten over my giggles from her tackle hug before she resettled by my side. I joined her in lolling my head against the back of my couch. We rested that way for a few minutes, simply enjoying the renewed comfort and recovering from her physical attack. At last, she pivoted her gaze back my way, her whiskey eyes bright but probing. "You're terrifyingly calm about all this."

A long sigh. "Oh, don't worry. I'm freaking out on the inside."

"Do I get elaboration on that?"

"Well, I'm not ungrateful," I went on. "Not for any of it." I squeezed my eyes shut. "But the last time Sebastian and I actually talked about...things...was when I delivered his lunch on Monday."

"And?"

"We agreed to take some time. He said he'd give me space."

"If this is the new definition of 'space,' I'm applying to NASA."

Oddly, her soft chuckle gave me deeper comfort, and I leaned my head to rest on her shoulder. "He agreed to my terms but then redefined them."

"Which is a bad thing why?"

"I didn't say bad."

"Okay. So what is going on here?" she asked softly.

I threw the back of my hand over my eyes. "I don't knooow."

She took a turn at the heavy sigh. "Come on, Abs. Just say what you're thinking."

"I wish I knew. Honestly. He was out of the country for a long time, and his schedule's been jam-packed catching up ever since. Also, judging from the blueprints and artist renderings on the conference table, they're preparing to break ground on the Edge soon."

"So he's really going to build it?"

"Looks like it," I confirmed. "And as strongly as I've been tempted to stop and gawk—because the artist renderings look stunning—all I've had time for is just stopping and dropping the food."

This wasn't normal for me, being emotionally exposed for so many days on end. I wanted all my walls back, and I wanted them now. Not likely with where my mind instantly went, recalling every "stop and drop" I'd made to Bas this week. Fleeting or not and implied "space" or not, I remembered every damn one of those moments. The way his intense stare raked my body. The need clearly painted across his sculpted face. The white-hot energy crackling on the air while I was in the room. It was all branded into me, searing my memory like a lighthouse's flash across a stormy night sea. So brilliant but desperate. So urgent, yet so perfect.

I'd never been happier about hearing Rio clear her throat. "Well, I know you don't want my two cents right now . . ."

"You're right," I returned, turning and reaching for her hands. "I need at least a dollar's worth at this point, Rio."

She gave my fingers a solid squeeze. "Can I really just shoot straight with you?"

I squeezed back. "Please."

"For starters . . ." She dipped a quick nod. "I can tell you're scared about what's going on."

"Scared?" My punctuating *pssshhh* didn't cause her to flinch by a millimeter.

"But I don't think you're being honest about what's causing the fear itself," she insisted.

I responded by repeating, in a harsher croak, "I wouldn't say I'm . . ."

She tilted her head harshly. "You wanted the whole dollar. Has Shark tried calling you this week? Or tried texting?"

A tight frown. That so wasn't the question I expected. "No."

"All right. Has he made any other attempts to contact you,

aside from acknowledging the lunch deliveries?"

Only those lighthouse looks in the office…that felt impossible to describe, even to her.

"No," I bit out, though more to myself than her.

"And has he come here at all? Camped out on your doorstep for one second?"

I sent over a new scowl. "No, damn it."

She tick-tocked her head from shoulder to shoulder. "Then from my seat in the bleachers here, this is a boy who decided he liked a girl and then took the time to learn about what she liked and enjoyed. Then the boy used that information to please the girl."

"You're making it all sound so simple. So why do I still feel so confused? Like I don't know which way is up?"

Rio pushed to her feet and circled around to stand face-to-face with me. "Abbi." She sighed, tears in her eyes. "Be young. Be carefree. Dance in the clouds. Be happy. Stop overthinking everything like a sixty-five-year-old man."

I groaned while I stood and dropped my head in my hands. "I just didn't expect falling in love to be such a confusing mess." I quickly shot my gaze up to meet hers. "Or whatever. You know what I mean!" I dropped my head again, not wanting to see whatever look was coming after my slip.

"Ahhh." She stroked my hair. "I see now. You thought all these feelings were going to be neat and tidy."

"They're not going to be?" I jerked my head up, slanting a challenging smirk. "I mean, they're mine, right? There should be boundaries. Definitions. I need the damn boundaries, Rio. Does that make sense?"

At once, the woman kicked into full gentle mama mode, swaddling me in a tight hug. "We all know your fondness for boundaries, baby," she soothed. "Maybe that's why it made sense that you picked Sebastian for your first time."

I burrowed my snuffle into her shoulder. "What . . . does that mean?"

"His walls meant you could keep yours up and they'd go unnoticed. You got to have the fireworks and then leave before the gunpowder sweep-up."

"Damn," I finally blurted. "So busted."

"Mmm-hmm," she cooed and stroked my hair.

Again, Rio with her knowing, comforting sounds and movements. Despite knowing, deep in my belly, that every feeling I qualified as "comfortable" would never be that again.

Everything had changed. And I'd done it to myself.

I'd lusted after a player. Had then slept with that player. Consequently, expected the end game from that night to be by the man's standard playbook.

Wrong.

Because Sebastian wasn't playing.

Not now.

Had he ever been?

My gut knew the answer to that too. At once, my head careened and swooped from it as this new epiphany took root.

He hadn't been playing.

Everything he'd said and done . . . every stare and whisper and caress and growl . . . had really been him. From inside him. From all those meaningful places he kept telling me I'd stirred and touched . . .

To which I'd responded no better than a tabloid reporter. Someone who'd already made up my mind about everything he was, based on what everyone told me to believe. Yes, even after his heroic gesture, standing up to that asshat at Vela's soccer game. Even after knowing how he grew up with nothing and faced adulthood so young.

And even after everything that happened between us afterward.

"Sheez-usss." Rio's exclamation, soaked in her astonishment, was a lifeline back to reality. As I hung on for dear life, she sent over a dazed, "I still can't believe all this."

"The thing is, I can." I gulped. Then again. "Or should I say, maybe now I do?"

She pivoted, making me squirm under a new dose of her tender scrutiny. "And you've come to a conclusion about it?"

"Yeah," I confessed. "I mean no. I mean— Ahhh, I have no damn idea what I mean!" I dropped my face back into my hands. "Help me, Obi-Wan Kenobi. You're my only hope." I moaned. "What would you be doing, if you were this damn confused?" And lost. Completely off-keel and taking on more water by the second . . .

But all Rio had for me was a soft, rueful, utterly unhelpful stare. "Oh, honey, how I wish I could answer that—but Sean isn't Sebastian, I'm not you, and the world sometimes isn't as clear as a Thin Mint craving." She winked, backing up and straightening her clothes.

"Or a pleasure cruise about to capsize." The metaphor still felt perfect, so I stuck to it while dragging my hands along the sides of my head. As I yanked the hair tie out of my ponytail, an unmistakable sting pressed the backs of my eyes. Damn it.

"You're going to figure this out, Abs. And you know I'll be here to listen through every second of every hour of every day."

Astoundingly, a long giggle tumbled out of me. Still, I drew away for fear of getting my fresh tears all over her pretty ensemble. "I love you more than every Thin Mint in this kitchen, sister."

She laughed so hard, her curls bobbed against her cheek. "Damn. That's a lot of love."

I shoulder-bumped her. "Freakin' right it is."

"Well, at the risk of being downgraded on the cookie scale, I'm officially late." She checked her buzzing phone with a wince. "I was only supposed to stop by on my way to date night. Your brother is getting mighty impatient."

"Can't blame him." I gave her an approving once-over again, actually happy about the interruption.

"Sean had a job interview downtown this afternoon and actually dressed in a suit and tie for it. Now we're meeting at Kincaid's."

"Oooo. Fancy."

"Right?" Her eyes twinkled with golden joy. "We're going to slurp oysters, watch the sunset, and do interesting things to each other under the table with our toes."

"And you're really leaving me on that note?"

She waggled her brows. "Maybe it'll give you a few ideas."

"Actually . . . it does."

With that resolve, I was already pulling up Sebastian's screen on my phone while walking Rio out. By the time I hugged her and thanked her for the fifteenth time for the visit, on top of promising her I'd never go so far to emotional ground again, I had a text composed and ready to send.

After a huge inhalation, I jabbed the green arrow that would shoot the words across town to him.

The words that would turn this night into a beginning I never dreamed or an ending I'd never forget.

Hey there. Can we talk?

His text response raced my heartbeat three times faster than all his gifts combined.

I thought you'd never ask.

He'd gotten more perfunctory with the messages after that, and I could all but read the mind-set that had driven him to be that way. He was anticipating bad news and suspecting I wanted to "soften the blow" by giving him the home court advantage. And damn it, I hated making him feel that way, even for the ninety minutes it took to drive through the city and get to Calabasas.

Forcing myself to get out, I walked to the mansion's massive front door. "Out on a limb" wasn't far off the mark of my mood as I stood in a puddle of gold light from the ornate lantern overhead. The glow, while warm and evocative, was a useless barrier against the aural glory of the Calabasas boonies at night. Unnamed critters scuttled through the bushes. A light breeze fluttered through the cypress and eucalyptus trees. Nocturnal birds called to each other but stopped when a canine howl soared on the air, along with answering yips.

I started counting to sixty. Sebastian had one more minute to come to the door, and then I was out of here.

"Thirty-three, thirty-four, thirty-fi—ahhh!"

My yelp was an unthinking reaction to Bas's fierce swing of the door. As terrorized birds burst from the trees, I had a chance to regain my breath—for about a second. Then the full sight of him registered in all my senses. And between my ribs. And at the crux of my thighs. Oh God, especially there.

"Holy. Hell."

Yes, I rasped it out loud. No, I didn't regret it. I dared

any woman alive to have refrained from the same burst when suddenly face-to-face with the sight of Sebastian Shark in nothing but charcoal track pants, a sheen of sweat, and a stare that could drill its way through an obsidian wall.

"Uhhh...hey." I locked my teeth while tapping a toe at the smooth travertine beneath my feet. "I—I mean hi."

I decided to stop when he stepped all the way outside next to me. With two graceful moves, he took me from slightly unsettled to totally unbalanced. His presence was part of mine now. His scent, a mix of perspiration and the warm sweetness of his cologne, was swirled into every inhalation. He was close enough to touch. And Christ, how I wanted to touch.

"Good evening, Miss Gibson."

His voice, pure velvet on top of raw virility, made me scoot back. Fortunately, he didn't press forward again. "I—well, I"—*get your crap together, Abbi*—"am I...interrupting anything?" I congratulated myself. There was just enough volume to give the illusion of confidence. "I just invited myself up here and never thought to ask if you—well, if you—"

His gaze intensified, the midnight blue becoming luxurious cobalt. "If I what?"

I exhaled. "If you were busy or—"

"Did any of my texts give you that idea?"

He growled it this time. Fiercely. I stumbled back again. Trouble was, I did it with a lot more gusto. The motion finally had me teetering off the stone step.

Oh, shit, shit, shit.

Luckily, I didn't end up flat on my backside—

Because the shirtless god became my salvation then too.

His reflex was a quicksilver miracle. Before I could blink, he caught me by my shoulders. I gasped as he yanked me back up, the veins in his biceps jutting from the effort. I whipped my arms out on sheer instinct, until I was digging my fingers into the mesmerizing flesh of his chest.

For long seconds, we were trapped like that.

Frozen in time. Staring deeply into one another's eyes. Further than we ever had before.

No longer resisting. No longer denying. No longer contesting.

At last, Bas tugged me harder, molding my lower body against his. I sighed with blissful completion. He felt so perfect. More destined to be than the amber moon and summer stars overhead. More inevitable than the cosmic explosion that had sparked their existence.

"All—All right," I finally spluttered. "Your point is solid . . ."

"Oh, no." As he drawled it, he slid his hands down the backs of my arms. He stopped when he was gripping me by the elbows, a perfect point of leverage for him to fit my lower body tighter to his. "You have yet to know what 'solid' feels like from me, Red."

I took in a ragged breath, head spinning as much from his proximity as his promising words.

"Can we talk? I won't keep you too long."

"Of course." He allowed air to pass between our bodies again, though he clearly wasn't happy about it. It actually appeared physically painful for him to move away. I was beginning to empathize with the sensation.

But the speech I'd rehearsed during my drive was nothing but dust on my tongue. The muteness was worse when I witnessed a tic in his jaw. Above that, his eyes glimmered with brighter emotion . . . maybe even a strange uncertainty.

"Abbigail."

And now, with his normal husk replaced by a pleading rasp, it was all I could do to stay upright, let alone form words. At least I had a perfect excuse to grab for him again, seeking balance for my precarious senses. I was a damn hussy about it too, stroking up the burnished skin of his torso, reveling in the rippled muscle beneath my fingers, before murmuring, "I . . . I got the peonies," I finally managed. "All of them."

"You drove all the way out here to tell me that?"

I lifted a little smile. Well, tried to. But the intensity of his stare made it barely possible to breathe, let alone twist air into new words. "I— Well, they're gorgeous. My place smells heavenly now."

He angled up one of his decadent dark brows. "No longer a funeral home?"

"Hmmm. Maybe a little. But not a lot." My smirk felt more authentic now. It boosted my confidence to stretch up and kiss him. Just on the cheek with chaste brevity before muttering respectfully, "Thank you. So much."

His demeanor changed once more. The anxiousness wasn't gone, though an invisible burden on his frame seemed to lift. Hints of warmth crossed his face, blooming to full heat when they permeated me. The balmy summer night suddenly felt like a sauna, and I was more than ready to sweat it out with this man.

Christ. Was this how it would always be with Sebastian? This sense of the world burning away but never feeling better? With more and more certainty, I knew it was what I wanted—especially when he inched so close again, bending his whole upper body to stare into my eyes. His bright blue eyes were so incandescent in the moonlight, our passion seemed to flare with enough wattage to light up the city far below this windy hilltop.

"You like them better than the roses."

He spoke it as fact, in his arrogant baritone, making me smile and worship him a little more. Sometimes he was a router saw, able to carve out the truth of a person with dangerous dexterity. And why did that turn me on?

"Peonies were my mom's favorite," I finally whispered.

"That's not what I said," he growled.

My heart rate sped. My blood sizzled with a million little sparks of energy. "Yes," I admitted. "I like them. I—I love them, actually. Much better than the roses. Truly. Thank you."

"Good. I'm glad." His gaze re-warmed to a rich cobalt. I should have reacted with a new swoon, but a goofy giggle bubbled up my throat instead. That had him shaking his head with a smile. "What brings you by, Abbigail?"

Because I still hadn't really told him that part...had I?

I bought a few seconds to regroup while poking at the porch tiles with my toe. "I...I had this whole speech planned out while I drove here. I was going to march up to your door, thank you politely but sternly, of course..."

"Sternly?" He jumped in the second I stalled, breaking out the full force of his panty-melting grin.

"Yes," I rebutted. "Sternly. While I can't express how lovely all the gifts are, they're also unnecessary." Though I added a smile, I couldn't meet his careful stare while piecing together my thoughts. This was the part I should've rehearsed better. "You don't have to do those sorts of things for me, Sebastian. But you already know that."

He sobered the grin, replacing its lines with a thoughtful look. "And if you already know that I know..." He leaned against a column, all shirtless indolent male about it. "I'm actually going to get redundant here." And then swung over one of his lazy-but-not-really stares. "Why did you drive across the city on a Saturday night to tell me this?"

I emulated his pose, folding my arms in front of my chest. "Seemed like the point needed to be made in person."

He barely shifted out of position. Likely because the bastard knew exactly how incredible he looked there, with the porch lantern stamping golden light patterns across his gleaming chest and the night wind playing at his dark, damp hair . . .

My freaking God . . .

"And have you accomplished that?" he finally queried. "Properly made your point?" he clarified. His voice had its perfect lilt on the rich summer wind, turning my senses into heaven but my logic into a mess.

"I'm . . . not sure yet," I stammered back. "I'm having trouble organizing my thoughts, quite honestly. And—"

"And what, Abbigail?"

"God, I feel so awkward around you sometimes. And so damn tongue-tied." I felt the flush clinging to my cheeks. Thank God for the dimly lit stoop.

"Tongue-tied?" He rasped it when he stepped in closer, sliding our bodies back together. He didn't stop there. He dipped down so close, his breath fanned across my mouth. "That sounds . . . dangerous."

"I . . . I suppose it could be," I whispered back. "I mean, serious injury could result."

"Oh. We wouldn't want that."

"No?"

"Definitely not. I have plans for your tongue, Abbigail."

I swallowed roughly. "You—you do?"

He dipped a steady nod. "Think you're up to the challenge?"

"Yes?"

"That a question or an answer, Little Red?"

I didn't waste time speaking my reply. Instead, I just showed him.

Starting with a straight surge forward, stopping only when I'd seized his nape with one hand and his hair with the other. I kept going by twisting my fingers and pulling hard, ordering his lips to slam mine. I answered his hot, sweeping tongue with erotic stabs of my own. A heavier sound escaped as he took command of my ass, gripping it hard enough to hoist me off my feet as he spun around and reentered the house.

Somewhere in that cavernous space, Sebastian finally set me back down—yet I still felt several feet off the marble floor. I was floating on breezes, a feather wrapped in the buoyancy of his magnificence. And it was just the start of my new dizziness, as the air-stealing, Mount-Olympus-dwelling male turned his stare fully upon me.

Without a backward look, Bas kicked the front door shut and whisked me back off my feet. Instinct guided me to wrap my arms around his neck as he enveloped me in his capable arms and set a course straight for the staircase.

"I—I haven't been on the second floor before," I said quietly once we'd reached the top. How was that the only thought that tumbled out of my mouth?

"No, I suppose you haven't." He smiled through every word, gazing down at me while practically gliding down a long hallway.

"Do you get lonely here? It's so big. For just you, I mean." I was rambling, letting my nerves get the best of me.

"I'm not here that much. Work consumes most of my time."

"You can put me down, you know. I can walk on my own."

"Hmmm. Okay."

I yelped as Bas obliged me—by flinging me onto the hugest bed I'd ever come into contact with. My head sank into luxurious pillows of all shapes and sizes. The fabrics were fine enough to swaddle royalty. But the most surprising aspect of the room was the color. Correction. Absence of. Everything was white upon white, giving me the sense of actually floating in the clouds—until the god himself brought me back down to earth. Sebastian pulled on my ankles, hauling me across the comforter toward him.

"Tell me, Little Red. Where are we now?"

I looked around, mildly confused. "Your ... bedroom?" I propped up on my elbows, trying to gain a better view while he pulled off my sneakers and socks.

"Yes, obviously." He tilted his head, eyeing me past quirked brows. "But I mean your head. Your heart." He pressed firm thumbs into the arch of my bare foot, stroking the underside that absorbed so much of my day's abuse in the kitchen.

"Ooohhh God, that feels so good." I let my eyes drift closed. The bastard was not playing fair.

Especially when he stopped.

"Talk to me, baby. Tell me where things stand between us. Last time we discussed it, you wanted space. Time to think. I don't want to assume or rush—"

I cut him off before he could say anything else. "I want to be here with you."

"Out of obligation?" He bored his stare into me, seeking an honest reply.

"No. Why would you think that?"

"The gifts, for one thing. You said you came here to thank me."

He crawled up my body and hooked his fingers into the elastic band at my hips. Apparently, even if I was there out of some sense of indebtedness, he was going to collect my payment.

"Good Christ. I've been dying to see your pussy again, Abbi. To touch you . . . taste you . . ."

"Sebastian . . ."

Just like that, my voice was nothing but a whisper. Bas didn't let my husky need go unanswered. He bent in, shadowing my body with the carved grandeur of his, before dipping his head and taking my mouth again. Our kiss started sweetly but intensified quickly. I squirmed beneath him, my blood heating and my core aching. My lust swelled from the second his erection pressed into my belly. He was already so thick and hot, and as the kiss intensified, I bucked up, silently pleading for more friction from him . . .

Meaning I was not a happy camper when he pulled away instead.

"Bas!"

"*Ssshhh.*"

He grabbed the bottom of my T-shirt. With one quick motion, he ripped straight up the middle of the cotton. His powerful stare fixed on mine as he tore my bra away too. A gorgeous growl left him as my breasts spilled free.

"Hmmm." His low vibration was like a direct caress on my clit, making me shiver all over. He sat back on his heels and surveyed me, letting me view all the hunger painted across his face.

"You look so fucking perfect in my bed, Abbigail." He stared a few moments more before leaving said bed with a graceful swing of muscles. He strolled over to a dresser, leisurely deposited his watch into a drawer, and took out something else. My view was hampered by the pillow nest, but I hoped like hell he was returning with condoms. I needed to feel him inside me. The ache was immeasurable.

"Bas..."

"*Ssshhh*, baby."

"Come back to me. What are you doing?"

I sat up fully so I could see him. At the same moment, he turned back to face the bed.

With his pants dropped.

A weighted breath rushed out of me. Couldn't be helped. Oh yes, his penis was as stunning as I remembered. And now it was nearly within my reach...

As he approached the bed, he fisted himself. He didn't stop when I gave him the full attention of my gaze. My sigh transformed into a greedy moan as I watched his confident fingers pleasure his swollen flesh.

I needed more. I needed him.

But at the same time, I was still terrified of both. Of turning myself completely over to him. This passion wasn't going to be like our first time. Now I knew how good he was going to make everything. And how much more addicted I'd be to it. How I'd have to fight being completely drowned by it.

"Touch them." His dictate was my salvation, reconnecting me to the sizzle of my body instead of the fear in my head. He nodded toward my chest. "Your perfect tits..." His voice grew rougher as he stretched out each descriptor. He also lengthened and intensified each pull on his flesh, coaxing a perfect white pearl to the slit on his cockhead. "Pinch them for me, Abbigail." He paused, watching with narrowed eyes, before giving the next direction. "Now twist them. Fuck, yesss."

But as he hissed it, his face contorted and his shoulders tensed. He reached down to brutally squeeze his balls.

"Yes?" I challenged, trying yet failing to bring some lightheartedness. "Wh-Why don't I quite believe you?"

Bas tipped his head. "You don't believe there can be pleasure in pain, Little Red?" He released himself, sliding those stunning fingers up my body and over my left nipple. Without pause, he pinched the pulsing bud and then scraped across it with his thumbnail. "I do. One hundred percent," he murmured. "Now more than ever . . . because that's what every second away from you has felt like."

For long seconds, I couldn't formulate a reply. My attention was sucked in, centered on the delicious stabs of pain he brought with every tug and scratch to my nipple. When he added his other hand, doing the same thing to my other breast, I could barely remember what words were.

But like a roller coaster breaching the top of the highest hill, there was nothing we could do to stop it. I accepted that now. Happily. "It won't happen again," I whispered, cupping one of his cheeks.

He kissed me again. This time, not as a sweeping invasion but a tender possession.

His lips were slow and sensual, prodding and patient. Every ministration coaxed me into a thicker, beautiful fog. It had to be the truth, since I only half-registered the crinkle of foil and the slick of latex as he sheathed himself. Somewhere, Lady Irony had to be laughing her head off. Look at us: the eager sexual newb and the lothario who could glove up one-handed. There was an epic joke waiting to happen here, but I didn't care about the punch line. All that existed in this moment was him.

All that gave me air were his words, whispered as he lingered his lips along mine. "Christ Almighty. I need to fuck you, Abbigail."

I circled my arms around his neck. Curled one leg across his back. "Yes."

He shifted, aligning his body with mine. "Hold on tight, baby."

"Yes," I rasped again. "God, yes."

"'Sebastian' will do."

But I only had time for the sparsest laugh before he swiveled his hips, working his demanding cockhead into my trembling, swollen slit.

He notched in a little deeper. Deeper.

"Oh, Sebastian."

I rocked my head back, feeling my hair fan out as wave after wave of perfect heat swirled through me, softening my core for his ultimate subjugation. But even as I widened my legs and let him in deeper, I gazed into his steel-blue eyes—and at last embraced the truth. So simple. So incredible.

He was vanquished as thoroughly as me.

"Please," I heard myself begging. "Please...Bas... more..."

"Patience, little girl." He started it as reproof, but the shudders beneath his breath told me otherwise. "You're soaked, baby, but you're tight. And I'm—"

"The one who's going to bring me pleasure and pain." I enforced it by digging my thumb into his chin. I splayed the rest of my fingers along his jaw. I didn't stop the clawing until he visibly winced. "I want the pain."

At this point, probably even needed it—though I had to be careful about revealing all of that to him at once.

A goal that lasted twenty seconds.

Right up to the point that he pulled out far enough from my channel for a fresh coat of my arousal . . . and then seized my hip like an archer notching his arrow . . .

"Oh, fuck!" I screamed it as he drove his shaft all the way to the target, igniting places low in my belly. As he continued to ram me, the fires raged higher until going off like rockets up the center of my being. As a moan exploded from my lips, there was a smile with it—but not just from how his glorious cock filled so many aching spaces inside.

"Fuck." I grated it as he added little circles to his motion, heightening our sensual rhythm. His erection stabbed me in new places inside. Corners I never knew existed . . .

Bas pushed away by a couple inches, enough so that we could stare at each other fully again. "Does it hurt?" The edge was back in his regard—the one that said he'd know it if I was lying and wouldn't be happy about it.

"A . . . A little," I confessed. "It's so full. So big. Ahhh!"

He fucked in on a straight shot this time. He didn't stop until his balls slapped against my ass. He dropped his head back down, his forehead slick on mine, his heaving chest smashed against my engorged breasts.

"I'm a sick bastard, Abbigail—because fuck me, it feels so good to make you hurt." He bit into my lower lip, dragging his teeth along my pouting flesh. "And to make these pretty lips scream." He pumped again, conquering my channel in brand-new ways with every full, fierce lunge. "And to make this beautiful cunt tremble around me."

By now, my lungs were working as hard as his. Between my ferocious efforts, I raised my head and returned his sensual bite. As he growled from the pain, I soothed it with a long lick of pleasure. "But I need to come, not tremble."

He narrowed his gaze. "I know exactly what you need, Red."

His smirk was the true perfect shot here. That sensual expression was better than tequila for making my head swim and my pussy burn. I gasped as the shadows of his bedroom tilted and flipped. The sound became a hoarse moan as he dropped his head and then his shoulders, preparing to drive into me with purpose.

Consummation and chaos and cosmic fire I'd truly thought I remembered wrong. In a bizarre way, it wasn't untrue. In so many ways, my memories had been wrong.

Because this reality was better.

Fuller. Harder. Deeper.

"Oh! Oh, Christ! Sebasss..."

I faded away, consumed by his primitive groan and his thundering heartbeat. The organ in my own chest raced just as fast. Holy shit, he knew exactly how to move inside me. He knew exactly what to do with that steely length, sliding and grinding me toward a shattering climax. Could I even handle this? My chest was nearly exploding. My fingers and toes were numb.

But no way in hell did I want him to stop.

He trailed a series of nips along my jawline, his stubble awakening even deeper pools of my lust. "Jesus," he erupted. "You're a dream, Abbigail. My responsive, sexy little girl. I can feel every quiver in your tight, sweet cunt."

"For you." It was romantic mush and I knew it, but it also

felt so damn right. "All for you."

"And we're just getting started, baby." He whispered it between kisses along my cheeks and over my forehead. "I want it all from you, Abbi. Everything. Don't hold back on me."

I tilted my head up, slanting my lips over his in an openmouthed bite. "Hurt me, Bas," I begged, my teeth bared. "Fuck me. Do it. Plea—ohhh!"

My scream gashed the air as he did the same to my body. Every shred of my senses was filled with the pressure of his punishing stabs. I was mindless. Thoughtless. Weightless. There was nothing but Sebastian, bruising me from the inside out.

"Abbigail. Oh, Abbigail. Jesus. Oh, fucking Christ . . ."

And then taking me beyond that with his dirty, husky litany. And his brutal thrusts. And his spiraling heat—

Until I was blindly exploding.

"Draw it out, girl." His snarl sounded far away, a demand through the golden haze of my orgasm.

I nodded eagerly, ready to obey. As long as he kept shuttling his cock like that, I was good. So damn good.

"Don't stop, Abbigail. Don't stop. I'm there. I'm— Fuuuckkk!" he roared with his release spurting thick inside me. He swore softly as he began to slow, restoring us to normalcy by gradual increments. If there was ever going to be a thing like "normalcy" in my world after this.

For now, I let my eyes drift closed while I enjoyed the calm. When Bas finally dragged up to rest on his elbows, I forced my gaze to reopen.

"Do I dare ask what that is all about?" I twirled a finger in the direction of his face. The gorgeous bastard was grinning as if he'd discovered a secret swimming hole on the hottest summer day.

"No need to ask, Little Red. It's all about you." He gave me a tender kiss. "A lot of it's about you these days."

I didn't hide my own grin. "So I'm forgiven?"

"Forgiven?" Now a scowl from him. "For what?"

"Oh, let's see . . ." I called his frown and raised him by a pair of arched brows. "Being a skeptical shrew this week? Treating your gifts as stunts and not heartfelt gestures?"

"So you were wrong. We'll agree on that. But you came to your senses and admitted it, so we're squared up, okay?"

"Squared up." I couldn't help quirking my lips again. "Meaning that you won."

"Baby, I think we both won."

My laughter took over as he punctuated his words with a blatant glance down. No mistaking what he was getting at, considering his dick was still buried deep inside me. "Well played, Mr. Shark. Truly well played."

"Who says I'm playing?"

I pushed some dark strands off his forehead. "I know you aren't."

He was silent for a long second. No, more than that. Cautious? As I mentally pursued the right word, he tilted his head back to maneuver my fingertips into his mouth. After treating them to a few soft suckles, he locked me back down with his stunning blue stare.

"Stay with me tonight."

I pulled in a long breath to buy myself some time. The decision wasn't as easy as just hauling back the comforter and diving under the covers with him. Some—*most*—women would be labeling me a fool for second-guessing a sleepover invitation in this bed, but being my own boss had taught me that dream offers were rarely "dreamy." Or easy. They usually had strings attached. It freaked me out that I couldn't figure out Sebastian Shark's "strings."

"Sebastian—"

"Abbigail."

"Just hear me out, okay?"

"No. That's my line this time. God save us from backtracking on all the progress we've made here tonight." He rolled his eyes heavenward. "I have a confession—"

"Confession?" I felt my brows jump with my tone. "About ... what?"

"That I didn't send you all the gifts this week for purely noble reasons." He took his turn at the extended inhale, again raising my awareness of how deeply joined our bodies still were. Holy shit. Did the man have a flaccid mode? "They were also my way of keeping tabs on you."

Well, there was the key for wanting him out of me as fast as possible.

"Excuse me?"

"Abbi—"

"Did you seriously say 'tabs'?"

He rose, peeled off the condom, and lobbed it into the trash can next to the nightstand. When he returned to the bed in a confident descent, I dropped my jaw. How was he so unaffected about what he'd just told me?

"You asked for space." He said it as if declaring the earth was round. "And I gave it to you the best way I could, but—"

"You found it necessary to spy on me regardless?" I used my heels to punch my body back against the headboard.

He expelled a heavy huff. "I wasn't spying."

"Right. 'Keeping tabs.' There's such a big difference there."

His nostrils flared. "In this case, yes," he gritted. "In case you don't remember, someone attempted to implicate me in what would've been a second woman's death. Less than ten days before that, I was flat on my back in the ER due to being purposely poisoned." He scooted over, positioning himself right in front of me. His stare was nearly a glare, and he wasn't giving me an inch of aversion from it. "I haven't had a chance to fill you in on the developments of the last week yet . . . but let's say that in light of those, the deliveries were the less invasive choice of an action plan."

I swallowed. Pretty damn hard. "Developments?" I repeated, forcing myself not to stammer. "What kind of developments?"

He reached for my hands. I willingly let him cradle them. As he lifted his head, I prayed there'd be a gotcha smirk across his face. With his lips still set in a firm line, he supplied, "Nothing as crazy as the Cinnamon suicide-note-that-wasn't, but nothing I can't ignore either."

He finished by shaking his head and sighing.

"It's mostly been prank phone calls; people telling Terryn they're from City Hall or calling themselves one of my trusted associates, only to play strange music on the line once I picked up."

I sat up straighter. "Strange music?" I demanded. "Like what?"

With a new grimace, Bas rolled his shoulders. "Like . . . love songs, I guess," he finally responded. "Not stuff I'm familiar with."

I studied him carefully. "And this stuff . . . in these 'prank phone calls' talked about being in love?"

He shrugged again. The move was tighter now, betraying

his frustration. "Yeah. Honestly, I never listen for long."

I bit my lower lip. "So do you think it's all related? The calls . . . the poisoning . . . the bogus suicide note?" Which was still hitting me as the creepiest and most confusing act of them all. "Or maybe it's part of Terryn's weird little crush, and she's hoping to brighten your day from the other room."

I swore Bas turned an appropriate shade of green before he grabbed me by the waist and hauled me flat across the comforter again. At once, he flattened his whole body over mine again. The force of his ire joined the size of his body to lord over my senses. His snarl took over the inches between our faces.

"That's not a subject to joke about, Abbigail."

"Sorry." I stroked my knuckles across his jaw. "I really am."

He brushed his lips across the end of my nose. "I know."

"My sense of humor is a strange and dark thing sometimes."

"Strange. Dark." His eyes gained velvety seduction. "Like me."

"Hmmm," I purred. "I can't wait to learn more, then."

"But you can't do that if you don't stay over."

"Ohhh. Well played once again, Mr. Shark."

He responded by nestling his body against mine in all the right places—with all the right pressure. I gasped and bit my lip again, accepting the beautiful torment he brought to my most sensitive tissues.

"You like that, baby?"

He worked his erection against my cleft. Shamelessly, I let my thighs fall open for more of the contact. "Baaasss."

"Uh-uh." He leaned in, taking my mouth in a brief but hard kiss. "That's supposed to be 'Yes, Bas, let's start the sleepover now.'"

I moan-giggled. "You do not play fair."

"Life isn't fair, baby."

"Says the man who just won the big round?"

He dipped his head in and regarded me with glittering eyes. His gaze was beautiful all the time but devastating when he wanted to play dirty. "Tell me who wins tonight after you've hit double digits on the orgasms."

My jaw fell open. "You're so full of it, Shark."

He added a smirk to his naughty devil's scrutiny. "Challenge accepted, Red."

CHAPTER FOUR

SEBASTIAN

One of my favorite features in the twelve-thousand-square-foot expanse of my Calabasas home was the built-in coffee station in my master suite. Sometimes the little things in life were truly the best things. Not having to trudge downstairs and across the house to the kitchen for that first cup was something I thanked my sister for daily.

I had to admit, when Pia first showed me the plans for the master suite, I'd had a good laugh. It had all seemed so over-the-top, especially given the way we grew up. After our father died, we'd been lucky to have heat and running water. Fortunately, Southern California winters were mild. On the rare nights when our place got too cold, a few of the neighbor women let us sleep on their sofas. We never got too comfortable though. I got tense taking handouts from anyone, seeing the tally marks from those debts add up on my invisible survival tote board. I also didn't like the families getting too attached, dreamily latching on to the idea of taking care of us. Of "saving" us. If we were "saved," there'd be obligations. And obligations meant trouble with Child Protective Services. And CPS meant the distinct possibility of separation from Pia, which had been my worst fear and completely unacceptable.

As unacceptable as the thought of parting from Abbigail.

I returned to her, pausing beside the bed to gaze at her still-sleeping form. Good Christ. She was more beautiful now than when she came to me last night, if that was even possible. Her hair was a mass of wavy flames against the pillows. Her face was soft and innocent, such an anomaly of texture from her normal animation and expression. The repose made me focus even more on the full pillows of her lips, just slightly parted as she floated in dreams.

I only had to take another step before setting Abbigail's cup on the nightstand next to her. While circling around to the other side with my own cup, I grabbed my smart pad off the dresser to check on emails. Morning rituals were hard to break—some absolutely necessary. But I didn't want to wake her if she still wanted to sleep. Seeing her soft body snuggled in my bed was giving me an entirely different list of morning habits I'd like to get into, though.

It wasn't long before the coffee aroma started rousing my beauty. I leaned over and kissed her forehead through her sleep-mussed red mane.

"Good morning, baby." My voice was deeper and quieter than I expected. Having her beside me was affecting me completely—and I liked it.

She smiled but didn't open her eyes. On any other woman, I'd interpret the move as manipulation, a cat masquerading as a kitten. On her, it was simple magic—especially when she turned to nestle into my hip with her nose. I stroked her shoulder and back, her bare, creamy skin exposed where the covers fell away.

"I think I could get used to you naked in my bed every morning, young lady." I closed the iPad and set it on the nightstand. I was kidding myself if I thought I'd be able to concentrate on anything but her now.

"Just the mornings, though?" she asked playfully, still not opening her eyes.

"Mmmm," I groaned as twenty new and naughty thoughts jockeyed for pole position in the 24 Hours of Le Mans of my imagination. "Nights too." I stroked her hair off her back and lightly scraped my nails down her spine, at least as far as our positions would allow.

"Mornings and nights," she said, stretching onto her stomach and tempting me with the full length of her toned body. "But there are a lot of hours left in between. Mr. Shark." She turned her face into the pillows after a slow, sweet smile. Fuck me. Okay, better than a kitten. She was my adorable little fox, with that fiery mane and her furtive, innocent ways.

Motivated to movement by the thought, I straddled her hips with my body. Once there, I offered, much less playfully, "I could tie you to my bed and never let you leave. That would solve the whole problem."

Though I couldn't see her reaction, I sure as hell felt it as her body tensed beneath me. My cock swelled again. I let primal instincts flow, gathering her hair up into one mass of red glory. I pushed it up, piling it above her on the pillow. So damn perfect.

"No sassy remark for that idea?" I goaded while settling my weight onto her ass and hips. My action pressed her deeper into the mattress. I reveled in the savage satisfaction of the moment.

"Ummm..." I sensed her hard gulp. "Too early to be sassy."

I scraped a few stray tendrils off her neck and wasn't

gentle about it. "And that's your whole truth?"

"And . . . what you're doing feels too good to think straight."

"Mmmm. Much better," I hummed. I massaged firm strokes from the base of her spine up to her shoulders and back again, rocking her entire body with mine while doing so.

"Oh God, Bas. That feels so good." She moaned again after I repeated the motion a few times.

"Yeah, it does." I shifted my weight off her body. It was only temporary. The pants had to go before I drilled through them to get to her heat.

"Hey! Where are you going?" She lifted her head in protest when my motion made the bed dip.

"Just taking my pants off, girl." I slid the track pants off and remounted her the exact way I had been before. The only thing separating our skin now was the cool cotton of the flat sheet. I leaned closer, fitting my mouth to her ear. After a few kisses around the sensitive area, I murmured, "Something seems to have come up that needs to be addressed." I illustrated the problem by grinding my erection into the seam of her ass.

"Oh. Ooohhh." Her first sigh was nervous. Her second was breathier . . . sexier. As she relaxed more, allowing my shaft to press against her entirely, we exhaled together.

"Christ. Even that feels good."

The abject astonishment in her voice had me chuckling. "Even?" I teased, ending it with an extended growl. "Oh, baby. I have so many things to teach you." And there was no better time than now. To prove the point, I repeated the motion several more times, keeping up the sensual treatment until my gorgeous little fox was rolling her hips beneath me . . . with me. As thoroughly as I wanted this tidal wave to build and grow, I cut it short by gently pinching her hip. "*Ssshhh*, baby. Be still.

Let me play with you for a while. Let me make you feel good."

Couldn't say I didn't expect her petulant mewl. "Bas. I already feel good. Can't we— I mean, won't you—"

So damn cute. So innocent. She still wasn't comfortable with her raw desire, let alone expressing it. Asking to have her needs met, much less knowing what all of them were, was a foreign concept to my sugar-and-spice girl. We'd get there though—and it was a journey I was very much looking forward to.

"Spread your legs for me."

As she obeyed my command, the heady scent her arousal filled the air—and jacked all my senses. Hell, yes. So damn good. I inhaled so deeply, I was temporarily dizzy. Until—

Ding dong. Ding-ding dong.

"What in the actual fuck?" I dropped my head between my shoulder blades as the question left my tight lips.

I sent out a silent prayer to Mother Nature for lightning to strike whoever was at my front door, apparently determined to break the goddamned doorbell. Pop-up thunderstorms were a thing in SoCal, right?

Ding dong. Ding-ding dong.

"Fuck!"

As I rolled off Abbigail, I glared at the clock on the nightstand. It wasn't ridiculously early, but I wasn't expecting anyone either.

Ding dong. Ding-ding dong.

"Bas?" Abbi raised her head all the way. Her hair was a magnificent scarlet tumbleweed around her face.

"I'll be right back. Do not move. I swear, if it's those devil's disciples selling wrapping paper again..." I let the sentence trail off as I hopped from foot to foot, trying to put my pants on. "But if they want to talk grade-school fundraisers, I'm sure this boner will be a quick conversation killer."

"Don't you dare!"

"I said don't move."

My menacing glare was losing its mojo with this one, because she shot me a censuring side-eye, rolled off the bed, and searched for something to put on.

"I said stay." I gave her a glare through squinted eyes. "I'm not finished with you yet."

Ding dong. Ding-ding dong.

She giggled and stabbed a finger toward the tent in my pants. "You cannot answer the door and talk to anyone—especially children—like that!" She swiped my T-shirt and her panties off the ground and hopped into them as we covered the length of the hallway.

Ding dong. Ding-ding dong.

"I'm coming! Settle down!" My voice bounced off the soaring walls and ceiling as I descended the stairway and reached the foyer floor.

Swinging the front door open in a seething bluster, I huffed, "Bloodthirsty little shits, aren't y…"

My voice was strangled by a stunned gape.

Then a hoarse cough.

Then a wordless stare.

This definitely wasn't the mini sales team I expected. Not even close. But a ghost? Couldn't say I was expecting one of those either.

"Sebastian. Hi."

A ghost that spoke. But didn't most of them do that? Admittedly, my knowledge on the subject was limited.

I focused on shoving coherent syllables to my lips. I was

finally able to get out a couple and stuck to the key ones.

"Tawny?"

Shifting her weight from one foot to the other, then checking over her shoulder, she asked, "Do you mind if I come in?"

"I do, actually." It barely got past my lips as Abbigail pushed her way between me and the doorframe.

"Whoa," she whispered and placed her hand on my arm to calm me. "Of course. Come inside."

Tawny Mansfield, she of postmortem notoriety, jogged up one side of her thin mouth. "Thanks," she offered to Abbi in a mild tone. But my poor girl was still just as confused as me.

"Aren't you . . . dead?" Abbi slapped her hand over her mouth.

I gave her a sideways look before turning my attention back to the woman huddled inside my front door.

"We need to talk," Tawny replied.

I answered that by raising an eyebrow and then closed the front door, sliding the lock and dead bolt home. Photographers routinely camped out in the neighborhood, and there were often drone cameras zipping around as well. The hazards of counting a number of celebrities as neighbors, in addition to the paps targeting my own driveway routinely. The last thing I needed was more news coverage related to this woman.

As soon as I turned on the woman in my foyer, I dictated, "Get to explaining and at a quick-time pace. This is some fucked-up shit, lady." Despite latching a hand around Abbi's to keep her close, I couldn't take my eyes off the brunette who'd entered my home. Tawny moved like a wraith.

What the hell had happened to her?

I'd already started inner speculations while pinning

Tawny with an expectant stare. I didn't get very far because Abbi immediately shifted into hostess mode. "Can I get you some coffee or something?" she asked Tawny. "Tea, maybe?"

Tawny darted an openly confused look between Abbigail to me.

I quickly interrupted, "This is my girlfriend, Abbigail Gibson. But honestly, you need to start talking before we all sit down for a game of Canasta. What the fuck is going on here?"

"Bas." It was a verbal version of Abbi's tight twist around my bicep.

"'Bas?'" Tawny added a small smile, but I couldn't tell if she was being sweet or snide. "That's so adorable."

And there was the word that did it—mostly because I couldn't tell if I liked it or abhorred it. "Stop fucking with me, Tawny. In case you haven't kept up with the news, you've caused some serious shit in my life lately."

"I know."

"But I guess that's what you were going for, yeah?"

"Please, let me explain."

"I'd love nothing more." I shrugged off Abbi's hold and started a forward stalk toward our new "guest." "Because I don't think you really understand. Maybe you need some enlightenment about how it really feels to have the whole world wanting to put its hands around your neck all at the same time. Here, let me help you underst—"

"Sebastian!"

Abbi's terrified scream was the successful lasso on my temper, despite how Tawny held out her hands, flat palms supplicating me. "Sebastian, I wish I had an hour to stand here and apologize to you," she said. "Hell, even longer than that."

I clenched my jaw. "But you're just popping by on your

way to fuck over some other generous john?"

The woman took a second to compose herself, breathing in deep. "I realize I'm probably the last person you expected to see on the other side of that door this morning."

I folded my arms.

"But I've come to warn you."

"Warn him?" The retort belonged to Abbi. She was more beautiful than ever, but I couldn't appreciate the look because my gut clenched in matching increments to her forehead. "About what?"

As I joined her in swinging sights back to Tawny, the woman returned an equally direct stare. I wasn't known for my patience or acquiescence, and she'd be smart to remember it now.

"You really need to listen to me, okay?"

With an impatient huff, I answered, "I didn't shut the door in your face, did I? And really, after the maelstrom you've created, I really should have."

"Again, I'm ... I'm truly sorry for that." Some of Tawny's conviction drained out with the repentance. "Honestly, Sebastian. I don't know what else I can say to make you believe me." She paused, once more going for the back-and-forth stare between Abbi and me. Undoubtedly finding a more sympathetic audience in Abbi, she stammered, "Can I, uhhh, take you up on that tea? I could really use something to calm my nerves."

"Calm your nerves?" My bark was a result of my own damn nerves, goddammit.

"Of course. Let's go into the kitchen." Abbi put her arm loosely around Tawny's shoulders, bringing on a new conflict of kiss-her-or-spank-her for me. It only worsened as she guided the woman toward the kitchen, quickly looking at me over Tawny's shoulder.

In response, I shrugged curtly. Right now, only Tawny could provide answers to about a hundred of my questions. So throwing her out, while exceptionally satisfying, wouldn't serve any practical purpose.

"I'll put some water on. Bas, do you want another cup of coffee?"

"No, babe. I'm good. Why don't you sit and I'll get the kettle started?"

She gave me a grateful smile while joining Tawny at the breakfast bar. It didn't take her long to realize that she didn't know her way around my kitchen yet, despite her natural instinct of shifting at once into hostess mode. Or maybe the look was for a different reason—that she was thankful I hadn't pointed out the newness of our relationship in front of a woman I'd shared a past relationship. "Relationship" being a really loose term here...

Good God. How humorous this whole situation was.

Except that it wasn't.

On that note, I grabbed a variety of teas for the women to choose from and placed them on a small plate along with the cream, sugar, honey, and lemon. Christ, how did a cup of tea become such a production? I should've just tossed Tawny a bottle of water, demanded she answer my questions, and then sent her packing. By the time they finished with the tea, Abbi and I could've been into our second orgasm.

More small talk between the women until the water was ready and I'd filled two cups. I set them on the bar ... and then took a determined stand across from them.

"Thank you." Tawny's voice was still abnormally serene,

considering the announcement with which she'd arrived. She chose a tea bag with equal grace, practically reminding me of some Victorian poet as she dunked it.

"Yes," Abbi concurred. "Thank you for this, Bas."

She used the chance to catch my gaze with hers, but I answered with a frustrated scowl. I didn't have a single answer for the curiosity on her face, and that was maddening. I had to do something—had to move.

Obeying the instinct, I fumbled at the apparatus to open the blinds covering the kitchen windows. Since they faced east, a substantial swath of golden sunlight poured in, promising another day of weather perfection for Southern California.

"You really have no idea how lucky we are to have these weather conditions until you have to live on the streets for days at a time." Tawny's voiced thought accompanied the gentle steeps she gave her tea bag.

"Explain."

"What's to explain?" she volleyed.

"Can I ask how you two met?" Abbi interjected.

"I was a dancer," Tawny explained with a rueful smile. "He would come into the club I worked at every now and then."

"Listen, as nice as a cup of tea and a stroll down memory lane may seem to some, it's not really my . . . well, cup of tea." I stared at her with pointed intensity. "And frankly, Tawny, I don't really remember you." I winced the moment the words left my mouth, but it was the truth. Tawny wasn't like Cinnamon. She was pretty but in an ordinary way, especially dressed in a dingy hoodie and faded leggings. Clearly she didn't have the other dancer's ballbuster attitude.

"I'm not surprised." Though the woman's shrug did hit me as a surprise. "From what the other girls always said, you're a pretty detached john."

Abbigail pushed back from the counter. "Maybe I should leave you two to talk in private." She had a look of repulsion on her face. It couldn't be interpreted any other way. It made me sick to my stomach, especially because there was nothing I could do about it. Because I'd fucking caused it.

"Abbig—"

Tawny cut me short by raising her hand. "No." And then lowered it around Abbi's wrist. "Please don't leave on my account."

Abbi twisted her arm free. She held her hand against her middle in blatant self-protection. "It's all right. I have to . . . well . . . do something upstairs."

"Abbi!" I said it louder this time.

"I'm sorry if that made you uncomfortable," Tawny rushed to insert. "Because there's no reason to be." Before Abbi could finish laughing about that, she blurted, "God. I'm not doing any of this right. I should've started out by saying there's a good reason Sebastian doesn't exactly remember me." Before I could react, she went on. "We never slept with each other."

Abbi halted. "Oh?"

At the same time, I brought the flat of a hand down on the counter. As the teacups finished their residual clatters, I demanded, "And that didn't seem like the better place to start . . . why?"

"I'm so sorry," Tawny babbled again. "I've—I've been so scattered . . ."

"Too scattered not to listen when I introduced Abbigail as my girlfriend when you came in? After arriving to my house on a Saturday morning—uninvited, I might add?"

"I'm really sorry—"

"As I'm already aware." I was a solid case of livid—with the woman and the situation. "Because so far, you've been nothing but a troublemaker."

"Forgive me." It was barely a rasp from Tawny, matching her timid fussing with her tea. "I—I only meant that—"

"That what?"

"That it didn't surprise me that you didn't remember the girls you sleep with, since you have a reputation of being emotionally uninvolved when you do."

I was furious with myself for forcing the answer. The torture got worse as I looked back to Abbigail. She seemed enthralled with every word out of Tawny, nodding as the woman spoke. I couldn't imagine what she was gleaning from the conversation, but she looked as though the dancer was imparting the damn Da Vinci code.

"Okay. Let's just cut to the chase here." I pinched the bridge of my nose for a long beat. Begging for some sort of calm. "Why the fuck did you write that suicide letter?"

Tawny opened her mouth, but Abbigail beat her to the punch on actually forming words. "More importantly, whose body was pulled from San Pedro Bay if you're sitting here?"

Though it made my head threaten to blow into a million pieces, I couldn't negate the question's validity. Crossing my arms over my chest, I waited for an explanation. The details she owed me, damn it.

Tawny rapidly stirred some sweetener into her tea. "I'm going to give you an abridged version of the story."

I flared my nostrils and sucked in air. "Just out with it."

"I came to California with a lot of dreams and no cash to back them up. Needless to say, I racked up a good amount of debt shortly after moving here. For one thing, it's hard to find a job in this town. For another, it's expensive to live here." She took a long look around my gourmet kitchen, and her shoulders dropped even farther. "Though I guess you wouldn't know much about struggling to make ends meet."

As she gave a watery laugh, I lowered my head to level our stares.

"Do not presume to know me." But aside from my small nod of emphasis, that was all I'd offer her right now. "Continue."

"After a lot of dead-end jobs, I fell back on the oldest profession known to man—or woman, I guess—to pay the bills. In the meantime, I got mixed up with some shitty people. When I was in too deep, both with owing debt and favors to all the wrong people, they came knocking to collect."

"Who did?"

But the question—which seemed the most obvious one to ask at this point—was overlapped by another query from Abbi. "They literally made you fake your death?" she asked with an incredulous rasp.

"In a nutshell." As Tawny supplied that, she winced. She looked ten years older than the picture they'd been flashing on the news a few weeks back. "But it seemed like the perfect answer," she finally went on. "They said they would handle everything, and I didn't have to actually do anything in return. It was the perfect deal . . ."

I used her tearful trail-off as a perfect chance to tighten my scrutiny with furious force. "There is no such thing. Business 101."

"But all I had to do was disappear . . ."

"And I rest my case."

Abbi looked confused. Instinct told me she was deliberating whether to glare me down or ignore me. She quickly chose the latter, giving Tawny even more of her focus instead. "What happened after that? How long did they take to make this 'perfection' happen?"

"A day, I guess," Tawny replied, blinking. Maybe she was really starting to recognize how batshit her story sounded—only now, it was too crazy not to believe. "Maybe a day and a half. It wasn't long. They had all the details taken care of. The body, the note, the information leak to the press. They gave me all the stuff I needed to go to ground—the papers, new IDs, some cash, and . . . well, all of it. They made me sign papers, swearing I'd never resurface. In exchange, they would handle all my debt and obligations I'd dug myself into." She jogged her head up, and the brimming tears in her eyes caught the light from outside. "It seemed perfect. A fresh start. A clean slate. No more worries . . ."

"But what about your family? What did you tell them?" Abbi tried to hide her continuing fascination by taking a sip from her mug. But it was more than that. My Little Red always worried about how everyone else would be affected.

"That's just it. Don't have any." Tawny shrugged, looking more desolate now. "No one would even notice if I disappeared."

As Abbigail set down her tea and closed the space to the woman, clearly intending one of those girl hugs, I could no longer keep my reaction quiet. "Okay, can we get serious about all this?" I yelled, at once tempted to do it again. Self-composure was pathetically overrated. "Do you have any idea how this stunt has fucked with me, Tawny-of-the-tearful-apologies? Do you know what chaos you have wreaked on my whole damn life? Did you stop and think about anyone but yourself in this entire, insane scheme?" Though her tears welled heavier, I didn't fall for her sad-sack, crocodile bullshit.

"I—I really am sorry," she blurted as soon as Abbi loosened the hug. "No. I didn't think this through at first. Not really."

"You were scared about the debts, and they probably made threats," Abbi offered.

Once more, the key question seared through my mind. *Who are they?*

"But afterward, when it was everywhere...my death, I mean—God, every news channel, every paper, magazine, website..." She folded and unfolded the empty packet of sweetener, not able to look at me for even a second. "Yeah, then it hit me. I started feeling really guilty about what it was doing to you, Sebastian. And...your life..."

"My whole fucking reputation!" My bellow caused both women to jolt. "I've worked tirelessly in this town, day and night." I sucked air through my nose, trying to settle down a notch. I wasn't very successful, since talking about my journey compelled me to remember where it began. Those grungy days when Pia and I were scrabbling...for everything. "Because, whether you believe it or not, I do understand the desperation that led to your decision. To struggle to make ends meet. To worry if there will be food for the next meal or where I'll sleep at night. But I clawed my way up from the gutter. Inch by inch, I made myself into what I am today. And I'll be goddamned if you will take that away from me because you were looking to take the fucking easy way out!"

"Sebastian!" Abbigail matched my volume decibel for decibel, only her intent was reproach instead of anger. How I even knew or cared about that difference was an astounding little factoid, but I shelved it for later.

"What? It's true. Every word!"

"He's right," Tawny croaked, tears filling her eyes.

I longed to call out every drop as the bullshit it was, but Abbi's empathy for the woman was palpable, which somehow ramped my aggravation higher.

"I'm—I'm so sorry. I truly am."

"That's not good enough," I snapped.

"You don't have to keep apologizing," my girlfriend comforted at the same time.

I glared at her, willing her to heed my silent decree—my house, my dictate—but she wasn't obliging with so much as a glance my way. The whole time, Tawny looked into her mug of tea and said nothing. Fantastic. Now, she'd succeeded in disrupting my personal life too.

"So was this your idea of an encore?" I finally snarled. "You just decided to show up on my front porch and cause some more problems for me now?"

"Bas—"

"Why, goddammit? I need to know that. You could've just stayed dead, and we could've gone on believing it. Why did you feel the need to come here and stir up more shit?"

I pounded a step closer to Tawny—an irony if there was one, since I was damn good and ready to put this entire fiasco behind me. Things were going well now. No, better than that. Everything was fantastic since Abbi came back last night, and then just the beginning of this morning was . . .

I closed my eyes for a second, forcing back the imagery of her sleep-mussed hair and lust-swollen pussy. None of that was going to be mine within the next five minutes. Not with this giant albatross setting up shop in my kitchen. And continuing to dunk her damn tea bag.

"Like I said when I first got here, Sebastian—I felt like I

should warn you."

"Warn me?" At least I maintained a half-civil tone—a miracle, considering I was ready to strangle her instead. "About what?"

"About . . . them."

"Them." I grinded teeth on the word. Well, hell. Now that her chin wobbled like a tuning fork, I wished she'd return to playing with her tea. "Them who?"

"The people who set this whole thing up. They're very dangerous."

She waited for a reaction, silently staring at me from across the counter. I was positive I'd lost a few layers of tooth enamel by now but finally spat, "And do these 'very dangerous' people have names?"

"If I knew that, don't you think I'd have gone straight to the police instead of enduring all of this?" The way she seethed on the last word actually hiked my esteem for her a little. I knew the self-will it took to find one's spine even in times of pure terror. And whether Tawny was embellishing her truth or not, I did believe her fear was real. "I wouldn't have risked a bigger media blowup and endangering your plans for your new building again for a simple apology. But since everything has taken this crazy course, whatever it is, they've been trying—" She interrupted herself with an audible gulp. "Well, they've been—" Then dropped her head into her hand.

"What?" Abbi clutched Tawny's forearm. "It's all right. Just breathe," she exhorted, though her words trembled as well.

"Th-They tried to kill me. Twice, actually. And I mean for real this time."

"What?" I growled.

"The first time, it was messing with my car brakes. I grew up around cars; I know sliced lines when I see them. The second, they weren't so subtle." She gulped hard while pulling down the hoodie's zipper. Underneath the jacket, her torso was covered by a faded "I Heart LA" T-shirt—and a neck full of purple bruises.

"Oh my God." Abbi gasped.

"This morning." Tawny zipped back up just as quickly. "I woke up, and there was a guy in a ski mask over me. And his hands were already there, squeezing."

Abbi gasped again. "Are you okay?"

Tawny wobbled her way through a nod. "I—I think so."

"Did you see a doctor? More importantly, have you gone to the police?"

Insanely, I was on the same page as Tawny now. We swung pointed looks at Abbigail, filled with the same message.

Are you fucking serious?

My fiery redhead gave back as good as we gave her, planting hands on her hips. "Oh, I'm sorry if my normally law-abiding-citizen ways seem ridiculous to you both. But there are lines, and then there are lines."

I circled to the other side of the counter to stand beside her. I nudged her up off her chair, replacing my body onto the seat and pulling her to stand between my thighs. I didn't care if Tawny gawked while I gave my girl some attention. I wouldn't care if Tawny whipped out her phone and recorded our affection to use in getting her next quick buck. All the tension in the room was getting to me, and I'd spent way too many minutes without touching her.

"I happen to enjoy your lines," I crooned against her forehead. "Very much."

"Hmmph." But it didn't sound like Abbigail meant it. At least not yet.

"All right…then I'm sorry if I insulted you." I held her face between my palms before placing a soft kiss on her lips.

"Forgiven," she whispered at last and kissed me as chastely in return.

"This morning didn't go the way I thought it would," I said against her lips. That earned me a soft giggle, though Tawny ruined the moment—imagine that—with a subtle clearance of her throat.

"I'll…ummm…get out of your hair now," she murmured. "Thank you for the tea. And just for listening. It was never my intention to cause you so much trouble, Sebastian. I just wanted to tell you to watch your back. I don't know why these people want me out of the way or why they think I'm a good conduit to you." She shook her head. "But I'm pretty clear about one thing. You are definitely their end target."

Her declaration hit the air like a mallet against steel. Even thirty seconds later, the reverberations didn't stop. Part of me registered the impact, especially because I could still feel the vibrations through every inch of Abbi's frame.

And despite Tawny's helpless and haggard face, I had to take this information seriously. Very seriously. She wasn't the only fly that had flown into my soup lately. When I cocked back and studied all the pieces, it was starting to look like a complete picture. The fake suicide threat from Cinnamon. The bizarre phone messages. Even the miles of red tape at City Hall through which Grant was still hacking to get the paperwork straight for breaking ground on the Edge.

Goddammit.

These cockroaches—if they were even real, because

God only knew what was really going on behind this woman's glassy stare—might even be the bastards standing in the way of the biggest dream of my life. Bigger now because there was someone in my life to share it with. Someone I could see as part of that dream.

"Wait." I barked it with such violence, Tawny froze in place. "Not so fast, little bomb dropper." As she turned and actually threw me a glare, I went on. "You know that I'll be relaying every word of this to Elijah Banks, my personal private investigator, right?"

She shrugged. "Of course. And you should."

"So you know he'll have additional questions and need to get in touch with you. Where do I tell him you're staying?"

Her chuckle wasn't surprising. "I'm...in between addresses."

"A cell phone, then?" I asked.

"I told you already; they took my phone."

"Maybe a relative's number?"

"I just explained that too," she retorted, and the tuning fork chin returned. "I don't have any family."

Without faltering my stance or my tone, I leveled, "Well, you can't expect me to just let you disappear again."

"Seriously?" She forced a laugh. "Why not, Shark? Who am I to you?"

I knew how I wanted to answer that. Instead, pretty damn sure I would kick myself for this later, I said, "You'll stay here, then."

She turned that glassy gaze into a lemur-worthy gawk. "Huh?"

Even Abbi whipped around, her green eyes huge and gorgeous with surprise. "Sebastian?"

"Not in here," I growled. "But in the pool house for a few nights. Until you feel safer and are ready to move on."

But as the words spilled, I instantly tagged them for their special brand of bullshit. My place on the World's Biggest Bastards list was safe. I had no idea what possessed me to make the offer, but it wasn't from any magnanimous notion about her well-being. It had more to do with preventing her from slipping through my fingers before Elijah could interrogate her properly.

"I . . . I don't know about this . . ." Tawny hugged herself while taking a step toward Abbigail and me. Before she froze again. Then slowly turned back toward the patio windows.

In response, Abbigail and I did the same.

"What is it?" Abbi asked.

Tawny stepped backward. I was about to counter by rolling my eyes—could the woman be any more melodramatic?—but I was more preoccupied with how she swung her chin to her right and stared harder out the windows, across the pool deck. There was a crazy urgency to her motion—almost a fear—that made me nudge Abbi back from where she still stood between my legs, allowing me to stand and get a better view out the window.

"What in the actual fuck is that?" Tawny added to my trepidation with her careful, almost fearful, enunciation.

At first, I had no answer for that—and the realization was comforting. Maybe the woman was truly strung out and had simply cloaked it better before now. All I saw was a vibrating dark haze, standing out in the perfect cerulean morning sky. Most of the lots in the neighborhood opened up on the backside to unincorporated county land. It wasn't unusual for wildlife to stray into the boundaries of the housing development.

"Looks like a murder of crows," I said, ducking down to see past the valances that lined the kitchen windows. "There's probably a dead animal close by, and they're looking for breakfast."

I turned back toward the spot where the women stood.

And came face-to-face with both their horrified looks.

"What?" I scooped up Abbigail's empty mug and walked it to the sink while I explained the situation. "It's nature, ladies. The circle of life and all that shit. It's not a big—"

"They're getting closer!" Tawny was now nearly flattened against the French doors that led out to the pool deck, still fixated on the circling birds. "Look."

"Oh, for the love of—"

But this time, I interrupted myself.

While at the sink, I could see clearly across the pool deck. I didn't want to alarm either of them, but it became gruesomely apparent what the scavenger birds were feasting on. And Tawny was right. Horrifically so. The object wasn't beyond the property line. It was in my own backyard. Right on my goddamned pool deck, as a matter of fact.

"Stay inside." I issued the command before covering the distance between the sink and the back door in two long strides. I whooshed the door open, and a dozen blackbirds took flight from their carcass feast lying on the patio.

When I stopped abruptly, Abbigail collided into my back, trailing so tightly on my heels she didn't have time to stop. I whirled and hissed, "I said to stay inside!"

"What's going on?"

"Damn it, Abbigail."

"Oh, come on!" She clearly had no intention of retreating. Worse, Tawny followed right behind her. Damn headstrong women.

I muttered several colorful incarnations of my favorite profanity, but taking the time to rip out appliance cords and tie them both down wasn't a luxury right now. Not with what I had to contend with here. Which, after years of handling complex contracts, tricky negotiations, a thousand hostile competitors, and one delightfully spirited niece, wasn't ever on my radar of possible "situations" to face.

As we carefully approached the enormous, gray, bloated, and foul-smelling tiger shark sprawled across the pool deck, the remaining crows dispersed in a flurry. Wings flapping and batting, their caws rang off the stucco of the surrounding mansions.

"What the fuck?" I finally growled. I prepared myself for similar outbursts from Abbi and Tawny, meaning I was pathetically taken aback by what my woman actually did instead.

"Oh my God!" Abbi sobbed. "This . . . this poor baby!"

"What?" I sputtered.

"Huh?" Tawny got out at the same time.

"Is it still alive?" Abbi insisted, crouching down. "Can you tell? Is it alive, Bas? Can we get it into the water?"

"What water?" It sounded as lame on my lips as it had in my head. "Abbi, the pool is saltwater, but how would we move the thing . . ."

"Okay, so maybe get the hose and wet it down. Come on! We have to try!"

My sweet, amazing woman. She was sputtering question after frantic question. While I wondered if she was serious about them, my gut already told me the answer. She really was.

"Babe." I gently pulled on her shoulders. "Come on. I'm

pretty sure it's dead."

"Oh goooddd." Tawny's moan jabbed through the air. She clamped a trembling hand over her mouth and nose. "God, that smell! I'm—I'm going to be sick." She dashed over to the grassy area of the landscape and then folded at the waist. She'd reached the lawn just in time to heave dramatically.

"Clearly she's never cleaned out spoiled produce from a walk-in," Abbi mumbled as we walked around to the other side of the huge mammal. Once we were there, her shocked gasp took the place of her brief levity. "Wh-What is that?" she queried, pointing at the long length of silver steel protruding from the shark's upended belly. "A spear?"

"A harpoon," I supplied and did it with confidence. Years of doing business in every international shipping lane on the planet gave a guy some basic knowledge of the tools used on ships, big and small. "Fishing line only catches the big biters. More stabby things are needed to haul in a big fella like this."

Despite my sarcasm, my tone was solemn. Making light of a situation only went so far when one had gone through a huge bout of trouble and effort to bring the "situation" to a guy's backyard.

"So that's how it was killed?" Abbi bounced her big green stare back and forth between the dead shark and me. "But... but who would do something like this? Or why?"

"I doubt this was how they actually killed the beast," I answered. "I think the hardware is more for dramatic impact than anything."

I trailed off the end of the assertion, noticing a piece of paper stuck to the end of the spear like an advertisement banner flying from the back of an airplane. I reached to grab the note, but Abbi's sharp yelp stopped me.

"No!"

I locked my teeth again. "Abbig—"

"Wait!" She twisted her hold tighter. In other circumstances, I'd chuckle at the cute assumption she could restrain me, but I didn't have the heart. She was as speared by agitation as Mini Jaws was by that harpoon. I couldn't entirely blame her. This day was getting more freakish by the minute. "I really think we should call the police, Bas. This is your house. Someone was on your property, doing this. And that's evidence."

"Solid point." I used the moment to arch a brow Tawny's way. "Perhaps even while I was being distracted by the dead woman at my front door."

The woman bared her teeth. "You think I had something to do with this?" she spat. "After I just fertilized your lawn with everything in my stomach?"

"Another solid point," Abbi said. She pivoted back toward the stinking carcass. "Further verifying why you shouldn't touch . . . it."

Her guttural pause before that final word was my impetus to tug her close once more. I was certain she was seconds away from giving the damn thing a name instead of "it." I had to provide distraction before she started looking up shark burial services on her phone.

"If you're calling the cops, I need to disappear." Tawny stepped over again but kept her mouth and nose covered. "I don't want to be anywhere around when they show up."

I pinned her with a glare over Abbi's head. "Not happening."

"Excuse me?"

"You heard me," I stated. "I'm going to insist you stay

here, Tawny."

"But—"

"You've walked into this one, woman. You said it yourself. You're 'between addresses.' Besides, there's more than enough room." I turned in a semicircle, pointing out the obvious. "You can stay in the pool house, as I said before," I insisted. "It'll be adequate for your needs."

She narrowed her gaze. "You can't just keep me prisoner—"

"Of course not," I cut in. "You will have the freedom to come and go as you please." I stared at her, pressuring her to respond. "It's just until the danger is eradicated."

And I get the information I need from you.

Thankfully, it only took her the space of a nod to respond. "All right." She sighed. "I see the reasoning behind your call."

I kicked up one side of my mouth. "Of course you do."

"And if you're sure I won't be imposing..."

"I wouldn't offer if you were."

"Well, then." She nodded again. "I gratefully accept. Thank you, Sebastian. I really didn't expect it when I came here this morning. Or any of this." She grimaced, glancing once again at the dead shark.

Her gratitude was making me uncomfortable. "Do you have belongings somewhere? I can send my assistant to retrieve them."

"No," she laughed. "I'm traveling pretty light these days. I just have the backpack I came in with. It's in the kitchen."

"Good enough. Why don't I go ahead and show you the pool house now so you can get settled? There's a full bathroom in there as well."

The woman still cocooned against my chest stirred. "I think I'm going to go get a shower, okay?" Abbigail pushed away but looked over her shoulder, her gaze unreadable as she headed back inside.

"I'll be up in a minute."

I gave her a promising stare as she turned back once more to say goodbye to Tawny.

One abbreviated tour of the pool house later, I was sprinting up the curved marble staircase in her wake.

I didn't pause for one step in making my way directly to my bedroom and then right into the master bath. But when I came into the steam-filled bathroom, she was already shutting the water off.

"I hurried as fast as I could." I let my shoulders slump. Maybe I could play the hard-up sympathy card here, though her answering grin told me nothing about the chances.

"Well, you know the saying, Mr. Shark. You snooze, you lose." She stepped from the shower enclosure with a white towel wrapped securely around her body. Her hair was swaddled under another towel piled high on her head like a turban. She looked pristine and pure yet sensual and fuckable, all at the same time.

I stepped up against her, walking her back until her ass rested against the vanity's edge.

"So, Miss Gibson." I hiked her off the floor and set her fully atop the smooth surface. She yelped when her bare ass met the cool marble.

With her impossibly wide green eyes staring at me, she gulped in surprise. "Mr. Shark!"

"Do you believe me now?" I spread her knees apart and slid between her legs.

She looked up and down the length of my body. "Regarding?"

A low moan vibrated from my throat as I trailed kisses along the delicate skin of hers. When I reached her ear, I rumbled, "The gravity of the situation."

"Uhhh...which situation, exactly?" Despite our proximity, she managed to work her hand between our bodies. With bold little strokes, she rubbed the front of my track pants. My erection answered her every touch, straining to be free. "I mean, really. There are several situations of which you could be speaking."

"Well." I closed my eyes and pushed into her palm one last time before grabbing her wrist to stop the torment. "While this situation is becoming desperate, we do need to focus for a minute."

"Okaaay." She angled backward a little, partially supporting her weight on one hand. Goddamn. She was so dewy and fresh and delectable... "What's going on, Bas? I mean, besides the not-dead woman in your pool house and the totally dead shark on your pool deck?"

We both laughed at the absurdity of her statement. Just for a moment, but those few seconds felt so fucking good. In truth, what else could be done? Laughter was as ludicrous a choice as any right now.

"Elijah's on his way over in a while to talk to Tawny. He'll also handle the police to whatever extent they'll allow. I'm sure they will insist on talking to me, however, since I own the property and am the obvious target of all this bullshit." I scrubbed my palm down my face.

"Okay." I didn't miss the hints of disappointment in her response. "I should get dressed, then. Do you want me to leave before they get here?"

"Great question." I pulled her close and kissed the top of

her nose. "The answer is part of what I wanted to talk to you about. The more significant part, actually."

Abbi tilted her head in blatant confusion. The move reminded me of a little puppy, and it was the cutest damn thing. I couldn't help grinning again. This woman, amazing and bold and honest, had made me smile more in the short time I'd known her than I had in the past ten years.

"Hmmm." She pressed her palm to my cheek. "Another smile."

I leaned my face into her hand, accepting the comfort of her touch. "Yes," I murmured. "Another."

"I like it when you smile," she said softly. "You're so beautiful, Sebastian."

"Beautiful?" I broke out a new scoff. "I don't think I've ever been called that before."

"Well, I hope it's one of many firsts we share, then."

"Deal." I took her hands with the same resolution lining my voice. "But there's still an important topic here."

"Oh, no." But she laughed it out. "Not important. Significant."

"Exactly," I said. "Now before you say anything, hear me out . . ." I paused anyway, predicting she would protest before a single word came out of my mouth. But she surprised me and just quietly stared back, waiting for me to speak.

Well, damn.

Because the one and only time an argument might actually help my nerves—and Christ, why was I so nervous?— she decided to be amenable. I just went for it and said, "I think, for your safety and my sanity, that you should also come to stay here."

"No." The retort was swifter than her prim pop off the

countertop. "Thank you, though." With equal efficiency, she brushed past me and into the bedroom. Her overnight bag was on the floor where I'd dropped it last night after bringing it in from her truck.

"That's all you're going to say?" I huffed, following her back into the bedroom. "Just no, and carry on about your business?"

"Did you need more?"

"Yes, damn it." As she lifted the bag to the bed and pulled out her toiletries and clothes, my ire climbed. The thought of her covering her body, on top of shutting down her thoughts, was like a spike through my brain. "I think we should at least discuss why you're being irrational."

She took a second to arch a brow. "Irrational?"

"You're in danger, Abbigail. What about that don't you understand?"

"It appears you're the one in danger, Sebastian." She emphasized my name with the same impatience I had given hers. "Not me." She pulled the tank over her head, only breaking eye contact while the fabric passed in front of her eyes.

"Exactly. Therefore, by association, so are you."

I studied her carefully, clinging to tendrils of relief while the pieces of my logic—or at least the start of them—seemingly clicked into place. I nearly fell to the floor in gratitude. The reality of our situation was finally coming together for her. Or so I hoped.

As she bent over to tug on a long, pale-green skirt, I was definitely praying. And ordering myself not to tilt my head for a better view of her ass as she did. Jesus, the perfection of this woman's ass . . .

She straightened, and the skirt fell into place with the

hem brushing the floor. "Are you going to shower?" she blurted while nodding in the direction of the bathroom. "I mean, after being near that—fish?"

For a long second, I was lost for a reaction. While she was clearly attempting to evade the subject again and was more emotional about the dead creature downstairs than she wanted to let on, her more practical instincts were taking over. She scrunched up her nose so tightly, her entire face pulled with it. And God help me, even that expression was adorable on her. But if I kept standing here just mooning because of it, I'd be enduring a police interrogation smelling like the back lot of SeaWorld.

So yeah, she was evading. But she was also right.

Damn it.

"We aren't done with this discussion." I whipped my shirt over my head as I stalked toward the bathroom. She followed me with her gaze while wrapping a worn brown leather belt low around her hips. As she tied the long rawhide strands into a knot at the center, she followed me into the bathroom. Her steps were just as determined as mine—and so was her comeback.

"Last night, we didn't even know if we were going to continue seeing one another. Now you're asking me to move in with you. No, telling me I should move in with you. Do you hear how ridiculous that is?" She raised her voice over the running water I started, emphasizing with an upsweep of her arms, as well.

I should have shut her down by ignoring her and climbing into the stall. Instead, I pivoted and hooked my fingers into her thick leather knot. The belt provided perfect leverage for yanking her body up against mine. And damn, did she feel right there. Completely, absolutely right.

"Only one of us was uncertain how we felt last night." My voice was deep and just shy of warning. As her pupils dilated from the impact of my growl, I leaned forward to kiss her— but stopped just short of following all the way through on my intent. I dipped down, biting into her lower lip instead. Oh, yesss. She was so juicy, so sweet. I tugged her soft flesh between my teeth until she inhaled with arousal. When I finally released her and pulled back, she tracked my actions with her glassy, wide stare.

I stepped under the steaming spray of the showerhead without looking back at Abbigail. I could still feel her gaze on me, drenching my tight muscles and throbbing dick more thoroughly than the water. After a few minutes of that, I finally cobbled together the strength to turn and look at her again. She was in the same spot in which I'd left her, fingers pressed to her swollen lower lip where I had possessed her with my teeth.

Well, damn.

Usually I liked to linger in the shower. It was one of the few places I could escape the outside world and do some of my best thinking. But with Abbigail waiting for me just beyond the enclosed space, I was motivated to cut this one short.

As I got out and dried off, she left the bathroom. Correction. She hurried out of the bathroom like I'd just showered in fire instead of water.

"What the hell?" I muttered, cinching the towel around my waist and following her. She was sitting at the foot of the bed, texting feverishly. She didn't even look up when I strutted in, despite how I scooted the towel as low as possible across my abdomen. Seriously? The Sebastian Shark happy trail was on display in full glory, and she couldn't be bothered for a glance? She'd better be dealing with an E. coli outbreak at the kitchen or something close to it.

"Everything okay?" I asked, finally getting her attention.

"Oh, yeah." She smiled at last, taking in my mildly damp body from head to toe. "But Jesus, you make it hard to focus when you look like that."

Oh, that was so much better. I grinned, nudging her legs apart so I could stand between them once more. "Then just focus on me. Right here."

She wrapped her arms around my waist and looked up. "I'd say your wish is my command, but we both know that's not true."

I moved in tighter and pushed her back on the bed. Or tried to.

She stiffened her spine and started angling away. "As much as I love that idea, I need to go." She lifted her face, thrusting out a little frown. "My eldest brother wants to meet me for an early lunch."

"You don't look too enthused."

"I think I'm just confused," she clarified, stressing the last word. "It's out of the ordinary."

"Why? Because he's married to your business partner?"

"Well, that's part of it, of course." Her face tightened, her gaze seeming to jump someplace far away.

"Well, if you think you can wait until after the police are done here, I can go with you?" I offered.

"No, I should go alone. He doesn't even know we're—well, shit—what are we? What do we call this? No matter what we call it, he's not going to like it. All my brothers are fiercely protective." She stood up and smoothed her skirt into place. I hadn't noticed, but her bag was neatly packed and sitting beside the bed.

"Will you be coming back here when you're done? To stay, I mean?" I was done beating around the bush.

"I understand why you're worried about my safety, Bas. I do. And I'd be lying if I said all of this craziness hasn't freaked me out a little bit. I just think moving in with you is a big step. And it's one I don't think I'm ready to take."

Frustration was jockeying for center stage in my emotional theater, and I was doing my best to rein it in. I quickly pulled on a pair of jeans and T-shirt while we talked. "Can I propose a compromise?" My brows were hiked up into my hairline with hope, the new player trying to battle for the spotlight. I took her bag from her hand when she tried to carry it along with her handbag as we left the master suite.

This piqued her interest. "I'm listening," she said while we walked downstairs toward the front door.

"Let's consider the move-in a temporary arrangement until things settle down and the authorities figure out who's behind all these stunts. No long-term commitments, no change of address with the post office." She nodded as I spoke, so I forged ahead, bolstered by her seeming acquiescence. "You can just keep a few weeks' supply of clothing here, swap it out as needed. Of course, my staff does laundry as well. Whatever is easiest for you."

We were beside her truck, and she opened the door. "All right. So, let's do this," she said, taking a deep breath. "I'll stay here for a few days to start, and we can work up to more as needed."

"Done." The word rushed out of my mouth before she changed her mind, and I gripped her face in my palms and kissed her so swiftly I stole the oxygen from her lungs. She grabbed my forearms for balance, and I deepened the kiss, finding it difficult to break away at all.

"Wow. I may never want to leave if you keep that up." Her eyes glittered with excitement as she climbed in behind the wheel and let me close the door to the cab. "I'll go by my place after I meet up with Sean to pack up some things, and then I'll meet you here later this afternoon?"

"Oh, don't worry about it," I said, knowing a small bomb was about to go off and I was intentionally waiting till she was about to drive away to trip the wire.

Confusion twisted her gorgeous face as she tried to work out the meaning of what I said. Finally, she asked, "What do you mean, 'don't worry about it'?"

I winked, grinning like the bastard I was. "Elijah's at your place right now, packing for you." I gave the driver's-side door a hearty double thump, turned on my heel, and strode into my house, quickly shutting the front door behind me.

CHAPTER FIVE

ABBIGAIL

"How is this my life?" I asked of my reflection in the window at Belmont Brewing Company, where Sean was meeting me for lunch. It was one of our favorite places to meet, located on the ocean halfway between his home and mine.

Well . . . the place that used to be mine.

"It's only temporary," I muttered—for the fifth time since leaving the Calabasas city lines. I didn't care about the weird glances I got from the smoochy couple at the table across the way. Right now, I was the lunatic lady mumbling to herself. I felt that crazy anyway.

But damn it, I was completely justified.

While I wasn't champing at the bit to hear whatever Sean wanted to talk about, the invitation couldn't have been better timed. It was the perfect excuse for getting away from ground zero of Crazy Town.

"No, I'm meeting someone." My brother, greeting the hostess in his naturally husky voice, broke into my meandering thoughts.

I stood up and waved him over.

"There she is. Thank you," he said to the young hostess situated near the door. When he was closer, he spread his arms and practically glowed. "Hey, Abs!"

I forced a smirk and batted his big shoulder. "Hey yourself!"

He bent and wrapped me in a warm hug. Oh God, he was big and strong and familiar. And home. But damn it, I must've clung to him a few seconds too long. As soon as he pulled back, he gave me a head-to-toe inspection.

To head off any questions, I quickly said, "Well, you look handsome—but if I tell you that, your head will just get bigger and bigger, so . . . option B."

Sean chuffed. "Which is?"

"I'll just eat chips." I stuffed another crunchy tortilla into my mouth, savoring the extra salt I'd added to the whole basket before Sean arrived.

"Oh, dear God. You destroyed them already?"

I grinned and shoveled another one into my mouth. "Maybuh," I said around the mouthful.

Sean narrowed his gaze. "Aren't you bound by some chef's Socratic Oath not to ruin perfectly good food?"

Our waitress saved me from having to respond to that when she paused in front of our table, placed cardboard drink coasters in front us, and drew out her pen and pad.

"What're you drinking, Abs?" Sean deferred to me.

After all the events of this crazy morning, something from the bar sounded perfect. "A Bloody Mary, please. Spicy." I gave the woman a thin smile.

Sean ordered a Guinness, and the server set off to fill our order.

"So." The guy spread his hands atop the table. "What's new, sister?"

"Oh, you know." I tried to act nonchalant, but he rolled his eyes, not buying a second of my act.

"Okay, if that's how you want to do this." The aged leather of his seat squeaked as he resettled his weight. "I asked Rio how your girls' visit went last night."

I picked up a new chip, breaking it into smaller pieces to make the goodness last. "At my place?" Rhetorical question in every way, so I moved on. "Was more like a flyby than a visit, but if you insist..."

"Rio's answer was... interesting." He twirled his drink coaster, using it as his focal point. In short, totally avoiding my gaze.

"Should I be afraid right now?" I finally uttered. But I already knew that answer. "Interesting" was Sean-speak for several different things. He was either intrigued, incensed, impatient, or in the dark. Maybe all four. At least that was the vibe I read in the firmness of his face and the inquisitive intensity of his gaze.

"She said you might have some interesting news... about your love life."

I tilted my head. Cocked the sassy little grin, perfected since childhood, that usually derailed Sean from giving me the third degree about everything from spilled milk to skipped homework.

But not this time. Not even a little.

Time for a derailment.

"I thought you and she were having a date night. Why were you discussing my love life?"

"We had a wonderful date night, thank you for asking. And it had a very happy ending." He smirked while the waitress dropped off our drinks.

I groaned and sucked down a lot of mine in one gulp. "Guess I walked into that one."

"Surely thinking you'd be escaping my actual question."

I waved a hand toward the attentive blond waitress. "I think we're ready to order."

"I'll have the smoked salmon flatbread, and a kale and quinoa salad."

I joined the girl to impale him with a new gape. "You're having what?"

"The bacon mac 'n' cheese is really good today." But the waitress's suggestion didn't go anywhere.

"Clean fuel is better for the engine," Sean stated.

"Oh, Christ," I muttered.

He bounced up both brows. "That's what you're ordering?"

"No, I think I will have the chicken alfredo."

His darker scowl, clarifying that we'd really descended from Celtic warriors, had the waitress hurrying off to put in our order. Just as well.

"Okay, bruiser," I finally drawled. "Just what the hell is up with you right now?"

Sean took his time sipping on his Guinness. He squinted over the rim of his glass, briefly noting the score of the Dodger game, but that had him grimacing too. "You stealing my lines now?"

"Puh-lease," I scoffed. "Like there's anything to steal."

I dropped my gaze. Instant mistake. The reaction, practically sewn into my DNA, was a surefire tell for anyone who knew me. And Sean definitely knew me.

My mind roared at me, forcing me to accept the inevitability of this moment.

It's time. You can't shove this off anymore, Abbigail.

Rio had respected my right to keep the "Shark Shocker" in the information closet until I could choose the right moment.

But there was no time to wait for that anymore. I was out of moments.

Get out the key. Unlock the diary. Tell him the secret.

"What would you say...if I told you Sebastian Shark asked me out on a date?"

I forced myself to look at him and was relieved by the waitress's quick return to our table with our food.

Sean took a quick bite of salad and finished chewing before issuing an answer as chill as the low tide on the sand outside. "That depends, I guess."

"On...what?" Shoveling in some pasta at least gave me something constructive to do. Best of all, the mouthful of garlic and alfredo sauce was heaven.

"On whether you're asking because you're hoping he'll ask or because he's already asked and you're in a tizzy about what to say."

I managed a grimace around the pasta. "Is there an option C?"

Sean swirled a kale-laden fork. "Does there need to be?"

Now, not even my food could be a mask for my apprehension. Still, I faced the admission in full. It wasn't as hard as I thought, which gave me courage to carefully tuck my fork along the side of my plate.

"We've already been out," I finally declared. "Several times, actually. And—"

Sean cut me short by jabbing his free hand up between us. "Well, fuck. When you say you need an option C, you're serious."

"And that means...what?"

He pulled his hand back in and flipped it around to hammer its heel into his temple. "It means give me a damn second, okay?"

I dropped my hands into my lap. "Okay."

"Shit. I'm sorry, Abs. You're being a grownup here, and I'm snapping like a jerk."

"Just tell me . . . are you mad? That I didn't say anything sooner? Or that . . ." I ordered myself to stop there. No use detailing even more sins for the guy.

But as my big brother took a chomp of his flatbread, he did so with contemplative purpose. He leaned back, slowly chewing, and took to futzing with his coaster again.

"Has the guy been treating you with respect? Making sure you're safe?" he finally asked after a tense moment.

"Well, of course."

"Not 'well, of course.' To be transparent, we're all painfully aware of the hormonal torch you've been carrying for the guy, Abbi."

"Oh my God." And there went my hope of getting in a stress-free bite of pasta.

"But I'm trusting that you know to make decisions with the head on your shoulders and not the zings between your thighs."

"Sean!"

"Abbigail?" He twirled some kale into his mouth with a sublime grin. "Just answer the question."

I took a few seconds to focus on breathing. "I can tell you, with every certainty in my soul, that my safety is Bas's number-one concern." I reached over and wrapped my fingers across my brother's meaty hand. "He drove me home from downtown one night because it was late. He walked me all the way to the door."

Sean's face was a combination of sanction and supposition. "And then all the way inside too?"

"You really want to know the answer to that?"

"Fuck." He glowered at my saucy reply. "No. For God's sake, no."

I tossed my head back, giving in to a gloating guffaw.

His eyes danced like a leprechaun's as he settled fully back into his seat again. "You're enjoying the hell out of this, aren't you?"

"Absolutely and completely." I smiled. "But I wasn't expecting you to be all calm waters about this."

"You're an adult, Abbi." Sean averted his gaze, seemingly trying to align his swirling emotions with the words he wanted to relay. "Eventually we're going to have to release the hounds on some poor fool. You get that, right? Better off some guy who can hold his own—like Shark—than some idiot who will get eaten alive by your pack of overprotective brothers."

"He certainly can do that. Hold his own, I mean," I agreed before stuffing more pasta in my mouth so I didn't say anything else I would have to explain. Time for a subject change. "So, anyway, tell me about the new job you applied for."

With that, Sean was off and running, excitement glittering his eyes while he told me all the details about the new employment prospect.

We finished our meals, and as tempting as chocolate, sugary goodness sounded on top of all the carbs I'd just ingested, I knew I didn't want to pay for it on my next run. "I think I'll pass," I said, smiling as I slid the waitress my credit card with the dessert menu. She gave me a quick wink, letting me know she understood I wanted to pick up the check without a lot of posturing from my brother, and hurried off to take care of settling the bill.

In the parking lot, after one final "make sure he treats you well" type of warning from Sean, we went our separate ways. I climbed into the truck, took a deep breath to clear my mind for driving, and started the engine.

As soon as the Bluetooth engaged with the car, the dashboard display lit up with an incoming call to my cell.

I'd never been so happy to see Sebastian's number.

"Hey." I recognized my failure at hiding the exhaustion from my voice.

"Hey yourself." His voice, so rich and confident and masculine, filled the cabin's air. I almost inhaled it. At this exact moment, he was my opium. "What's wrong?"

"Nothing. Just tired. I had pasta and I'm in a carb coma." I attempted a light laugh, but he cut in.

"Why don't I believe you?" He didn't wait for me to get in even a breath of reply. "Do you need me to come to pick you up? I'm going to come pick you up."

"No." I sighed heavily. "Bas. Stop. I'm . . . I'm fine."

"Abbigail." Again, like he was barely bothering to listen to my words. Like he had already gathered his wallet and phone and was heading to find his driver.

"Hmm?"

"Tell me what's going on. What's happened?"

"Bas, stop. I'm fine. I'm just exhausted. It's been quite the day. You have to admit, things have been a little crazy. But I need to get on the freeway before traffic gets heavy."

"All right. Are you sure you don't want me to come? I can send Joel, if you're more comfort—"

"Really, Bas," I broke in. "It's fine. I'm fine. I'll be there before you know it. Thank you, though."

"Abbi?"

"Yeah?"

"You're turning me a little upside down here. Are you sure you're okay?"

"Yeah." I cleared my throat while tracing a finger along the circle of the steering wheel to settle my thoughts. They finally centered enough so I could murmur, "You know, Mr. Shark . . . I think I'd better be careful here."

"Careful?" His voice was sultry, corresponding to the similar notes in mine. "Why's that?"

"I may wake up and find this has all been a dream."

He growled, but it was like a wolf getting a belly rub. Still, his response was thoroughly and beautifully rugged. "Don't you believe in dreams coming true, Red?"

I went still again.

Finally, he stated, "I'll see you when you get home. Drive safely, Abbigail."

As he clicked off the line, I was stunned at the awareness of a smile on my lips. I had no idea why. His last words had bordered on firm commands, and he'd used that word—*home*—like I was supposed to start accepting the permanence of his mansion over my place.

Yet, I was smiling and I couldn't stop.

And I didn't want to.

His kindness and compassion had worked its way through all the crazy stress and overwhelming challenges thrown in my path today. And the stupid, silly, overwhelmed smile stayed in place the entire time.

Even as warning flares shot off in my brain.

And, even more brilliantly, in my heart.

Already I could see the potential for utter devastation from continuing on with Sebastian Shark. Beyond the fact that a supposedly dead woman had shown up on his doorstep this morning, alive and well. Beyond the dead fish that had appeared minutes later on his pool deck, as a creepy message of warning. Even beyond how he'd convinced me to move in with him less than twelve hours after reconciling with him.

But what a reconciliation . . .

Sebastian somehow already had the power to decimate my existence. My very heart and soul. The things I'd sworn I'd never hand over to the care of another human being.

But it didn't matter if I was a willing donor in this setting . . . because Sebastian Shark was the kind of man who came into a situation and *took*.

And the whole time made you believe it was what you wanted too.

CHAPTER SIX

SEBASTIAN

"Where the hell is that stuff?" I muttered while dropping to all fours and leaning into the cabinet under my bathroom sink. One wrong move and I'd face-plant into the storage space completely.

"Aha!"

I grabbed the dayglow pink bottle and backed out. Or so I thought. I rose too soon and smacked the back of my head on the edge of the cabinet door casing.

"Motherfucker! Fuck!" But that was all the self-pity I had time for. Minutes were ticking by, which meant it was time for me to suck it up.

I plugged my phone into the speaker system in the bathroom, surfed to a relaxing playlist, and adjusted the volume on the speakers. All that was left to do was light the candles I had set around the room. I finished while listening to Craig greet Abbigail as he opened the front door for her.

She didn't spend much time on pleasantries with my assistant, opting to head straight toward the stairs.

Making her way to me.

But my balloon of obnoxious pride was pierced as soon as I laid eyes on her.

She looked exhausted. Her mouth was tight and her

posture weary. Her eyes were tired. The same eyes that found me when I got to the midpoint on the marble stairs.

"Hey there." She attempted to lift her lips, but the energetic smile that usually illuminated an entire room was a dim shadow instead. But weirdly, her dim energy drew me faster toward her. By the time I got all the way down the stairs, her chest rose and fell in perfect rhythm with my steps.

"Hey yourself." I didn't stop advancing. Not until my arms were around her waist, pulling her against my body. My lips found their way to the satin skin of her neck. The woman had the silkiest flesh my tongue had ever explored.

Her sigh, sounding like a mix of relief and bliss, warmed the base of my throat. Her body slackened, allowing the purse on her shoulder to drop to the crook of her elbow. I slid the burden all the way off her arm and then continued the motion, tucking her hand around my bicep.

"Come with me," I directed and then led her back up the stairs.

I had run the bathwater hotter than usual, calculating for the temperature to be perfect by the time she got settled up here. With all the blinds closed and the sun moved over to the other side of the house, the master suite and bathroom were mostly dark. The candles were the sole light source across the bathroom. In my rush, I could only find about fifteen randomly shaped and scented candles, but it was enough to do the job. The room smelled like a cross between a flower garden and fresh linen, but the ambiance was still relaxing. And, at least I hoped, romantic.

"Bas." As Abbi breathed it out, the curves of her face were a candlelit collection of delight. I couldn't help being clear about it, since she turned and dazzled me with it while cradling my face in her hands. "This is . . . perfect."

I was damn grateful for the muted lighting, hoping it concealed the color that rushed to my face. I refused to call it a blush.

"Not sure about the execution," I muttered. "But 'perfect' was the ultimate plan."

She rose on tiptoes and softly claimed my mouth with hers. "I can't wait to get in—but only if you'll join me."

I raised my brows. "That was definitely the plan." And then moved in for another kiss, longer and more languorous.

When we finally untangled our tongues from each other, I tugged the tank top over her head and dropped it to the floor. I stepped back, but only far enough to untie her wide leather belt. I added it to the small pile.

"Now you," she said shyly—though she wasn't too bashful to pull my shirt off. She stepped out of her sandals while I unfastened my jeans, not confident I could withstand her innocent hands fumbling around so close to my hard-on.

"Oh! You even have bubbles." Her impish expression was eclipsed by the sight of her succulent breasts, bared for my appraisal as soon as I unclasped her bra. "Impressive, Mr. Shark."

No. "Impressive" was definitely this pair of gorgeous tits— but I managed to restrain my inner rogue. "Well, if that's all it takes to impress you, my dear, I'm getting off easy tonight." I braced my hold to her hips and pulled her back against me. "Though to be clear, I'll accept 'getting off' in any way I can."

In one motion, I swept her skirt and panties down, puddling them at her feet. "Bas!" she yelped, and that sound alone had my cock jumping again.

"Yes?" Somehow, I got it out with normal inflection

instead of an aroused groan. While my body betrayed how I already craved to skip the bath, she was more than a sex toy to me—and I was about to prove that if it killed me.

I helped my effort by taking more action. As I squatted at her feet to help her step totally out of the clothes, she steadied herself by holding my shoulders. "So chivalrous," she murmured, adding a light laugh.

"Not for long," I growled.

"I'm all yours, Mr. Shark."

"Come on. Let's get in before it cools off too much." I helped her climb into the deep tub, and she sank to her shoulders into the bubbly water.

"Oh, God," she groaned. "This is fantastic."

I stepped in as well. "Move forward so I can sit behind you." When I was settled, I pulled her back against my chest. Cradling her like this, surrounded by the warm water and the candle glow and the mellow music, significant weight started to melt away from my psyche—and my body. I drew lazy circles on her stomach and arms, and she lightly scratched her nails up and down my thighs.

Finally I said, with quiet care not to disturb the bubbles or the ambiance, "I've never done this before."

"Taken a bubble bath?"

"Taken a bath," I clarified. "Let alone with a woman. Or just sat still like this. Just . . . existed." I chuckled. "I think I can hear myself breathing."

"Is that . . . a good thing?"

"I think so. It's nice."

"Yes. It is." Abbi meshed her fingers into mine, and we both watched tiny suds emerge from the contact. "Thank you for doing this for me. Your timing was perfect."

"Do you want to tell me about your lunch date?"

Another minute passed. Two. Abbi took several deep breaths. Just when I thought she'd speak up, she'd stop.

"You don't have to talk about it if you don't want to," I offered at last. "I just thought it might help to get it out of your head. Sometimes it's the only thing that helps."

"Is that how you handle stressful stuff?"

I laughed, really meaning it this time. "Hell no. That's just shit Grant always says to me. Thought I'd try it out."

She joined a soft chortle to mine, though she dropped it to a groan as I stroked my free hand up her arm and focused on the tension in her shoulder. With my thumbs, I found matching knots on either side to work on. She was happy to give me nothing but relieved sighs for a few minutes before finally speaking up again.

"When Sean asked me to have lunch, I had no idea what he'd want to talk about."

She let out a low moan when I applied deeper pressure to a particularly stubborn knot.

"Feel good, baby?"

"Yeeesss. Don't . . . stop."

She extended her joyous groan while I chuckled and rubbed harder—and forced my mind away from an image of her making the sound under different circumstances.

"So what did you and your brother talk about? Everything okay with your family? Your sister-in-law?"

"Everything's fine. Really good, actually." Abbi's head lolled side to side on my chest before she let out a long yawn.

"Do you mind if we get out? The water has gotten cold."

She turned back to look at me—sort of—before sitting forward. I was right behind her. Once I gained my feet, I grabbed one of my bath sheets and wrapped her in it. I didn't set her free. I caged her arms along her sides and held her tightly.

"Hey? Abs?"

But she wouldn't look up.

It was time to bring out my dominant baritone.

"Abbigail."

That worked—at least to snap her attention for a second.

"Baby, what's wrong? Talk to me."

"I think I'm just exhausted. Everything that's happened over the past couple of days seems to be catching up to me. All the emotions, you know? Like a tidal wave." She swiped a tear off her cheek. "But I promise, I'm fine. Will you—"

I waited for her to finish, but she just swallowed roughly, having trouble asking for what she wanted.

"What? Anything. Anything I have. It's yours. But you have to tell me what you need."

"Just hold me. Please."

She rocked into my chest, clutching tightly under my armpits and then around to my shoulders. She gripped me so tightly, I could only fill my lungs to half capacity.

But that was okay. Because she needed . . . me.

After a few minutes, she loosened the clench. She slid her arms lower until encircling my waist. By now, because of her cheek snuggled to my chest, I was acutely aware of both our pulse rates. I willed mine to maintain a calm, steady rhythm.

And that was okay too. Because she needed me.

Several minutes of silence. The air flowed with the music and whispered with the candles. And I just let it, ready and willing to cradle her all night like this . . .

Until she shifted, wordlessly but tenaciously, against me.

Knowing I was still only covered by a big bath towel and very aware that she was only covered by the same. But then she was moving in that quiet and insistent way yet again. Probably aware, as I definitely was, that the plush terry sheets were matted down from our tight, continuous press. That meant there was only a thin barrier between the dewy heat of her skin and the aching desire of mine.

Barricades dissolving more by the minute . . .

By the second . . .

I wanted to be noble at that moment. I ordered myself to be. To do the right thing. To step back and let her have this moment.

But I barely achieved an inch of that because Abbi gripped my waist tighter, forcing me back toward her radiant softness and warmth. In the same moment, she lifted her face and locked her mesmerizing emerald stare to mine.

In an unsteady voice, she admitted, "I need you."

Nobility? What the hell was nobility?

Let alone the infinitesimal shred of decency to which I'd attempted to cling.

Gone—all of it—in a damn flash. Incinerated like dry kindling in a forest fire.

I crushed her body closer and did the same to her mouth with a full and passionate kiss.

She yielded, letting me sweep my tongue between her lips while walking her backward with the advancement of my own steps. I didn't halt until she bumped into the counter, and then I hiked her up onto the vanity.

"Yes," she groaned as I went at her skin with seeking, fervid lips. I explored every inch of bare flesh I could, from her forehead down to where the towel nestled safely between her breasts.

When we were both panting from wild hunger and spiraling need, I abruptly stopped. With brusque urgency, I angled her farther back on the countertop and then took a measured step back.

"Show me," I dictated, my tone coarse.

"What?" She took a moment to raise her eyes from where my erection was trying to escape between the overlapping towel edges.

"Drop the towel and show me your body," I told her. "I want to look at you."

She went to wriggle off the counter and even reached her hand out for support. "Let's go to the bed, maybe?"

"No."

That one finally seemed to sink in. Abbigail halted at the edge of the counter and shot her gaze up to mine. All the candles flickered with the air disturbance. I watched the different flames reflect back in her eyes.

"This is an excellent position," I stated. "Now drop the towel, or I'll do it for you, Red."

She raised her chin. So defiant. So radiant. I cocked my head to the side and studied her for a long second. I was intrigued by the sudden shift in her demeanor—and unsure about how to proceed because of it.

But I didn't want her to be scared. At all. I just wanted to take her mind off the shitty day she'd had.

Reaffirming the goal, even to myself, was my new motivator.

Because I knew—with ridiculous confidence—how to blow the doors off a woman's psyche.

I started by reaching back in, just by the few inches required, to deliver one quick flick between her breasts. With that, the white cotton fell away.

"Jesus, woman." Drinking in her naked form was more intoxicating than closing a high-stakes business deal. That was the best rush I could think of. Before meeting her, at least.

Now, standing in front of her, taking note of every detail, I was more totaled than ever. Her damp, flame-red waves. Her gorgeous, graceful neck. And dear God, all that flushed skin, dusted with the freckles I longed to connect with my tongue—along with one very perfect mole just to the left of her navel. I had already discovered that darling dot while making my way toward her pussy before. Though I was single-focused at the time, a mental image of her unique little mark popped back into my mind at the oddest times—like during quarterly sales reports reviews or listening to Vela's details about her latest boy band obsession.

Needless to say, no way I could look and not touch for another second. Regarding that mole or any other delectable part of her.

I eagerly coaxed Abbi's mouth back open, slamming her with a fresh and forceful kiss. I held her there, palming the back of her head with one hand while using the other to stroke her collarbones in continuous, sensual slides. I kissed and petted her neck, shoulders, and arms—all the while ignoring her breasts, and doing it quite intentionally.

Finally, a moan slipped from her between our thorough kisses.

"Please, Bas," she blurted. "God, please!"

"Please what?" I murmured. "What is it, baby? What do you need from me?"

"You're teasing me, and you know it!"

I rose far enough so she watched me point to myself,

slathering on mock disbelief. "Me? I would never do such a thing." I dared her to refute me by hardening my features—and then determinedly nudging my way between her legs. A gasp escaped her as I trailed my index finger from the hollow at her throat, down her sternum, and then lower.

"You're lying," Abbigail accused in a whisper. "And you're doing it terribly."

"Abbigail." I trapped her gaze in mine and savored her sharp inhalation of response. "I'm about to blow your mind."

She instantly picked up the warning in my words and gave me a sexy hitch of her breath to prove it. With an answering smirk, I continued the pursuit toward her sex.

I already claimed a minor victory as soon as she sat up higher to watch my progress until I stopped mere inches from the soft, inviting cleft of her need. Though her heat was tangible, already beckoning to my fingers, I asked, "You want to be filled, Abbigail? Here?"

Her sighing response wasn't of much consequence. I already knew the answer—confirmed from the second I ran a light touch over her swollen pussy. She jumped as though I'd Tased her.

"Easy, baby."

I ran my finger deeper through her wetness. She moaned but sank back, resting onto her bottom and leaning her shoulders against the large mirror. To make her position more comfortable, I removed my towel and positioned it behind her. "Better?" I murmured.

"Yes. Thank you. But you know we could just go—"

"Hush, baby." My command, as things like that went, was gentle. Not the case with the swift swat I delivered to her mound. At once, she lurched from the invisible Taser again.

Just as instinctively, I clamped her thighs with spread fingers.

"Oh!" she yelped.

"Be a good girl," I admonished, dropping to my knees in front of her. I spread her wider, worshiping the tender pink folds of her slit with my greedy gaze. "Stay still, Abbigail. We don't need to end the night with a trip to the ER." Her ass was perched at the edge of the counter, and too much squirming would land her on the marble floor. But the sight was amazing. Her succulent cunt contrasted with the hard and shiny countertop. Perfect.

My dick was throbbing, an urgent reminder of my rising desire. The effort was boosted by how she responded so well—so naturally—to my dominance. Verbally binding her with my instructions clearly heightened her arousal. With every passing second, her pussy pulsed and gleamed in new and captivating ways.

I rewarded her—and myself, to be honest—for the compliance with a full swipe of my tongue up the center of her folds. She trembled and sighed as fresh wetness slicked her entrance. The taste combined with her potent feminine fragrance to arouse all my senses.

Even the music on the air conspired to help my cause. The smooth tracks I'd selected were finished, and my phone automatically clicked to a new collection of songs—all chosen specifically to fuck to. Oh, hell yes. Throbbing bass lines, passionate lyrics, and deep, sensual melodies added another layer to our growing stimulation.

My pulse sped up to the new beat as my instincts zeroed in on Abbi's spicy taste. Within seconds, it became the center of my existence. I needed more. I'd obsessed about her all day. Even through the seemingly endless police interview, my mind wandered back to her. She was a fire inside me. A pull on my body. A call to my mind. An ache in my soul. But most of all—best of all—the awakening of her sensuality. Her outward shyness but the burning passion that constantly overrode it. The bravery with which she drove past it, driving to satiate her natural needs.

"You're so fucking sexy, Abbigail." I spread her pussy open with my fingers. "So wet for me, baby. So ready for everything I'm going to do to you."

"Yessss," she sobbed out. "Oh yes, Sebastian. It feels so good. Don't stop. Please, don't stop."

"No, baby," I assured her. "I'm not stopping now, girl. Not until you come for me. Maybe twice."

"Mmmm," she moaned. "Oh...okay..."

"Say it for me, Abbigail. Tell me what you're going to do for me."

"I'm..."

"Say. It," I demanded.

"I'm going to come for you. Maybe twice. Oh...oh, please..."

And that was enough talking. Thinking.

I dived in, licking and sucking and savoring her. Covering every last bit of her delicious cunt with my tongue and lips. She was perfect. So. Damn. Perfect.

There were so many things I wanted to do with this girl. Wanted to try with her. But at the very core of it all, I just wanted to please her. Her moaning and keening were letting me know I was off to a solid start.

"Are you close, baby?" I finally prompted, though I kept my mouth fixed to her clit. The vibration of my voice helped me keep the promise of pleasuring her.

"God, Bas." She moaned in time to my words on her most sensitive button. "That's . . . that's so good . . ."

"Yeah, it is," I husked back.

"I . . . I need . . ."

"What?" I prompted. "Tell me, sweet girl."

"I need you to fuck me," she finally said. "Please . . . fuck me. It feels so good when you're inside me."

But as good as that sounded, I wanted to taste her orgasm on my tongue. No, I needed it. But if I was reading her correctly, the emptiness was what was keeping her from going over the edge. "Don't be a cock slut, Abbigail," I prodded when she whimpered again. "I want you to come on my tongue."

I enforced it by firmly licking her swollen nub. I added demanding nibbles until her legs spasmed involuntarily.

"Fuck, Bas! Christ!"

"Come on, baby. Come for me. Let me taste you."

I rammed two fingers up into her tight tunnel. I pumped roughly but never relented on my fast tongue flicks over her erect clit. At last, her walls clutched around my invading hand. She wailed and ruthlessly gripped my hair. I hungrily lapped at her trembling sex, continuing to finger-fuck her through the wild, screaming release.

As her yells calmed into ragged breaths, I praised her. "That was so hot, Red. So fucking hot."

"Oh . . . wow," she rasped. "Jesus . . . Sebastian . . . wow."

"Now show me again."

"Wh-What?"

"Again," I challenged, even as her gaze went from half-lidded to cartoon-wide in a fraction of a second. I ignored the shock, choosing to rise to my full height while keeping my arms wrapped around her. I made sure she was steady on her legs before loosening my hold.

"Wh-Where are we—"

"Shower," I voiced, yanking her in the direction of the stall.

"We just had a bath," Abbi croaked. "Can't we just crawl into bed? I'm ready to pass out."

"We need to rinse off first."

She sighed, but it was the distraction I needed to get her into the glass enclosure with me. Once the twelve chrome heads throbbed to life, she groaned in new pleasure.

"Oh, God. Your shower is such heaven."

"You mean our shower?" Before she could concoct a quip for that, I directed, "Turn around so I can wash your hair."

For some reason, she stared at me like I'd just spoken in another language. "Sebastian, I can wash my own hair," she finally said.

"I'm aware. But I'm taking care of you, remember?" I pushed her to sit on the teak bench that was built into the corner. While I grabbed the handheld sprayer, I instructed, "Tilt your head back."

Wasn't like the task was a chore for me. Abbigail's hair was the most fascinating color of red. When the water soaked it, plastering it to the milky skin of her back, the shade deepened to merlot. I worked the shampoo from her scalp to the ends over and over until even her feet and toes seemed to go limp. The multiple showerheads kept her warm while I worked on her hair.

After rinsing the shampoo suds, I used the conditioner Pia gave me for my last birthday and repeated the treatment. I rarely used the stuff on my own hair, but it left Abbi's so silky in my fingers, maybe I needed to rethink my routine. Before replacing the sprayer, I passed the water over her shoulders and back to make sure she was free from suds.

My beautiful, content woman let out a happy sigh when I shut off the shower. At once, my chest constricted. A strange feeling overcame me, a tightness I couldn't connect with at first. And bizarrely, it had nothing to do with my continuing erection. This was much different. And it wasn't physical.

Holy shit.

It was emotion. Raw, unannounced, unintended feelings.

Sensations that swelled further when I grabbed a couple of towels from the rack outside the shower stall and then wrapped the first one around her body. While unfolding the second, I instructed, "Bend forward."

"What?"

"Just do it, please," I growled good-naturedly, though I added a teasing dig of my thumbs into the creases of her hips, causing her to let out an ear-piercing squeal. "Well, what do you know?" My grin spread impossibly wide. "Someone has a ticklish spot."

"Don't get any ideas!"

"At least I know one surefire way to make you bend to my will."

I raised a brow in challenge, discovering it was all I needed to make her comply this time. She finally bent forward, shaking out all her wet hair. I wrapped the towel around her tresses and twisted the end until it folded down on itself like a turban.

"Stand up."

She reached up and ran an assessing hand over the towel piled on top of her head and grinned. "How, or should I say, *why* do you know how to do that?"

"Vela taught me." Just the mention of my favorite little

person's name made my heart swell even more. "But before that, there were the years I took care of my sister. But you know that worn-out story already."

Abbigail wasn't laughing anymore. She seemed absorbed by my words like they weren't all that worn out. She flattened her fingers right over my heart before saying, "You're an amazing man, Sebastian Shark."

Every pore of my being was trampled anew by that odd, tight sensation. "Not really."

She didn't say anything.

Neither did I.

We stood in that position longer than we should have, with our bodies close and our stares entangled, until I couldn't stop the rest of my words from coming out.

"But something about you, Abbigail Gibson, makes me want to be better."

Her answering smile was full and kind. From its light alone, I could feel the sincerity of her trust and honesty. "Bas?"

"Hmmm?"

"I'm glad I'm staying with you."

I smiled too—glad she was standing where she was, how she was. She'd be able to catch my heart in the next three seconds, when it burst all the way out of my chest. "I'm glad too, Red," I managed to utter in the meantime.

"I mean…I'm not happy about the situation that's brought me here, but I'm very happy to be here nonetheless."

"I'm not thrilled with the extenuating circumstances either," I admitted. "But this way, I know where you are and that you're safe." I slid my hand up her toned thigh to the sexy curve where her leg met her ass. It was one of my favorite places on a woman's body. Especially hers. "And there are some key extra benefits to having you here too."

Her blush was more stunning than any peony I could ever send her. "Well, yes. There are definitely those."

As loudly as my cock screamed at me to park her back on the vanity and fill her pleas of fifteen minutes ago, I restrained myself hard enough to order instead, "Sit down here, and I'll brush out your hair. It's easier to do while it's wet. And yes, I've learned that lesson the hard way."

"Let me guess," she said as she sat. "Vela once convinced you to let her go right to bed after a bath?"

I chuckled. "See? You are such a smart girl."

"But once was all it took, right?"

I grunted. "Last time I listen to a five-year-old."

"See?" She giggled. "You are such a smart guy."

I winked at her while taking out the "miracle brush" that Pia made me keep here. The thing worked wonders on tangled wet hair. Without another word, I got to work on Abbi's long mane. Once more, our timing worked out well with the rotating playlists on my phone. One of my favorite songs began playing over the speakers. Then another. As I got lost in the task of taming Abbi's fiery mane, I absentmindedly sang along with the soul-heavy soundtrack—

Until I was caught short by a reflection in the mirror.

That of Abbigail's full gape.

"Red?" I nearly dropped the brush. "Did I hurt you?"

"No, no," she insisted. "It feels amazing."

"Okay..."

As I drew out the word, she paused to clearly measure her next words. "You...can sing."

I frowned. "Uhhh..."

"I mean...beautifully." She was quiet, giving me another

unnerving stare down. "I mean, holy crap," she blurted. "Is there anything you can't do, Mr. Shark?"

Fortunately, I was hit with a fast answer. The sooner I distracted her from this track, the better. "Crochet."

As she snorted out a laugh, she quickly covered her face and its new flush. "So ladylike," she mumbled from behind her fingers—which had me nailing her with a strengthened scowl.

"Abbigail," I ordered, gently tugging at her wrists. "Don't hide any parts of yourself from me. I want to see it all, woman."

She stunned me a little—all right, maybe more than that—with the force of her newly raised stare. Dear God. Her irises were evergreens, so ethereal and entrancing. But because of that intense hue, I could also tell she was working up the courage for her response to me. It was going to be honest. Yes, to the point of cutting. I'd seen this look; I knew this look. It always came before a stinger.

"Hmmm."

Especially when she added that kind of a *hmmm*.

"You know, it's interesting." She looked down at where her hands toyed with the edge of the towel but then back up to pierce me with a pointed gaze. "You want to see every part of me... Yet the moment I complimented your singing, you changed the subject quicker than a hooker changes panties."

"That's different." I brushed all her hair back with an efficiency to match my tone before separating it in three equal sections.

"How so?"

Her charge was just as no-nonsense. Clearly she wasn't going to let this go—so why not give her what she wanted? I would just lay it out there, and then she'd feel like shit. At least then we could move on to pretending it never happened.

Story of my life.

"My mother used to sing. All the time. To Pia and me. Around the house, in the car..." I drifted for a brief moment, focusing on schooling my features so she didn't have to witness my pain. "It's not easy to think about, so I don't like talking about it. But there you go. Now I have."

I finished the single braid—the one hairstyle I could accomplish—and grabbed Abbi's hair tie from the vanity. After securing the end, I stepped back to give her room to stand. As soon as she did, she returned her hand to the middle of my chest. Her stare was even more luminous now. And harder for me to confront.

"I'm sorry," she whispered.

I pried her hand free but kissed her knuckles to declare a truce—though I wasn't quite sure what from. "It's fine." I just knew I needed the pressure across my lungs to stop now. "Really, it was a long time ago."

"I know." She finally showed me mercy, lifting an adorable little smile. "Can we go to bed now?" And again with the change of subject. "I'm so relaxed after all this pampering. Thank you for spoiling me."

Obeying my surging impulses, I swept her legs out from beneath her. She let out a yelp of surprise while instinctively wrapping her arms around my neck. I carried her into the bedroom, meaning to give her a tender kiss before I lay her down on the bed—but the moment I felt her lips beneath mine, the beast inside me roared back to life. Her body called to mine with its perfect, yielding curves. Her passion awoke mine with its needy manifestations: the way she tugged on the ends of my hair and sneaked her tongue between my lips, seeking deeper heat from me.

I followed her down onto the bed as though our bodies were already joined. The thought of being separated, even to go around to the other side of the bed, was unbearable. I was long past the point of desiring her, evidenced in full by my aching, swollen cock. My erection was turning my towel into a tent—a really useless one. My brain and heart were no longer talking for me. The time for all the emotional shit had passed. I was solidly back in my comfort zone—carnal cravings, unadulterated pleasures.

"I need to be inside you," I growled into the pit of her ear. As she mewled in response, I grinded my hips against hers. But not for long. With a determined snarl, I pushed her legs apart with my knee. "I need to feel you, baby." Pulling the towel from her body, I tossed it to the ground beside the bed.

"Yes." She arched her back as I bit into the underside of her breast, then sucked and licked the same spot. I crudely kneaded her flesh while hungrily moving back up to her mouth.

"When are you going to learn I'm not actually asking, baby?"

Abbi tugged the towel off my waist and tossed it off the bed. She stroked my back and ass in greedy desperation. Her nails were exquisite scrapes across my skin as she explored every peak and valley of my torso.

Until she found the courage to venture between my thighs.

Her tentative touches from behind were enough to rip a harsh groan from my chest. Her eagerness was replaced by carefulness, and when I pulled back from our kiss to search her waiting gaze, I couldn't quite read what I found there.

"What is it?" I rasped, lust scratching my throat like fire.

"I ... ummm ..."

"Abbigail?"

"I just . . . well, do you like . . . that?"

"What's that, baby? Be specific. There's very little I don't like, especially when you're the one doing it."

"Me. Touching you. There."

"I love when you touch me." I thrust my dick against the inside of her thigh again to illustrate just how much. "I'm so hard for you, Red. I'm fighting the urge to just drive into you."

"Why?"

"Why? What do you mean, why?"

"Well . . . I want the same thing." She held my gaze while whispering it. "Please, Bas. Fuck me. Just do it."

I choked again, more vocal about it, when she widened her legs in welcome. Ohhh, yes. Little Miss I Swear I Was Just a Virgin planted her succulent pussy directly in line with my cockhead—and then completely blew my mind when gripping my whole shaft and stroking it through her wetness several times.

"Fuuuccckkk. Abbigail." I grabbed her wrist, but that didn't dislodge her grip. "You're playing with fire, girl." Nearly literally. She held my shaft in a mind-altering squeeze. It was heaven and hell in one excruciating moment.

"Then burn me, Bas. Light me up. I'm dying here."

Correction.

Now I was in both heaven and hell.

I swatted her hand off my cock. Truly lined myself up at her entrance.

And then thrust forward.

A garbled scream escaped from Abbi. I almost apologized—my size was likely a lot for her to take all at once—but I was past the point of checking my baser instincts. The madman in me took over. I began pumping in and out of her like an animal.

"Shit! Bas!" She wrapped her legs high around my waist while I fucked her harder. I fused our mouths together, stealing her breath as she stole my sanity. I couldn't get deep enough. I would never have enough of this woman.

I pushed her knee toward her chest, so her foot rested beside my hip. Her channel opened even more for my invasion, which helped me regain a semblance of control. I slowed my pace. One languid slide in and then another back out, almost to the point of leaving her body altogether.

Again.

Then again.

And one more time before she clawed even harder into my shoulders. I grunted, certain she was breaking the skin. I welcomed the surety. I craved her mark on me. If only she realized the claim was more than skin deep. Would that admission scare her the way it terrified me?

I banished the thought by refocusing on her body—and how it was affecting mine.

I withdrew from her heat. Kneeled up over her. She popped her green eyes wide. They were drenched in glittering arousal.

"Turn over. All fours."

My growl was dark and deep, without an inch of room for debate. Abbigail rolled to her stomach, her braid lying down the center of her back. The view was beckoning to me to yank her up to her hands and knees. The lightning-fast argument I was having with myself was decided when the sassy brat led her next transition by lifting her ass up off the bed. The movement was for no other reason than to entice me. If she wanted to poke the beast, she'd feel his bite. I gripped her braid in one hand, tugging her head back at a sharp angle. She scampered up to her hands and knees to ease the slant, but I just took up the slack in the braid by pulling back more. With my other hand, I gave her a few quick slaps on her ass that now rested against my thighs. I could feel how soaked her pussy was along my leg when the cool air of the room blew across my skin.

"You're soaked, Abbigail. You love the way I fuck you." I spanked her ass again, and she moaned. "Do you want more, baby? Do you need to come?"

"God, yes! Please, yes. I do."

I pushed two fingers into her and lazily pumped in and out. "How's that? Better?"

She attempted to move her head from side to side but couldn't while tethered by her hair. "No, no, that's not." She pushed her ass back into my hand for more, and I quickly added a third finger.

"How about now?" I taunted beside her ear while picking up the pace of the finger fucking.

"Bas! Why are you teasing me?"

I used my thumb to rub her clit roughly while I fucked her with my hand, pressing down to stroke her G-spot.

"Fuck! No! Shit! Oh . . . Bas! Oh my God!"

I couldn't take any more. I needed to finish us both off.

I released her hair and pulled out my fingers, wiping her slickness across her ass. Before Abbigail could process much, I filled her again. With my cock.

"Give it to me. Give it all to me. Let me feel you come on my dick, Red." Sweat formed on my forehead, a similar sheen evident across Abbi's back. I dug my fingers harder into her hips, pulling her back onto my length as much as I thrust into her. Our bodies made a solid *smack* each time we collided.

Finally, as I felt the prickling sensation in my lower back and around to my groin, I slowed my thrusting. The ecstasy in my psyche was too damn good. The heat in my blood was too damn perfect. The pressure in my balls was too damn painful. Oh, yes. Agony to the point of ecstasy. I never wanted it to end. But at the same time, I already knew how good this orgasm was going to be.

"Come, Abbigail! You have five seconds. I'm blowing in five."

"God, yes!" she cried.

"Four." I thrust deeply, swiveling my hips when I bottomed out against her ass, rubbing against her swollen clit.

"Oh!" she cried out again.

"Three," I warned, repeating the thrust and swivel.

"I'm close. So damn close, Bas."

I reached over her hip and snaked my arm beneath her to find her clit. I squeezed the bud between my thumb and index finger. She bucked forward, but I held her steady. "Two!" I shouted, my orgasm boiling up from my balls.

"Fuck, fuck! Yes! God, Bas!" Her pussy pulsed and clenched around my dick as I shot my load deep inside her. I stilled completely while the inside of her channel seared me with her creamy release. Mixed with my own, we were a wet, sticky, well-satisfied mess.

At last, I rolled to the side, pulling Abbigail with me. She settled into the space in front of me. The little spoon to my big spoon. The puzzle piece that fit mine. I'd always wondered about all that bullshit when Pia made me sit through romantic movies, but now I knew. It was a perfect analogy, actually.

"You are ridiculous," she finally said through a yawn.

"I was thinking more along the lines of amazing," I replied dryly. "But magnificent would also suffice. I'd *settle* for outstanding."

"Okay, ridiculous it is." There was a soft smile in her voice.

I buried my nose in her hair, enjoying the smell of my shampoo on her more than I cared to admit. "In that case, you're also ridiculous." I held her quietly for a minute and then added, "Thank you."

She turned to face me. "Good night, Mr. Shark. Thank you for everything tonight."

"Always, Ms. Gibson. I will do whatever is in my power to make your days—and nights—the best they can be."

She kissed my nose and smiled, eyes already closing.

"Night, baby."

She turned over again, getting comfortable to sleep, and very faintly, so quietly that I couldn't be sure my mind wasn't playing tricks on me, I heard her mumble, more to herself than me, "I could definitely love you."

CHAPTER SEVEN

ABBIGAIL

"Abbigail?"

"Hmmm?"

"You do know they sell things like this already finished, right?"

Sebastian scraped his wooden stool across the stained concrete floor of the do-it-yourself pottery painting studio as he plunged on. "Completely ready to use. I'm serious, in all kinds of designs and patterns. It's pretty cool."

"Oh, now where's the fun in that?" I retorted cheerfully.

"But—"

"Heard you the first time, Mr. Shark. And the second. And now the third."

And if he made it a fourth, I still wasn't letting him off the hook. He'd told me to pick something to do for a date night, and we were painting pottery if it killed us.

Judging by his behavior, I thought it might. In a few ways, I understood his squirming. For a man who was used to the world marching to his beat, it was difficult to relinquish control—even over something as simple as the activity choice for a night out.

Emphasis there on out. If it were up to Bas, we'd be locked away in his palace even now, fucking each other on every available surface. Not that that would have been a hardship, but I'd needed to get out of that house. I'd been going stir-crazy. Even with their ridiculous size and stature, the walls were closing in on me. Not literally, but close enough that I was feeling like it. The craziness surrounding us—Tawny in the pool house, uncertainty in the air, Elijah and his team following every step I made—was more intense pigment in the paint bucket of our lives. And while I'd never had any illusion that life with Sebastian Shark would be simple, this routine was stifling. For close to two weeks, we went to work during the day and came home right after. A decadent dinner was followed by incredible animal sex until we collapsed into mutual unconsciousness. The next day, we awoke to do it all again.

Needless to say, I'd been giddy as soon as the words "date night" spilled from Bas's oh-so-sexy lips.

"So what did you choose to paint?" I asked, looking over the supplies on the high-top table we shared. "I'm making a utensil caddy!"

If nothing else, I'd at least showed him how this kind of stuff was done. Overzealously leading by example, and all. Sebastian definitely got that part, a conclusion based on his grin getting wider.

"That's an unreasonable amount of glee over kitchen tools, Ms. Gibson," he observed, going for droll with his own mien.

"Not for a girl who spends the majority of her day in a kitchen," I volleyed. And this time, it was my truth. I was the girl who got giddy when I walked into the home goods store. The utensils and gadgets aisles were my Mecca. Some girls liked shoes and handbags, I drooled over small kitchen appliances and cutlery. Rubber spatulas and cookware brought butterflies to my stomach.

"You make a very good point," Sebastian conceded, his smile easing into casual angles. "I guess I didn't think of it like that." He studiously watched the way I wiped my bisqueware with a moist sponge and copied the process with the dinner plate he'd chosen.

"Well right now, you've got to think about something else," I stated while gathering both his sponge and mine.

"Something besides you?"

I bit my lip and gave him what must've been a simpering smile, but I didn't care. Okay, he got major date night points for that, not that I was about to admit it, however. "We have to let these dry completely before painting, but by the time we get our paints, they'll be ready. Now's the time to narrow down your color choices. Do you know which ones you want to use?"

He blinked slowly. "Colors?"

"Yeah." I laughed. "You know, the stuff that makes things a little more interesting? People use it to liven up stuff like their clothes and—" I stopped short, taking in the view of his formfitting black T-shirt and jeans, paused, and then spurt out more laughter. "Okay, moving on. You can't leave your piece totally naked—"

"Why?" He tucked his hand beneath the table to squeeze my hip. "Naked is good. Sometimes . . . very good."

"Sebastian."

"What?"

"Focus on your colors."

"No."

"Attitude!" But my teasing tone and arching eyebrow only made him slide out a sexy smirk. "Follow me, Padawan." I made another attempt at prying his hand off my hip and using the momentum to tug him to his feet. "I'll show you all the choices."

"Padawan?" He choked on the word but acquiesced to trailing behind me, heating my back with his gaze. I'd worn a top that only connected at the neck with a bow. The rest of the fabric wafted in the breeze as I walked, billowing out from my body in alluring ways. I'd paired the loose top with skinny jeans that left nothing to the imagination on the bottom. The denim hugged my ass and hips before tapering to my ankles, where I finished with an open-toe ankle boot. Since my hair was in desperate need of a trim, it was piled high on my head in a messy bun, which also showed off the blouse's bow detail.

The paint station girl was absent for a second, doing refills for a kids' birthday party, so we had the corner to ourselves. I picked up the kiln-fired sample tile and turned to Sebastian with it, already explaining how the colors would be darker when our pottery was finished, but the words drizzled to a halt in my throat. He was all but radiating with pure lust, turning every thought in my head to dust.

"I can't think straight when you look at me like that." My voice came out in a needy, hoarse moan.

"Goddamn, you smell good," he growled in the pit of my ear, pressing fully against me. "What are you wearing?"

"H-Hey," I husked, trying to take a step back. But he held me tight with a hand at the small of my back.

"Easy there, pal. This is a family establishment."

"That's not my concern at the moment." I felt his cheeks tighten with his knowing grin.

"Bas . . ." And I was back to barely getting one syllable out. The effect he had on my body was unnerving. "Focus."

I grabbed a few different pinks and reds, thinking I would try to paint peonies on my container. Usually my ideas were bigger than my artistic ability and I ended up with a simpler design than imagined, but I always liked the process of trying. Bas grabbed a few paints—I wasn't sure if he even looked—before we went back to our table.

I reached and scooped a pencil out of the brush caddy. "I'll try to sketch this out first. Or maybe I'll see if they have a stencil." I nodded, thinking that might be a better option. "Thank God my kitchen isn't *Pokémon* themed."

I'd barely started to sort out my supplies when Bas swiveled that quietly incisive gaze back on me. "Your kitchen," he echoed, tilting his head. "A pretty important place?"

I smiled softly. "Well, yes. Of course."

"When did you discover your passion for cooking?"

My smiled wobbled. But how could I refuse him a response? Especially right now, after he'd pinned me with his full attention.

"I used to help my mom cook dinner for the family on Sundays. I mean, I did it on other days of the week too, but Sundays were special. My grandparents would come over, and sometimes my aunts and uncles and cousins if they weren't busy. As we got older and everyone had sports and school commitments, it got harder for everyone to come together."

I paused, wondering if it would be hard for him to listen to stories like these.

"What was that like?"

"What do you mean?"

I hated asking, because there was genuine intrigue in his voice. His face was filled with the same. But I couldn't help it. I was equally as curious. Did he want menu details? Or know how we had to mix up the seating arrangements? Or how my mom never let me miss Sunday dinner, even if Monday was a holiday and I could have longer sleepovers with my friends if I skipped?

Fortunately, he didn't leave me to fill in those weird blanks. "I don't know," he said with a shrug. "I mean, having that many people around. All in your house at one time."

A small laugh spurted out. "Loud."

Clearly he was mystified by the concept. "Did everyone get along?"

"Well, sure." I emulated his shrug. "I mean, for the most part. Mostly they're happy memories," I admitted. "Sometimes, my mom and her brother argued—especially if my uncle was drinking. And we're Irish, so let's be honest. There was beer and whiskey at every occasion."

In typical Bas fashion, he didn't skip a beat before plunging into the task in front of him. I watched as he painted his plate with steady, even strokes, marveling at how he approached everything—even something as unfamiliar as painting pottery—with such confidence.

And why did that infuriate me and arouse me at the same time?

He looked at his plate from another angle and made a confused grimace. "How am I going to get the underside?"

"Most people don't worry about the underside."

"Most people aren't me."

I bit back a full grin. I couldn't argue that point in any form. "You have to wait until it dries. But it will dry quicker than you think. Are you painting the whole thing black?"

"You worry about yours, and I'll worry about mine." He didn't break his concentration to grab even a second of eye contact with me. I had a feeling he lived his life similarly. Why glance to the side when he'd always had his most important things and people in front of him? His thriving business, his dream building, his sister, and his niece. What and who else did he really have to worry about? It seemed a simple concept, but thinking about it now in light of all my memories, I felt a little sad for him. But at the same time, perplexed. He'd come from nothing and now had everything—but in so many ways, his world had remained exactly that small.

My rumination must have extended my silence longer than I realized, because Sebastian rammed his brush into the rinse bowl with a loud clatter. "Are you upset now? For Christ's sake, you can't really be that sensitive, Abbigail."

I whipped my head up. "What are you talking about?"

"Why are you always trying to make small talk instead of talking about your family?"

"What was all the sharing just now about the Sunday dinner memories?" I gritted my teeth in frustration. "But way to have a hissy fit, chief."

He quirked a brow. "A hissy fit? Chief?"

"That's what I said."

"Explain."

I was tempted not to—but for the first time, he made the word a request instead of a demand. "All right, fine." I set my own brush down and turned to face him better. "You act like a bratty child when you don't like what's going on around you," I asserted. "And I suppose it's always worked for you, and that's why you continue doing it." As I paused to think for a second, I shrugged again. "But I have to admit, it's hard to imagine Grant or Pia tolerating being manipulated like that."

His gaze nearly matched the pigment on his plate.

"Woman. What are you talking about?"

Well, well, well. It appears I've struck a nerve.

I straightened my spine and set my chin. "It's pretty elementary psychology, Sebastian. You have to consciously know what you're doing when you behave that way. All that bluster?" I waved toward his discarded paintbrush, as well as the dirty rinse bowl water he'd spattered across the table.

"Please," he snickered. "Enlighten me."

"Don't patronize me either. It's rude. When you throw those fits, you think you'll intimidate whoever you're trying to bully at the moment with your show of dominance. It seems so obvious to me. I suppose it works on a lot of people. I think it probably even worked on me more than once." Heat spread across my face as I flushed at the admission. I was pretty sure he saw it too—but reading his reaction past his shadowed gaze and tight frown wasn't a remote possibility.

We sat in silence for a few moments.

Long damn moments.

We ended the standoff by simultaneously retrieving our paintbrushes and then resuming our painting.

For a second, I tried looking at the bright side. At least he didn't insult me again by trying to deny my assertion. Nor was I going to apologize for what I'd said. I seriously hadn't been trying to start an argument, but he'd pushed until I vocalized my theory.

The longer we stayed silent, the higher our tension mounted.

Eventually, Sebastian broke the silence. "How long has it been since you've been back east?"

I squinted my eyes in concentration. "I think it's been a year already. Wow, that's crazy. Sometimes time passes too quickly, doesn't it?"

"You have no idea." He shook his head but smiled. "I remember when Vela learned to walk. And also said my name the first time. And her first day of kindergarten..." He set down his paintbrush again, but this time it was with a gentle motion. "That feels...strange," he murmured. "To admit that. Christ...time is slipping away faster than I can deal with."

I slid my hand over his. "Your face lights up in the most magnificent way when you talk about your niece. It's beautiful that she's so deeply entrenched in your heart."

His scowl wasn't the reaction I expected, but it wasn't a shocker. "I don't know about beautiful," he returned. "Terrifying seems more accurate."

I tightened my fingers across his. "Well...that's love for you."

He shifted in his seat from my bold declaration. And here was the response I'd fully anticipated—though his follow-up, so blatantly real and soul-felt, was nowhere on my agenda at all.

"I've learned more about the world—and about myself— through that child's eyes than I ever thought possible," he confessed. As punctuation, he raised a negating hand. "Before you even ask me to cite examples, I don't have specifics. I just know I've felt like I've been kicked in the nuts on so many occasions from experiences with that kid. It's a special kind of terror."

His grated words wove even deeper into my spirit, making me glad for the moment he took to simply shake his head. A faraway look took hold across his face, and I took a secret stab at nailing the motivation. Wonder? Bemusement? Disbelief, maybe? Or perhaps it really was what he claimed. Sheer terror.

"Do you think this is dry enough to do the other side?"

His subject change, erratic as it seemed, couldn't have been better timed. I needed neutral conversational ground right now. My heart was ready to file a whiplash claim with my psyche, dealing with his switch-ups between silken lover and conniption-fit control freak. But his artistic confusion was doable to deal with, as he looked from my project to his and then back again, maybe gauging if we were progressing at the same pace.

"I think so," I answered him, touching a fingertip to the surface of his plate. "It looks and feels like it is. Are you really doing the backside all black as well?"

"Yep."

"I like it," I said slowly. "It's very . . . black." I tried keeping a straight face as the words came out, but when he stared at me for two seconds too long, we both burst out laughing.

"You're a terrible liar, Abbigail." He laughed it out and then continued with the sound. With a start, I realized I'd never really heard him make the noise before. Not like this. An actual, unguarded, thoroughly genuine laugh.

"I was honest!" But he clearly didn't buy my plea. I looked back at my pink caddy, realizing I wasn't any more impressed. The flowers were going to be the tricky part, and I wasn't feeling confident they would be recognizable as peonies when I finished.

"I'm going to get a bottle of water up front. Would you like something?" Just as I asked, Sebastian's cell phone vibrated between us on the table.

"I need to take this. I asked Elijah to check in on Tawny," Bas said, looking at the caller ID.

"Water?" I asked again, leaving to give him some privacy.

He gave me a quick nod, and I headed toward the front of the store where they sold light snacks and drinks for their patrons to enjoy while they painted. I lingered a bit longer than necessary, checking out finished projects the store displayed for inspiration and trying to give Sebastian time to take the phone call with his private investigator.

By the time I returned, he was off the phone and back to work on his dinner plate. "Everything okay?" I asked, setting a bottle of water beside him.

"Thank you."

Sebastian cracked the seal on the lid and tilted the bottle up to his lips, capturing my full attention. How did the most ordinary acts become so sensual when he was the one doing them?

Noticing how he basked in my blatant attention, I flipped my regard back to the unfinished piece in front of me. It needed at least two more peonies, but I was seriously more interested in the fresh subject at hand.

"So what's up with Tawny? Have you seen her around the house?" This weekend marked two weeks that she'd been staying in Bas's pool house, and as far as I knew, Elijah was no closer to knowing who'd threatened her—and, if her assertions were right, who were still after Sebastian, as well.

"Not really." Bas was back to studying his plate as a convenient focal point for his gaze. I wasn't surprised, given the traces of tension beneath his tone. "I think she's trying to stay out of the way. Elijah keeps track of her comings and goings, of course. He said she only leaves the property a couple times a week."

An extended breath left my lips. "Normally, I'd call his spying a little creepy—but right now I'm glad he's keeping an eye on her." I frowned while mixing some white and fuchsia shades, creating a silky carnation color on my palette. "Shit, I don't know how I feel about the whole thing," I confessed. The soft paint hue wasn't wrapping my nerves in a drop of its pretty serenity. "It's all so strange. Have the police come up with anything?"

"No," Bas responded. "I don't expect they will. And even if they do, I doubt they'll share it with me."

I compressed my frown tighter. "Why do you say that?"

"Baby, I'm not exactly their favorite citizen."

"But you still have the civil right to be kept safe." I huffed hard, incensed by the idea that the police would discount his safety because he may have pissed them off in the past. That was a tiny effort compared to staying even about his follow-up: a grin that quickly turned into a full chuckle. "What's so funny?" I challenged.

"Nothing."

"No. Tell me."

"It's not 'funny,' necessarily," Bas explained and lifted my knuckles to his lips. After bussing them thoroughly, he let the open affection spread across his face. God, how I wanted to freeze-frame the moment and cherish it for a bit longer. Just an hour . . . or five. "I just lo—uhh, admire—your idealism," he went on. "It's so endearing. So purely . . . you. It's one of the things I adore about you. You can't recapture that once it's gone, and I think I envy you for still possessing it at your age."

While talking, Bas wasn't sitting still. He flipped over his dry plate with one hand and used the other to squirt white paint into one of the palette divots. The sight of the stuff was so surprising, I wasn't shy about my curious gawk.

"I need a pencil. Be right back."

"A pencil?"

But he'd hopped off his stool and bounded away by a few steps before I was done blurting it. I watched him cross the shop with the same authority he traversed his own office, his steps effortless and effectual, before he paused at the supply area. The young woman in charge of the station was back from helping another customer and seemed especially happy to lend a hand. I rocked back a little, watching with amusement as Bas gave the girl the usual abrupt treatment he gave most strangers. Who was I kidding? He acted like that toward people he knew, too.

He strode back toward me with his trademark confidence, twirling the pencil between his fingers like a practiced juggler with a baton. Fitting, since the girl behind him started resembling a deflated balloon. Not that I was going to make him aware of my little spy job. The second he turned back, I busied myself with the last peony on my caddy.

"Get what you needed?" I asked, trying to sound carefree.

"Yes. Apparently, you have to use a special pencil or the lines will show after it's been in the kiln," he said with authority.

"Good to know."

"And what, may I ask, are you grinning about now, Ms. Gibson?"

"I'm curious what you're going to do on that black canvas you've created." I angled my chin toward his piece while dipping my brush in the darkest magenta on my palette.

In lieu of an answer, Sebastian simply started sketching with the magic pencil. But he rendered the drawing so lightly, it wasn't until he began going over the lines with the white paint that I could make out what he was doing.

"A skull?" I blurted. "Really? I didn't peg you for a

memento mori kind of guy."

"A what?" he asked, concentrating on the lines of his design.

"Memento mori. Directly translated from the Latin, it means, 'remember you must die.' Historians believe that in the fifteenth century, people wore skulls, on jewelry and clothing, to remind themselves of their own mortality."

His snort-smirk was a damn gorgeous volley. "Honestly, I just thought Vela would find it amusing on a dinner plate because she gives me a lot of shit about my cooking." And at once, his lips lifted a little higher, back into the unique because-of-Vela smile, and I couldn't help a light laugh of my own.

"I bet she'll love it, then." I set my brush down with a flourish and announced, "There. Done. It's hard to tell what the colors will really look like until it's fired, but I saved the first blob and am proud of the rest." I held the caddy up and back, rotating the thing just to be sure I hadn't missed any key spots. "I think this might be my best work yet."

"Yet?" Bas remained focused on his piece, going over his design with a second coat of white. I didn't have the heart to tell him that his skull would likely look more like a zombie because of the lighter color on the dark background, especially because he followed up by murmuring, "So . . . you come here a lot?"

"Hmmm. I wouldn't say 'a lot.' A few times a year, I guess."

"Other date nights, then?"

I yelped out a laugh before it could be helped, and several patrons whipped their gawks in our direction.

"You're seriously asking that, knowing the 'extent' of my 'experience' before we met?"

Bas ducked his head until his face filled the space in front of mine. His gaze was the shade of steel; his cheekbones formed bold slashes against his taut skin. "I live in a lot of boxes, Red, but under no rocks. Maybe you've been here before with guys who were happy with taking you here and leaving the fire in the kiln." He dipped his gaze, studying my nose, my lips, and finally farther, searing the exposed skin of my cleavage with his indecent intent. "I, on the other hand, plan to light up every fucking inch of your body this evening."

My first instinct was to step back, mostly because I yearned to straddle him here and now. But his audacity inspired mine. I stepped between his legs instead and watched the roguish grin take over his lips as he discarded his project and framed my waist with his knowing grip.

"Magnificent plan, Mr. Shark."

"I'm glad you're on board, Ms. Gibson."

Clearly knowing what a needy storm he'd whipped through my sex, he swept his gaze across our projects on the table. "They really do look good," he complimented. "Very impressive." His smirk became a pout as we shifted apart, pulled back to reality by a discreet harrumph from a nearby mother. "So . . . uhhh . . . how long does it take them to bake these?"

I laughed at his choice of words, grateful for the redirection back to some casual fun. "I'll swing back by in a week, maybe five days, and pick them up."

"Don't worry about it. I'll send Craig to do it. He runs out of things to do."

"I find that hard to believe, especially with your house occupancy currently bumped by two."

While Sebastian put the finishing touches on his skull design, I walked our used palettes and brushes to the sink that the staff used for cleaning up. As I stepped to the basin designated for customer cleanups, he joined me. Just like that, as we washed our hands together, we were back to thinking about doing other things beneath running water. Things involving a lot less clothes and curious bystanders . . .

It was wonderful.

He squirted some liquid soap into my hands and then his own. He began making a soapy lather between our palms. His fingers worked the suds between each one of mine, paying close attention to my fingernails.

Wonderful.

I couldn't tear my eyes off his face while he worked, breathing in the mix of the tropical soap and his rich cedar smell.

Quietly, I said, "I enjoyed this. Thank you for being a good sport."

With a smile of gentle pleasure, he moved my hands under the warm water with his. "It was my pleasure. I like discovering new things with you."

I giggled softly. "We didn't really 'discover' painting pottery, though."

"It was a new discovery for me," he defended. "And I learned a lot about you tonight."

"You did?" My bafflement was genuine.

"Well of course. It's nice to just spend time, just the two of us."

I couldn't argue with a word of that, so I didn't. It was much easier to gaze at Bas in his smooth surety, even as he performed something as basic as reaching for paper towels. After pulling a few out from the dispenser beside the sink, he dried my hands first. While he grabbed a couple more to dry his own, I noticed another studio employee stepping over to our table. She was no less smitten with Sebastian than the paint station girl, proven by her flitting mien as Sebastian handed her his black credit card.

I fought down a grimace. If I didn't want us to be sealed away in his mansion like butterflies in jars, I had to get used to moments like this. The inner pep talk lasted for all of fifteen seconds before I gave in to the urge to press my hand to the middle of his chest and insist, "You know, I'd like to discover new things about you too. This shouldn't be just about me."

A wave of subtle feeling crossed his face, but I couldn't decipher the mixture of shadows and shifts. "You already know Pia, Vela, and Grant." He scooped up my purse and handed it to me, obviously grateful for the busy distraction. "There isn't much more to tell."

As soon as I accepted my bag, he visibly stiffened again. Sebastian Shark did not like talking about himself in any way, shape, or form. But another glaring clarity? If we were going to have any sort of relationship, his resistance needed to end. Only...how? This was my tenth gentle prod in just as many days at the issue—and his tenth sweet but stern brushoff.

Despite that, I was so tempted to push again, just this once. Whether he realized it or not, most people found Bas fascinating.

The dilemma dogged me as Joel pulled the car up and we climbed into the back seat. As soon as we were shut in and private, Sebastian pulled me close. A million promises danced in his eyes, filled with sexy and passionate intent—but I was compelled to stick to my courage now. Just this once...

"Okay. I...uhhh...thought of a question for you now."

"Why does this suddenly feel like *truth or dare*?" he

deadpanned.

"It shouldn't. I thought we were just getting to know each other. Like we have been all night. Plus, I'm curious." I paused, studying his features one more time before introducing my question. "Why is there so much bad blood between you and Viktor Blake?"

Tense muscles. Sharp inhale. Stiff posture.

Were those his reactions or mine? A little of both, maybe? Confirmed reality and not my imagination though, when he pointedly slid away, causing an unwelcome chill to creep across my whole body.

I longed to take back every stupid word of the question. To rewind time and go back to the warmth, safety, and strength of his embrace.

"It's not something I want to talk about," he said tersely, and I wanted to respond with all the "right" kinds of things, like compassion and understanding. Instead, my teeth locked and my nerves frayed.

I clamped back the command I really wanted to finish with.

Explain.

The intent must have glinted in my eyes anyhow, because when I pulled up and repositioned to face him, Sebastian rivaled a warrior statue for stony resistance. But seconds before he answered, the stone crumbled at the edges. Only the edges.

"I just do not want to talk about it, Abbigail."

"With me or in general?"

"That's a redundant question."

"So you're telling me they're one and the same?"

"Are you telling me they're not?"

The massive stone to which I'd compared him rammed to the center of my chest. "I guess I was telling myself I had moved out of the 'general population' category," I croaked as all the light in my spirit shrank, inch by agonizing inch. "But thank you for letting me know my place in your world. Much appreciated."

Sebastian seethed. "Why are you doing this? Did we not just have a pleasant evening? Did I not just sit and paint fucking pottery with you for three hours of my life that I will literally never get back?" The glare he sliced my way could have cut a glass pane with razor-sharp accuracy.

"Sebastian." With every new word he spoke, meaner and more cutting than the one before, he was pushing the hilt further. On cue, tears welled in my eyes. They pricked, burning hot, in the corners. I rolled my eyes heavenward, begging for the damn drops not to fall.

Not now. Not now. Don't give him the satisfaction. He's trying to upset you to turn the attention away from himself.

The admission wasn't startling. This was standard operating procedure for him. I knew this by now. This was how Sebastian Shark, master mogul, stayed safe from the world at large, not just me. He lived in a kingdom of his own, where no one could hurt him. Until that happened, he just dealt with people who got too close by smiting them with his mighty tongue. In none of the good ways either.

This man didn't do relationships. Didn't do anything more than the good old-fashioned *wham, bam, thank you, ma'am.* At least until now. Or so he kept telling me. And so I kept telling myself not to believe—until somehow, in some way, I had—and then acted on it by grabbing for more like a needy girl. Despite the solid proof that he was really trying here, giving me a night of fun and adventure instead of his usual workaholic act. But I hadn't been satisfied with the simple gratitude for that. I'd gunned our relationship engines for more emotional road than he had and not paid attention to all the signs. And they were right there, in caution yellow and stop sign red.

Stupid, stupid, stupid.

But now, because of my constant need to push for the next achievement, attain the next goal, and rise to the next level in all things, there might be only one road sign left to heed. The scariest one of them all. The one I feared we'd finally come upon.

Pavement ends.

CHAPTER EIGHT

SEBASTIAN

"Joel."

"Yes, Mr. Shark?"

"Pull over."

Abbi twisted her hand into the back of my shirt. "What are you doing? You can't get out of the car in the middle of the street!"

Panic drenched her voice. Still, I was tempted to laugh. Did she think she could physically hold me back from this? From doing anything I really wanted to?

Damn, how I admired this woman's tenacity—among so many other things.

"Don't be ridiculous." I finished with a scowl because this whole conversation still had me pissed. I didn't want to be in a shit mood, yet she'd thrown me headlong into one by bringing up Viktor fucking Blake. What was with her and that bastard, anyway?

"You're the one being ridiculous right now." She flopped back against the seat, furiously folding her arms.

"Joel! Pull over!"

"Of course, Mr. Shark."

I ducked my head back toward my woman—if she was still that anymore. Why the mere thought of the alternative halted my heart and made me break out in a cold sweat, I had no idea.

"I think we need out of this car before one of us says something we won't recover from." As soon as I gritted it out, I released a rickety breath. "And I don't want to do that, baby. I really don't want to screw this up, Abbigail—and I feel perilously close to doing that."

Only silence from her side of the car.

I tried to pry her hand from where it was tucked under her arm. She wrenched away with a censuring glare. I dropped mine back into my lap, clenching my teeth against bellowing a string of profanity. My temper would only thicken the air in here, which was already stifling.

And goddammit, no matter how hard I tried, I knew that relief wouldn't be happening anytime soon. The confines of the back seat were getting hotter by the second, and I took no measure to hide my desire to get out. Why bother? Abbi was already staring like I was a caged creature, igniting her obvious fear. She even found extra space on her side of the car and used it to scoot farther away from me.

At last, Joel eased the car into a parking space. Before he was done killing the engine, Abbi and I had our doors flung open. We bailed like kamikaze bombers changing our minds on a final mission.

I paced along the side of the car, rubbing my neck to relieve my tension.

I needed to apologize. It was one of the few feats in this world at which I was complete shit.

I rounded the trunk of the car. Slowed my determined stomps into cautious steps. She had her back hunched to me and was scrolling on her phone.

"Red—"

"Don't," she retorted. Once more, I didn't begrudge her the anger.

"Can we just talk about all of this?"

"That's not necessary, Sebastian. You've said more than enough already."

"Abbi." Hard inhalation. Deeper exhalation. "Please."

Well, that got her attention. A word she'd heard less than six times since we met—but like rain in LA, certain words had special effects when they were finally uttered. I watched as her arms went slack and she let them drop to her sides.

"Please, Abbi." So maybe I was exploiting the effect now, but I didn't care. At least her gaze was full of me and not her cell screen. "Come here, baby. I need to apologize to you. I—"

My throat clutched, cutting off the rest of the words. I needed her to be the one taking the steps now, coming the rest of the way to me. Showing her forgiveness. Making the final move and stepping into my open embrace.

A moment stretched by.

The wind kicked up a little more, tossing some strawberry curls across her cheek.

Come to me. Say I didn't totally fuck this up between us. Come to me, baby.

Her shoulders sagged.

If she hadn't heard my soul's plea, she'd at least seen the evidence of it in my unblinking gaze.

Thank God.

Finally, she stepped forward. Only one step at first, though her stare was planted firmly on mine. Then another step as she let out a heavy sigh, seeming to give up some internal fight. Her last three strides were quicker before she collided into my chest. The force had me bracing against her impact but doing so with a face-splitting grin. I'd accept her clutch even if she had a bomb strapped to her back.

She wrapped her arms around my waist and pressed her cheek against my chest.

And I held on in return. So fucking tight.

I wrapped my arms around her shoulders, all but burrowing my fingers into her skin. She was shivering and covered with goose bumps. The night temperatures had dropped considerably since we'd come out of the pottery studio, and she hadn't brought a jacket.

"You're cold."

"Hmm, yes." She sighed into the base of my neck. "Better now, though." And then snuggled tighter against me.

"Let's get back in the car." But I made that semi-impossible by burying my face in her hair. I couldn't get enough of the spicy scent. I breathed deeper, working to mix the sugar from her skin into the redolent mix.

"I'm so sorry."

I sucked in a sharp breath. While letting it out, I leaned back to fully see her face. "Stop," I ordered.

"But—"

"You have nothing to apologize for."

"I do, Bas," she persisted. "I do, and I need to—"

"I said to stop."

But my growl didn't deter her. She kept up with the clutch around my waist, and this time I was the one giving in. Why try to coerce her when it felt so good to hold her in my arms?

What the hell is happening to me?

I couldn't understand it. Sure as hell couldn't explain it. What did this woman have that all the others hadn't? How had she already embedded herself so deeply into places I'd locked off from world?

I'd never felt like this before in my life. Utterly lost without. Perfectly whole with.

And beyond unsettled with those admissions.

While I was indulging those selfish ruminations, her teeth began to chatter.

"In the car," I commanded. "Right now. Before you catch pneumonia." With her still in my squeeze, I shuffled toward the back door of the car, refusing to hear an argument about it. "Turn up the heat back here, Joel. And give us some privacy."

"Ready to head home?" Joel asked, turning in his seat as soon as we were inside.

"Just give us a few minutes here."

"Of course." He disappeared as the privacy divider completed its ascent.

For the better part of a minute, the only sound between us was the forced warm air from the vents and Abbi's brisk hand rubs. Fortunately it didn't take long for her to start taking more relaxed breaths. Still, I waited until she was visibly cozy before speaking up again.

"Listen." And so much for either of us lingering in the land of comfortable. I doubled up on my cringe, realizing my tone was already more abrupt than I intended. "Sorry," I blurted, reacting to the defensive look she shot over. "Sorry. That was more aggressive than I intended." I sighed, gripping my nape with deeper fervor.

My on-theme line earned me at least a softer scowl. "We don't have to keep beating this up, Sebastian. Honestly."

I halted the self-strangle but didn't drop my hand. "Also not my intention."

"I realized my overstep the minute I made it." She hugged

herself. I couldn't tell if the action was spurred by a new chill, a new miff, or both. "I should know better than to push you beyond your comfort zone."

"Which shouldn't have really mattered," I countered. I expected her puzzled glance and addressed it at once. "I told you I'd try, remember? That I really want to try with you. And the first time you asked for more from me, I flipped my shit." I shook my head. "That doesn't seem like trying, does it?"

"But it's at least a step." Though her tone was encouraging, she made no move to reach for me again. Maybe that was for the best. "You recognize it now. That's better than before."

"But it's not good enough." I had to clench my jaw to hold back from scooting toward her. "Yet I can't promise it won't happen again. You have no idea how foreign this all is for me. Just . . . no idea, Abbi."

She believed me. It didn't make anything easier, but I could see the certainty of it in her eyes before she replied, "I think I have a pretty good idea, actually." She pivoted so we faced each other a little better. "I haven't been in a ton of relationships either."

"Yes, but you've had normal interactions with people your entire life. I can't even say that."

"You've had Pia," she interjected. "And what about Grant?"

"But I'm not in love with Grant!"

The moment I realized what had just leapt from my lips, I rushed to undo the startling damage. "Well, you know what I mean," I spewed. "Not in love, per se . . ."

And I was just making everything worse. The furrow of her brow and the frantic bounces of her chest were clear signs of that.

"Not sure I do know what you mean," Abbi challenged through gritted teeth. "Per se...?"

"I mean...referring to Grant." It sounded as jittery as I felt. Jesus Christ. This all just went from shit show to clusterfuck in the blink of an eye. "I mean, he's important. I... care for him. But he's not family. Not like Pia and Vela."

"Sure," she murmured, rubbing her upper arms again. "I get it. Your family gets your love, and the rest of the world gets whatever's left over."

I leaned my head back on the seat. Rubbed my eyes with my thumb and forefinger. I pressed into the sockets until stars danced behind my lids.

Shit show.

Clusterfuck.

What was the next step after that?

Because I was pretty sure I'd just taken us there.

There was an escape hatch. But just one. I had to distract Abbi with the information she'd originally wanted. A diversion from my disastrous slip. Goddammit, I hated being backed into a corner, especially because I was the one who'd put myself here.

I took advantage of the moment to get in a heavy sigh. But there was no mental break along with it. It was time to dig deep, dropping my mind into a hell I hated visiting.

My childhood.

"All right." My ensuing exhale was so loud, I was surprised Joel didn't hop out to check if we'd just gotten a flat. "Here we go," I muttered.

"Go?" Abbi softly queried. "Where?"

I disregarded her. The memories started coming, hard and fast—and relentless.

"I've known Viktor Blake since I was a kid." I tick-tocked my head while I worked out the number of years. "Probably since I was eight or nine. He's a couple years older than I am, but not by much."

"Bas." She was back at my side in seconds, her touch at the middle of my chest, her warmth so near. "Really, Bas. You don't have to get into this. I—"

"This is what you wanted," I insisted, but I could already hear the pain in my own voice. Christ, what must it sound like to her?

She remained silent now. Though she kept her hand on my chest, her energy was resigned to the verdict I'd just meted. Felt like a damn good word for the occasion.

"He was always a prick," I said then. "Even when we were kids. His father owned half the city, or at least it seemed that way to me and everyone else in our school." I tensed but took no measure to hide it. "I seriously hated school. But I tested into an advanced learning program the school offered, and the district wanted me to attend a different campus than my own neighborhood school to help their stats. They promised not to turn my father over to Child Protective Services and fed us twice a day in exchange for me playing the grades game. Everyone got what they wanted."

"Only not really."

"Not after the Blakes joined the parent-teacher organization."

She swallowed. "What happened then?"

"They moved in—and took over. And Viktor was well aware of the immunity he'd gained because of it. He played every shred of it up like the playground bully he was."

"I believe you." Shadows took over her eyes. "More than I

178

want to admit."

I wanted to press for details on her knowing tone but tucked the comment into a mental file for later—though not too far in the future.

"No one was safe. Blake was the kid who took whatever he wanted whenever he wanted it. Lunch money, sanity, dignity— nothing was off-limits for the asshole. He'd push weak kids down and hold his foot on their neck while they cried for help. He cheated on every test and threatened to knife a guy's mom for refusing to write a research paper for him. He had a group of boys who followed him around as if he were a deity. Grant and I just tried to stay far away from him."

She jerked her head up by an inch. "You and Grant were already friends at that age too?"

"Yeah." I smiled while summoning memories of the skinny, too-tall-for-his-age kid that I'd met in a rat-infested alley on the east side. "We became friends during our daily bus rides to the west side. We were misfits and didn't fit in with any of the other groups, so we made our own group. Just the two of us."

"So what was the issue with Viktor?"

"What wasn't the issue with Viktor?" I rebutted. "Like I said, we attempted to steer clear—and succeeded. Most of the time."

"Most of the time?" Her smile faded.

"Well, he was a big guy—and not just in terms of his dad's money. But we were smarter and faster. We were usually able to outrun the bastard, but it pissed us off that we had to. So we'd play tricks on him. Just when he had one figured out, we'd change up the ruse and make him fall for another." I laughed at the memory.

But Abbigail stared as if I'd just confessed to sticking my head in a lion's mouth. "What did he do about that?"

"Honestly? Not much. He was always up to as much mischief, if not more, than we were. Reporting us meant the possibility of getting his dad involved—and let's just say the asshole apple didn't fall far from the tree in that family."

"Okaaay," she finally drew out while sliding her hand down into mine. "That all makes sense . . . if you're ten. But you're grown men now. How has that playground rivalry carried into your adult lives?" She pursed her lips. "It seems petty."

"And it would be," I concurred, "if all the bullshit had stopped there."

"It didn't?"

"Hell, no. The antics grew as we did. I'm not proud of it, Red, but you wanted the truth, and this is it. As we grew older, the stakes got bigger and the plots got more complex."

And here we were. The part of our history I hated revisiting the most. Once again, the school-aged me and the grown male part of me were merged too closely in my mind. And once again, there was nothing I could do about it. As usual, I was paying unearned fines for my father's dereliction.

"The summer before fifth grade, Viktor's father bought the home my father rented—'home' being a loose term here." I gritted my teeth and compelled myself to go on. "My dad was always late paying the rent. When Blake Senior came around to collect the money, he'd bring Junior with him."

A soft groan from my exquisite, empathetic woman. "Sounds like that was as much fun as a root canal."

"Indeed." I frowned, the memories flooding back like bile repeating after a bout of indigestion—bitter and acrid to swallow. "Viktor used every detail from those house calls as ammo at school. He couldn't resist telling everyone how poor I was, in full-color detail. He took great pleasure in detailing how my father was a drunk loser, barely able to pay the rent."

Her face twisted, and a furious little huff spilled from her. As strongly as I longed to kiss her for the compassion, I ignored it. Because it resembled pity—with a bitter amount of accuracy. Ignoring her reaction was the only way I was going to finish this.

"At first, I was able to get even by just playing sneakier pranks on him," I said. "And it was all fine. In grade school, no one even knows what that shit means, so I escaped with some dignity intact for a couple of years." I took another fortifying breath. "But in junior high, everything changes."

She tucked her head into a terse nod. "Yeah. It does."

"I was becoming a young man," I continued. "And pride was a major part of my psyche." I averted my gaze out the window in order to vocalize more. "And Blake's bullshit really started to sting."

"Oh, baby." Abbi all but sobbed it out. She stroked her hand higher on my arm, but I shrugged away from her touch.

I recoiled from her pity.

And instantly felt like shit for it.

I battled away from that moment too, consciously softening my gaze. "It still smarts, Abbigail. That probably sounds like he and I have taken the pissing contest too far, but it's the truth. Some shit just doesn't just go away—especially when it comes to bullies who grow up into assholes. And believe me, Blake's become just that. In some fucked-up ways, though, I'm glad he's gotten worse over the years. It's validated me. Driven me."

Her brows bunched together. "To do what?"

"To bury the motherfucker in business. No...correction. To bury him in every way I can."

I looked away again. But why? To erase the ugliness of the admission? To undo the years of dirty play on my part as well as Viktor's that had led to it? Worse, that Abbigail was still sitting there wanting to give me comfort and care instead of revulsion and rage?

"Stop," I finally bit.

"Stop what?" She already knew that answer. "Bas—"

"I said stop."

"You were a child. A child who had the weight of the whole universe piled on your tiny shoulders." She bypassed my grunt at her adjective, continuing on. "For any person, let alone an adolescent, to have to go through what you did..." The liquid sheen in her emerald eyes drew my focus back to her expressive face. "It's not okay."

"I never said it was."

"It's just that I—well, I care about you, Sebastian." Her gaze glittered brighter. "And it hurts my heart that someone else hurt you."

This time when she touched my arm, I didn't pull away. But I also didn't shy away from the subject into which we'd dived so deeply. "Yes, I was hurt. By Viktor Blake, Abbigail. He's the cruel son of a bitch we're talking about right now."

She flinched and then blinked. "I had no way of knowing you had this sort of history with him. You realize that, right?"

"Of course I do. But does it make more sense why I have such a visceral reaction at the mere mention of his name?"

"Yes," she conceded. "Somewhat."

"Somewhat?"

I was incredulous. Empathetic tears still threatened her

stare, but she was still defending the asshole.

"You have no damn idea what that man is capable of, Abbigail. He's a savage and has only gotten worse with age. The stories that float around this town about him would make your blood run cold."

"Wh-What do you mean?" she blurted.

"What do *you* mean?" I practically bellowed the pronoun. "And why do you keep pushing for more on this? Why can't you just take my word for it?"

"Because the man I know doesn't seem like a 'savage.'" She visibly squirmed, but the erotic implications I normally enjoyed from the move were far from actualizing right now. "It just seems a bit... I don't know..." She shrugged. "Dramatic, I guess?"

"Dramatic?" I hauled in air through my nose. "Right. That's me. Dramatic."

"I mean, I do get the sense there isn't something quite right about the man." As she continued as if my snarl had been silent, I was also robbed of the chance to fume about it. She was actually making sense now. "There's an undertone about him, you know?"

"Yeah," I snapped, disregarding her self-dismissive wave. "I do know." I snatched her upheld fingers and squeezed. Hard. "Go on." I wasn't gentle about that part either.

"There's a—" She huffed, seeming to realign her thoughts. "Well, the best way I can describe it is... He has a darkness to him. There's something almost..."

"Almost what?"

"Sinister," she offered at last. "And one time, when I was at his office..." But she trailed off, flashing me a glance but nothing more, clearly as afraid of my reaction to her words as what she'd really spoken.

Wise girl.

Because I was furious. The anger burned an instant hole in my chest. I could only imagine what my face looked like. "What did he do?" I seethed through gritted teeth.

She gulped. "Bas—"

"What the hell did he do?" I exploded. "So help me God, Abbigail. If he laid a finger on you . . ."

She recoiled from my intensity. Very wise girl. "No," she spurted. "He didn't touch me." For a fraction of a second, her racing thoughts were visible across her face. "Well, he did . . . but—"

"Fucker!"

"But that's not what I'm talking about—" Her volume was cranked to my level now. "I can handle myself, Bas! You don't have to worry about me!"

"Not a decision you get to make."

"Bas—"

"He. Touched. You?"

"Bas! Calm down!"

"Also not a decision you get to make." I fished out my cell, forcing myself to prioritize the reinforcements I'd call in. "I swear to all things holy, I'll destroy that motherfucker. He has tangled with me for the last time."

"Sebastian." She surged into my lap, seizing me by the biceps. Her grip was brutal. Her voice was desperate. "Stop this. You need to calm down!"

"When was this? When, goddammit?"

"Please listen to me. Listen to the whole story. I said he didn't do anything to me."

I clamped my jaw, uncaring if it fell off from the tension.

"You said he touched you."

"And I'll explain—if you'll let me. Jesus Christ, Sebastian!"

Her chest was heaving. So was mine. I pulled an arm free from her grip long enough to stab a hand through my hair. Grabbing a bottle of water, I offered another to Abbi as she settled back on the seat beside me. We each chugged half before contemplating words again.

"Please tell me what happened with Blake," I requested, calmer than before. "So my imagination doesn't make up twenty scenarios that end with you trapped beneath that bastard."

She exhaled with composure to match mine, though a spirited light still blazed from the depths of her eyes. "I went to deliver his lunch. It was the day I rearranged my schedule and hit the route early. You'd been avoiding me, so I wanted to catch you off guard. Do you remember that day?"

"Of course I do." I quirked a small smile. God, how I admired and adored her tenacity.

"So, I took Viktor by surprise as well. People get used to a certain schedule when you do the same thing day after day." She waited for me to agree and then continued. "Anyway, just as I was going to enter his suite, a woman came rushing out of there instead. At first I thought they'd just been wrapping up a meeting... but she had a huge red mark on her face and she was crying."

I dropped my hand. Before it hit my thigh, I'd fisted it. "Did you know her?"

Abbi shook her head. "Even if I had, I don't think she would've stopped. I barely had a second to confirm that—"

"That what?" I asked.

Once more, her breaths came in harsher spurts. "The

mark—the bruise—it was a fresh handprint. I'm not mistaken about this, Bas."

"I don't doubt that, baby."

She darted her tongue over her lips. "She'd been slapped by someone."

Divine intervention—because that was the only feasible excuse—helped me keep my mien impassive. "Yes. Probably."

"By...him?" she rasped.

"Probably."

The air audibly snagged in her throat. "Did you...were you...aware of all this?" Her voice pitched higher, riddled with incredulity.

"Not about this specific incident." I let her see more of my fury now—but not too much. I had to walk this precipice carefully because complete rage wasn't going to help anyone here. Over a decade of dealing with Viktor Blake had taught me that lesson well. "But this is what I've been trying to get across to you. Well, one of the things. He's a monster, Abbigail. He abuses women on a regular basis. He has a reputation across Southern California for it. He's rarely seen with the same lady on his arm twice. He's so hard on them, they don't come back for seconds."

"You can't be serious."

"I've never been more serious."

"But why haven't any of them come out? Spoken up?"

"Because fear and money are phenomenal motivators."

Her face fell. Despite the vindication of watching her accept the truth, I hated being the one to cause her such distress. "Oh my God," she whispered.

I steeled myself, preparing to issue the next question. "After you saw the woman with the bruise...what happened?"

She flashed a fresh wince. "I ... went into his office. To deliver his food."

"Christ."

"And he was as cool as a coastal breeze." She was clearly bewildered about the assertion. "You would think he was having an ordinary day at the office. I remember ... being mollified by that. My logic literally wouldn't let me put the facts together. If he had just physically accosted the woman I saw in the hall, it hadn't affected him in any way. And that didn't make sense."

I sucked in a long breath. "Of course it didn't."

She drew back a little. "It's so bizarre."

"And that's why I don't want you anywhere near him," I insisted. "He's dangerous, baby. Physically, mentally, emotionally. The man's a psychopath. There's your 'logical' explanation. Did you ask him about it?" I couldn't help but wonder. "About the woman who'd just left?"

If I knew Abbi at all, I knew she would never stand by and watch another woman—another human being—be mistreated and not say something in her defense.

"Of course I did." She jerked her chin in righteous defense.

"And what lie did he tell you?"

She dropped her elbows to her knees and then her face into her palms. She slowly shook her head, though I couldn't tell if she was denying me my answer or herself the whole truth.

"Abbigail." I stabbed it harder into the air, intending to break her from her thoughts. "What did Blake say about the woman? About her injury?"

She lifted her face and looked at me with open regret. "He said she hit her face on a filing cabinet and got lost looking for the first aid office."

"Christ Almighty." I shook my head, knowing she felt like she'd personally slapped that woman. "I'm sorry, baby."

"Why? Why on earth are you feeling sorry for me?"

"Because you had to witness that at all."

"Well, I don't deserve it. Any of your comfort. What about that woman? I—I should've done something. I knew, deep in my gut, that Viktor was lying. I knew he had probably just struck that woman. And that he'd done it so hard, she'd have a welt the next morning. And like a damn coward, I went in and set up the bastard's lunch. I stood by and did nothing!"

Her agony gutted me all the way open. Without thought, I just reacted. I reclosed the distance between us and hauled her into my arms. Thankfully, she let me. She let me hold her, stroking a hand up and down her back. She didn't fuss when her hair broke free completely from its bun and tangled with my fingertips. I sighed when she pressed her face into my chest, releasing another heavy breath while she snuggled into a comfortable spot.

"I'm seriously shit at this date-night concept," I mused into our contented silence.

"Huh?" she mumbled. "Why?"

"I've pretty much ruined the night for you." While I infused my tone with heartfelt remorse, I doused it with equal sarcasm. It was well past time for the tension to lighten in here.

Abbigail leaned back to look up at me. "You haven't ruined it for me," she chided. "I've had a wonderful night." She touched my cheek gently, smiling as I covered her hand with mine. "Thank you for opening up about the situation between you and Viktor. It goes a long way in helping me understand things. The vehemence between you two . . . it makes complete sense now."

I turned my head and kissed her palm. "I'm not used to talking about my past, Abbigail. It's not easy for me. Or comfortable."

"I know. I get that." Her eyes glittered, gorgeous and catlike, in the halogen light that shone through the car's tinted windows. "And thank you for trusting me with your history."

"My antagonism was never a personal thing against you."

"I get that too," she assured me.

"It's just the opposite," I stressed. "I want you to know things about me that other people haven't. And when I get frustrated or feel like I'm being backed into a corner, I come out swinging. And I know I can say some pretty harsh things. I also know that those words hurt. I saw the look on your face, and I hate being the cause of that pain or fear."

She compressed her fingers tighter, working the tips into my hairline. "This is still new, for both of us. The whole idea of being in a relationship, let alone really giving it a go. It's going to take work." She smiled deeper, bringing out the sweet dimples in her cheeks. "People I've known, who are in relationships for years, like Rio and Sean and even my parents, say that relationships constantly evolve. They're works in progress that require maintenance. It's like taking care of a machine, because of the moving parts. Nobody can expect to get it right on the first try or every single time."

I responded with a determined nod. "All right. Fair enough."

"The thing is, we have to be willing on the 'trying' part. To keep at it and not run away when it's hard. Because some days will be hard, Bas."

I reached for some stray curls that had tumbled into her eyes. "And the other days?"

"Will be even harder than that."

Instead of tucking the strands along her head, I held on. I contemplated how perfectly these shiny red strands fit her. So many fascinating turns. So many brilliant depths. "How did you get so smart about all this?" I softly asked.

"Mmmm, I don't know." She laughed lightly, pulling my hand down to her lap. There, she entwined our fingers. "My mom always told me I was a born nurturer. It's why I enjoyed cooking so much. That I inherently love caring for people and making sure their needs are met. I'm still not one hundred percent convinced, but as I get older, it seems like she may have known what she was talking about."

She finished with a big, unabashed yawn.

"My exhausted little girl." I murmured it against her forehead before pressing a kiss there. "Are you ready to head home?"

"Hmmm." She smiled wistfully. "Yes. I was just thinking how nice that shower of yours would be right about now."

"Of ours," I corrected before leaning forward to tap on the privacy divider to signal to Joel we were ready to leave. Since the night had already been unusual, he lowered the partition to confirm my request.

"Let's head up the hill," I stated.

My neighborhood sat atop of one of the canyons in Calabasas, meaning we had to wind through a few other residential areas to get there. The trip didn't take long. About fifteen minutes later, we pulled into the circular driveway in front of the house—and for the first time in a long time, I was content about thinking of it with another word.

Home.

As I helped Abbigail from the car, I told her, "I want to

walk around the back and check in with Tawny before we call it a night."

She cocked her head. "Is everything all right?"

"Probably," I answered. "Since my conversation with Elijah earlier, I've just been thinking it wouldn't hurt to check in on her. He said he hasn't seen her all day. Though she's been keeping to herself, that's a little unusual."

"Of course." The woman's usual compassion took over the curves of her face. "She's been through so much. Best to make sure she's just regenerating and not going stir-crazy."

I fingered one of her curls again. "You know, your mom was right. You have a real gift for getting people."

I was rewarded for the compliment with one of the most glorious smiles across her full lips. "Do you want me to come with you? Maybe she'd like a woman to talk to."

"Good idea." I stretched my arm back, and she clasped my hand, so I tugged her close to my body. We stood chest to chest under the lamppost near the large eucalyptus tree beside the patio gate. I pushed more hair back from her face before pressing my lips to hers in a grateful but demanding kiss. Her lips parted for my seeking tongue, guaranteeing her moan vibrated through me while I thoroughly explored her candy-sweet mouth.

When we separated, she stood with her eyes closed for a few seconds longer. She swayed in place until I scooped my palms beneath her elbows.

"Open your eyes, silly girl," I whispered beside her ear.

"But I didn't want that to end yet."

"Well, the sooner we go speak to our houseguest, the sooner we can be in the shower together."

"Oh, I like that plan."

"I think you're probably really dirty tonight too," I husked. "All that paint, going places it shouldn't. All your secret, naughty places..."

"Oh, now I really like the plan."

"I always have the best plan. It would do you well to remember that."

I tweaked her nose before stepping away. With a chuckle, I dodged the smack she aimed for my shoulder, but I managed to grab her hand once again. We strolled our way through the gate and into the backyard, still sharing soft laughs—

Until we came to the open expanse of the lawn.

And slowed down at the same pace, undoubtedly struck by the same unease.

Something was out of sorts.

Maybe a number of somethings.

At first impression, and even through the second, I inwardly called myself a pussy. None of the normal backyard lights, usually switched on at dusk by the automatic system, were fired up. I'd blame the malfunction on a basic outage, except that being on the edge of the canyon like this made a massive backup generator a necessity. On top of that, not every light was doused. Some significant wattage was still working out here. As in, the pergola perimeter lamps, the patio sconces, and every halogen possible over the tennis courts down the hill were on. But the lawn, pool house, pool deck, and the pool itself? All as dark and cryptic as the Mariana Trench.

As if someone had wanted it exactly that way.

But why?

I hated the messages my body sent as answers.

My spiked neck hairs. My jacked heart rate. My coiled clutch around Abbi's hand, tight enough to yank her a little closer.

Not that she fought me on it. As I tucked her in, there were already tiny tremors up and down her form.

"Bas?" she stammered. "Wh-What's . . . going on?"

I scanned the backyard more closely, trying and failing to penetrate the shadows with my stare. "Not sure, baby. Not yet."

I wanted those last words to have more emphasis, but a growing din on the air eclipsed that possibility. The strange sound blanketed the normally calm atmosphere, almost like thick static from a public address system.

"Do you hear that?" Abbi beat me to the question by two seconds. She looked up at me just as fast, her face twisted in confusion.

"Yes." I tucked her even closer. "But I have no idea what it is. It's normally so peaceful back here."

She visibly shivered. "It's . . . eerie."

"I'll say . . ."

"It sounds like it's coming from the pool."

"Agreed."

But at once, I regretted my intense focus on the noise. It was too easy for her to step free from my hold and start inching toward the water for herself.

"Maybe there's something stuck in the filter?"

"Babe," I ordered, noting the purposeful quickening of her steps. "Hey, don't get close. You need to wait for me. In case—"

Her horrified scream cut me off.

Panic stabbed me into a sprint. I'd never heard such a terrible burst from her before. I'd turn over millions to never hear it again.

Thankfully, I reached her side in seconds—

Just in time to catch her limp—and unconscious—form.

"Fuck!"

Whatever she'd glimpsed in those ten tentative seconds... had literally stolen her senses.

I repeated the oath while readjusting my stance to accommodate her weight. Thank God the woman hardly seemed heavier than Vela, though sheer puzzlement still had me a little dazed. What had rendered Abbi limper than the towels that overflowed from the patio hamper? For that matter, why the insane pile of linen in the first place? No way had Tawny—or anyone else around here—thrown a raging pool party tonight, but my house staff wouldn't have left this many wet towels out to gather mildew for days either.

What the hell happened here?

And why did my skin crawl with the surety that the answer was in the pool—which had already given up a clue so vile, it made Abbigail pass out?

Mysteries were piling up higher than that mountain of towels.

But I had one priority. The woman I cradled in my arms.

I searched frantically for a place to lay her. The chaise longues in front of the pergola were my closest option. I bent over and placed her on the reclined seat and slid onto the cushion too.

"Abbigail!" I shouted. No response. Even in the amber glow of the pergola's lights, I could see how she'd lost all her normal color. "Abbi! Abbi, damn it." I lightly tapped her cheek with my palm. Two beats passed. Four more. At last, she started rousing. "Baby? Come on, babe. That's a good girl. Open your eyes."

I kept my face in line with hers. I didn't waver the angle until she focused steadily on my face. "Oh, thank God." I didn't pay homage to the big guy often, but this time he deserved the gratitude.

"Bas? Wh-What..." She tried to sit up but fell back to the cushion immediately. "Whoa. *No bueno, señor*," she moaned wearily.

I laughed. Not hard and not for long, but her adorable declaration had me grinning like a full loon. I broadened the smirk as she squinted, looked around the backyard, and asked, "Wh-What happened?"

"I'm not really sure. We walked back here to talk to Tawny, and we heard a strange noise. You thought it might be coming from the pool, and then—"

"Oh, God." Her shriek wasn't as loud as the first one but ear-poppingly close. "Oh God, Bas!" She clutched my arm and sprung upright, sitting up fully. "I—I remember now. Ohhh, Gooodddd!"

"Abbigail." I punctuated it with a grunt as she drove her face into the center of my sternum. "Ssshhh, sweet girl. It's all right...it is, I promise."

"The...the smell," she sobbed. "And all that—that stuff... floating around...in the w-w-water..." She gripped me tighter. Her body convulsed as if she fought nauseated heaves. "What was it?"

"Abbi—"

"Did you see it? Is it—was it—human?" She yanked back. Buried her face in her hands. Started slowly rocking herself in place.

"I didn't see anything." My reply was as stiff but quiet, attempting to calm her. "I got to you just before you face-planted on the concrete and then brought you over here."

"Oh shit," she blurted back. "Ohhh, holy shit—then you

probably should call the police."

"Why?"

"Because there's definitely something in the pool." She raised her head, revealing a look of fear and concern. "Something awful, Bas."

I twisted in place, following the line of her sight. But from here, only the curved stone coping of the pool was visible. "More awful than the dead shark on the deck?"

"Just call the police, okay?" She gripped my arm, frantically shaking her head from left to right. "Don't go back over there. Please!"

"Abbigail." I chuckled along with the chastisement, mostly to ease my own nerves. I gently pried her fingers from my arm. "You've got to let me look, sweetheart. I have to have something to explain when I call the police." Though I still didn't know if that was the right action here. But the excuse gave me leverage to loosen her hold, at least.

As soon as she allowed me to stand, I cautiously re-approached the pool. I registered that the humming din had settled a little. Not that the same was happening for my nerves, however.

"At least the noise level has quieted," I commented.

"That's weird," Abbi replied. "Because that sound was still going on when I first walked over here—and it was definitely coming from the pool. It looked like the entire thing was a boiling hot pot."

I stared harder. Because of the lack of light, it was difficult to see the pool water in general, but I could tell it wasn't its usual turquoise clarity. Debris was scattered throughout the murky depths, but it was tough to identify what the junk was.

"Can you tell what all that is?" She pointed in an all-encompassing motion to the water.

"Not really."

"But I'm not going crazy, right? It's like some bizarre stew...or something...right?"

"It definitely seems to be moving beyond basic wind ripples."

"I mean, what could be in there? Fish, do you think? It is saltwater."

I turned at her question and immediately winced. Her pallor was worse than before. Maybe even a little green.

"Fish," she echoed, managing a shaky nod. "Yeah, I think you're right. But if so, why are they in there? What does this mean?"

As I stepped—well, stomped—backward, I balled my fists. "It means someone's been on the property again."

Goddammit.

I kept the oath to myself but not its source—my mounting rage. What was I paying my security team for, if these criminals were able to just come and go as they pleased? And now, in my mind, this was criminal activity. Even if it was just a bunch of neighborhood kids—though everything in my instincts said it wasn't—what was their end game? And if this wasn't just some bored teens pulling a summer prank, who'd done this? And what message were they trying to send?

I had more questions than answers. But I was certain of one thing. Abbi didn't look willing or able to help me probe for facts. Shit, my own guts were churning like the waters at which I gazed.

"I'm...I'm going to go see if Tawny's okay." Abbi's declaration was stamped with strength, despite how she still clutched at her midsection. "I have a bad feeling in my stomach about all this."

"Good idea," I encouraged. "Maybe she saw or heard something."

"Maybe you should call Elijah," she ventured.

"I was just thinking the same thing," I growled while following Abbi over to the pool house. We knocked on the door of the casita several times but didn't get an answer. I sorted through the keys on the ring in my pocket until finding the spare for the door in front of us. When we got inside, the place was empty.

And in complete shambles.

Light furniture was toppled. Small décor items were in pieces on the floor. A few pictures were askew, albeit still hanging on the walls. It looked like a skirmish had ensued inside the three small rooms.

"Wow." Abbi swept her gaze around the room. "I wouldn't have pegged her for a slob, for some reason."

"She isn't. Elijah's checked in on the place a few times since Tawny's been staying here. He's told me that she's kept everything neat as a pin." As soon as I uttered it, a defined dread rose in my psyche—and a string of profanity gritted from between my teeth. "Don't touch anything," I dictated. "I mean it, Abbi. Stand back. Someone else has been in here. Something's really wrong."

As I spoke, I yanked out my phone. I finished the command while jabbing the Send button, zooming my text to Elijah.

Something's happened to Tawny. She's not at the pool house, and the place looks ransacked. Pull the security tapes from the last twelve hours and get over here.

I'd barely tapped the Send key when his response buzzed through.

Be there in ten.

"Let's get out of here," I advised Abbi. "We shouldn't disturb anything."

I gently pulled her toward the door, making a mental note to never agree to another date night as long as I lived. Talk about an evening that had become a disaster.

"Sebastian?"

I looked down to where Abbi was again burrowing into the crook of my arm. She met my stare fully, though hers was bottomless with pensiveness.

"Red?" I tightened my hold. "What is it?"

"I'm beginning to think you were right," she said. "About holding off on calling the cops." She worked her bottom lip under her teeth. "We still don't know what's going on over there"—she darted a glance at the pool—"or with Tawny. Wherever she is."

I lowered my brows. "Explain."

She hauled in a deep breath. "Are we going to look guilty when we admit that she's been here all this time and we never told anyone?"

"I don't know what we'd be guilty of." I was sincere about the assurance. "She was thought to be dead, not evading arrest—or committing a crime. We weren't aiding and abetting a criminal."

"I know, I know." More lip chewing, which had me tempted to halt her by simply kissing her. But her stress was palpable, making her shiver all over again. She stepped back to start pacing back and forth across the deck, but I grabbed her around the waist and steered her inside the main house.

Elijah knocked on the front door a few minutes later.

"Banks," I greeted, nothing but business in my tone.

"Good evening, all." There was nothing but charm in his—but most disturbingly, the shit was authentic. That wasn't always the case with Elijah, but right now he was in full, gregarious, unassuming mode.

"Ms. Gibson," he drawled. "I don't think we've formally met yet."

Abbi bit her lip, giving off her exclusive mixed air of suspicious and charm, as Elijah took her extended hand and bent his lips over it. "Nope. I don't think I've had the—"

"Pleasure," he finished for her, lifting his head and flashing a wink. "And it is one . . . indeed. I'm Elijah Banks, Mr. Shark's private investigator."

He finished by placing a soft kiss to the freckled back of her fingers. Just as swiftly, she shot her stare up to me—missing his mischievous smile. That was fine by me. More than fine.

Elijah jumped his regard from her to me, obviously checking if I'd caught his entire move.

Oh yes, Mr. Banks. I see. I rarely miss a trick where you're concerned, buddy.

Nevertheless, I warned from the rumbling depths of my throat, "Elijah."

Like that moved the needle of the guy's game—or what he imagined it to be—by a millimeter. "Hey, Bas," he greeted as if I wasn't still brandishing a get-your-hands-off-her-now glower. "How's it going this evening?"

"I've had better," I answered curtly. "And as I've already communicated, someone's been in the pool house. Besides Tawny."

His features, rugged and handsome when relaxed but next to Satanic when he was pissed, darkened to something in between. "You're sure about that?"

"I will be once we look at the security cam footage. Did you pull it?"

"Of course," he stated. "But I didn't have a chance to look at it because I came right over. Do you have a laptop I can put the drive into?"

"In my office." I jerked my head toward that end of the house, as if Elijah couldn't track his way to the room blindfolded by now. "Let's go."

I led the way for a couple of reasons. Most importantly, we still had no idea what was going on here. If the creeps who'd messed with the pool were lingering somewhere, it made sense for me to be their first—and hopefully only—target. Neither Abbi nor Elijah deserved to be on the wrong end of their fuckery.

"Did you pull video from the whole day?" Abbigail asked when we were inside my home office.

"Yes, ma'am." Though Elijah answered as if giving deference to a superior officer—which was funny, given that the guy's street smarts made him more lethal than most special ops personnel—he jerked a questioning brow my way. Maybe now he'd start realizing just how vital Abbi was in my world.

When the drive mounted, I opened the file with today's date. The monitor came to life, filled with five fixed views of all the backyard areas. "When was your last check on the property?" I directed Elijah's way.

"Around four p.m.," he offered. "But like I said in my earlier text, there didn't seem to be anything out of the ordinary—except that I hadn't seen Tawny all day."

"Did you check on the pool house?" Abbi posed, bending her stare toward the bottom left corner of the screen, where the structure was displayed. As of ten o'clock this morning, nearly twelve hours ago, all still seemed quiet on the casita front.

And for the next five minutes and then the next, it continued that way. The three of us continued watching every corner of my serene backyard in the midmorning sun.

"Shit, we need popcorn for this action," Elijah said dryly.

"Right?" I then tapped the fast-forward key. While the footage zoomed ahead, with birds flitting and trees blowing at five times their normal pace, I specifically kept my gaze on the gate between the lawn and the front driveway. Somehow, I sensed the intruders had chosen that route instead of the house. Less chance for detection and a clean escape route.

"We looking for anything in particular?" Elijah posed as I sped past high noon on the footage. There was still nothing to see but the breeze in the trees, the birds on the fence, and a couple of wayward ground squirrels dashing across the lawn.

"If I knew that, I would have told you," I supplied. "But right now, we only know that Tawny Mansfield is basically missing again—and my pool house is turned upside down."

"Maybe she just didn't straighten up before she left," he commented.

"The scene is beyond not straightening up," Abbi volleyed. "I grew up with four brothers. I know messy. What happened in that casita is..." She shook her head and frowned before blurting, "Well, it's chaos."

The conviction of her statement appeared to sink into Elijah. He ditched the charm-and-awe for fixed-angle focus, his stance firm and his arms folded. "And goddammit...this footage is going to show us nothing."

"Why do you say th—the hell?"

I repeated the last couple of words and for good cause.

The security cam footage, which I'd only sped past the two p.m. mark, suddenly jumped to eight thirteen.

"Wh-What happened? Wh-Where did the rest of the afternoon go?"

As Abbi stammered that out, I flipped the video to rapid-rewind mode—and, once arriving at two o'clock again, to normal speed.

At exactly two thirteen p.m., the image jumped forward by six hours.

"I yanked the footage at nine thirty-three," Elijah muttered. "No more than a minute after you texted, Bas."

"Which means what?" Abbi interjected.

I spewed the F-word so powerfully, it was more a snarl than a syllable. I lurched to my feet and stabbed both hands through my hair. "It means that after those assholes messed with the pool, they tampered with the stored video footage in my system."

"And before that, they messed with the lights in the backyard." Abbi sounded like she'd rather be disclosing news of a bomb threat.

I turned and slammed my laptop shut. "So we're really not dealing with neighborhood punks here."

Abbi pushed her way back against my side. While her nearness eased the twist in my gut, no way was my tension fully dispelled—nor would it be. At least not tonight. "I think losing consciousness made me rule that one out already, baby."

"Losing what?" Elijah dropped his arms. "As in, you passed out? Why? From what?"

She snaked a trembling grip around my waist. "You'd

probably better just show him, Bas." But she pulled back with equal distress, a new look of impending nausea across her face.

I pressed my palms to her cheeks. There was a burning pressure in my head as I dipped it low, aligning my gaze with hers. "But that doesn't mean you have to come along, baby."

"Baby?" Elijah taunted beneath his breath. I ignored him. It was easy as long as Abbigail's face consumed my vision.

"I—I want to come with you," she said, once more in her miserable bomb-threat voice.

I took her lips in a gentle kiss. "Okay, but I don't want you near the water."

The first time she'd lost her shit, I'd been terrified of her tumbling into the muck. I took her hand and followed Elijah back outside. The man knew his way around the lighting control box since he'd been the main decision-maker about its purchase and design. In less than a minute, he had punched in new directions for the system.

Still, while hovering a finger over the blinking green Ready button, he swiveled back toward me. "Your neighbors might disinvite you from their Christmas party list for this."

I hiked a brow. "And you thought they weren't already doing that?"

His lips quirked. "All right, just so we're clear, I've programmed the full electrical enchilada here. Your yard's about to look like Chavez Ravine on night seven of the World Series."

Wordlessly, Abbi twisted her grip against mine. I felt her impulsive heave on top of it.

And that was what changed my own mind.

"One second, buddy." As I held up a finger for Elijah, I wasted no time in rounding all the way on Abbigail. By the time

I had her shoulders in my grip, she was visibly trembling. Her jaw was clenched.

"Bas," she bit out. "Can't we just get this over with?"

"Sure," I answered with smoothness I didn't feel. Not while confronting her distress so fully now. "We're going to do just that—Elijah and me."

She snapped her head up. Her gaze raked my face. "But—"

I stopped her with a couple of fingers across her lips. While Elijah remained quiet, I could practically feel his disgusted groan on the air. The Austen novel move was a shock even for me, but I got over myself fast. The shit gave me an opening to speak, and I took it.

"You're a formidable woman, Abbigail Gibson. One of the gutsiest and strongest I've ever known." Only my sister had ever heard those words from me before now, but that didn't need to be shared. "There's nothing more for you to prove here. Not to yourself, to me, or even to Elijah."

After a glance at Elijah, who backed up my assurance with a nod, she pinned me again with her wide, gorgeous greens. "M-Maybe it's a good idea . . . if I do sit this one out."

I leaned in and kissed her. What was meant to be an approving peck turned into much more. While we didn't end up sucking total face, I had no other way of conveying the rush of relief she'd just given me—a surge that served yet more surprise to my psyche. There were words that came with it this time. Pledges I whispered once I walked her back inside, out of Elijah's earshot.

"This isn't me tossing you aside, Abbigail. This is me never wanting to hear you scream in fear again." I tucked my head down, pressing my forehead to hers. "If I did, I'd probably jump in that water and kill whatever's in there with my bare hands."

"Bas!" It was half gasp and half laugh. She clamped her fingers to the sides of my face. "For the love of God, don't you dare go in that water!"

"I'll stay out of the water if you promise to get your ass upstairs and rest—and trust that I'll give you every detail of what we find."

"I promise."

The soft smile with which she finished that was my last glimpse of heaven—before what I knew was going to be hell.

As I paced back out to the patio, Elijah met my grim stare with a quizzical one of his own. "You want to fill me in on your theory about this?" he pressed. "Because clearly you have one."

I rubbed at the back of my neck. Turned and walked closer to the water's edge again. I really didn't want to say anything else, even to one of my closest friends.

But I did anyway.

"I think Tawny Mansfield's body is somewhere in here."

"Fuck." Elijah grunted. "But yeah...me too."

"And I don't think it's going to be in one piece."

Or even a number I could count on one hand.

Elijah muttered our favorite profanity again. But this time, there was no "me too" at the end.

"All right, man. Give me the whole damn stadium."

As soon as he punched the button and flooded the backyard in garish white light, I closed my eyes for a couple of seconds, knowing I had to be ready to confront Tawny's dead, pale stare—and probably a lot of body parts in the same condition.

When I finally looked, what I got was worse.

Much fucking worse.

CHAPTER NINE

ABBIGAIL

"Monday morning riff-off! You up for the challenge?" Rio chirped as she pulled down a stack of stainless-steel mixing bowls.

"Hmm." Twisting my mouth in a thoughtful grimace. How many songs did I know containing the word Monday in the title or lyrics? "What are we playing for?"

Rio waggled her brows. "Winner asks the loser five free questions." A bigger eyebrow dance from her. "Free," she repeated. "As in, must be answered."

"You're merciless."

"So you told me an hour ago." She laughed evilly.

The last thing I wanted to do was play a silly game with my competitive as hell sister-in-law after little to no sleep. Especially when I would be the one who ended up in the hot seat when I lost.

I decided to change the subject altogether. "Are you sure we have all the ingredients for this order?" I scrutinized the printout she'd handed me a few minutes ago. "This is for fifty people. Do we have everything for the main course?"

"There isn't a main," she returned. "It's all hors d'oeuvres. Anniversary party, I think. Came in through the website at midnight."

"Who plans their anniversary party at midnight for later that same damn day?"

"People who had sex and made up instead of getting divorced and burning down the house?"

She giggled while I scowled. It was good to see Sebastian and I weren't the only couple with crazy problems at home every night.

"Sometimes I seriously worry about you."

"*Pfffft.*" My sister-in-law pulled the clipboard off the peg in the wall and studied the rest of the orders for the day. The fact that she flipped through so many pages was both exciting and stressful.

"Beefing up the functionality of the website has really stepped things up, don't you think?" I asked her.

"Agreed. But I think it's a little too early to tell if it's the new norm. Might just be a coincidence, with us popping up on timely keyword strings." Rio shuffled across to the oven and set the temperature to preheat the appliance. "But if the pace stays like this, we may need to think about hiring another person."

"On the same page with you." After debating it for half a second, I decided to go for the gusto on feeling out another topic. "I was actually going to talk to Bas about it last night, but things got a little crazy, so we never had a chance."

"Bas? As in Sebastian?" She looked back over her shoulder but didn't move from her spot in front of the oven. "Sebastian Shark?"

"Yes, Rio." I laughed to emphasize the tease. "That's who I'm talking about. Why are you acting surprised?"

"Well, it's just..." She shrugged. "The way you said that 'things got crazy,' it sounds like you had...well...a night. A whole one. Like..."

"Like what?" I had to press, despite noting the firm line of her lips and the tension at the corners of her eyes.

"Like you slept over with him."

"And what if I did?" I pushed out half a laugh.

"At his place?"

"What does that have to do with anything we're talking about?" I managed a new laugh and breathed a little easier when she flashed back a full smile.

"You're totally right." She put her hand up. "It's not my business. One has nothing to do with the other. I think Sean and I are still trying to get used to the idea of you as an adult with a boyfriend, let alone that you're with Shark."

"But really, Rio. Besides being my boyfriend, the man runs a successful company of his own. Several, actually—if you count the subsidiaries."

She made a face that was difficult to identify. "I'm aware of that, Abs."

"He probably could share a lot of valuable business advice with me."

"I'm aware of that too."

"What?" I finally demanded. "What is it?"

She set down the puff pastry sheets she'd pulled from the freezer and stared at me. "I feel like you're hiding something from me." She unwrapped the dough with sharp tugs and tears, exposing the frustration she hid from her tone. "Something that has Sebastian Shark's name all over it."

"Okay, you're going to have to stop this. Every time his name comes up, I don't want you to assume I'm keeping something from you."

"Only when you are."

"But this isn't one of those times."

She narrowed her brown eyes to slits. "With all the love in my heart, girl . . . bullshit."

I sighed heavily. "Listen to me. Please. Bas is a high-profile man."

"That's the part you don't have to explain, Abs."

"Then you also get that there may be things going on in his world that I can't talk about, even to you. Even if I'd love nothing more."

"Of course," she murmured. "I get it."

"You do?" I didn't hide my skepticism.

"Yes, Abbi. I'd do the same if it were me with Sean. I really do see where you're coming from." She kept her eyes pinned on me. Still delving. Assessing.

"What?" I charged.

"Nothing."

"Now I'm calling bullshit." I wasn't willing to back down anymore. "You're still not dropping whatever you're building up in your imagination. I can see it on your face."

"But does that matter?"

In return, I opened my mouth—but just as quickly snapped it shut. My racing heartbeat helped to confirm my commitment. No backing down. If I was going to continue in a relationship with Bas, and I had every intention of doing so, I needed to set a clear precedent with my sister-in-law, and that meant parameters and boundaries. That had to happen now.

And God, did it feel nice. Really nice. My time with Sebastian, while still so short, was changing me—and in some positive ways. Just a month or two ago, that exchange with Rio would've ended with me caving and spilling everything on my mind. I'd probably have gone to tears while doing so. I was stronger now. Tougher. I had Bas to thank for those things.

He was teaching me to believe in myself. Because he saw my strength and courage, I saw them too. No matter how things ever turned out between us, those were things I would walk away with. Physically intangible gifts but more valuable by all accounts.

As I loaded up the delivery coolers, I shored my decision of sticking to my guns about creating a new paradigm between us.

"I'm loading up the van and then heading out," I called to her. "After the lunch runs downtown, I'll head straight out to Thousand Oaks for the anniversary party. Figure I'll just take the van overnight and leave my truck parked here."

"What?" Rio turned from where she'd been drying the last of the pots and mixing bowls. "Why?"

"Well, Thousand Oaks practically sits on top of Calabasas," I replied with efficiency that matched my movements. If I didn't get on the road within the next ten minutes, traffic was going to be hell. "There's no point in coming all the way back here. It's totally backtracking."

By the time I finished stating it, there were literally five different things on my mind—to which I added a horrified sixth. But realizing my mistake didn't recall any of it.

I'd just outed my current living arrangement to my sister-in-law in the most honest way possible.

"Abbigail." And with the announcement of my name, as if she really were my parental substitute. As if I were a damn child and she'd busted me for breaking curfew.

"You know what, Rio? I'm pretty much over this weirdness with us right now."

She politely folded the towel in her grasp. "I'm not the one making it weird, Abbi."

"Once more, I say bullshit. And I've been nice about every second you've dealt it so far today. The looks. The tone. The judgment." I copied her stiff stance, though added a marginal tilt of my head. "I'm an adult, remember? Twenty-two years on this earth, and I've somehow managed to make it on my own." I spread my arms wide, turning in a semicircle. "I even own and operate a successful business. In one of the largest cities of the world!"

"Which is remarkable, Abs. Incredible," she emphasized. "And I'm not here to discount a word of what you're—"

"Actually . . ." I cut her off by wheeling back around, my arms still akimbo. "That's exactly what you're doing. And I know you're doing it with all the love in your heart and best intentions in your soul, but you need to stop. And you need to hear me." I dropped my arms and leveled my gaze. "After twenty-two years of saving my virginity and protecting it like King Tut's tomb, I'm shacking up with my boyfriend. And I have been for a couple of weeks." I gave my shoulders a hefty shrug. "There it is. Happy now? Is that why you've been giving me your best stink eye all day? Hoping your death ray eye glare would force the truth from me?"

"Sweetie, I only want you to be happy."

I toyed with the van keys. "Well . . . I am." And then tried showing her how much I meant it by meeting her gaze once again. Her eyes turned to soft sable, but a strange light still lingered in them. Doubt? Worry?

There was no time to dawdle in hopes of figuring it out. Even if there was, I wouldn't have taken it. The woman claimed she wanted me to be happy but still eyed me like the truth police even when I came right out and declared it to her.

"I need to get going," I mumbled. "I'll see you tomorrow."

I punched the button that set the metal door rolling upward. Its loud clanging provided the perfect excuse to consider our conversation over.

During my drive up the 110, my phone dinged. The sound was unique for texts from Rio. It would have to wait until I parked downtown. I did, however, crave a check-in with Sebastian. I was raw right now, and he was the only balm that would help.

Through the van's Bluetooth interface, I used the voice command to connect me directly to Bas's desk. Anytime I could bypass talking to Terryn, who seemed stranger by the day, I did. The phone rang four times. If it went to five, I'd just tell the system to disconnect the call. I hated interrupting him when he was busy—but when wasn't he?

"Shark."

His deep and determined voice echoed through every corner of the van.

"Hey." I breathed it more than spoke it, which made me pull the car off to the shoulder and take a few deep inhales. Seriously? Could I have sounded any more wanton? "Uhhh . . . hey. It's me."

"Little Red." His smile drenched his husky voice, relieving some of my awkwardness. But only some. "I was just thinking about you."

He dropped his words into a purely seductive range too, ensuring he wouldn't be taking care of my lust so easily. Not that I was complaining. Not by a single syllable.

"Oh yeah? Well, tell me more, Mr. Shark. Was I naked in your thoughts?"

Holy. Shit.

Where on earth had that all come from? I couldn't believe

it had been my own brain. Not just the thoughts but the bravery in voicing them. This was so new. And exhilarating...

"Of course you were." Oh, definitely exhilarating. The way his voice dipped into a timbre usually reserved for the bedroom was my beautiful confirmation. "And just an FYI, imaginary you is banned from wearing clothes. Ever. Except for knee socks. Those are always allowed."

"Knee socks?" I repeated. "That's a new development."

"Not inside my mind."

"Interesting." The line went quiet for a few seconds except for our heavier breathing—corresponding, I assumed, to our mutual thoughts of knee socks. Me, wondering where I could pick up a pair or two to surprise him. I hoped his had to do with envisioning me in them—as he spread my legs wide and prepared to roughly screw me.

The rougher the better...

"Abbigail?" His voice was gritty and strained.

"Yeah?" Mine was breathless and lusty.

"What can I do for you, girl? You called for a particular reason, I assume—beyond giving me an erection in the middle of the day?"

With a little laugh, I pressed the button to lower the driver's-side window. The freeway was noisy, but I needed the fresh air to help me refocus.

"Well, I had to leave just as you were coming to bed, and I figured the last thing you'd want to do was give me the play-by-play." I groaned. "It's already been a long and crazy morning..." I tugged at my lip with my teeth again, deliberating about dumping on him about the tension with Rio. "I can't believe it's not noon yet," I stated instead. "And I guess I just wanted to hear your voice."

"You know I'll never turn down hearing yours," he answered in that same low, intimate tone. "No matter how painful it makes my pants."

He'd turned me to mindless mush with that romance book narrator voice, so all I came up with as a response was "So... what's going on with the hunt for Tawny? Any leads from Elijah or the cops?" I gulped hard, switching out some of my desire for some old-fashioned dread. "And what's going on with whatever was in the pool?"

"I have details," he disclosed, though he changed out his own tone for something between careful and guarded. "But I'd rather tell you everything tonight at home."

"Good idea," I returned. "Because lunch delivery has to be a flyby today."

"Why?" There was a rustling sound, denoting he'd surged up from his chair. "Is it that last-minute job Rio called about? Will you be really late?"

"Nope. I'll probably beat you home, if I hit decent traffic," I explained. "After the downtown deliveries, I'm dropping hors d'oeuvres trays for an anniversary party in Thousand Oaks. Rather than backtrack to the kitchen in Inglewood, I'm just taking the van home overnight."

"Outstanding," Bas stated. "Makes much more sense rather than sitting in traffic all night."

"That's what I thought too—although the logistics switch put Rio hot on my trail about my current living arrangements."

"Hot on your trail... how?" he asked with a bit of growl.

"I shut her down before she got too preachy about it," I qualified. "I know she loves me. I also know she means well. I can also see that part of me let her become too maternal, especially after I first moved out here. She wants to be a mom so badly, and my own died right when I needed her most."

Bas huffed, but it was more an expression of contemplation than frustration. "And now the situation is different."

"And now the situation is different." I deliberately stressed the verb. "She doesn't need to be so concerned about my life anymore. I'm capable of making my own choices. I want to be making them. It's time for her and my brothers to respect that and back off."

My volume grew and intensified, and I realized I needed to dial down the lecture. Bas didn't deserve it. He wasn't the one judging me on the subject.

"Good for you, Abbigail," he said once I'd gotten in a full breath again. "I'm proud of you. You're standing up for yourself this time, not just for the business or your loved ones."

"Thank you," I said quietly. It felt good to hear him praise me. Probably a little too good, but I didn't want to wreck the moment by overanalyzing it.

"Anyway, let's talk when we get home. I'm going to try to break out of here a little early today."

"Early?" I laced it with sarcasm. "Umm, excuse me... who are you and what have you done with the hot and sexy Sebastian Shark?"

His hearty laugh filled the speakers. "Ohhh, he's right here—and now has an incentive to get the hell out of here before the sun sets."

I sighed loud enough for him to hear. "I'd love to enjoy the sunset with you, Mr. Shark."

"Good." His voice dipped back into its sultriest baritone. As all my pores burst into new flames because of it, he continued. "Let's make something on the grill and really enjoy the summer night. I'll have Craig get everything we need, considering you've been at the meal prep thing since the ass-crack of dawn and still have deliveries."

"I appreciate that," I murmured. "It'll give me time to make a stop for knee socks."

"In that case, I'm leaving the office now."

He waited out my extended giggle and then a few beats beyond that. When he finally spoke again, the seductive baritone was gone. In its place was a chest-deep sibilance I'd never heard from him before.

"I miss you already, Abbigail Gibson."

But ohhh, how I wanted to hear more of it. So much more.

"I miss you too, Sebastian Shark."

"Drive safe." Just like that, he was back at the height of dictatorial CEO mode. "It's Monday. The pricks have taken to the freeways like migrating lemmings."

"And there's one whopping visual for the day."

"Damn." He infused the word with abject apology. "I should have remembered your tender stomach."

"It's fine," I rushed to state. "Well, not fine but better." While raising the window again, I started looking for an opening to remerge into traffic. "I hope you and Elijah were able to figure some stuff out last night."

"Yeah." He let a noticeable pause go by—and then another as he cleared his throat. "I've got a lot to tell you."

Though we exchanged another pair of mushy goodbyes, that was the declaration clinging hardest to my brain a few hours later when I pulled into the circular driveway of the Calabasas mansion owned by my boyfriend.

I stopped while exiting the car.

My boyfriend.

The words had rolled through my brain like gentle rain

instead of a lightning storm, and I wasn't sure how to react. Giddy grin or silent freak-out? But the mental jump was reasonable, right? I was staying at Sebastian's house full-time. I had not one but three keys, each granting me access to different parts of the property. I'd moved a bunch of my belongings here and had only been back to my place in Torrance once since he'd insisted I remain here—and only long enough to pick up more stuff. Granted, he'd mandated the plan was for my personal safety, but it had absolutely been a command, not a request—and came only a month after he'd refused to be my first lover.

So yeah... it all still felt a little strange. "Strange" being really relative these days.

And just the start of an explanation about what we'd been through together since. Crazy shit that belonged more in a summer suspense movie than real life, which only intensified my doubts about it automatically landing us in the boyfriend-girlfriend territory. But that was to be expected, right?

The stress compounded with the realization that I had no one to talk to about it. Not right now, at least. After the way I'd stood up to Rio earlier, I was confident my relationship with her had shifted gears too. We'd work it all out—or so I hoped—but I was certain about not wanting to continue in our current roles, either.

The conclusion set in as I paused outside the truck, absorbing the warm beauty of the August afternoon. The air smelled like sage and oaks and wildflowers and probably would be like this until past Halloween. There really was no such thing as autumn in Southern California.

A smile lifted my lips, despite my hit of nostalgia for the glory of the changing trees back home. My mom had always said peoples' lives were like the seasons. They changed. Things within them transformed. Grew. Matured. But while they altered on the surface, the important stuff stayed the same underneath. That felt like a good descriptor of where I was right now. Changing seasons. And the more I thought about it, the more I was perfectly fine with the idea.

Once inside the enormous front door, I looked around for Sebastian. While I'd been sure I'd beat him here, it was clear he had actually proved good to his word and left the office early. His presence was practically a touchable force on the air. I breathed in, savoring the lingering notes of his cedarwood cologne along with the fresh orchids that graced the middle of the foyer table.

He usually lounged back by the pool if he was home, but I couldn't bring myself to walk out to the lawn and deck by myself. Not yet.

It was a relief to find him just beyond the open sliders that made up most of the far wall, bustling around in the outdoor kitchen area. He was mixing a pitcher of sangria and blending his soft humming with the quiet twilight air.

Correction. He was humming most of the tune, which sounded like Sam Smith's most recent release, though I couldn't be a hundred percent sure. He only knew part of the lyrics. The parts he didn't know, he hummed.

He was so damn cute—and so unspeakably beautiful.

And yes, that was the only term that perfectly fit him in this moment. I really couldn't speak. I almost cried. After holding up through the bizarre turns of last night as well as every damn pressure of today without a drop rolling down my cheeks, this sight would be my breaking point. This man. The soft spell of his voice. The perfect strength of his presence.

The sublime joy of knowing he was mine.

Especially when he turned a little and noticed me standing there. A brilliant smile breached the sensual angles of his lips, and his eyes lit up in cobalt glory. That was a good thing, since I'd likely have fixated on the rest of him otherwise. Black track pants hung low on his toned hips, giving me a wonderful eyeful of the muscled vee leading to his groin.

"Hey, Red."

"Hey there," I somehow managed to blurt. Damn, he was glorious. My fingers ached to explore his body.

He grinned with cocky confidence, watching me closely. Could he read my lustful thoughts that easily? After rounding the bar and coming to where I stood, he grabbed my hips and pulled me tight against him.

"Welcome home." He kissed me without any other words getting in the way. He mastered my mouth in seconds, his tongue seeking and taunting, tangling and twisting with mine. I instantly wished there weren't any clothes between us. His sure movements spiked my blood and raced my heart. He kneaded the soft flesh at my waist, dipping just beneath the waistband of my pants, as though he just needed a small rub of my warm skin beneath his fingertips. And the way it instantly pebbled for him in return.

"My God," I whispered when we separated, touching my lips to ensure they were still intact. "That's the way I want to be welcomed home every single day."

"Deal."

He moved in again and planted a kiss beneath my ear. I moaned and gripped the bulges of his shoulders. God, they felt nice—but as he nipped my earlobe, my grip slipped to his defined forearms. Okay, so those felt even better.

His muscles flexed under my greedy clutch as he

murmured, "Can I pour you a drink?"

I schooled my grin long enough to answer, "Yes, please." I didn't hide the journey of my gaze down to his swollen crotch while he poured me a tall glass of the wine he'd just mixed up.

"Guess I should've asked if you like sangria first," he said while handing me the punch-filled glass.

"I've learned I like pretty much everything you do, Mr. Shark."

"And that was definitely the right answer, Ms. Gibson."

I interrupted our exchange of smirks to take a sip of the beverage. "Oh, this is fantastic." I took a more enthusiastic drink but not just because of how delicious the wine was. "How was the rest of your day?"

"Much the same," he answered while pulling a plate of skewered meat from the refrigerator. "And yours? How did the delivery go?"

I didn't answer him. I couldn't. Because he'd taken the meat and walked out to the grill with it. The grill . . . located between here and the pool. Which, technically, wasn't a pool right now.

"Abbigail?" As soon as Bas's voice registered for me again, I knew it wasn't his first iteration. "Talk to me. You okay?"

I set down my drink, realizing I was close to dropping the whole thing. "B-Bas?" I pointed to the water. Well, lack of it. "What's going on?"

With a tight expression, he covered the meat. "Yeah. About that . . ."

"About that?" I laughed—or intended to, at least. But this maniacal sound escaped instead. "The water's been completely drained?" I ended with a stunned gape. The pebble-bottomed crater looked unnatural in the middle of the backyard's landscaped perfection.

Sebastian pulled in a long breath. Released a longer one. "So maybe we should do this now."

"Do . . . what?"

"Talk about what happened last night. It'll help clarify . . . why that was necessary."

Though he tried to be casual about motioning toward the pool, my nerves skittered worse than the pair of lizards that popped over the crater's edge. "Necessary," I repeated in a four-part stammer. The expression on his face concerned me more than his words. It was nervousness for sure, but there was something else I couldn't quite identify. Fear? Worry? Dread?

"Come here." He moved to one of the padded seats next to the fire pit and then patted the cushion at his side. "Come sit with me." He looked up, confronting my cautious gaze with the dark entreaty of his own. "Please."

Well, damn it. He'd said please. That one was going to get me every time with this guy.

I snatched my drink off the bar. I had a sinking feeling I was going to need the fortification. "Do you want yours too?"

"Yes, please."

There it was again.

"You want me to bring plates out, as well?" I asked. "Will we be eating outside?"

"No," he answered, "I had Craig set the table inside. You likely won't want to sit and look at the empty pool. Especially after I explain."

He was even quieter during the last few words, and my apprehension grew into emotional lizards again.

"All right," I finally snapped. "I can't take it, Bas. Just get into it. Please. No sugarcoating." And now I was the one adding more "pleases" than necessary. I plunked down next to him. "Obviously it's bad. I see it; I feel it. So just say it, and we can go from there."

As I ranted on, Bas simply watched me. At least until amusement—or what I guessed to be an emotion close to it—pulled at the corners of his lips.

"Am I amusing you?" At once, my nervousness morphed into annoyance.

Sebastian wrapped a firm arm around my waist. He tucked me close. Then closer. "Easy, Little Red," he said against my lips before settling deeper into the soft cushion with me right beside him.

I swung a look around the backyard as the lighting system kicked in, back on its regular timing. That included the pool lights, which made the dry hole look like an alien moonscape. "Still no Tawny in sight?"

Sebastian discernibly stiffened. "I have an update about that," he explained. "But the information is not good."

I forced down a full breath. "How 'not good'?"

"It's likely going to ruin the night." There was an unspoken apology in his voice. "I just wasn't overly anxious for the day to end this way. Can't blame me for that, right?"

"Of course not." I pivoted to face him better and gently twined a hand with one of his. "But let me be the judge. How does that sound?"

"Fair enough."

I waited as he took a long second after that, draining the second half of his sangria in one gulp. He extended the pause by keeping his eyes closed, and I let him do that too. Even gripped by obvious tension, the man was captivating. His eyelashes were ink-dark crescents against the sharp blades of his cheeks.

Some of the wine lingered on his full lips, tingeing them with lush color.

At last, he grated two words into the still air.

"Tawny's dead."

My exhalation was rough. "I wish I could say that was unexpected."

"Her body, or what was left of it, was the flotsam we saw in the pool water."

"Yeah," I rasped. "Also not unexpected. Wait." I pinned him with a double take. "Th-That was a lot of debris."

"It was." Bas scrubbed a hand down his face. "Apparently, the noise we heard when we first came into the backyard last night? As we suspected—was from the water."

"Because of … what?" They were the most tenuous words I'd ever uttered—a caution confirmed by the full shudder that overtook Sebastian.

A shudder.

Up and down *this* man's form.

At last, he spoke again. "Once we turned on the lights … we found close to four hundred piranhas in the pool. Well, give or take. We couldn't get an actual count."

"Piranhas?" Though I got the word out in one croaking try, the syllables didn't settle totally into my comprehension. "You—You mean … like … little fish with big teeth and killer appetites?" Images bombarded my mind. In Southern California, there were a lot of them, from the comical to the dramatic, used to market everything from surfboards to microbrews to yoga pants. But never the real things. Not that I knew of, anyway. And certainly not in a backyard swimming pool.

Slapping my hands to my burning cheeks, I asked, "Who'd

do such a thing? Who'd even think of it?"

Sebastian surged to his feet. "That's what I've got Elijah working on," he explained while retrieving the pitcher of sangria and refilling our glasses. "And I've authorized him to hire a team to help out. These fuckers won't be able to hide under their rocks for too much longer."

I took a long and grateful gulp of the fruity wine. My shock-parched senses needed it. "I—I thought that was a myth . . . piranhas attacking humans. So they really do?"

"Yes and no. Apparently humans aren't their prey of choice. But if you starve them long enough and then chum the water with blood, it gets them on the scent. Then they'll attack anything." Sebastian paused to look out over the yard.

"Oh my God." I dropped my hands to cover my mouth. I was suddenly really thankful he'd held off on starting dinner. "Did . . . did you see them . . . doing it? To her? Was she still . . ."

"Alive?" he filled in. "No." While there was no repeat shiver, his tension remained tangible. "By the time we turned on the lights, there was nothing . . . significant . . . left."

Crazy as it sounded, a spike of hope hit me, and I pushed to my feet. "How can we be certain it was Tawny's body, then?"

Just as quickly, Bas quashed my momentum. It wasn't deliberate, but his gravity wasn't dubious. "Some bones and teeth were trapped in the pool's filter," he disclosed. "And the forensics team had enough to match DNA with some items they collected from the pool house."

After a minute of stunned silence, I could finally speak again. "She's really dead?"

"It would appear so. For real this time."

I sat—fell?—back into the cushions of the fireside chair. "Wow."

"Yeah." Sebastian stayed on his feet. His energy turned nervous, like a rainstorm ready to burst from a black cloud. "Wow."

"I bet you had a lot of explaining to do." That definitely clarified why he hadn't come upstairs until nearly four in the morning.

"A bit, since the cops thought they'd closed the Tawny Mansfield file after they thought she 'dived' off the Vincent Thomas bridge." After air quoting his verb, he drove his hands into the deep pockets of his track pants. "But it was a lot less drama than I expected. I don't know; maybe the evidence they had from the Vincent Thomas incident had been flimsy all along. It also helped to have Elijah with me while they asked their questions."

"Why is that, do you think?"

"For one thing, he knows just about everyone on the police force. For another, not many people fuck with him. He knows how to answer questions in ways that don't leave much room for follow-ups. When that doesn't work, that bastard can charm his way out of a paper sack."

I absorbed that in silence since it made complete sense—though it was the only factor about all this that truly seemed to. All this new information was dizzying.

"Where does this leave us now?" I asked pointedly. "Do you have any idea who would do something like this?"

Bas's face darkened. "Still none," he muttered. "And yet, several hundred—which is why I've got Elijah hiring a small army." He shook his head. "I've pissed off a lot of people over the years, baby. This could be any one of them."

"Or it could be none."

"Either way..." He faced me fully, his demeanor as

inscrutable as what he'd just said. "I'm concerned, Abbigail. Deeply concerned."

I shook my head, refocusing from thoughts that had gone a thousand directions at once. "Of course you are. I get that."

"No. I don't think you do."

I tilted my head in question.

"Because what—who—I'm most concerned about...is you."

"Me?" For some reason, or maybe for a thousand of them, it was difficult to keep my voice calm. "I...I don't understand. You've got this person—or these people—doing all this crazy shit to you, and—"

"What about you?" he cut in. "What about your safety right now, Abbigail?"

"I still don't understand."

"Someone's been here, Abbigail. Twice now. There's a damn good chance they know you live here now too. That means that if someone is trying to hurt me, they'll try to twist the dagger in more by hurting you. It's the oldest trick in the book."

His next actions were surreal. Any other day, any other surrounding circumstance, it would have looked like something else was about to happen. Every girl's dream come true...

Sebastian dropped to one knee in front of where I sat. He took a deep, fortifying breath and reached for my hands, gripping them so tightly in his own, I winced. Whatever he was about to say was going to be intense.

"Will you consider taking time off from Abstract so I can ensure your safety?"

I jerked my hands away and retracted my head equally as

abruptly. "Be serious..."

"I've never been more serious about anything in my life."

"Then you know how serious I am, as well. I'm a business owner and operator, Sebastian. I don't have the luxury of a sick day, let alone an undefined sabbatical waiting for your 'all clear' decree." The last of it sounded bratty, if not outright insolent, but I felt backed into a corner. "I know you're feeling out of control right now, Bas, but putting me in a gilded cage isn't going to solve the bigger issue here." I stroked his cheek to try to soften the blow of my rejection.

"Is that what you really think?" He moved in tighter, taking up every inch of my personal space and making it even harder to breathe... to think. "That I'm using this as some kind of a control move?"

I moved my head to the side, deliberately avoiding his beauty. "There's not a lot about this situation you can control right now," I said softly. "And maybe you're using my 'safety' as a way to rectify that." Before his answering growl could get too far, I rushed on. "These bastards have come onto your property twice—and those are the times that you know of. In broad daylight, I might add. It would seem it's not safe here either."

"I wasn't planning on you staying here."

I snapped my sights back up to him. Correction. My total glare. "Excuse me?"

"Calm down, baby. I'm not talking about Siberia."

I widened my gape. He actually started grinning, as if giving the idea more consideration.

"You don't get to consider anything." I jolted back to my feet and stalked back toward the pergola. "Do you get that? You don't get to move me around like a pawn on a chessboard,

Sebastian." I folded my arms and hunched my shoulders. "Not now. Not ever."

"I will if it means keeping you safe."

Cradling my face in my hands, I muttered loud enough for him to hear, "You're crazy."

"I'm in love with you."

I kept my face covered with my hands while his words sank in. One beat. Two. At last, I spun back around. Lifted my face clear of my fingers. "What did you just say?"

He was waiting for me—so ready with his sapphire eyes. The intensity of the hue matched the emotion in his voice. The combination of the two nearly took me to my knees.

"I'm in love with you. I will do whatever I have to do to ensure you are safe, even if that means tying you down somewhere with guards posted outside or handcuffing you to my own body. If it means knowing where you are all day and night, so help me God, I will do it. Until I find out who is trying to fuck with me, I will not lose you as collateral damage." He had covered the distance between us so the last words were said with his two large hands on either side of my face.

I opened my mouth. Snapped it shut. When I finally summoned speech again, all I could manage was one utterance.

"S-Sebastian."

"Do you understand me?"

"But . . . but there has to be a more reasonable way."

"Do you understand me, Abbigail?"

All I could do was shake my head in disbelief. How had my seemingly simple life turned into this? I squeezed my eyes shut, trying desperately to organize my thoughts while keeping the tears that were coming hard and fast from spilling out and down my cheeks.

Fail. Big, fat, emotional fail.

Each time I thought I knew what to say to get through to him, I'd pull up short when I met his fixed cobalt stare.

"Do you understand me, Abbigail?"

"Yes," I finally croaked. "It's becoming quite clear."

CHAPTER TEN

SEBASTIAN

The next few days were quiet. Granted, "quiet" in my world still looked like chaos to most, but not having dead marine life or human beings on my property was my current—and welcome—definition of quiet.

From my penthouse office, I watched Los Angeles wake up and stretch its wings. These moments were still my psyche's version of a sunrise yoga workout. The mental warrior pose necessary for aligning my goals with my action plans.

Lately, this mental exercise hadn't just been routine. It was necessary. An affirmation that there were still things in my world I could control. Grant would be up here soon, helping to reconfirm that—sort of my sun salutation stand-in. The guy always centered me on both business and personal footings. Starting my day this way was my proverbial namaste to the universe. The emotional and mental "I see and acknowledge you, world." Oh—and my written-in footnote: "I'm coming for you, so watch your back."

The door to my office popped open, and the devil of the hour strode in. Twombley was—unsurprisingly—half dressed. There was an unknotted tie around his neck. He'd draped his suit jacket over his forearm. Crosswise over his chest was the strap of the Louis Vuitton overnight bag I gave him for

Christmas. His light hair was still wet from a recent shower.

I battled to suppress a grin, but it got the best of me by the time he set his stuff down on the sofa. "Do I even want to know?" I asked, raising a brow.

"Probably not." He punctuated with a demonic grin while popping the collar of his dress shirt into the position to tie the tie properly. "On second thought . . ." He rubbed his unshaven jaw. "Maybe you do. Is Elijah coming to this meeting? And if yes, is he here yet? Because that bastard would definitely enjoy the young lady I just spent the night with."

I looked at my phone to check the time. "He'll be here in fifteen minutes. I wanted to talk to you alone first. About some personal shit."

"Well, of course you did."

I ignored his comment, continuing the subject at hand. "I'll be more than grateful if you tell him about your newest 'friend.' That means he can shift his attention off mine."

Grant knotted his tie and raked his fingers through his hair a few times, using my office window as a mirror substitute.

"Coffee?" I offered, making myself one while he changed into his dress shoes. He'd walked in wearing his casual loafers, which he usually kept at the office for jobsite visits or taking the Metro lines around the city.

"Yeah, that sounds great." He hustled over to the sideboard and joined me in front of the coffee machine. While adding cream and sugar to the cup I'd poured, he stated, "So let's get to it, then. What's on your mind, man?"

I took a bite from one of the cranberry scones Abbi had left with yesterday's delivery. Turned out my girl liked to bake off her stress. While I hated the reason behind it, the pastry was one of the best things I'd ever tasted. "We've been like ships passing in the night lately, Twombley."

"Awww." Grant grabbed one of the scones too. "I miss you too, honey. But if you want your big-ass building to break ground soon, that's likely to be the case for the next few weeks, at least."

"And I appreciate every second of your hard work," I assured him.

"But you're digressing." He stopped to chew his scone in obvious appreciation. "Aren't you?"

I drew in a defined breath. "A lot's happened lately . . . that you don't know about."

"Well, you got me now."

"As you do know, Tawny Mansfield showed up at my house about two weeks ago." I took a long drag on my coffee, eagerly seizing the chance to organize my thoughts. "Well . . . a few nights ago, we found her dead in my swimming pool."

Grant had just taken a taste of his own coffee, and my shocker caused the liquid to go down the wrong way. He choked and sputtered but raised his hand to fend me off when I advanced to smack his back in aid.

"Christ, man." He looked down at his shirt, inspecting for spatter damage. "You want to give a little heads-up before you drop bombs like that?"

"Because you're not used to this from me now . . . why?" I volleyed. And yeah, I guess a better man would've apologize for the bad habit—but these days, I was saving my human development moments for the times I had with Abbigail.

"You had Elijah pull the security cam footage, I'm assuming?" he asked then.

"As soon as I knew something wasn't right," I concurred. "But the assholes knew how to screw with the feed. They either erased the footage or jammed the cameras."

"Damn. Are you kidding me? So you don't have a single video lead?"

"And not a lot of physical evidence from the backyard either." I grunted. "There was a strong breeze off the canyon that night. And last I checked, piranhas can't be dusted for fingerprints."

"Dude." Grant's gaze bugged. "Are you shitting me right now? Piranhas?"

I gave myself a warm-up on the java. I wanted to be firing on all cylinders for this conversation. "Wish I were making up even half of this," I told my friend.

He swore again, beneath his breath. Aloud, he said, "This sounds like a bad B-movie plot."

"Right?" I returned. "Abbi and I went on a date night—"

"Okay, now you're really making things up."

I narrowed my gaze but only a little. "If you want to talk bad movie plots, we can discuss that whole disaster later."

"Oh, and we will," he promised, chuckling.

"Anyway, when we came home, we thought we'd go out back and check on Tawny. Neither one of us had seen her in a couple days. And, I'm not joking, the entire pool was bubbling like a Jacuzzi."

"Uh…I think I've heard enough." He clutched his midsection. "Just picturing that is giving me stomach cramps."

"The crappier part of it was the noise," I admitted. "I think it's going to haunt me for a long time." I kicked at the nap of the carpet. "I had to have the pool drained and sanitized. Since the debris was human remains, the county is insisting on the health department doing an inspection or some bullshit before I can fill it back up."

He snorted into his cup. "Pia's never going to let Vela in that pool again; you realize that, right?"

"I thought the same thing." I grimaced. "I haven't told her about the whole mess yet, but she's surprised me with crazier decisions, so never say never."

"I will be completely shocked if she does, but you know her best." While issuing that diplomacy, the guy cruised over to his usual spot on the black leather sofa. When he sank down low on the seat, making all the usual sounds preceding his typical attempt at kicking up his feet, I let a growl gurgle up my throat.

Just before his foot hit the table, I warned, "Don't put your feet on the table." I swore under my breath as I sat down opposite him.

"Jesus Christ. Do you nag Abbigail like this?" He shook his head and rearranged his long legs.

"No. First of all, she doesn't act like a barbarian. Secondly, she can do whatever she wants." I grinned, knowing I was opening a Pandora's box of "pussy whipped" comments, but it was the perfect segue to what I really needed to discuss right now.

"Is your tailor really busy right now?" Grant asked, seemingly out of the blue.

"My tailor?" Confused, I grimaced and said with annoyance, "I have no idea. Ask the psycho who sits at the desk out front for his number and call him. Why are you asking?"

"Well, I figure without your balls, all your pants are having to be altered. That would keep him pretty busy for a while, yeah?"

"Ohhh, I see." I feigned discovery while Grant snickered at his own joke. "That was your lame attempt at witticism. Shit,

Twombley. Your game is way off. You've been living in luxury too long. When we were street urchins, you could spar much better than that." I shook my head and chuckled. "Really, man. That sucked."

"Apparently so does she, and quite well. You wouldn't be this far gone otherwise. Can't say I've ever seen you like this, Bas."

I lurched forward on the sofa cushion. Screw that. I surged to my feet and loomed over the bastard, pointing right in his face. "You don't get to say shit like that about her. Ever. Am I clear?" I stabbed my finger farther in, uncaring that his eyes were practically crossing. "One hundred percent off-limits." I waited for his gape to raise back up. I kept my stare leveled to his for a few beats and then backed off. Though I sat back down, I didn't relent the pin of my scowl.

"All right, killer. Settle down. I was joking." Grant lifted his mug to his lips with a smirk. "Shit, Sebastian." Using my full name was his unwritten code for an apology. After the better part of a tense minute, he finally muttered, "Dude. You've got it worse than I thought."

I sent back half a smile. Unknowingly, the guy had given me an opening to drop the most significant mortar in my bomb bay.

"I'm in love with her."

From Grant, a slow swallow. Then the steady flow of his hands, lowering his porcelain cup to the tabletop.

Well, damn it.

Where was the drama I'd hoped for?

Instead, my lifelong best friend honored me with a smartass slow clap, a wide grin breaking out across his face. "Welcome to the party, bonehead. Glad you could join us.

You're the guest of honor but the last one to show up! I swear to God, Bas. It's like everyone around you knew you loved that woman weeks ago—everyone but you."

I wanted to glare; I really did. Every instinct told me to scowl and stomp and insist he was acting like an asshole. But I couldn't muster the expression or the behavior. It wasn't authentic, and I'd just showed my hand, so why bother with the grandstanding?

"I'm so out of my comfort zone with all of this." I made a wild hand gesture, encompassing the entire notion of being in love. What did my profession mean, when all was said and done? What did it change?

"Any of us would be, man. And that has to be okay. Because you don't have a choice about any of it. Fate has you by the balls now. You just have to roll with it."

"Roll with what?" I retorted. "Honestly, man. Do you know how foolish that sounds to a guy like me? 'Fate'? And 'being okay' with it? I mean, do you hear yourself right now?"

"Of course I do. I don't even like the sound of it, and I'm about thirty percent more in touch with my feminine side than you."

"Thirty?" I chuffed. "More like sixty-two."

"Which isn't a random number or anything."

"I don't do random, Grant."

"Of course you don't."

We both grinned as if we were in the alley of our childhood neighborhood instead of easing back on sofas in my penthouse office suite. But our easy silence only continued for a beat. I sat back up at the sound of someone moving around outside my office door.

During the workday, when the office was bustling with

people, I wouldn't hear or care about such a sound. But because Grant and I were probably the only two people on the entire floor and security hadn't called to say Elijah was in the building, the sound instantly raised my hackles.

Grant jumped to his feet at the same time I did. We shoved at each other, battling to be the first out the door to investigate.

Grant rounded the doorway first. He skidded to a halt at the sight of a feminine behind, bent over at a complete ninety-degree angle to the floor.

"Terryn?" he guessed by the view offered.

I stepped around him, homing a baffled stare down at the curvy brunette still crouched next to her desk. "Why are you here already?"

The words definitely weren't a sunshiny greeting and likely teetered on the edge of asshole, given that the woman was always here a few minutes after six in the morning—but I couldn't bring myself to care. Even weirder, I was less irritated by Elijah's lateness than by Terryn's very presence. In my head, I told myself to be grateful for having such a dedicated employee.

But my gut was saying something else.

"Oh! Hello, Mr. Twombley." She stood up, straightening the red button-front blouse that had come untucked from her black pencil skirt. Though she'd already glimpsed me, she took care to peer around Grant's frame while "smoothing" the blouse over her bosom. "And Mr. Shark...good morning. I wanted to come in a little early in case you needed me. I've been noticing how early you come in, and I thought...well, I just thought...you know..." She dropped her hands and wrung them. "Well, since you're getting your days started earlier, maybe I—I can help you."

She finished by plastering on a smile that made me want to crawl out of my skin. Instead, I turned on my heel and went back into my office. There was something off about my "sweet" little secretary, other than the fact that she had no life to speak of. Between dealing with "minor" life issues like a dead shark on my patio, a dead woman in my pool, and a crazy little thing called love, I hadn't yet had a chance to ask Elijah about looking deeper into Terryn—so for now, the greater the distance I could put between my location and hers, the better.

I sat back at my desk. From there, I could hear Grant making small talk with Terryn for a few more minutes before he casually strode back into my office.

"Close the door," I said without looking up from the email I was responding to.

"Dude, you are so rude to her. What's your deal?" He folded his arms while leaning against the back of the sofa nearest my desk.

"You do remember the shit she pulled at Club Delilah?" I prompted. "Tracking my phone?"

"Yeah, but you said you took care of that. It seems like she's really trying to make it up to you."

"Tip of the iceberg," I mumbled, hitting Send on the email.

"Huh? I'm not following you," Grant answered. "Surprise."

Ignoring his derision, I continued with my explanation, "That stunt was just the locomotive of her crazy train, mark my words." I sat back in my chair and met Grant's steady gaze. "I'll bet you twenty large that once I have Elijah look into her, he comes back with way more on that little nut burger."

He held up his hands, palms out. "Ah, no way. I'm not taking that bet. Your instincts are much too sharp when it comes to reading people. But you've definitely been keeping

Banks busy, haven't you?"

"When it rains, it pours, my man."

"Meaning?"

"That the closer a man gets to becoming King of the Hill, the more people line up to knock him down."

"Truer words have never been spoken."

"I'm aware."

We sat quietly for a minute before Grant shot to his feet. "Coffee refill?"

"Thanks," I murmured, passing off my mug to him as my phone vibrated atop my desk. It was a text message from building security, letting me know Elijah had finally arrived.

"Speak of the devil," I said while tapping out a quick thanks to the guard.

"Elijah's here?"

I dipped a cursory nod. "Wonder why he's so late. Bastard better not have been bothering Abbigail."

"Wouldn't she already be at work?" Grant posited.

"And that would that stop him why?" I rebutted. "You know how our buddy can be once he's on the trail of something—or someone—interesting to him."

"Hmmm." Grant cracked a knowing grin. "Almost worse than you, my friend."

"'Almost' being the operative word."

Before Grant could get in a responding quip, our conversation was interrupted by Terryn's telltale knock. After Grant crossed to the door and opened for her, the woman barreled right past my COO.

"Is Mr. Shark okay?" she damn near demanded, rushing in. Elijah followed about four feet behind. "Oh, there you are," she exclaimed, looking relieved when she saw me in my usual spot behind the monitors on my desk.

"Here I am." We stared at one another for a few awkward moments before I raised an expectant brow.

"Oh!" she said as if she'd been lost in thought. "Ummm... Mr. Banks is here to see you. Do you want me to order some breakfast? I didn't realize you had a full conference this morning. Your schedule only shows your appointment with Jacob Cole in an hour."

Christ, she was acting cagier than usual—and that was saying something.

"These two can fend for themselves." I motioned at Grant and Elijah. "They aren't staying. Just let me know when Mr. Cole arrives."

Grant and Elijah stood motionless, watching the exchange between my assistant and me. After I finished speaking, you could have heard a pin drop in the room.

"Terryn?"

She jerked again when I called her name. Her ensuing smile was more awkward-meets-uncomfortable than before. "Yes, Mr. Shark?"

She leaned her hip on my desk, definitely going for a come-hither vixen vibe with her reply. Problem was, the gesture was beyond inappropriate. I couldn't just toss it off as her misguided helpfulness. I pointedly looked to where her body rested on the furniture and then slowly raised my eyes until they were level with hers and directed through gritted teeth, "That will be all."

For. The. Love. Of. Christ.

I had no idea what sort of game she was playing, but it needed to stop.

The woman was odd. She always had been. But ever

since the phone-stalking incident, she waffled between overly subservient, coquettish, and skittish. She was never just a normal human doing her prescribed job. There was always some bizarre behavior or comment hanging in a gray area of possible misunderstanding.

Elijah followed her to the door as she scurried out, ensuring it was closed entirely behind her. He even engaged the lock for good measure. After spinning on the heel of his expensive Prada loafer—the man had a shoe habit to rival many ladies in this town—he strode over to the opposite wall of windows. "I will never tire of this view. What will you do with this property when the Edge is built? Sell it to me?"

"Dream on." I steepled my fingers but shot him a cocky smirk. "I might consider leasing to you, though. My other tenants say I make an excellent landlord."

Normally I'd milk such a moment awhile longer, but I felt lighter already just having these two guys parked in the same room with me. It felt fucking terrific, actually. I'd trust either of these two with my life and had literally done so on more than a few occasions. They knew all my secrets. Where all the proverbial bodies were buried. If I ever needed to dial a lifeline, it would be Grant's or Elijah's numbers on my speed button.

"So... Banks..."

"What?"

I indulged one more short grin at his sour grimace. "Grant tells me he has a new toy you may be interested in playing with."

Grant spun and shot me an incredulous look. "Really? You just word vomit like that?"

"What?" I spread my arms, not feigning my confusion.

"You said yourself that he would like her."

"Oh yeah?" Elijah straightened. At once, his lemon seemed to become a succulent strawberry. "Do tell. Apparently, I won't be getting anywhere near the sweet and gorgeous Abbigail. Shark's gone all broody possessive like an old married man over her."

"She and I have enough challenges of our own at the moment without you and your monster dick getting involved," I retorted. "So play nice on Twombley's playground for the foreseeable future."

"Challenges?" Grant cocked a quizzical glance over his shoulder. "Hold up. After your first array of shock-and-awe announcements for the morning?"

"I think I'm going to have to relocate her."

My torpedo hit a double wall of silence.

"Who?" Grant finally pressed.

"Abbigail." At least Elijah was able to follow the logic.

"Wait," Grant blurted. "What?"

"Yeah. I think he means Abbigail."

"Dude . . ."

"I'm serious." I rose and joined my friends in front of the windows. On the streets below, cars and pedestrians were growing in number as the workday got underway.

"I don't doubt that you are. But she's not a possession, Bas. She's a per-son." Grant broke the word into two distinct parts, as if sounding it out for a very young child.

"You don't think I get that?" I growled. "But whoever's fucking with me is serious about this crap. That means they'll start fucking with Abbigail soon."

"You're sure enough about that to send her away," he volleyed. "Besides, the police—"

"Are worthless," I groaned, looking to Elijah. "Banks, you were there when the police finally arrived at the house and started investigating. Did you get the impression they thought I was the innocent party? Because I sure as hell didn't. There were moments, albeit brief ones, when I felt like they had my best interest at heart. But for the other ninety-eight percent of the interrogation—"

"You mean the investigation," Elijah cut in. "Not the interrogation, Bas."

"You think I care?" I spun from them, hiking my hands to my hips. "And you think they really do?" I scuffed my toe against the carpet in resignation. "The LAPD's made themselves clear. To them, I'm the spoiled billionaire with the food poisoning that wasn't. In their minds, they've got bigger issues to deal with—so I'm on my own for trying to figure this shit out. But it's just a matter of time before this asshole and his friends crawl out from under their rock again—and what if they've figured out that the quickest way to me is through Abbi? I need to keep her safe above everything else. It seems like the easiest way to do that is take her to ground."

I drew in a long breath at last. With sharp scuffs, I pivoted back around to stare at the two men. Only then did I realize that I was actually awaiting their feedback.

At last, Elijah posed, "What does she think about all this?" He slid his hands into his front pockets, rocking back on those damn loafers like a modern-day Perry Mason.

"Well, clearly she's not happy."

He hiked his eyebrows. "Right. Clearly."

Grant moved forward again. "What about Pia and Vela? Are you going to safehouse them too? They'll be equally big targets as Abbi."

I shook my head the minute Grant mentioned my sister's name. He knew better than to make such a ridiculous suggestion. My sister's strong will damn near bettered mine. Shark genetics, at least in the texture of our skulls, ran strong.

"He has a point, Bas," Elijah said. "Why do you disagree?"

"I don't disagree at all." I firmed my jaw and leveled my gaze. "But you've both known Cassiopeia since she was a little girl. Tell me, what do you think her response to something like that would be?"

Grins spread across both their faces—likely the result of them picturing my sister castrating me via various methods. I almost rolled my eyes, but I had only myself to blame for their hell spawn smirks. I'd walked right into that one.

"Oh, please let me be there if you make mention of it." Grant clasped his hands in front of his chest like a begging choir boy.

"You're such an ass," I muttered.

"True, but not the point," Elijah interjected. "Pia is a smart woman. And if she thought Vela was in an ounce of danger, she'd be the one coming up with a plan to get her to safety. We all know that. So it may just be a matter of how the problem is presented to her, Bas." He let me digest his words before continuing. "You go into a conversation with your sister blustering and demanding and ordering her to do something? Hell yeah, she's going to dig in and object."

"Go on," I urged—if only to examine Elijah's mien a little more. If I wasn't mistaken, I saw a glimmer of adoration, maybe even respect, in my friend's eyes as he addressed the subject of my sister. My protective hackles didn't like it, not one bit, but what he was speaking about also made a ton of sense. Logic I likely needed to hear right now.

"But if you plant seeds of fear and danger, she will let them germinate and thrive."

"Okay, Confucius." Grant twisted a frown as if Elijah had pulled out a garlic clove and unpeeled it. "What the hell's your point? You advocating that we keep all of this a secret from Pia?"

"No." I rubbed my knuckles against my chin. "He's saying exactly the opposite."

"So . . . tell her everything?"

"But carefully," Elijah stressed with a nod. "With selective messaging." He tilted his regard back my way. "And before you know you it, she'll be strangled by vines of maternal fear."

I turned my hand over, scrubbing it up my face. "That's devious as shit," I growled. "But damn it, I like it."

"She'll be packing their bags within two days tops." Elijah folded his arms across his chest as he finished.

"Dude," Grant deadpanned. "That was fucking beautiful." He pretended to sniff and wipe a tear away from the corner of his eye. The two gave each other a dramatic hug. When they parted, they stared expectantly back at me.

"So many times," I muttered while throwing a pleading look up at the ceiling. "So many times I ask myself why I'm still friends with you two jackasses."

"Because of my pretty eyes?"

"Because of my awesome ass?"

I shook my head, unsure to be amused or worried that they'd thrown out the taunts in unison. "No comment, Tweedledee and Tweedledum," I finally said. "But I can recognize a good plan when I hear one—and now I'm thinking maybe this one should be taken a step further . . ."

Elijah filled my pointed pause with his steady nod. "You

think the same tactic will work with Abbigail."

"Oh, snap," Grant inserted. "Damn. That's brilliant."

"She's very headstrong too," I commented. "And I don't necessarily want to change that. It's one of the things I love the most about her."

Elijah snapped his stare to Grant. The guy nodded sagely. But before we could discuss my declaration of love, now out there for both of them to churn up, tease out, and openly debate, my desk phone sounded with the internal intercom. In two long strides I was in front of my desk, answering the page from Terryn.

"Shark."

"Jacob Cole is here." Shock of shocks—yet a pleasant one at that, thank Christ—her voice was cool and polite, all traces of previous strangeness gone.

"Give me two minutes, then show him in." I released the speaker button and addressed my buddies. "All right, kids. Party's over. The architect for the Edge is here, and I have a shit ton to do after the meeting. Twombley, are you staying for this, or do you actually have work to do?"

"You know I live to serve you, Sebastian." He rolled his eyes before giving me his serious answer. "My first appointment is at nine, but it's here in the building. I can sit in for a bit if you want me to."

"Outstanding," I responded.

"And I think that's my cue," Elijah put in. "I'll get out of your way—but before I do, to safehouse or not to safehouse?"

"That is the damn question," I said from gritted teeth.

"I can put out preliminary feelers," he offered, already brandishing his cell and scrolling down his contacts list. I didn't even want to know how many world governments would kill for that directory. "See if someone's got something decadent but discreet nearby."

My nod was terse. I hated feeling like I was sneaking around on Abbi as well as Pia, but this shit was necessary. I'd certainly faced—and approved—uglier missions before. "Thanks," I finally murmured. "That's a good idea, man."

"Catch you later, then." Elijah called it over his shoulder while walking out. His gaze hadn't left his cell screen—and I was grateful. I paid that man an obscene hourly rate, but on days like this, he was worth every penny.

"His approach just might work," I said to Grant. "For both of the women."

My friend sucked in a lot of air through his nose. "Just be careful, dude. The minute either one of them senses you're playing them, they'll fuck up your world bad. Baaaddd. Seriously, you won't know which end is up."

I shoved away from my desk. "Yeah, yeah," I growled while crossing to the conference table. "I know, goddammit."

"Please don't make me hold your hair while you're puking from the bender you will most definitely go on."

"All the more reason to make sure they never suspect a thing."

Two quick raps on the door ended our conversation. A second later, Terryn stuck her head in. While she'd outwardly returned to the realm of demure respect, her gaze still gleamed like a character from *American Horror Story*.

"Now if I could just figure out what to do about this little nutcase," I commented solely for Grant's ears. A second later, I was lifting my head with professional command. "Jacob Cole. How are you?"

I offered a hand as the young architect came in the door.

He had blueprints tucked under each arm and a leather briefcase slung over one shoulder. We shook hands in greeting, and when Terryn hung in the doorway, I gave her a quick scowl so she would leave. I turned to introduce Jacob to Grant, but they were already shaking hands.

"You must be Grant Twombley?" Cole asked.

"Yes." Grant narrowed his gaze, obviously curious. "Have we met?"

"Not formally," Jacob explained. "I did some research on the company when I was bidding the job, so I recognize you from the website."

"Hmm." My friend rubbed his chin in thought. "And you're sure we haven't met somewhere else? You look very familiar."

"Maybe I just have one of those faces."

"Can I take something from you? You look like a pack mule."

"Thanks," Cole replied as Grant flashed his congenial grin and pulled out the blueprints. As we completed the stroll to the conference table, he and Grant continued to chat.

"Damn," Grant said. "I guess you do have one of those faces."

"Or maybe it's just something in the air today." Jake thumbed over his shoulder toward the outer office. "Your assistant just grilled me for five minutes, insisting the same thing."

I clenched my teeth but did my very best to keep my voice level while asking, "What was that about my assistant?"

"She kept insisting I looked familiar," Jacob answered. "And that we must know one another from somewhere. I tried explaining that I studied abroad in college and didn't grow up in LA. She's a little odd, that one." He laughed. "I mean, no offense. I'm sure she's awesome at her job. Otherwise you wouldn't keep her around."

"Yeah." Grant sighed. His wistfulness was as sincere as a hooker at confession. "She's a real gem, our Terryn."

But his humor was no help. The literal straw had just broken the camel's back and, with it, my patience. "Siri, page Terryn."

"Do you mean fucking Terryn?" the computerized voice replied.

Grant burst out laughing. I sent an apologetic glance Cole's way.

"Yes," I answered, rubbing the aching furrow in my brow. Jesus Christ, this woman was going to drive me to the 5150 ward—likely right on her heels.

"Yes, Mr. Shark?"

"Call the HR director and set up a meeting in our first mutually available slot, please," I instructed.

"Can I tell her what it's regarding?" Terryn asked, and the pain pounded harder at my forehead. Was she being nosy, or was that a reasonable question? And why the hell was her odd behavior causing me to question my perception of everyday matters?

I was seriously pissed now.

"It's an employee situation," I bit out. "I can't give more detail on an unsecured line, so that will have to be enough. If Wendy asks, tell her she can call my direct line."

"Will do. I will add it to your calendar and send you a notification."

"Great."

As I ended the call, Grant caught my gaze with his. I shook my head with subtle inference. I definitely didn't want to discuss my assistant in further detail in front of our guest.

"Sorry about that, gentlemen." I forced a smile while giving the architect my full attention. "So, Jake. Ready to show me the changes you came up with since we last met?"

"Yes," he replied. "But first, I wanted to share some great news."

"I could use some. Let's hear it."

"Yesterday, I was at the city planning office, checking on some drawings I needed to have stamped. Honestly, the backlog in that department is out of control."

He shook his head while scowling. I nodded. I could appreciate his frustration with the city's system of handling the building process.

"While I was there, I figured I may as well check in with DCP and see where we are on this project, especially with your groundbreaking target date looming so close."

"Please say you have good news." I didn't hide my overt hope from the guy, though it was only cautious optimism. I was afraid to even admit to that, optimistic after the unending disappointments and red tape courtesy of City Hall.

"I'm happy to report that things are in great shape, Mr. Shark."

"Are you shitting me? Uh ... I mean ... fill me in." I wasn't so opaque about the anticipation this time.

"There's just one action item with Public Works"—Cole referred to some notes on his smart pad—"and if I had to guess the reason, the fire inspector's backlog is likely to blame. On new construction, there is a concern with fire hydrant spacing and fire lane placement on the street level. I have both clearly marked on my plans, but I'm sure you've noticed those." He pointed to the symbols for the valves spaced at regular intervals around the perimeter of the structure. "I suspect fire lanes could be on this street here, here, or here." He swept his capped pen across the blueprint in conjunction with his directions. "Or possibly all three, based on the maximum occupancy of the building." He quietly studied his drawing for a few moments before adding, "But ultimately, that's up to Public Works to decide, along with the fire department. That'll be another small holdup, I suspect . . . once the inspector sets eyes on the print." He teetered his head back and forth. "But I shouldn't think it'll be too much longer."

At last, Cole looked up from the detailed prints. He glanced back and forth between Grant and me for feedback. I noted his concern, but Grant was fixated on the intricacy of the drawing.

"This is really thorough, Cole."

I let him hear the admiration in my tone. I couldn't really throw anything at him that he hadn't covered thus far. There was a good chance Jacob knew that already, but he nevertheless beamed like a kid with a fresh A on a test.

"There's a secondary plan review with the state fire marshal, which is customary for high-rise buildings over a certain height," he went on. "But your DBS concierge will most likely hand carry the plans through, getting one stamp right after the other. I mean, that would be ideal, right?" He added the last part when Grant and I remained silent.

"Forgive my ignorance," Grant said with a self-deprecating wince. "DBS?"

"Department of Building and Safety," I supplied. Still, I admitted to feeling a little inferior around Jacob and his vast building process knowledge. It was rare I felt less than another man in any arena. The sensation was unsettling—but not enough to prevent me from making my next statement.

"Once again, Mr. Cole, you've really impressed me. I know we haven't gone through the change list yet, but your knowledge astounds me. That's a rare occurrence." I peered at him more carefully. He was a good-looking guy, with overall coloring similar to mine but a leaner build and a shaggier haircut. "How long did you say you've lived in this city?"

He shrugged. "Going on about six months now."

"Six months," I echoed. "Yet you've already learned the ins and outs of the city's planning and permitting departments, as well as being nothing less than brilliant at your craft here."

As I emphasized the point by tapping on the blueprints, Grant tossed in his approving vote with a sturdy nod. "Bas is right," he declared. "I've only just met you, Cole, but I'm impressed. I think Bas has made an excellent choice putting you at the top of this project."

Jacob flushed with another hit of humble pride. "Thanks, man. That means a lot. I know we'll be working together more as the project takes off. I'm looking forward to it."

"Ditto," Grant returned and stepped around to shake Jacob's hand again. "But right now, I need to head out and prep for another appointment."

"Understood." Jake nodded. "Don't let me keep you."

"Thank you for everything you've done so far. I look forward to sitting in on more of these meetings in the future." Grant walked his coffee mug over to the kitchenette. "But I'll see you at the groundbreaking?"

"Damn straight you will," I stated—only to be caught short by Jake's defined wince.

"About that…" Oh, yeah. It was definitely a wince. The guy was now radiating discomfort too.

"What is it?" Panic returned with a familiar drumbeat at my temples. "Is there an issue? A delay?"

"Oh, no," Jake swiftly rectified. "Nothing like that. Not at all. I just wanted to let you know that I won't be able to attend the ceremony. I received the invitation to my office late last week but wanted to give my regrets to you in person."

"Oh, that's really too bad. I was hoping to introduce you to the press," I said, not hiding my disappointment.

"I appreciate that. Any type of PR is appreciated. Unfortunately, I'll be in Barcelona."

"Well, damn," Grant teased. "That's a real hardship, man."

"Okay." Jake put a hand up in concession. "Wrong choice of words. I meant that it's unfortunate I'll miss the event. But I am definitely happy to be going back to Spain."

"Back?" Grant pressed.

"Yes. I'm attending a reunion with some close friends. I committed to the event several months ago, right before coming out here. The travel arrangements have already been made."

"Ah. That's too bad," I mused. "I would've offered you use of my jet as a gesture of my gratitude."

"You have a jet?" It was Jacob's turn for the unmasked reaction. Surprise dominated his face. "Annnd that was probably a dumb thing to ask. But I could never accept something like that."

I exchanged a private glance with Grant. Yes, from all the way across the room. Yes, because Jacob Cole was as rare as a unicorn in a town like Los Angeles. Talented as a leathered rock star yet as humble as homemade apple pie.

"Of course you could," I nearly growled at the unicorn, who still stood there nervously fiddling with his pens. I almost wondered where his pocket protector was but refrained from cracking that particular zinger. "And next time, you will. I insist."

As I held up my hand to stop his mounting and useless protest, Grant made a point of striding back over to add in a stage whisper, "Eventually, you'll learn not to bother arguing."

With that as his parting jab, Grant turned and rushed out the door. As soon as he shut the door, Jacob posed to me, "So . . . you two have known each other for a long time?"

"Our whole lives," I supplied. "We grew up together. Why do you ask?"

"I just feel the brother-close air between you." He lifted a quixotic smile. "I haven't seen a lot of that around here. In this town, I mean. People are nice enough, of course—peace, love, sunshine—but it just seems like everyone is so . . . driven." He paused, clearly not nailing what he wanted to say with that either. "Motivated," he finally pronounced. "And focused. And all of that is great too, but there are key human things that seem to be missing in most of the people I've met so far."

"People." As I repeated the word with slow care, I examined Jacob Cole with even deeper regard. The telling flash in his gaze gave away the truth I sought out. "You mean women. Or maybe men?"

"Ahhh." The guy chuckled, clearly put on the spot but confident enough to handle my incision. "Definitely women." He tapped the end of a pen against the tabletop. "Not that the definition helps," he confessed. "I'm . . . just not really sure I'll ever meet the right one in this city."

"Were you hoping to?"

I asked it with raised brows but inwardly questioned my move. Why was I even going there with the guy? Small talk wasn't something I usually engaged in. Not enough time, not enough patience. But Jacob had such a unique "little brother" quality about him. He just reeled me in. Made me want to care about him, for some reason.

"Nah," he said but with speed that gave up even more of his game. Or, in this case, lack of it. As in, not even wanting to play it. "I guess not. No, definitely not," he rushed out. "I mean, I already met her—a lifetime ago. When I was in college, up north."

"So what happened? If she was 'the one,' I mean, why aren't you married with two-point-five brats and a Pomeranian that you push around in a dog stroller?"

"Complicated story." But his laugh was too loud and too agitated. "No, that's bullshit. It's not complicated at all. I got offered a dream apprenticeship in Barcelona—"

"And ergo, the reunion," I inserted.

"Right," he commented. "And she insisted I accept it. She wasn't able to come with me due to having a super-controlling family."

"Whom she refused to stand up to?"

His features, already carved and pronounced, tightened to the texture of a stone statue. "It was a little more complicated than that."

I nodded, pretending to commiserate—until realizing, with shock, that I actually did. "As most things are," I murmured, meaning that too.

"We stayed in touch at first, but well . . . you know how it goes." He shrugged and leaned heavily against the table's edge. "She grew distant and then ghosted me after about nine months. Cut off all communication. I never heard from her again."

"Damn." And yes, I meant that too—but I'd have to be made of the same stone he looked like to phone that one in. "That's cold."

Cole grunted softly. "By then I was so brokenhearted and bitter, I just threw myself into making the most of my studies in Barcelona."

"And the pussies of the local España girls?" The lighthearted crack was my attempt to ease the guy's moroseness. It hung over him like a shroud.

"Not for a long time," Jacob asserted. "Took about a year after the last time I spoke to her to even sleep with another woman. I loved this girl with every breath I took. We grew up together in college, you know? We shared our dreams and planned what our lives would be after graduation. So when she cut me out of the very dreams we shared, it eviscerated me."

"Dude." It was all I could offer in the way of sympathy. Admittedly, empathy and compassion were not my strong suits—or at least I'd assumed until now. Until Vela came into my life, I thought I was incapable of feeling the emotions at all. And actually displaying them? Like, possibly, in a situation like this? No way. At all.

Yeah . . . just . . . no.

Yet, here I was. "Dude"ing all over Jacob Cole like we were sharing our inner spirits with each other two days deep at Coachella. And I was fine with it. More than fine, actually.

"I know, I know. To a guy like you, I sound like a big fucking pussy." He shook his head in embarrassment while looking down at the floor. "I mean, you're Sebastian Shark. A legend, just about. And I'm standing here talking about a woman who literally dumped my ass, and I sound like I'm still hopelessly carrying a torch for her."

I pulled in a long breath. As I let it out, I laughed. Long and hard. At this whole conversation. But most of all, at myself. I hoped Jake saw that, because I didn't want to stop. It felt too damn good.

At last, I stopped long enough to spurt, yet again, "Dude."

Jacob narrowed his stare. "Uhhh . . . huh?"

"I get it." I clapped a hand atop his shoulder. "I really get it, okay?"

"Uhhh," he stammered again. "Okay . . ."

"Actually, just very recently, I've had the unreal experience of feeling emotion at the same magnitude."

He popped his gaze. "Seriously?"

"Seriously." I laughed again. Not so loudly but just as deeply. "It's actually taken me this long to find it, but maybe the wait was worth it." After jostling him for a long second, I raised my hand and raked it through my hair. "I just know one more thing," I admitted. "It's scaring the living shit out of me."

Jake broke out in a grin. "Yeah, that sounds about right."

"Shit." I raked my other hand through my hair. "I'm not sure I'm man enough for all this—for her—either."

"Yep, that sounds about right, too."

"Not helping, Cole." I side-eyed him.

"Sorry, man," he offered, still smirking.

"It's good. Let's get back to work before we're hugging it out or jaunting off to paint pottery together. I can't lose all my street cred in one fucking appointment." I motioned toward the work awaiting our attention.

"This all stays right here. You have my word." There was pure honesty in the guy's gaze. I felt nothing but trust in my blood at his declaration.

"You've got yourself a deal, my young friend." I smacked

him on the back, probably a bit harder than I needed to, judging by the way he lurched forward, and I couldn't help but chuckle when he gave me a sideways glare. We both turned back to the blueprints on the table and got back to business.

CHAPTER ELEVEN

ABBIGAIL

His large hands easily kept me still on the bedroom floor, even though I bucked and wriggled beneath him.

"Sebastian. God, please. You have to . . . you have to . . ."

"Oh, baby." His croon was low and sensual—and exasperating. "You know I love it when you beg so sweetly."

"But . . . but you're not listening!"

"Of course I am."

I begged to differ—and actually was—but again, back to the maddening-man-not-listening factor. He'd been feasting on my pussy for what seemed like an hour. A woman's dream come true, right? Not when said attention had spiraled me well past my third orgasm and the room had started spinning around me.

"Bas, please," I panted. "Stop. You have to stop!" I wanted to thread my fingers into his thick, dark hair, intending to pull his wicked tongue, lips, and teeth away from my protesting clit. I wanted it so badly, but damn it, he'd ordered me to keep my hands flat on the floor beside me—and clearly my acquiescence was the man's aphrodisiac. In a huge way. Never had he eaten me out with such unbridled fervor—and unequaled talent.

"You don't really mean that, Abbigail."

Nor had he ever purred at me with such unmatched sensuality.

I couldn't even launch a logical argument. Because he was right. With every exquisite word. He brought me so much pleasure, I never wanted it to end. Any of it. Not just the panty-incinerating sex or his caring, considerate love. By now, I was even smitten by his demanding, overprotective, all-consuming nurturing.

I wanted all of it.

I wanted all of him.

Forever.

My musings pulled my focus off Bas's ministrations for a few seconds. Vital ones, since I resurfaced to discover he'd moved up my body to hover his beautiful face above mine. I gasped roughly, my nostrils flaring with urgency. Oxygen. I needed more oxygen and then realized why. His hands were locked around my throat, clutching lightly but enough to hamper my already labored breathing. When I lifted my hands to pull at his hold around my throat, he raised a menacing brow, all but threatening me to return them to my sides where I had been instructed to keep them. Or else.

I slammed my arms and hands back to the floor, flattening them alongside my thighs. Just as I returned to the position, Bas pushed inside my throbbing pussy. I arched my back, jerking my hips up to meet his ferocious thrusts. I cried out with a primal quality in my scream.

Bas released his hold on my neck. He supported his weight with both hands, using the leverage to assist his pumps into me.

"Fuck, baby," he grunted. "Always so wet for me."

"Always," I echoed, my sigh dreamy but husky.

"You can't get enough of my cock, can you?"

"I always want more." Oh, how true it was. In so many, many ways.

My pledge summoned a sound of feral satisfaction from the middle of his chest. He backed out entirely and then slammed into my body again. Again. Yet again. I welcomed every commanding thrust, hoping he saw how he wasn't just invading my body. He was inside my soul . . . my heart.

After several more lunges, he settled far inside me. Our breaths mingled as our bodies thrummed. He looked peaceful but intense while swiping the tangled hair away from my forehead and then planting a tender kiss in its place.

"I love you, Abbigail."

I couldn't do anything but smile. Even after a month, my heart swelled when I heard those words from his lips. It usually took a moment to recover before I could respond in kind. This one was no different. "I love you, Sebastian."

"And I love fucking you." He groaned while dropping his head. The sound deepened as he bit a stinging trail down the side of my neck.

"Mmmm. And I love the way you fuck me." There was always dirty conversation to be had while we made love. "God, every bit of it."

"And I love all of you." He rolled his hips, ensuring every inch of my tunnel felt every contact of his engorged length. "But right now, I love this cunt, girl." He rotated again. Added a pair of shallow but erotic thrusts. It was the most amazing friction my pussy had ever felt. Every membrane was turned into a shivering star; every muscle clenched in aching arousal.

"Holy hell." My eyes rolled back involuntarily from the jolts of pleasure he brought beyond even that. "Bas!"

"What, baby?" He slowed his body and fixated again on my face. "What's wrong?"

"Nothing," I blurted back. "God. Not a damn thing. Feels

so good. So good!" My breath sawed in and out as my climax neared.

He sped up his passionate pace. "Are you close?"

"Yes." I pushed it out between wild pumps of my lungs. "Y-Y-Yes. Oh, holy shit, I . . . I can't believe it."

"Good Christ. I can feel you fluttering all around me."

But even with the possessiveness and passion in his gaze, I couldn't believe it. Climaxing once, even during the days when I did this stuff for myself, was close to a miracle. My brain could never let go of enough details to make it happen. But Sebastian Shark made the details inconsequential. He made the whole world go away.

And right now, he spurred my body on to an impossible explosion. I climbed higher and higher, reaching for that miraculous moment of absolute ecstasy.

"Right there," I whimpered. "Bas, yes. Oh, please!"

He hunched his shoulders. Pressed his face back into my neck. "Closer, baby?"

"Don't stop!" It was bossy and demanding, and I didn't care. Nothing else mattered but the power of his body and what he was doing to me with it. "I'm going to come," I finally blurted. "Holy . . . God . . . I can't . . . ooohh . . ."

But then I did. Oh hell, how I did—while I shattered into complete, carnal bliss. My body was a collection of spasms and shivers. My brain felt short-circuited. Everything went dark. My body slackened as Sebastian hammered into me, finding his release right after me.

"Fuck, Abbi." He timed his chanting with the pumping of his hips. "Fuck, fuck, fuck!"

At last, he began to slow. He finally came to a full rest with his forehead nestled between my neck and shoulder. Sweat covered both of us like a fine mist on a spring morning. It cooled me instantly when Sebastian rolled to the side and the air conditioning hit my skin. Goose bumps erupted across my body, and it didn't escape the notice of my ever-observant man. He pulled a coverlet off the bed we'd never actually gotten to.

Suddenly, a giggle bubbled up out from my lips. Bas regarded my reaction while tucking the cover around our naked bodies. "Have I fucked you silly, woman?"

"Maybe." I snickered. "I was just laughing at the two of us here on the floor, when the perfectly amazing bed is right there."

"Hmmph," he growled, though humor still glittered in his gorgeous blues. "Mattresses are overrated." He took my lips in a slow-burn kiss that literally curled my toes. "Better traction on the carpet."

I rolled my eyes, but just talking about "traction" had the man's penis jerking anew against my thigh. Before he could start with the magical hip rolls and do something about it, I pinned him with a more sober stare. "How are you doing?" I ventured while stroking a hand up and down his muscular back. "Are you excited about tomorrow? Nervous?"

"A little of both."

His admission came as a pleasant surprise. Not the words but the comfort level with which he'd given them. Our conversations had become so much simpler lately. More authentic. The openness wasn't just a necessity anymore, forced by the hand of fate—not to mention the faceless forces who were trying to get under Sebastian's skin.

While they had yet to succeed, it seemed I had—at least a little. It felt like he gave me a bit more trust with each passing day. He was also freer about sharing exactly what was on his mind. Bas was letting a lot more of his guard down around me, though I could tell that the gesture wasn't always easy for him. But he was trying, and that fact alone gave me more hope for our relationship's future than anything else.

"Well, that's honest," I supplied.

"Damn straight it is," he stated, attempting another hopeful nudge against my thigh. For the moment, I ignored the action. The subject at hand was important here.

"I appreciate it," I told him and meant it. "And I also empathize with where you're at. You've been working for this moment for so long. At last you're breaking ground on the Edge. So yeah, I'd think some nerves would be expected, even for someone like"—I dropped my tone to a teasing manly man bass—"the mighty and powerful Sebastian Shark."

At that, a low snarl rumbled out of Bas—as he dinged a silent timer on the wait time for rolling back on top of me. He covered me completely with the weight of his body, enforcing the domination by stretching my arms above my head. "Are you making fun of me, Abbigail Gibson?" His voice was lethally calm as he pinned my wrists harder to the floor. Instantly and shamelessly, my core pulsed. My eyelids felt heavy and drugged. Lust spiked my entire system.

"Bas." My voice was barely a whisper.

"Oh, Little Red." He dipped in and kissed me, slowly working my lips apart with his. "What kind of spell do you have on me?"

He pushed his tongue inside my mouth as though we hadn't been kissing and fondling and fucking just seven minutes ago. My whole body trembled beneath his again. My pussy ached for his attention.

"I don't know what's happening either," I confessed. "It's

madness." I pushed my hips up to him but wanted to offer more. So much more.

"Madness. Hmmm. Well, that's one way to describe it. But in a very, very good way."

He finished that with a devastating smile. My lips inched up in response. I couldn't help myself. His grin was so boyish, irresistible, and sexy. I acknowledged the continuing meltdown of my bloodstream, feeling my self-control slip away. The new heat across Bas's face was another encouragement. I was seconds away from giving him the words he visually demanded.

Do it. Fuck me again.

But I gulped the syllables back down into silence. I really wanted to give him the opportunity to talk about the Edge's groundbreaking ceremony. It was less than twenty-four hours away now—and even now, with our lust practically spoonable on the air, I could see the gears in Bas's head at work. He had at least five mental lists going at the same time. I wanted to be here for him with more than just my pussy. To listen if he had any logistical or motivational concerns. To assure him he really was going into this important day with his best foot forward.

"So, tell me what you're nervous about."

For the trouble of my honesty, I received a narrowed glower. "What makes you think I'm nervous?"

"Because you're still trying to redirect my attention with the power of your . . ."

His eyes glittered brighter. "Say it, baby. My cock." He pressed his wakening erection into the inside of my thigh. "Is it working?"

"Sebastian." I drew out the middle syllable with deliberate chastisement. Maybe his physically controlling position would make it okay for him to admit emotional vulnerability. Even now. Maybe especially now.

Sebastian let his eyes slide closed for a moment. Then two. I waited through the pauses, sensing him switching mental gears.

"I just want everything to go well," he finally confessed. "The press loves to hound me, you know?"

I feigned a shocked gape before deadpanning, "I had no idea. At all."

He meshed our fingers tighter while jacking his brows higher. The intensity of his gaze had me bracing for some kind of retaliation, but he chose to continue with the explanation— at least for now. "You've been doing enough private parties for enough rich assholes to know this by now. There could be twelve perfect parts about the event, preceding one aspect that isn't, and that one misstep is the night's headline. Nobody cares if it's the most insignificant detail."

I ditched the deadpan for an understanding nod. He was right; I'd routinely witnessed this nonsense. The press was a brutal bunch who knew how humans liked feasting on failure.

"Right," I murmured back to him. "I get that too."

"Thanks." He softly kissed the tip of my nose. "I know you do."

"Wish I could say I didn't or that it was hard to get. But when those primordial behavioral remnants get stirred in people..."

"When what?" Bas charged.

"It's common to most of us," I replied. "An innate instinct, almost. Humans really aren't that different from animals. We instinctually prey on those who are weaker than ourselves— survival of the fittest."

One corner of his mouth hitched up. Though it was likely

reflex for him, I was more than aware of—and heated by—the reaction. "I've been familiar with the concept for quite a long time, Ms. Gibson."

His drawl heightened my awareness of one more thing. The utter irony of my assertion, given our current positioning. "I . . . I suppose you are, Mr. Shark."

In the space of a heartbeat, threads of wildness reentered his sultriness. "And you like it."

My eyelids—and my sex—were heavy again. "And I'm smart enough to agree with you."

From above me, Bas broke his grin wider—with blatant mischief. "Smart girls are sexy."

"And horny boys are hopeless." I seized the chance to lighten up the moment, laughing while trying to buck him off me, but my effort was useless. The man was all muscle and pure determination. If he didn't want to be moved, he wasn't going to be moved.

The admission came just before he surprised me by releasing his grip and then rolling his body upward. His explanation wasn't long to follow. "As much as I hate to admit it, we should probably think about getting some sleep, though."

I hurled a playful side-eye. "Who are you, and what have you done with my give-it-to-me-all-night-baby boyfriend?"

He tossed his head back on a raucous laugh while balancing on his chiseled haunches. "Tomorrow's going to be a long day." He rolled up to his feet and then stretched out a hand. "Shower?"

"I think I'd rather just climb into bed and deal with it in the morning. That way I can have a fighting chance with my hair." I rolled my eyes up toward the wild mess around my face and shoulders.

"Sounds like a plan. Come on." He wrapped an arm around my waist to tow me to my side of the bed. With swift efficiency, he pulled the covers down for me. "I'll tuck you in, baby, but I need to check email one more time before bed."

"Nooooo," I protested and dug my grip into one of his beautiful forearms. "Just come to bed. If you get on the computer, you'll be up for two more hours." I slid my hand down until I could tug on his hand. "There's nothing you can fix at this hour anyway."

"Oh, you'd be surprised what I can do at this hour, Abbigail. The business world never sleeps."

His tone already made it clear who would win the debate, so I chose not to push the subject. Fact: certain subjects—all right, most subjects—just couldn't be argued about with the man. Also fact: business and the priority it held in his life were on the top of that list. But most important fact: now that I knew all the reasons why, there was no way I could or would change him. Not even in moments like this. The man who kissed me sweetly and then quietly walked out in his thousand-dollar track pants was still, in so many ways, the hungry kid from the east side in secondhand clothes. I loved him for the drive that had gotten him from one to the other—and yes, at times I also loved him in spite of it.

"Good night, beautiful," Bas tenderly murmured from the doorway. "Sleep well. I won't be long." As always, he'd left a soft light on in the bathroom until he came to bed, making it possible for me to watch him walk out into the hall. And what a sight it was. Despite how sleep strongly pulled at me, it wasn't hard to keep my eyes open for the captivating sight of him. The sleek muscles of his bare back. The determined set of his broad shoulders. The way his freshly trimmed hair caressed the back of his neck.

Wow. Even now, at complete rest, he was so breathtaking. So proud. So strong. So mesmerizing. So mine. Was this seriously my life now? It was still hard to believe at times. And then, like right now, it hit in a crazy rush of stunned awareness. I was really living here.

With Sebastian Shark.

My sexy-as-sin boyfriend.

In his palace-sized home in the hills of Calabasas.

Ohhh, yes. This was all really happening. And not just "for the time being." Not anymore. My lease had expired in Torrance two weeks earlier. After a lot of wine and a long conversation, Sebastian convinced me it was best, logistically and financially, to let it go. I'd miss dear old Mr. Blatt and the rest of the gang in the building, but Bas's logic resonated. I was paying for something I wasn't using—but, more significantly, for space that had always been a residence, not my home. On top of that, Bas was still convinced he could protect me better here than there. While the evidence to date didn't support that, I was ready to trust him on it.

Within hours of our talk, Bas had movers hired to pack and bring up all my things from the condo to Calabasas. They were now stored in the pool house, which had been steam-cleaned after the police finished picking it over. All I had to do was oversee the activities, which had taken just a few effortless, perhaps even anticlimactic, hours. It was all quite surreal.

But I knew not to get too comfortable yet. The real fireworks were just ahead when I explained my new living arrangements to Rio and Sean.

The strangeness of the thought got exacerbated when I broke things down a little more. Sean had been weirdly and pleasantly open-minded when it came to my relationship with Sebastian. Oddly, my sister-in-law was the one wielding more reservations. No matter how many different ways I looked at the situation, I couldn't understand where Rio's hostility was rooted. Clearly I didn't have some key information here, but intuition kept leading back to her issues with Bas's domineering side. Maybe that quality about him—which I did count as a quality, for more reasons than the benefits it brought me between the sheets—dredged up some unpleasant memories from Rio's past. But how did I get into that kind of conversation with her? And how did I look past the fact that my brother had a pretty wide bossy streak too? If Rio didn't respond well to that type of man, it made no sense why she'd married Sean. Of course, that just brought me back to square one. No matter how many ways I tried to rationalize Rio's disdain for Sebastian, the conflict didn't add up.

With all of those mental switches flipped, sleep was less of a sure thing than I thought. After tossing and turning for at least thirty minutes, I finally toggled all the thoughts back off and drifted to sleep.

★ ★ ★

The alarm went off much too soon, right before six a.m. It was way too early for a Saturday, but it was a big day for Abstract Catering as well as Shark Enterprises.

I quickly silenced the beeps so Bas could sleep a little longer. True to form, he'd come to bed far past midnight. I got a shower, dressed into my kitchen clothes, and sneaked downstairs to have my coffee in the quiet of the kitchen. Soon my day would transition to another kitchen. Rio and I were meeting at the Abstract prep space to check off the final tasks for the Edge's groundbreaking reception. The plan was to load and deliver the food to the party site by ten.

I'd already packed my change of clothes and makeup bag into my truck and would transfer it all into the Abstract Catering van so I could change after supervising the event setup team.

I'd also handpicked the setup and service teams for the event. Only top-tier staff members, with experience in high-end service etiquette, had gotten the call. While we'd briefed everyone in presentation specifics for each dish, I'd still be overseeing the garnishments and final touches for everything that got plated, with Rio overseeing logistics and service flow. We'd taken every measure to ensure things ran smoothly, including a pre-event run-through at the site. Barring any unforeseen catastrophes, the day would be a success from our end—but even if the sky fell, I could count on Rio to roll with it. The woman was an ace in a crunch and handled disasters like a champ. She promised that if anything crumbled apart while I was being Sebastian's very public date, I wouldn't even know about it until the next morning back in the kitchen.

I adored that woman. And I'd made sure to tell her, plenty of times, during the preparations for this important day. While things between us weren't completely back to normal yet, the quick prep for the groundbreaking had brought us together in a lot of cool ways, working toward our common goal. I hoped the new camaraderie would translate back into sisterhood soon as well.

I double-checked the contents of my work satchel, making sure I had all the essentials. Smart pad, charger, cell phone, wallet, and emergency kit. It was all there.

After stowing the bag into the truck, I made one last dash into the house to find my man. Along the way, I indulged a big grin. *My man.* The happiness of that thought would never get old. Nor would the anticipation of getting to see him in all his dark, confident resplendence.

I was hoping to add one more descriptor onto that— *naked*—but when I entered the master suite bathroom, he was already dressed and knotting his tie in front of the vanity mirror. But God, did he look good doing it—especially in the ensemble he'd carefully picked for today. Though he hadn't put on his tailored suit jacket yet, his crisp white shirt and dark navy slacks were breath-robbing statements on his ultrafine physique.

"Morning, handsome." Though I said it quietly, parts of me were doing giddy shrieks at the opportunity to come up behind him, flattening my hands across his stomach.

"There you are." He beamed at me via the mirror. "I was hoping you didn't leave without saying goodbye."

"Oh, bite your tongue, Mr. Shark," I said as he turned, leaving his tie to hang loosely around his neck.

"I'd prefer to bite yours, Ms. Gibson." He braced his hands to my hips and tugged me against him.

I laughed. But only a little. There was something to be said for the distraction of being held flush against Sebastian Shark's body. "Sooo . . . I'll see you at the site by . . ."

I purposely left the statement hanging open, openly fishing for his estimated arrival time at the groundbreaking site. After lowering a slow kiss to my lips, leaving me tingly from his mint toothpaste, he said, "I plan on being there by ten. And the press should start assembling by eleven. And then by twelve, I plan on you and I having our own private celebration . . ." Another slow kiss as he went on, moving my hair off my neck before kissing down the column of my neck.

"Baaaasss..."

I could barely rasp it out as he continued blazing a trail with the tip of his nose and then following with featherlight traces of his tongue. I moaned and repeated the protest, though my own skin betrayed me. Goose bumps rose on every inch of my body, as he noted when hauling me snuggly to his chest.

"But I haven't finished telling you about my schedule yet," he murmured against my ear while sliding his hands under my T-shirt. All too easily, he made his way up to my breasts. All too deftly, he palmed them into aching desire.

"Well, let me tell you about my schedule too."

"Hmmm," he hedged. "Okay."

"Not okay," I half-laughed back. "Because if I don't leave this house on time, your fantastic food isn't going to be ready on time. And if all the groundbreaking grub doesn't happen, all your guests are going to go home hungry. And cranky." I added the last part more for myself than him. It was getting harder and harder to resist his skillful, sensual touch. I'd already dropped my head between my shoulder blades, letting the lothario play me like a fine-tuned instrument. His private violin...

"Ohhh. The horror." The gibe was full of wicked promise, and Sebastian delivered by biting my nipple through the fabric of my bra. I gripped his face on both sides. My libido and my better sense declared war on each other. Hold him in place or push him away? Give in or start adulting?

As usual, the man went ahead and made his own decision. He lifted his head while righting my T-shirt. In the same fluid move, he straightened to his full height. But when our gazes crossed, he brought back my inner conflict. His indigo eyes were hooded and glowing with desire. I didn't doubt their accurate reflection of my own.

He heaved in a deep breath before finishing with "The presentation is set for eleven thirty. Everyone will be ready for food at noon."

"All right." Though that confirmation officially negated our own version of the "perfect nooner," I reached for his hand and gave it a reassuring squeeze. "You're going to be amazing today." This time I was the one who kissed him, deliberately lingering just a little longer than a peck. But I pulled back before we got carried away again. Remarkably, he seemed to appreciate it.

"I love you, Abbigail," he softly declared.

"I love you too."

"I appreciate all the support you've been giving me on this. On everything that's happened . . . on the way here. It's meant the world to me, Little Red."

"I wouldn't be anywhere else." Somehow I said it without a single teary tremor. "I'll see you downtown."

With our bout of mush giving me new wings of energy, I hurried downstairs and out to the truck. The man had gotten me behind—so worth it—but I did my best to make up for the delay by driving a little faster than usual. By the time I got to the kitchen in Inglewood, I was nearly back on schedule.

Inside the building, Rio was already swirling in her take-no-prisoners mode. I took a second to smile without her noticing. It looked like our pre-event timeline was proceeding without a hitch. Our plan was broken down by specific tasks, both at the kitchen and then on-site. We agreed I would break away about forty-five minutes before Sebastian's presentation, to give me time for cleaning up. He'd asked me to join him in mingling with the crowd—and while I'd instantly said yes, I was more nervous about that responsibility than catering the entire event.

"Good morning, sunshine!" I called out while hanging my bag on the hook by my desk.

"Hey!" Rio was chipper but brief about the response.

"What the hell time did you get here this morning? You already have half the list knocked out."

"I don't know." She shrugged. "I couldn't sleep last night. Just too excited. Seems like we've been planning for this day as intensely as the devil himself."

"Rio." I nearly growled it in solemn warning. "Not today."

"What?"

I was tempted—strongly—to turn the growl into a chuckle. Rio Katrina Gibson playing the innocent card was as believable as an altruistic politician.

Instead of pursuing the issue further, I just redirected my attention to the remaining tasks at hand, detailed on the clipboard lying on the countertop. It was best just to ignore her antics. When I really examined Rio's behavior, it was laughably immature. My sister-in-law was older than me by almost six years, yet she acted like a bratty high school troublemaker at times.

Maybe some music would help ease the tension. I flipped on a local radio station. The morning show gaggle of hosts bantered back and forth about television shows that had aired the night before, interspersed with the usual commercials and local news segments. Just another day in the City of Angels.

Thanks to Rio's frenetic efforts, we had the food prepped and loaded into the van with ten minutes to spare. We quickly tidied up the kitchen before heading across town to set up for the event. Although we didn't indulge in the luxury often, we'd hired an outside cleaning crew to come in and handle the more thorough cleanup. We'd both be downtown for the rest of the day and definitely too exhausted to deal with the mess here on top of the stacks we'd have after the ceremony.

Rio drove while I busied myself with catching up on returning email messages that had piled up from the morning. "Hey," she finally prompted.

"Hmmm? Hey," I returned. "What's up? Did we forget something?"

"No... No. Everything's fine," she said. "You're just so quiet today. Are you nervous?"

I chuckled through a heavy exhale. She'd returned to her kind, maternal tone for the comment—perhaps knowing how strongly I needed it today.

"Yeah, I think I am. Just a little. All right, maybe more than a little." It felt good to admit all that out loud. What felt even better was having my girlfriend back in the same space as me. I really hated it when we weren't on the same page emotionally, especially on a day as important as this one. "I know how important this is to Bas. I want everything to go well."

"Of course you do."

Her reply was still reassuring and gentle. Nevertheless, I crossed mental fingers that mentioning Sebastian wouldn't send her into a weird place again.

"It's not just the stress of our part in the event, you know? In fact, that seems like the easy part today. We've done this a million times." I waved my hand through the air like I was swatting at a pesky gnat. "I just get stressed when I think of all the other things that could go wrong. I have this crazy desire to shield him from all the bad stuff. I mean, not that I mean baaad stuff. Just…normal bad stuff. The usual insanity of something like this. You know what I mean, right?"

I forced myself to stop and inhale. I just wasn't sure how calm I looked about it. The financial district was relatively peaceful, meaning the woman had plenty of chances to rivet longer glances my way.

"Abs?"

Her somber utterance wasn't exactly the reaction I'd expected—or hoped for. Especially when she finished it off by ping-ponging an incisive look between Figueroa Street and me.

"Hmmm?" I said, having refocused on my phone again. Or pretending to.

"You're in love with that man." Her words were from the heart, soft and sincere.

"I know, sister. I know."

"I'd ask if he really makes you happy, but I think the people in Palm Desert can see your smile right now."

And with that, I beamed my smile even more.

"Do you understand that my reservations about him are directly related to my protectiveness and love for you?"

"Of course I know," I murmured, equally as earnest about my assurance.

"Showing emotion appropriately is something I've been working on ever since I met that amazing brother of yours." She eased the atmosphere a little more with her tender smile and wistful head shake. "Why he puts up with me, I will never know."

"Because he loves you, Rio," I stated. "You are an amazing woman, deserving of that kind of love. We both are. I will always be right here to remind you of that—even when you act like a total brat."

"*Moi?*"

She touched her chest, pretending to be hurt. I reached over and gave her shoulder a playful shove. While doling back a sisterly snort, she signaled to turn into the loading dock for the building next door to where the Edge would be built. We'd rented out and taken over the ground floor of the building as our prep and service staging area for the day. We'd brought in rented ovens, warmers, and refrigeration units a couple of days ago. The servers would have to trek out of that building and down a makeshift walkway to the construction site next door, where the groundbreaking ceremony and celebration were being held. The full staff "dress rehearsal" had included everyone taking practice laps on the walkway, and everyone was going to be wearing custom Shark Enterprises running shoes, so I was feeling good about our chances of getting through this without any major spills or falls.

"Once we get everything unloaded, I want to walk over to the actual ceremony site again," I told Rio.

"Good idea," she concurred, all the while executing a perfect back-in to the building's loading dock. "Just to make sure the platform hasn't gone wonky, and the décor has all been placed right."

"All right." I accented that with a deep inhalation once we were established in the kitchen. "We have exactly two hours before I have to cut out and get ready—so let's get this party started, shall we?"

Rio raised both arms like she was ready to hit an Ibiza dance floor. "Ohhh, we definitely shall, sister."

She lowered her hands into my solid high five. I was feeling more confident about the event by the minute, especially as she and I set about conquering the second part of our list. It was awesome to work with her like this again, as we moved together in well-oiled-machine mode.

By the time I needed to change clothes for the reception, practically everything was ready. I swung a dazed but thankful grin across the prep area at my sister-in-law, who still looked as pumped and ready for some catering fun as she had at the break of dawn. Though a zillion tendrils popped out of her ponytail and her face gleamed with sweat, her eyes were gilded with exhilaration, and she bit into her bottom lip with excitement.

"Okay, everyone," I called out, making sure our small staff army paused and gave me their full attention. "Listen up. Rio's officially in charge. But if anyone needs me, I'll be—"

"Getting ready to shine in that kick-ass outfit of yours," Rio rebutted. "So those inquiries should be coming right here." She directed both index fingers to her collarbones.

I huffed. "But—"

"Shoo!" she laughed out.

"Still. Just don't hesitate to—"

"Abbigail. Go! It's going to be fine. We've done this a million times, remember?"

I took another deep breath. My nerves were so frazzled. "I think I need a drink," I managed to laugh back.

"Not a bad idea. Not at all." She moved forward and gave me a quick hug before kissing my cheek and shoving me toward the door. "But right now, go and get beautiful for your man. The whole world needs to see what a lucky guy he is."

In the bathroom, I changed and piled my hair into a messy but trendy updo. Thank goodness for the beachy vibe of Southern California style, making it easier to deal on the fly with hair like mine. If I had to worry about straightening it and trying to make it look silky and smooth in the short time frame I had, I'd be screwed. I pulled the lavender slip dress over my head and grinned at my reflection as the silky fabric slid into place over my curves. Sebastian had helped pick out the dress, and he was going to love the way it looked with my hair pulled up off my neck and shoulders. I tugged on the matching strappy sandals before touching up my makeup in the small mirror hanging above the sink.

And now it was showtime.

I still wasn't sure I was ready.

But I had no choice about the matter.

Still on schedule, I made my way out into the crowd. The throng consisted mostly of press members. I found my dark and handsome boyfriend in their midst, holding court in the center of the construction site. The hazardous zone was fenced off to avoid any mishaps, and the large vacant lot was portioned down to a controlled area for the reception.

Sebastian's gaze heated as he spotted me making my way through the crowd. As I walked closer, his focus homed in tighter. His posture stilled. He was as beautiful and bold as one of the artworks in the Broad Museum, just a few blocks away.

The change in his demeanor was so marked, many of the men and women to whom he was speaking now turned to see what had captured his attention. The awestruck ripple effect caused similar shock waves through my system, not helping my nerves by a fraction.

Cameras clicked in a flurry as Sebastian wrapped his arm around my waist and planted a tender kiss on my jaw, using the moment to quietly tell me how stunning I looked in the dress we'd picked out. His adoration had me growing my smile without even thinking. The second that happened, the chain reaction began. The reporters pressed in. Their camera crews starting clicking and recording. Oh, yes, we'd likely be the lead piece for every news and entertainment show tonight. Nothing I hadn't expected.

So far.

I swiveled my gaze up to him. He returned my look with an expression that transformed him from handsome to devastating. "How's it going so far?" I kept my tone intimate, cherishing the moment as one of the few private ones we'd have all day.

"So far, so good." But his facile tone wasn't slick enough to cover the tightening corners of his eyes or the strange intensity he zeroed in on me. I could practically feel him yearning for the world to go away, but not for all the erotic reasons for which I hoped. His purpose was restless and fervent...

And...frightened?

But before I could dissect that anomaly, the moment was gone. Sebastian Shark, soon-to-be king of the LA skyline, was back in his beautiful, cocky glory.

"So, everything good on your end?"

"Yep." I bit into my lower lip in place of the kiss I longed to slather across his decadent mouth. "Rio has it all under control, so I'm all yours now."

And God, how I wanted to make that happen in every form of the phrase. He was so confident and stunning, a phoenix who'd risen from the east side to be a trailblazer in this vast metropolis. I was so proud to be on his arm for this triumphant big day.

"But ohhh, Ms. Gibson. That's where you're so wrong." He'd leaned in to husk it right into my ear.

I covered my lusty shiver with a light laugh. "About...
what?"

"You were all mine from the moment I saw you, baby."

Another enlightened tremble. Another stupid laugh to
cover it. "Never has there been a more true statement, Mr.
Shark."

And before the spiraling heat between our bodies
combusted us to dust in front of this crowd, I stepped back. Not
by far. Just a perfect distance for combating the heat across my
face by shielding my gaze with my hand. It was a good excuse
to change the subject too. "So...uhhh...I saw Pia and Vela
already. Is everyone else here? Grant? Elijah?"

"I imagine they're lurking here somewhere." He joined me
in surveying the crowd. "Last time I saw Grant, he was talking
with some of the board members over by the bar. Haven't seen
Elijah yet, though. He better not blow this off."

"I'm sure he won't. Maybe he's stuck in traffic?"

Bas made a displeased sound between a grumble and
growl, and I chuckled. If anyone could handle Bas's growly
wrath, it would be Elijah. The banter I'd witnessed between
the two friends was the kind found only between lifelong pals
who'd shared experiences good and bad.

"Let's head over that way, though," Sebastian suggested,
proffering his elbow to me. "I think you two are seated next to
each other for the official presentation."

Gee. I wondered why.

But I pushed down the snark and let Sebastian steer us
through the crowd. Along the way, he greeted most people by
first name. He introduced me to many, but also only by first
name. I was a little perplexed by the omission, which became
increasingly clear as deliberate, as we wove our way to the

stage. The journey took a long time, obviously longer than he expected, so by the time we got to Grant, he quickly asked the guy to "look after me" before he nervously looked toward the podium. I gave Grant a quick eye roll. Grant chuckled while turning to my man. Without hesitation, Grant stepped over and yanked Bas into a hearty squeeze of a "dude hug."

"Knock 'em dead," I added to the encouragement party. "I'll be cheering for you from my seat."

I kissed him again, making sure not to leave lipstick behind, and watched him stride to the front of the crowd. A small platform was elevated above the audience with a sleek stainless-steel podium, a microphone mounted on top.

My heart leapt to my throat. In all the best ways.

Holy hell, I was so proud of this man.

Everyone made their way to the chairs that had been set up for the presentation, and Grant escorted me to the front, where several rows had been reserved for special guests. Just as we entered the row, Elijah joined us.

"You're not going to believe who I just ran into out front. I tried to have security usher him out, but the bastard had an invitation in his hand. How the fuck did he score an invitation?" He was talking to Grant, with spitting emphasis on the "he" but not trying to shield me from the conversation.

"Shit. Do I even want to know?"

"Probably not. I just hope Bas gets through his speech before he sees him."

"Sees who?"

I already had a bad feeling I knew the name about to come from Elijah's lips, but the next second, he confirmed my worst fear.

"Viktor Blake."

CHAPTER TWELVE

SEBASTIAN

It was showtime. And I was ready. Damn it, I was born ready. Except for one huge difference. The show was better than I ever dreamed it would be.

I took a deep breath and looked out over the horizon of traditional and modern architecture. Then closer in, the streets streamed with sunshine and bustled with color. Then even nearer, to the attentive faces of the crowd in front of me.

For one more extended moment, I savored it all. Told myself to remember it all. Yes, the air was still peppered with the media crews' constant whizzes and clicks, a promise that every second of the day would be immortalized, but none of that recordkeeping would compare to how my spirit would permanently capture this. How my soul would keep it as a lasting treasure.

I straightened my spine, spread my arms, and gripped the outside edges of the podium—and started giving them exactly what they came for.

"Exciting times are upon us, my friends." My voice echoed back at me, booming up the heights and into the recesses of the surrounding buildings. "You are about to witness history in this great city of ours. Together, we are going to make Los Angeles even greater, to send it soaring on wings of innovation and vision."

I took a purposeful pause, letting those words sink into the crowd. It opened up a perfect chance to take in the enormous crowd once again—in particular, the front row. There were the people who mattered the most in my life. No. Who were the center of my existence. Every one of them looked to me with open veneration, adoration, and love.

All of the things, every damn one, that I felt for them.

Pia sat on the aisle with Vela's small hand clutched in hers. When my niece noticed my affectionate attention, she held up a hand to form our secret "half heart" sign, ensuring I could no longer hold back my smile. I prevented the expression from turning into more lump-in-the-throat mush by shifting my gaze to Grant, who sat on Vela's other side. The guy slung his long arm across the back of Vela's chair. On his lap, he formed his other hand into a solid fist and gave it a slight pump. I knew exactly what the bastard was saying. This was his solemn "you got this, man"—and I would be forever grateful for it. Twombley would always have my back. Always had, always would—simple as that.

Next, my gaze settled onto Abbigail.

My passionate, proud, completely perfect Abbigail.

How had I found this woman? How had fate decided I deserved this divine presence in my world? Had deigned I would have the privilege of nurturing her, believing in her, loving her?

I didn't have that answer, nor did I want to pretend to. I only knew that I had to preserve it . . . to hold on to it. And over the last several weeks, the key to that had become increasingly clear.

Holding on to her meant keeping her safe. And keeping

her safe meant keeping her hidden. It was going to be difficult—no, it was going to be hell.

But when everything settled down, after I worked with Elijah and his team to bring these fuckers down, I'd bring her home again. If she didn't understand why I'd done what was necessary—this ugly responsibility I was about to shoulder—then I'd sit her down and force her to understand. No matter what it took.

Because I knew, with one hundred percent certainty, that I was making the right decision.

Elijah was sitting on the other side of Abbigail. He sent me an assuring jog of his chin, much the same way Grant had, only the bastard decided to follow it up by pushing his cheeky luck. As I looked on, the guy leaned closer to my woman and then said something close to her ear. Abbi reacted with a chuckle before quickly turning her attention back to me. I pinned Banks with a subtle glower. He bounced back a cheeky wink. I almost faltered in my speech. Almost. He just might get an unexpected fist for that stunt later.

There were more important things to focus on here.

Much more important.

I pushed back from the podium and tugged sharply on my jacket. The actions were for optics as much as resetting my focus. With the fortitude of my family, I already felt like a triumphant Titan. It was time for the world to know that too.

But it was also time for them to know why.

"I know you've all come here today for our big reveal." I motioned to the large, covered architect's rendition of the building, "But first, I'd like to take the chance to share a brief story with you."

A soft buzz of curiosity worked its way through the crowd.

I waited for the figurative bees to settle before going on.

"Between the building's initial inception and now, many have asked me about the meaning behind the Edge's unique name. I haven't just picked the title because it sounds like the perfect descriptor for an icon—though that's certainly what this structure will be."

I secured one hand to the podium again. Well, hell. As public speeches went, this was definitely going to get filed into the what-the-hell-were-you-thinking folder.

Nevertheless, I persisted on my original track of intent. "As most of you know, I grew up on the streets of East Los Angeles. My first job was as a bicycle courier. I worked my way from that to the man you're looking at today. At the risk of dipping to the contrite, I applied a lot of blood, sweat, and tears to get to this point, as a leader in the international logistics industry. The culmination of all the challenges I overcame, hurdles I jumped, obstacles I had to traverse, and problems I solved—it's all represented right here."

With that, I pointed emphatically to the covered picture again. When I looked out among the attendees, I had everyone's rapt attention. I took another deep breath. And then another.

I was about to be more vulnerable to the world than ever before, revealing a piece of myself that people rarely saw. But damn it, this part was as crucial to my success story as the hard work component. I had to continue, if only for what my words would mean to everyone seated in that front row. "Success stories rarely include talk of the fears you face along your journey. I know, I know," I rushed out, holding up a hand as the crowd again got busy with their murmuring. "You didn't expect to hear me say that, right? But I wouldn't be honest if I didn't talk about the truly paralyzing moments when I thought everything was going to completely go to shit."

I was happy to make everyone break out in laughter at my creative phraseology. Right away, I continued on. "I remember vital shipments that weren't delivered on time, as well as huge financial risks I was sure wouldn't pay off. In the early days of Shark Enterprises, we stood a better chance of landing a real shark with a wooden fishing pole than we did getting a bank loan approved. Many times, cash flow couldn't sustain expenses or competitors outbid us for major contracts."

I threw my hands up to illustrate the precariousness of a growing business and observed many concurring nods of agreement throughout the crowd. People could feel my passion—because it was real.

"But business—and let's face it, life itself—is filled with facing fear. But it's not just about facing what you're afraid of." I made solid eye contact with each and every person in the first row who held a piece of my heart in their hands. "It's about having the courage to take on the challenge and to conquer it, as well." People in the audience murmured in support once again. "So, I want to leave you with one question today, before I show you the concept of this amazing building. And as it rises out of the ground, into the skyline of our city named after the environs of the heavens themselves, I hope that you'll be inspired to let your wings grow a little more and to face the key question here again."

I paused.

Breathed.

Drew on the love that filled my heart so fully now.

"What takes you to the edge? What takes you to the edge of where you're comfortable, into the abyss of where you're afraid?" I challenged them all. "Will you be strong enough?

Will you be brave enough to take on the challenge, to grow and learn so you can move ahead of your competition? In order to surpass your limits, you have to know what they are. You have to define your edge. You have to know it . . . and then push past it."

I stepped back once more. Watched every face in this throng move into personal acknowledgment of my message. It felt good—so damn good—to inspire others like this.

But the next moment was going to feel even better.

"And with that message, ladies and gentlemen, I give you . . . the Edge!"

I swept up an arm.

The big red curtain was pulled off the drawing with a flourish.

The crowd erupted into wild applause.

Jacob Cole's drawing was magnificent. At the enormous size we had printed for the reception, the rendering was even more colorful, detailed, and impressive. I felt just as fantastic. Hell, I felt ten feet tall.

This was everything I had dreamed it would be.

Confetti cannons shot millions of colored specks into the air. The music I'd preselected, a raucous rock anthem, played on cue. The crowd pushed forward to get a better look at Cole's inspiring drawing, along with four slightly smaller versions that were uncovered around the reception area. Abbigail had offered the idea from seeing it done at a similar event she had catered, and it was brilliant.

Food servers began circulating with trays of the appetizers custom-created by Abbi and Rio for today. The trendiest LA foods were represented, all topped by stylish curlicues of more tempting ingredients. The dessert finale consisted of chocolate slices shaped like the Edge, accented with molded cream clouds and glass sugar suns. The cuisine received as many delighted reactions as the initial unveiling of Cole's artwork. Everyone in the crowd eagerly plucked at the high-end snacks as they passed by.

Finally, I caught sight of the beautiful redhead making her way toward me. Her green eyes nearly glowed with happiness as I pulled her in and wrapped her in my embrace.

"Sebastian. You were amazing. I'm so proud of you."

Her words, so soft and sincere, filled me with more joy than anything else today. I surrendered to the rush and kissed her deeply. As onlookers clapped, I dipped her back without shame, pushing my tongue past her lips before she could say another word. She gripped my biceps while I sealed my mouth over hers. Our tongues dueled with bliss and lust. She dug her nails into my muscles while releasing a throaty, passionate moan into my mouth.

And into my being.

When we were both officially breathless, I finally stood her upright. "Oh, my," she panted, still clutching my upper arms to steady herself. "Mr. Shark . . ."

"Hmmm, Ms. Gibson? How can I be of . . . service . . . to you?"

"You think there's a way to top that?" She was incredulous and sincerely so. "Th-That was some kiss."

Her husky voice wrapped around my cock as if it were her actual hand. I craved more but was forced to resist. Half of Los Angeles was still waiting for me to walk over and shovel in some ceremonial dirt to the Edge's new site.

For now, I had to settle for leaning over and giving my woman a few lewd ideas for later. "I can't wait to get you alone tonight," I growled into the pit of her ear. "The things I have planned for your pussy are unspeakable . . . and irredeemable."

"Sebastian . . ."

She was interrupted by Elijah's and Grant's arrival. They stepped in, strategically flanking Abbi—and piquing my attention. Grant extended his hand, murmuring more words of congratulations. As we shook, his charming smile didn't change. But I was more agitated by Elijah's somber expression. Something was definitely not to his liking in the crowd. I already sensed it, even without him saying a word. Only then did I recognize Grant's grin for what it really was: a method to keep Abbigail distracted while Elijah jerked his head to the side, directing me away.

"Can I steal you for a second, Shark? Abbigail, forgive the interruption. I'll return him in just a minute. Promise."

"Of course," she answered with an affable smile. "This is a business event—and I know all too well that business comes first."

For a second, but just one, Elijah seemed surprised by her openness—but in pleasant ways. "Wow," he said, not taking his eyes from her. "You may have found the perfect woman in this one, my friend."

"Yeah, yeah. Stop flirting with my girlfriend, Banks." I socked him in the shoulder, possibly a little harder than necessary. His grimace confirmed what I guessed, but I added as we strolled away from the crowd a bit, "That's for being late, too."

"*Pffft*. I was here for the good parts, wasn't I?"

I chose not to go for a rebuttal as we moved off to the side. Though we kept Abbigail and Grant firmly in sight, I still didn't want to get too far. So much crazy shit had been going on, I really just wished Abbi had stayed home today. Not that she would've conceded. She'd put in so much time and care in getting the details right and ready for this celebration. Beyond that, selfishly speaking, I didn't know if my heartfelt speech would've happened without her here.

Still, I was beyond uncomfortable about things now. We were out in the open. Relatively exposed. Standing in the middle of a gathering with a lot of strangers. Yes, I knew most of the crowd, but not all. So many new and curious faces. Damn, I was getting tense about this. The sooner I could get her to a safe place, the better I would feel.

"So Bas—"

"Is everything set up for the move?" I cut in, positive we were out of earshot when I watched Abbi stop one of the waiters and give some instruction about garnishing the appetizer he was serving.

"Just about," Elijah stated. "I've got a few more details to lock into place, and then you'll be clear to make the move."

"Details?" I muttered. "Like what?"

"I need to get back to the house," he explained. "Pack her clothes and personal items."

I shook my head. Only once. But that was enough. "I'll do that. I don't want you nosing around in her stuff." My gut was already twisting, and not from mowing down too many appetizers at once. The thought of the man packing my woman's lingerie was an unsettling stab.

"Jesus, man. I packed a bunch of it when she moved from the condo into your place."

"That was before you wanted to fuck her."

"I can keep it professional. You know that."

"I said I'll do it."

"Fine." He raised his hands in surrender. "Suit yourself." The words, usually so casual, ushered his mien back into steady seriousness. "But none of this is the actual reason I wanted to talk to you alone."

"All right." I rocked on my heels, feigning that he and I were having a simple shoot-the-shit exchange—though unsure why my instincts screamed for that necessity. "What's going on, then? I could tell something was on your mind from the minute I saw you from up on stage."

Elijah opened his mouth, but I backhanded him into silence—the second I observed the dramatic shift on Abbi's features.

Pia and Vela had joined her and Grant, and she was engaging with the three of them with happy excitement. Her smile was radiant as she listened to my niece convey an animated story—

Until all the color drained from her face.

She stood taller. Stiffer. I immediately recognized her body language as defensive, even offended.

I knew exactly how she felt.

Because once I followed her line of sight, my own gaze landed on a very unwelcome guest.

"Mother. Fucker."

"Bas." Elijah wrapped an iron grip around my bicep. "Breathe, goddammit."

"What the fuck is Viktor Blake doing here?"

"That's what I was just about to tell you. I saw him when I arrived, and—"

"Well, consider me told." At once, I set a stomping course back toward Abbigail.

"Shit," my friend spat, rushing to keep up next to me. "So,

listen. He's on just as much of a tear as you, okay? I tried to have him thrown out on his ass, but he waved around an invitation like 'entitlement' was his new middle name. The rent-a-cops put up a fuss, and I didn't want to make a scene."

"Well, I can't guarantee the same thing right now."

I came to a halt beside Abbi, who immediately relaxed into my side as I wrapped a protective arm around her waist.

Protective. And possessive. Yep. definitely that.

Take a good long look at this, asshole. Because I'm not going anywhere when mongrels sniff around my woman.

Somehow, I pushed all of it into the realm of thought alone. Aloud, I decided to go for glib.

"Well, look what the wind blew in."

My bitter tone alerted Pia to the negative grownup vibes. She turned and said brightly, "Vela, did you see the beautiful cupcakes Abbigail made?"

"Cupcakes?" Vela squealed. "But wait, Mommy. I already had one of those pretty chocolate buildings too."

"Well . . . this is a special occasion. Maybe we can splurge."

"Ohhh, yay! Are they as delicious as your brownies, Miss Gibson?"

Abbigail bent down a bit to be closer to the little girl. "Mmmm, I'm not sure. Maybe you could try one and let me know what you think? They're chocolate too though, so it might be a tough decision."

"But life is about tough stuff, remember? Uncle Bas just said so." My niece ran over, tugged on my hand, and looked up to me with adoring eyes. "Uncle Bas, you gave the best speech I ever heard. You didn't even seem scared, though you also talked about being that way. Good job!" She put her little hand up for a high five, and I smacked it solidly.

"Thanks, Vel. Part of it was because I saw you right there in the front row, you know."

"Really?" Her round cheeks flushed with embarrassment, and my heart swelled with more love.

"Oh, yeah. Cross my heart." I crouched to her level and gave her a long, tight hug. "Your smile was so awesome. I just knew I could be brave." I leaned back from our embrace before saying, "And that's a lovely dress you have on today, Miss Shark."

"Thank you." She smiled wider, revealing a space where a tooth stood the last time I saw her. "We went shopping just for your special day. Mama said it was important."

My niece's admission had me pulling my sister into a hug too. "Thanks for coming, Dub," I murmured to her.

"We wouldn't be anywhere else Bas. I'm so proud of you, brother."

Vela began towing my sister through the crowd, in search of the second dessert for the day. Pia was a godsend for so many reasons—right now because of her ability to read a situation without words being uttered. Okay, most specifically, this situation. Of course, she was well aware of my history with Viktor. She'd grown up right beside Grant, Elijah, me, and the rude Russian bully. She knew all the trouble I'd dealt with over the years involving the bastard.

And now, speaking of the blue-eyed spawn of the devil . . .

"Sebastian Shark," Blake greeted with ease that, to any observer, looked open and diplomatic. "How nice to see you again, my friend. It appears congratulations are in order today."

He offered his hand, and I glared at the extended palm. I'd be damned if I would accept his gesture in front of the press and have it caught on camera. No way would I allow his intrusion to become the leading story for the day, instead of anything to do with the Edge. Because damn it, that was exactly what would make the cut with the media. Even the straight news stations went for the ratings-grabbing sensations.

"Cut the bullshit, Blake," I retorted past a clenched jaw. "What are you doing here?" I fought to keep my voice level so as to not attract any more attention. The people nearest to us had already stopped their own conversations. They turned and openly observed ours. Our rivalry was legendary, and we were rarely seen publicly in the same place at the same time—let alone talking to each other.

Viktor blatantly ignored my demand. "Abbigail," he drawled instead and pulled my girlfriend in close. He made a show of kissing each of her cheeks while saying, "What a surprise to see you here. You look lovely, as always."

As always? What the hell *does that mean?*

I heard Elijah suck in oxygen. It was a little reassuring to know I wasn't the only one galled by Blake's disrespect—or whatever the hell this was. I could feel Elijah's tension ramping too, likely in preparation for a fistfight.

I liked that idea.

I liked it very much.

There was a woman at Viktor's side. The leggy blonde had an aspiring actress vibe, with her pushed-up chest and too-tight dress. She slipped a coy smile my way while Viktor continued appraising Abbigail. The girl had no issue with the way he was admiring my woman.

I, on the other hand, could feel my blood pressure hammering through my skull.

"Enough," I seethed. "She's with me. And she's also mine—unless you haven't figured that out by now." I deliberately went with a term I knew Viktor could relate to. With a possessive arm around her waist, I tucked Abbi closer to my body. "Last chance to explain why you're here before I have you tossed out. I know for certain you were not invited."

"No, but my lovely assistant was."

"That so?" I arched a brow at the vaguely familiar blonde on his arm.

"She has ways of making things happen. But you probably already know that . . . right, Shark? You do remember consorting with Ms. Dobrochev before you 'claimed' Ms. Gibson?"

Dobrochev, who was nearly six feet and all leg, blushed and looked down at the ground. A mix of reactions hit me once. I was supremely uncomfortable for her—and for Abbigail. And hell . . . for me. I'd likely fucked this woman at the kink club both Viktor and I belonged to in Brentwood. But it must've been years ago, because I hadn't been to The Pike in a long, long time.

I hauled in a gruff snort through my nose, giving myself a couple of seconds to compose a decent comeback for the classless cretin. Thank God that was all the time Elijah needed to push in between us, averting the public train wreck toward which we'd been racing.

"All right, Blake. That's enough." As Elijah moved in on the guy's personal space, he coiled and uncoiled his fists. "Let's go before this gets really ugly. I'll show you to the parking garage, if you can't find your own way."

I shifted backward, though deliberately locked down my arrogant armor. Banks was handling this, and that was probably for the best. Though he and I enjoyed flinging a lot of shit at each other, Elijah ultimately respected the right side of the honor code—as strongly as he abhorred the wrong. The side Blake was trampling like an ox in a rice field right now.

Honest to hell. What was the man thinking? And how dare he try any of this right now? Insinuating the woman was one of my past conquests and doing it right in front of Abbigail—who, consequently, began shifting subtly at my side. Though I dug my fingers into her hip, molding her tightly to me again, she persisted in trying to put some space between us.

"Abbigail."

As soon as Viktor directly addressed Abbi again, she stiffened.

"You have nothing to say to her." My snarl was as rigid as my poor woman, who could've doubled as one of the nearby I-beams from the second her name tripped off his tongue.

"No?" Blake volleyed. "But this explains so much..." He canted his head as if I were just a tree in his forest, getting in the way of his prey. "Am I right, sweet Abbi?"

She jerked backward. Stumbled away from him like a fire-breathing dragon. But also, and very clearly, away from me.

"Don't call me that," she spat.

"Whatever I choose to call you... it doesn't change a thing. About why I understand so much more now." He circled his index finger between Abbi and me. "This... well, this explains a lot, actually. Definitely why you've turned down my advances so adamantly."

"Your what?" I shuttled a stunned gape between him and Abbi. "His what?"

A desperate grimace twisted her lovely face. My entire gut was given the same brutal treatment. "Sebastian..."

"Abbigail?" I fired back. "What. Is. He. Talking. About?"

"It's all right, Abbigail," Viktor crooned. "You don't really have to answer. I have the information I need now. And I

have it on good authority that your master can be a bit...
overbearing anyway."

"And controlling."

As the blonde muttered it in her Eastern European accent,
I gave up my empathy for her. But I directed my low, lethal
snarl completely his way. "Shut the fuck up, Blake. Shut up
right now, or you'll be spitting teeth." I punched a commanding
nod at Elijah. "Dispose of this trash before everyone gets sick
from its stench."

"Gladly," Elijah growled.

Viktor grinned, seeming to think he had the last laugh
despite Elijah summoning a pair of burly guards to usher
him away. I thought nothing of his bluff, until hooking a hand
around Abbi's and preparing to move in the other direction.

The bastard was calculated about throwing his final blow.

"Just be aware of what you're getting yourself into, Ms.
Gibson."

I wheeled back on him. "Last warning, Blake."

But the fool persisted. With a snakelike hiss, he finished,
"Like his namesake, this man is a predator. You need to
remember that. And Shark, if you're as serious as you claim
about her, it's time to level with her. About everything.
Including your past."

"Elijah! For fuck's sake." My friend and his buddies
started physically pulling Viktor away from the group, but he
still threw back over his shoulder one last leveling blow.

"Have you told her where all the bodies are buried, Shark?
All of them?"

So much for thinking I was done with uncomfortable for
the day. And unnerved. And on the verge of unhinged.

"I need to get out of here."

I readjusted my hold on Abbigail, meshing my fingers firmly between hers. I needed the increased contact of her strength and warmth—and selfishly sucked it all into my system so I could stride away from Viktor Blake without succumbing to the temptation to wrap my hands around his thick Russian neck and squeeze. And squeeze. And squeeze . . .

Ten minutes later, Abbi and I found our way to an empty office inside the building next to the construction site. While Rio and Abstract's staff still bustled in the kitchen a few feet away, all was blissfully still inside the little room with a steel desk facing a single chair.

I needed to decompress. Not that I thought even two weeks in Bali could do the trick for me right now, but at this point, I'd take what I could get.

I studied Abbi carefully. She was directing the same intense focus to her manicure. Apparently her nails had become the most fascinating thing she had ever seen. I'd challenge her on it, but the rigidity in her body hadn't dissipated since Blake had showed up with "Miss Dobrochev." Her posture was laced with tension as she leaned against the edge of the desk. I started pacing back and forth in front of her. It wasn't a good idea for me to consider being still right now. My pent-up fury felt like a bomb on a very short countdown timer.

"I can't believe he showed up here." She shook her head incredulously. "I mean, what was he honestly thinking?"

"He wasn't," I spat. "Because he's an asshole. Just trying to start trouble for me—for us—as always." It felt important for me to modify the statement as I had. She needed to start thinking of the entity as "us." I sure as hell was—and honored that commitment by taking a deep breath, determined not to misdirect my wrath toward Abbi.

"Do you remember when I told you I saw a woman leaving his office in tears? She had a mark on her face as though she'd been hit, but Viktor acted as though it was just another day at the office?" She waited for me to acknowledge the memory. It didn't take long. After I dipped a curt nod, she stabbed a finger in the direction of the event area. "Well, that woman—that blonde—was her!"

After a few moments of silence, in which we both processed that information, I muttered, "I wish I could say that surprised me, even a little bit."

"But it doesn't?" she countered.

I shook my head. "Not by a long shot."

"So was that the angle here?" She swallowed so roughly, I could see her throat struggling to work everything down. "What do you think he's trying to get at by doing this?" A new gulp, twice as labored as before. "That you know that woman too? That you slept with her? I mean . . ." A wince took over her face. "Have you?"

Well . . . hell.

I rubbed the back of my neck, attempting to combat the tension buildup. How had this day gone to shit so quickly? I'd been riding such a high after giving my speech. The celebration hadn't even lasted fifteen minutes before the interference from the rival I despised.

"Sebastian?"

"What?"

"Are you going to answer me?" she snapped.

It was my turn for the discomfited swallow. No matter how I answered this, it wasn't going to be good.

"I'm not really sure, Abbi," I admitted. "And that's the truth. I'm not even sure I know that woman. I mean, I might . . ."

"Which means what?"

"We used to roll in some of the same groups. Not at the same time, but six degrees of separation and all that shit, you know? I used to go to some of the same clubs that Blake does. That means there's a good chance we've had our dicks in several of the same women. I hate to admit that, but it's also the truth."

I cringed. The confession sounded as hideous as it felt. One look at Abbi, and I knew that as the truth too.

"Wonderful." After her bitter mutter, she dropped her face into her hands.

"Red." I compelled myself to stop, and stay stopped, in front of her. As torturous as the feat was, it was even harder to hold back from wrapping my grip to her shoulders. "We've been through this before. You know I have a past. I thought we'd discussed all those issues and put them behind us."

She released a heavy sigh while lifting her face to look at me. "But 'behind us' doesn't mean they get poofed out of existence—especially when they're thrown at me in front of a crowd of onlookers."

I exhaled too. Dipped in and pressed my forehead to hers. "I know. I do. And I'm sorry."

"I know you are. It doesn't make it hurt less."

Her tender tone was instant balm on my heart. I told her so by taking her lips in a gentle buss but didn't push any further. There was more weight on her heart here. I forced myself to wait patiently for her admission.

At last, she broke the stillness with a soft murmur. "Bas?"

"Hmmm?"

"Why did Viktor call you my 'master'? Exactly what kind of clubs did the two of you go to?"

"Do you really want to get into all of that? Right now, I mean?"

After two seconds, she threw her hands up, flattening her palms on my chest. "No, I guess I don't. At least not right now."

I took her hands in mine. Kissed her knuckles reverently. "I love you," I said, solemnity threading my voice. "I love you, and I love us, and I love what we've done to make this day happen. And I don't want all of it ruined by this bullshit. I want to look back on the memories of today and have them all be good ones."

"I want that too," Abbi vowed. "More than anything. You've worked so hard for this. Let's not allow him to take any of it away. If he does, then he wins."

I kissed her again. This time with a lot of tongue and passion. Because she deserved it. Because I deserved it too, damn it. "Sometimes I think you're too good to be true, Abbigail Gibson," I husked. "That I've been dreaming all this time with you and none of it was real."

"No, baby. It's real. I'm real. *We* are real." Yet the statements, all so heartfelt, were laced by something besides the conviction of her heart. As she pushed to her feet, I identified that force. It was the concern of her heart, as well. "But with real life, there are often real challenges," she said with matching deliberation.

"Challenges?" I countered. "Like what?"

She paced across to the door—all three steps—and then back again. But not into my arms. She maintained a distance that looked cautious...wary. "I have to ask you this, Bas, or it's going to eat away at me. What did Viktor mean...by knowing where all the bodies are buried? Was he being literal or figurative with that?"

"Abbigail." I tilted my head, wordlessly begging her to be serious.

"Sebastian."

"Goddammit!" I threw both my hands toward the ceiling. "Is that what you really think of me, then? That I could kill another man?"

Her gaze flashed emerald-green fire. "Do not with the righteous indignation, Sebastian Shark. Not with me! I know you're a ruthless man—but not for all the worst reasons. I know you would do whatever you had to do to protect the people you love, for one thing. And to ensure the success of the empire you've built, for another."

I shoved out a breath through gritted teeth. Those were both true statements, so arguing with her over them was pointless. Didn't stop an iota of my fury and frustration, which stemmed from the fact that we were having the conversation in the first place.

"If I were the kind of guy who just killed his enemies to make life easier, Blake would've been six feet under a long time ago."

"I know," she murmured before I was done with the snarl.

"No," I bit back. "I'm not sure you do."

"Sebastian—"

"We're not continuing this conversation." I pivoted and made my way to the door. "Not here, on this important day. But not at home tonight either." I said it all with finality and meant it. "No more of this bullshit, Abbigail."

I reached for the doorknob. She shoved in between me and the portal, her hands already planted on her hips. "This bullshit?" she challenged, borrowing my gritted seethe.

I clenched my jaw. "I believe I made myself clear."

"Are you saying this as my master now?" She glared at me with a fire in her eyes I'd never seen before. "And so it's just like that?" She leaned in and narrowed her gaze, a lioness in lavender, all but showing her locked teeth again. "You say how it is, and that's the end of it? Regardless of how I feel about it?"

I decided to ignore the *master* jab completely. It would only prolong this debacle, and I was trying to defuse it, believe it or not. "When the subject is whether I've really taken a human life and whether you'd really believe a truthful answer from me? Then yeah, that's it."

"You know I'd believe you," she volleyed. "But you also know that it wouldn't change a single thing about what I feel for you. About how deeply I love you and how thoroughly I'm committed to you."

I let a huge breath rush from me. But even that, along with dropping my head back and trying to drill an escape route through the ceiling with my gaze, didn't loosen the barbed wire ball in my belly—and my psyche.

"Sebastian?"

I realigned my head with my shoulders but still didn't meet the probe of her deep greens. She wanted that visual lock. The ferocity of her energy practically dictated it to me. She wasn't going to get it.

"We need to get back out and mingle, okay? People will think I'm fucking you in here."

"Yeah, well, you'll be lucky to do that in the next month at the rate you're going."

As she muttered it, she stomped back over and grabbed her clutch off the desk. Before I could process enough of what she'd said to even summon a rise of anger, she'd smacked the light switch, plunged the office into darkness, and left me behind to fumble after her. Though there were only two steps to the door, I managed to smack my shin on the end of a bookcase, ensuring everyone on her catering prep team got a fast lesson in my finest profanity skills. The woman, already two strappy-heeled strides ahead of me, didn't even pause.

Her sprint forced me to speed up. I quickly caught her in the hallway between the prep area and the throughway to the construction site. As soon as I had her elbow secured, I spun her back around and pinned her against the wall.

I wasn't brutal about the actions, though a great deal of my cock begged me to be. I was firm but smooth, directive but not domineering.

But when I tugged at her chin, there were unshed tears in her deep-green eyes.

Tears caused by me.

"Ah, Christ," I whispered and pushed in closer to her. "Red . . . baby," I begged into her ear. "I don't want to fight with you. Please don't cry."

She looked up at me with new glints in her gaze. "My tears used to turn you on," she said with biting challenge.

"Not when it's because you're sad. Never because of that." I dipped my forehead to hers. This day was moving from hot mess to dumpster fire at frightening speed. "Please. Can we just get through the rest of this event and revisit the subject when we get home?"

"You just said we wouldn't be discussing it when we get home . . ."

I pulled back and dropped my chin to my chest. "Okay, cut me some slack here."

"Sure, Bas. Whatever you want. That's how you're used to everything going, right? How you say, when you say. Right?"

Somehow, we made it through the rest of the reception playacting as the city's new "it" lovebirds. The crowd thinned fast, and Abbigail plastered on an authentic smile for them. As we did a few laps through the crowd, I was quickly swept back up in the mood I'd meant to have today. I was both exhausted and exhilarated all over again.

My woman, on the other hand, was still spoiling for a fight.

Silence draped the first five minutes of our drive back home. Then ten. Fifteen. She sat as physically far away from me as the town car would allow.

I finally sighed, deciding to put my billions where my mouth was. For the first time in my life, I was actually going to attempt some small talk. A desperate measure, but this was fast developing into a desperate time. I hoped I could soften her up enough to open her up.

"The food was fantastic today. Thank you for all your hard work, beautiful."

She pushed out soft air through her nose. "Well, thank you for paying Abstract so well for it."

"That's not where I was going—"

"I was just doing what you paid me for, Mr. Shark. A clear-cut transaction."

I groaned.

She huffed.

"Can we just stop all this? Please?" My vocal cords fought my brain to push out the nicer portion of it, but for naught. At the last second, a gritted growl took over me. "Before you say something you'll regret."

Abbigail angled her body enough to lean an elbow on the windowsill and then rest her head on a small steeple of her fingers. "And what is 'this,' exactly?"

"This," I spewed. "You know what it is, damn it. This...
this bitterness. I was giving you a genuine compliment. Why
are you being so testy in return?"

"This isn't testy, Sebastian. This is me, unable to do the
hot-and-cold thing with you, okay?" She shoved away from the
door but not by far. She was only leaning the distance it took to
make sure I got her point—and was ready to listen to the rest.
"I'm not wired that way."

I scowled. "I'm not asking you to rewire yours—"

"Bullshit," she retorted. "One minute I'm your girlfriend,
the woman you're smitten with like Romeo about to leap up to
the balcony. But the next, you're shutting me out completely,
telling me how your rules are now law, without room for
appeals in the courtroom. I'm getting whiplash here, and
my heart—" Fresh tears sprang to her eyes and strangled in
her throat. "My heart is too invested in this"—she motioned
between us—"to be treated that way. If that's a normal thing
with you, then it'd be a great idea to inform me now. I have to
decide if I can handle it, or if—"

"What?" I gripped the back of the seat, using the hold
to surge toward her. Not a velociraptor lunge but enough
movement to tell her I wasn't being merely suave and casual.
"Or if what, Abbigail?" I demanded again.

"If... I need to bail out now," she finally spurted and tacked
on a proud lift of her chin that unraveled my goddamned soul.
"Before I'm completely devastated from having to do so later."

Later?

Because she thought that if she did it now, we'd both be
just fine with it?

And this pathetic attempt at sarcasm, even unvoiced,
wasn't helping my cause. She didn't need that right now. But

to be honest, I wasn't sure what she did need. I was in an emotional wilderness with no damn compass.

I had to just take a stab. Follow my gut. Hope for the best.

"Well, I guess that's something only you can decide," I said quietly.

Pray I was halfway close to the target. Whatever the hell that was.

"What are you saying?"

Though by the looks of her startled jerk and Bambi-stunned eyes, all I'd drawn here was more blood. But I had to keep going. Had to keep working at this. Had to keep trying.

"I'm saying…only you can decide if what we have together, or what we're trying to build together, is worth fighting for." I edged out on a psychological limb, curling my fingers down from the top of the seat. As gently as I could, I stroked them over the curve of her cheek. "That it's worth feeling some pain for, Abbi."

Our stares entwined, and I treasured the schism of trust I still saw in the deep facets of her emerald irises. If we still had trust, even a little, then we had hope.

"You already know that life isn't always easy, Red," I went on. "Sometimes you have to go through some tough shit to get to the good stuff. But only you can decide if our 'good stuff' is ultimately worth it."

She was unusually quiet as I spoke, turning to watch the city pass by through the car window. Storefronts, speeding cars, and billboards whizzed behind her, but I hardly registered they were there. My only focus was her—and the twenty different ways in which her distressed features changed shape as the car climbed the rise into Universal City.

When we pulled into the circular driveway of the house,

she didn't wait for me or Joel to help her from the car. She threw her door open and got out like the fierce woman she was—and part of me yearned to cheer. Her independence was part of what made her so breathtaking, and the part of me that adored it was pumped about it being so vibrantly intact.

Hell, yeah.

My woman was still in there.

She judiciously avoided me for the rest of the afternoon and evening. I was looking forward to bedtime, when we could finally talk—

Until she announced, just after brushing her teeth, "I'm going to sleep in one of the guest rooms tonight."

"All right."

I murmured it while pulling a T-shirt over my head. I didn't like her call or the avoidance therapy it was enforcing but refused to give her a rise about it. We'd ridden that particular pony to death already today. And if she thought I'd jump onto her bandwagon just for the sake of sleeping with her, she'd be riding in that rig alone. I wasn't one to beg another for anything. Not even her. Especially when her decision was so clearly made.

"Well, if you change your mind, you're welcome back in our bed. I love you, and I'm not angry with you. I just want you to know that. I'll be more than happy to talk this through. I'm here for you, Abbigail. Any time, any day. I'll do whatever it takes."

Including this. Standing here with my soul in my eyes, my heart on my sleeve—

And a secret in my psyche.

A plan that was going to rip her apart.

Which did what for the goddamned olive branch I was

extending? Or my version of one, at least.

"Good night, Sebastian."

And maybe she already saw through that sham.

Which explained why her reply was only a sorrowful rasp . . .

With the power to crush my offering like a sad little twig under the weight of a lumberjack's boot.

CHAPTER THIRTEEN

ABBIGAIL

Toss. Turn. Flip. Flop. Breathe. Sigh.

You name it, I did it.

Everything but the verb I was in this bed for. And urgently needed.

Sleep.

My body was completely exhausted, but my mind was at full voltage. The gray matter was bettered only by my nervous system, which felt like a tangle of live wires.

One moment, I thought I had the whole situation figured out. The next, I was mired again in total bewilderment. I considered getting up and grabbing a glass of wine to relax, but when I looked at the clock and calculated the scant two hours left before I had to be up for work, that option was off the table.

And what was I mad about again?

I answered that with a loud laugh.

Because what wasn't I mad about?

Everything had started out so great. After Sebastian's presentation, I'd been so proud. My man had enraptured the whole crowd with his soul-filled words—his honest, open story.

And he was all mine. I'd known it with such blazing completion. Bas openly showed me off to everyone. Praised my culinary handiwork. Said he loved me on a routine basis.

To the outside world, I had it all—and more.

But did I?

My soul still said yes. Even my heart did.

But my spirit was deflated.

I loved him too. Admired him. Believed in him. Trusted him. Right now—literally—with my life. But did I want to be with a man who didn't respect me as an equal? Who thought it appropriate to order me around with the expectation of total compliance, no matter how "noble" his reasons for doing so? I wasn't talking about our dynamic in the bedroom, where he could dictate we'd screw upside down from the chandelier and I'd happily agree. Sebastian knew exactly how to make my body sing.

But spectacular sex didn't automatically bring emotional closeness. Or a relationship bond. Or the glue for a connection that would last forever.

And right now, I was wondering if we'd let the sex delude us into thinking we had the rest.

I'd seen a different side of him—or rather, a side I hadn't seen in a while—when he'd simply decreed that we wouldn't be further discussing Viktor Blake's accusations. Granted, the bastard's ballsy intrusion into the party was jarring, enraging, and unexpected, but in many ways, Bas's reaction was equally as disturbing. He'd opened a spillway of spite but then erected a dam of rancor. His finishing move? Surrounding it all with barbed wire, promising I'd bleed if I stepped within inches.

But the bossy shark behavior was just one issue. And not even the biggest hurdle to tackle here. What on earth was Sebastian really keeping from me? Viktor had thrown down at the party with a lot of cocky swagger. Was he bluffing? Did he truly have an empty quiver? If not, what was he getting at with his comments? His motivation had been crystal clear. Viktor was trying to fill me with doubt. Well, it had worked. Spectacularly. And that suffocating doubt was causing a domino effect on my confidence, forcing me ask one of the hardest questions I'd ever had to ask myself.

Had Rio been right this whole time? Had I dived headfirst into this relationship without really knowing the man behind the computer monitors? Had I given my body, heart, and soul to a man with more skeletons than I'd imagined?

I couldn't ignore the facts. My age and inexperience. His reputation and drive. They'd collided in the eye of a crazy storm, inciting us to move things fast in our courtship—if that was even what it could be called. Then there was the storm itself, careening around us. Bringing harrowing events and real danger. The Tawny saga. The false alarm about Cinnamon. The marine-life calling cards. All convincing motivation to move into his home—voluntarily parking myself deeper beneath his wing.

But what did it all mean now?

If not for the insane twists of the past few weeks, I would never have moved in here already. I'd have signed another lease at my condo. I wouldn't be without options for a place to stay now.

As it stood, I was basically homeless. Trapped. A pathetic damsel in a castle with a king only interested in doing things one way. His.

In some ways, I'd done this to myself. That general way of thinking worked for us in the bedroom—with mind-blowing goodness—but so far, so much of our time had been spent hot and horizontally. Had I let the smoke of our sexual fire cloud my judgment about everything else? Had I not realized that

Bas would demand—and expect—my acquiescence about a lot of other aspects too?

And if that was going to truly be the way of things, could I get on board with that?

I was young, but I wasn't stupid. Or weak.

There was a difference between trusting a man and then letting oneself be minimized by him. And that was really how things felt when Bas "put me in my place" yesterday. More than once.

Finally deciding sleep was not going to happen, I got up and took a fast shower in the guest bathroom. With equal swiftness, I got ready for work. To be as quiet as possible—for my comfort, not his—I skipped on making a cup of coffee. But as I pulled out of the driveway, I caught a glimpse of the blinds parting in the master suite. Apparently my mouse act had been for naught. I wasn't the only one who couldn't sleep.

As soon as I merged onto the freeway, my phone signaled with a text message.

Have a good day at work, baby.
See you at lunch.

Bas knew I didn't like texting and driving, so he wouldn't expect a reply. I did have to give him some credit for the gesture. At least he was trying.

But I still wasn't sure I could face him yet. More accurately, that I could keep my head separated from my libido long enough for a rational conversation with him.

Maybe I could talk Rio into making the lunch deliveries. Okay, so it was the cowardly way to handle the situation, but unless I had a moment of pivotal clarity between now and then,

I couldn't imagine wanting to talk to him at lunchtime either.

It was odd being the first one in the kitchen for a change. I checked the website's order portal to see if anything had come in that we weren't already aware of. Fortunately, no pop-up surprises. Most days we didn't mind the challenge, but with no sleep and a very preoccupied mind, I just wanted a routine day.

I tied my apron around my waist and got busy. Over an hour had passed when I heard Rio slipping her key into the lock. Hopefully she'd seen my truck when pulling in so my presence wouldn't be a surprise.

"The early bird gets the worm!" my sister-in-law said by way of greeting.

"So the saying goes."

As much as I fought to emulate her cheer, Rio halted hard enough to screech the floor with her Chucks. "Whoaaa, Abs, you look like shit. Truly, I mean no offense. Were you going for a Goth vamp vibe today?" She took a second look back over her shoulder while hanging her purse on the hook by the computer desk.

"Ha-ha," I deadpanned—nearly literally, if her assessment was accurate—and that woman was more observant than a seasoned FBI agent. "Just didn't sleep well last night. Guess I should've gone heavier with the concealer."

"Everything okay?" She asked it conversationally, but I knew better. Honestly, I felt bad for my future nieces or nephews. Nothing escaped this woman.

"Yeah," I replied, already knowing I rushed the snap. "Ummm, yeah," I repeated, hoping to correct the damage. "Just looks like the routine lunch orders today. Nothing new from the website either. Should be pretty smooth sailing."

"I meant with you, silly." She turned and faced me, hands

planted on her slender hips. "Nice deflecting though."

I shrugged sheepishly. "It was worth a try."

"So." She clapped her hands. "The event went really well yesterday, yeah?"

"It absolutely did," I declared. "Thanks, in no small part, to you. I can't thank you enough for all your help, sister."

"Just doing my job." As she pulled back, a wide smile graced her bow-shaped lips. "And loving every second of it, I might add. I would've never guessed this would be something I enjoyed as much as I do."

"I'm thrilled to hear that, honey. Seriously, that makes my heart happy."

"Well . . . I'm glad something is this morning," she volleyed.

"What do you mean?" Maybe playing dumb would work better the second time around.

"Okay, cut the crap, Abbigail. This is me you're talking to." She jogged her chin with fiery fervor. "Outside of your brothers, who knows you better than I do?"

"Fine. You have a definite point there." I sighed.

"Bet your ass I do." She leaned back against the counter. Folded her arms. "So spill it."

"I think I'm going to take a pass for right now. I'm so tired. Maybe later, though, okay?"

"Okay," she murmured. "You've got all the space you need. But I can only assume this is about your man, which means you're still sorting stuff out. But I'm here when you're ready to talk."

"I know." And I did—though to be honest, I still wasn't convinced she'd stay objective enough to give me solid advice.

"I think I have the steak and roasted veggie salad handled. Will you work on the pasta?" I looked to Rio for confirmation.

We often made a salad, pasta, and chicken option for our lunch regulars to choose from each day. Trying to keep the menu exciting, cost-effective on our end, and manageable—given the packaging and delivery constraints we dealt with—were just a few of the challenges of running a successful catering business. Eventually, if Abstract Catering became the in-house food service at the Edge, we'd have to think long and hard about continuing our lunch delivery offering. Our loyal customers helped us get where we were today, but managing a storefront that served three meals a day would completely change our business model.

The laptop computer binged. There was an incoming message on the computer program we used for order processing.

Rio, currently closer to the desk, yelled, "I got it!"

I checked on the meat but kept an eye on her too, hoping it wasn't a significant last-minute change. "Anything earth-shattering?" I queried.

She was already busy typing out a brisk reply. She wasn't amending with any exasperated groans or sighs, so I was hopeful. "Oh, this has your name written all over it," she finally commented.

"Dare I ask?" I said while portioning field greens into plastic containers.

"It's from Shark's assistant. She's requesting we modify the route so theirs is your last delivery."

Your last delivery.

I gritted my teeth as her last three words turned into ringing commands. Just like that, asking her to cover the lunch run was officially off the table.

"So what did you tell her?" I managed to keep my emotion

out of my tone. Barely.

"I said it was fine. I mean, it is, isn't it?"

"Yeah, sure." I shrugged with more forced insouciance. "Sebastian probably just has a meeting."

But like the veiled taunts from Terryn's message, my churning stomach warned me otherwise. I set the bowl of greens down with a clatter before cradling my face in my hands. *Please, no tears. No tears. No tears.*

Before I could pull myself together, Rio had rushed to my side. She tugged my hands away from my face. "Hey," she crooned. "What's going on?"

"Wh-What if he breaks up with me?" My voice squeaked pitifully on the terrifying admission. The damn thing had been like an ocean undertow. I'd battled it so hard, only to learn that fighting pulled me under faster. "Oh, God . . ." I couldn't believe I'd said it aloud—which made the possibility that much more real. "Is that . . . do you think . . . that's why he wants to see me at the end of the run?"

"Abs." Rio yanked me in, holding me tighter. "Come on now. Why would he—"

"I've really been a bitch to him, Rio," I sobbed. "What if he's finally decided I'm not worth all the drama? He's Sebastian freaking Shark. He can have any woman he wants. He certainly doesn't have to put up with"—I waved my hands through the air—"all of this nonsense."

"Okay, power down this jet cycle, babe." Her stern gaze brooked no argument. "First of all, your feelings are not nonsense. Any man—any person—who makes you feel that way isn't worth sharing the same air you breathe. Are we clear on that? All of it?"

I managed a sketchy nod. Not that I had a choice about it.

My sister-in-law was small in stature but a mighty warrior in spirit. I loved her like hell for it too.

"Secondly, where is all of this coming from? I watched the news coverage of the Edge's groundbreaking. That man adores you, Abbi. Anyone watching a TV screen last night could feel the heat from his gaze just by watching that footage—and if they didn't, they're a fool." She poked me teasingly in the ribs. "And you, Abbigail Gibson, are no fool."

I snuffled. "Thanks, Rio."

"Oh, shit!" She spun around, and I refrained from starting my Tasmanian Devil impression. "I've got to get the pasta!"

She dashed over, turned off the burner, and then carried a large pot to the sink to strain the fusilli. While she worked on her "alla vodka" recipe, I decided to cave about revealing what had been going on lately between Sebastian and me.

"The man lives in a world that you and I haven't experienced before, Rio."

She glanced my way while stirring the noodles in the pot. "I'm not exactly surprised by that, you know."

I leaned a hip to the counter. I needed the extra support for my deep breath hangover. Yes, I'd really pulled in that much air. And no, it didn't feel like enough for where I was next taking this conversation. "I'm not just talking about his nice things, his fast cars, and the crystal tower he just broke ground on. He's made enemies, sister. People want to hurt him. To legitimately destroy him."

"Are you talking about Viktor Blake?"

"Well, yes. But I have a feeling he's just the tip of the iceberg." In for a penny, in for a pound. I decided to go all-in about divulging the events of yesterday. "He showed up at the groundbreaking ceremony."

Her usually large, round eyes expanded in surprise. "Okay, now I'm surprised. Are you seriously leveling with me?"

"Yes! Can you believe the man's nerve? He proceeded to insinuate that Bas had slept with his date in the past."

Her face twisted. "Right in front of you?"

"Oh, no," I returned. "He said that directly to me." My voice kicked up at least an octave higher.

"Damn. And I was stuck in the kitchen while all of this was going on!"

I almost laughed. I wasn't surprised Rio was disappointed about missing all the fireworks while she was supervising the chaos of our on-site kitchen.

I held up my plastic-covered index finger. "But here's the kicker."

"Shit. There's more?"

"Victor made a really mysterious comment. Something along the lines of asking Sebastian if he'd told me where 'all of the bodies are buried.' Bas was furious. Grant and Elijah all but dragged him out of the venue, but..."

"But what?"

I rubbed my forehead with the back of my wrist. "I don't know, Rio. I really don't know what to make of any of it."

"Well, did you guys talk about it? What Blake might have meant with that comment?"

"Yes. Well..."

I trailed off for a number of reasons—but most importantly because I knew this was the part I'd most regret getting into with her.

"What?" She chopped the basil on the cutting board in front of her with a little too much enthusiasm. "Don't clam up on me now, girl. I'm on to you already. Whatever you're going to say is going to paint your man in a bad light. Believe me, I can take it."

She side-eyed my disbelieving glare while swooshing the chopped herbs into the simmering sauce. "Baby, listen. You're not giving me a news flash here. They all do and say stupid shit, your brother included. I'm sure they could say the same thing about us, especially if the heat of a disagreement gets mixed in. We don't always get it right."

She shrugged as if it were that simple. I took a turn at indulging a wide gape. Holy crap. Was it? I was so new to all this relationship stuff—and though technically Bas was too, he wasn't used to actually working on things either. His go-to stance was to be bossy and controlling. So maybe this was his norm. Maybe he wasn't actually hiding anything from me. Maybe he just didn't want to keep arguing about something he saw as ridiculous, and that was his way of putting an end to it.

And what had I done? Turned on the megabitch superpowers and iced him out.

So wonderfully mature, Abbigail.

So . . . was all this really that cut-and-dried? Were we just having an argument and said things we didn't mean? And if that was the case, now what? What sort of hornet's nest would I be walking into when I brought him his lunch this afternoon?

"Okay, okay. Bring it down a notch," Rio said, even though I hadn't said a word. Not out loud, at least. I'd been lost in my own thoughts for the past six minutes, at least.

"Huh?" I finally answered, ever so intelligently.

"I see what you're doing to yourself over there," she mused with a little grin on her lips. "You're not going to do yourself any good by raking yourself over the coals for whatever you said or did last night. Just go there today with his lunch, apologize, be sweet, and promise some sex. Boom, done."

I couldn't help but laugh. The woman had a way of making things seem so simple. It was a real gift she had. No matter what the situation, my sister-in-law just cut through all the extraneous crap and got to the heart of the issue.

For once, I hoped like hell she was on to something.

★ ★ ★

Of all the days I wanted the route to downtown to take as long as possible, it flowed shockingly smoothly. Traffic seemed light on all the usually congested streets, parking was effortless to find in front of every building, and even the elevators were ready and open for my arrival, practically goading me with their eager responses to the call buttons.

In short, the inevitable arrived sooner than later—and way before I felt emotionally shored up to deal with it. I took deep, fortifying breaths while being whisked to the top floor of Sebastian's building. They helped. I think. I hoped.

Oh, dear Lord. I was really being ridiculous. That was all there was to it. This was Sebastian. The man I loved. And just like Rio said, he loved me in return.

And what happened yesterday... It was a silly argument that we'd work through now. We'd both apologize for our parts in and then move past the speed bump. That was what couples did...right?

Now if my rioting nerves and clenching belly would get the damn message too.

"Get a grip, Abbi."

I mumbled it one last time as the doors slid open. After one more fortifying breath, I pushed my delivery cart into the main reception area of Shark Enterprises. I wished the trip were farther, at the end of some grand hallway, but the corporation occupied this whole floor as well as the twenty below it. If every office were laid out horizontally instead of stacked in this building, they'd be the size of a small fiefdom.

As I expected, Terryn sat dutifully at her desk in the main lobby. She regarded me like one of the Beefeaters at Buckingham Palace, guarding the bloody Queen's jewels.

Except that there was a more precious treasure beyond those double doors.

"You can go right in," she said without ceremony. Her directness was also an anticipated element. Her strange grin wasn't. "He's expecting you."

"Thanks, Terryn."

"Mmm-hmm."

I opened the door and peeked in first. I always made sure Bas wasn't on a phone call before dragging in my entire cart.

He wasn't on a call. But of course, he was deeply engrossed in work behind the three large monitors on his desk.

"Hey," I said quietly, feeling like I was disturbing him anyway. "Hungry?"

"Abbigail." He said my name on an exhale as if it were the first time he allowed his breath to escape the confines of his powerful chest all day.

I brought my cart inside the door and parked it off to the side. By now, my heart was thundering. My nerves were fraying. I hadn't been this thoroughly frazzled since the first week of engaging this man on a level deeper than professional.

He stood up behind his desk. Ran an appraising look over me. His blue eyes were darker than usual, probably from lack of sleep.

Bas prowled around to the front of his desk, stroking his unshaven chin with his thumb and forefinger. Had I ever seen him unshaven in this building? He'd never been more arousing to me than in this still, unsure minute.

I desperately needed him to say something.

"Close the door, Abbigail." He paused a beat. "And lock it."

CHAPTER FOURTEEN

SEBASTIAN

It was nearing lunchtime as I looked out over the city, taking in my empire. I'd been up since three forty-three a.m., when Abbi's truck had roared away from my house.

I snorted aloud at the idea of her thinking she had sneaked out on me. If Abbigail was going to skip out on me before daybreak, she'd better reconsider that monster truck she drove.

My cell phone chirped with an incoming text, and I eagerly dug it out, hoping it was Abbigail. But when I unlocked the screen, I was confronted by a text from an unknown number—with a really grainy photo attached.

"What the hell?" What was I even looking at? Maybe the text would help clarify.

It's not like you to be this careless.

I swiped back to the picture, and my blood ran cold. My darkest fears were coming to pass in the palm of my hand.

The image was of Abbi. She was unlocking the front door of her Inglewood prep kitchen. It was dark, though the slightest hint of dawn tinged the sky behind her. Still, the industrial park was all but abandoned at the early hour she had gone in to start the day.

My phone chirped twice. Two more pictures, both of Abbigail, taken on different days in different places. Places I instantly recognized.

In one, she was out jogging in our neighborhood—beyond the security gates and guard shack that should have been protecting her from this sick fuck. In the second—one that truly turned my blood to ice—she was in a utilitarian bathroom, in nothing but her bra and panties, getting ready to slip into the lavender dress I'd helped her pick out for the Edge's groundbreaker.

This was the moment everything changed. The moment I decided to change everything.

For the first time in my life, my heart was going to break because of a woman.

But there was no other way. I wouldn't risk her life in exchange for mine.

"Bas?" Her quiet query hauled me back to the present. I hadn't even heard her enter my office.

I swallowed hard. Gave my spine a direct command to stay upright. "Yeah, baby?"

"I . . . I just . . . Are you still mad?" She shifted her weight, using the cart as leverage. "I'm so sorry."

"No."

"No?" Understandably, she was more confused.

"Don't apologize. I don't want to hear you say you're sorry."

"You . . . you don't?"

Good God. Her wide, glowing green stare would be my undoing. I had to close my eyes to the magic of it.

"Why is that so hard to believe?" I forced my gaze open

and funneled its most authoritative force on her. "You didn't do anything wrong."

"I . . . what?" she stammered. "But I—"

I cut her off with a stern look. "Did you hear what I just said, Red?"

"Yes . . ."

"No." I slowly shook my head. "You heard me, but you weren't listening."

"Excuse me?"

"Now you're listening. Come here."

She stared at me for a few moments. Then glared. Clearly she had been examining our tiff from yesterday at every angle. But her body yearned to heed my demand, judging by the flush creeping across her chest and up her neck.

I had to capitalize on that.

I raised my chin and tilted my head to the side. Waiting— with a stare of blatant warning. "Abbigail . . ."

She shuffled forward, coming to a halt about two feet away.

With an impatient stab, I pointed to the space directly in front of me with expectation.

Her shoes appeared in my field of sight. "That's my good girl." The approving rumble emanated from the primal core of my throat. The completed whole of my spirit. Completion. That was what Abbigail was to me.

Connection. Salvation. Perfection.

I'd die for it all. Fight for it all.

And that plan started now.

But first . . . this moment.

I closed my eyes again. Inhaled her scent. Breathed in her presence. I didn't touch her. I only memorized the air around her. The heat flowing off her skin. The sizzle of her energy in the atmosphere. The light gleaming in the russet tendrils that had escaped her tight bun. She was eroticism and innocence, both spicy and sweet—just like her amazing personality.

Finally, I looked up again. Her gaze, focused and fervent, was waiting. Her eyes glistened like emeralds, replete with so much emotion. I detected arousal and anger in her dark-green irises, and the simmering mixture was a total turn-on.

Abbi shifted nervously. "Do you want your lunch?"

"No."

"No?"

"I just want you." I palmed her creamy cheek. "Will you let me have that, Abbigail?"

"You . . . you already have me."

"Take your hair down."

"Sebastian?"

"Do it."

"Why are you acting so strangely?" She lifted her hand to my face but thought better of the action when my harsh demeanor hit her in full. It all worked out well anyhow. Before she dropped her hand all the way, I caught it and lifted it back to her head.

Her gaze shifted from side to side, trying to examine every angle of my face. But she'd find nothing. I wore no clue as to how completely I was unraveling.

So I did what I hadn't allowed myself to do with Abbigail yet.

I dominated her. Controlled her.

And could I be blamed?

The sight of her . . .

The magic of her . . .

The entrancing completion of her . . .

Every one of those praises were bells in my head as I watched her pluck the pins from the coil at her nape. With equally graceful sweeps, she stashed them in her apron's front pocket. She shook her head to allow the long silky tresses to tumble down over her shoulders. As they fell, I was flooded with the scent of her shampoo. I let my eyes roam from her crown to her waist and then back again. She took my breath away. I would never let anyone hurt her. My resolution grew with each moment that passed in her presence.

"You are so stunning." I stroked her hair, luxuriating in the way it flowed through my fingers. "The most beautiful woman I've ever known. Fire."

I gathered her hair over one of her shoulders. I clutched the ends in my palm and then wrapped the length around and around my wrist. I didn't stop until I had her drawn close and tight, the warmth of our bodies mingling like the mahogany and copper striations in her mane. I yanked even tighter, using the gathered strands as a rope leash . . . now holding her in place merely an inch from my lips.

My breath was her breath. My sight was her sight. My scent, her scent.

I pressed my lips to hers—but didn't kiss her. Even when she whimpered for it. Even when she moaned.

Finally, I murmured, "Put your hands behind your back, girl."

A new whine. So damn sexy. A longer moan. So damn addicting.

"Bas," she protested.

"Hmmm . . . Yes, my love?"

"Why are you doing this?" she rasped. "Is . . . is this my punishment?"

"I told you." I parted from her mouth but only by a fraction. "You haven't done anything wrong. I'm doing this"—I drew it out in a wicked hiss—"because this is what I want to do. Need to do." I tugged her hair, and she whimpered. "Now do as you're told, beautiful." After another few moments of personal debate, she clasped her perfectly feminine hands at the small of her back. Watching her submit, even though—no, especially because she was struggling with each and every decision to do so was engorging my cock as though I hadn't fucked anyone in twelve years.

Each memory of what we were doing today would be crystalline and pure, high on the shelves of my disturbed mental library. One day in the future, when I was missing her skin and needing her touch, I'd be able to take out one of the delicate treasures and relive the moment as if it were happening all over again.

"Wh-What are you going to do?" she stammered. "To me, I mean."

"Fuck you. Eventually." My tone was flat and matter-of-fact. Still, I didn't miss her needy shiver because of my carnal promise.

"So why can't I touch you in return, then?"

"Too many questions, Red. You get one more for the whole time you're with me today. Use it wisely."

She made a show of pressing her lips together, and I nodded in approval. I was lured even closer by the glimmer that returned to her deep-forest eyes. My small display of praise sparked light back into her spirit.

It was time to claim those lips, that tongue, that husky moan. My erection pulsed at the notion too, so I ground into the softness of her stomach while holding her hips in place to steady her against my force.

"Mmmm," she moaned softly and stared at me while I pressed my lips to hers. Wasn't interested in soft here, not in the slightest. I needed to possess her mouth. Plunder and conquer. Mark and bruise. When Elijah would take her from me shortly, her lips would be swollen and tender from my kisses. Just the way they should be.

I swooped into her mouth with my greedy tongue. I tasted and explored every corner of her, inside and out. Her lips, naturally plush, were like heaven's gates parting for my demonic desecration. She chased my assault with one of her own, fighting to keep up with my fervor. So good. Christ, my Little Red was so. Damn. Good.

Nipping and biting, I moved down her jaw to her ear. I dipped to her neck, all but ripping the collar of her T-shirt to make a wider path for my exploration.

"Stay." I issued the one-word command while stepping back, finding the hefty stainless-steel scissors on my desk.

"No." Her eyes grew impossibly wide at the view of the sharp object in my hand. "Bas. No."

"Pardon?"

"What are you going to do?" she asked, panic-stricken.

"Last question. What a shame."

I made a dramatically disappointed face. It didn't matter one way or the other, though. I wasn't going to supply an answer or change my course of action, but she did just use the last question of her allowance.

"Be still now," I issued in warning, bringing the implement closer to her neck. As I slipped the cold metal against her collarbone, she shuddered. My dick surged. Oh, hell yes. "Such a good girl."

One snip of the thicker neckline of her T-shirt was all I'd really planned. I was just turned on by her trust in me, letting me indulge the mindfuck of having the sharp object near her throat. So hot. So erotic. I had it so bad for this incredible woman.

I stepped back to my desk to return the scissors before facing my woman again. She was still so breathtaking to behold. Her breath sawed in and out, making her chest heave up and down. Her breasts thrust against her T-shirt and apron bib with each inhale and exhale.

About both of those . . .

Two lengthy steps and I was in front of her again. My intent must have been searing from my gaze because she moved back by two matching strides. Nervous ones. "Sebastian," she chastised. "I have to have a shirt to wear, even just back to the kitchen. I don't know what's gotten into you, but—"

Riiippp.

Then one more yank. Downward this time.

Just like that, her tee was in two pieces, starting with the snip I had made at the neckline. The aggressive motion halted her protest. Shock and arousal battled for top billing on her features.

"You were saying?" I thumbed her erect nipples through the lace of her bra before taking each breast roughly in my hands. I kneaded and plumped their fullness in my palms. As I did, a new plan filled my mind. I acted on it at once, leaning closer to Abbi.

"Put your hands around my neck, baby."

This time, she followed my instructions without question. She kept her gaze fixed on mine, lusty need starting to override her natural inclination to investigate every angle of a situation or command. I cradled her by her backside, and she wrapped her legs around my waist. At once, I carried her over to the conference table. I nudged the chair at the head of the large surface, pushing it off to the side a bit, enabling me to stand at the end. I laid Abbigail onto the flat top. She shuddered when her skin met the cool surface but stilled when her eyes fell on my hands—as I got busy unbuckling my belt.

"I need to feel you" was all I could manage. My voice was strangled with the single-minded obsession. Once the seed of the idea popped into my brain, I couldn't focus on anything else. Just a few strokes, I told myself, and then I would tend to her more. Just to take the edge off—and then I could think straight again.

And then I would take care of exactly why I'd called her in here to begin with.

Abbi propped herself up on her elbows to have a better view of me standing before her. She watched with rapt interest as I maneuvered the button and fly of her jeans. She lifted her hips when I yanked the pants off her legs in one quick move. I dropped the denim to the floor in a careless heap.

"The bra." I held out my hand, wanting her to bare the final bit of herself to me. Instead of complying, she shot a quick look to the door clear across the suite. "Remember when I asked you to lock it?" I prompted.

My assurance, though a ruthless snarl, worked the trick of visibly relaxing her. After an audible but gorgeous breath, she reached behind her back and snapped the clasp. Her breasts, full and erect, spilled free from their lingerie confines.

As soon as Abbi handed over her lacey bra, I let it fall on top of her jeans. I stood to my full height and said, "Lie all the way back." As she eagerly complied, I murmured, "Next time I have a meeting at this table, I'm going to picture you lying here like this."

"Hmmm." Her hum was like music, silken and sweet. "Nice."

I moved around to push my executive chair out of the way. "Close your eyes."

After she did, I moved from the head of the table and went to take a seat closer to her head. I padded softly so she wouldn't know where to expect my voice to come from when I spoke again. I stroked my fingers down her cheek. She startled at first, surprised I was so close to her face.

"I don't think you realize how important you are to me, Abbigail." I continued my trail, dipping my head to brush my lips across her cheek several times. I kept going, down over her chin and throat before sucking and licking the hollow at the base. My voice was deeper when I spoke again. "To be honest, I don't think I even realized it until this week." I gave her more trails with my fingertips again, going gentle and slow across her collarbones. To me, that had always been one of the most delicate and perfect parts of a woman's body, especially hers.

But I didn't stop there. I couldn't.

I skimmed my touch down into the valley between her breasts. I applied my mouth to the effort again, unable to hold back my erotic hunger. I sucked her nipple into my mouth before giving the tender tip a nibble. She tasted so damn good, spice and salty feminine musk. At once, Abbi reacted with a sharp moan into the still air of my office.

"Oh, Sebastian! God, yes. Finally."

She sifted her fingers through my hair, and I decided to allow her the contact. I wouldn't be staying there long, so why not?

I licked around the stiff bud before biting again, only harder then. She arched her back off the table, pushing her sweet swell deeper into my mouth. With my palm, I flattened her back to the table. "Relax, Red."

She let out a sound of adorable protest.

"Patience, baby." I flicked my tongue over her flesh again. She went still but whimpered, not happy about having to be so still while I ruthlessly pleasured her. "Ah. That's better."

Despite my best efforts to hold it back, a deep groan spilled out. I let it linger on the air while skimming my fingers over her ribs, continuing my path down her body. When I spoke again, I returned to the serious intent of what I needed to say here— while I definitely knew she was listening, not just hearing.

"I want you to know, Abbigail, how much I think about you when we're not together." I skated my fingers across her abdomen and then kissed a wet trail in their wake. "How every decision I make is with you in mind. With us in mind. Because I think we're building a future together now. It's a whole new way of existing for me."

I got to her hips, where her bones stuck out in such a feminine way, they called to the male in me. Here, her body begged me to grip on to her and thrust into her with primal force. I had to move back to the end of the table and yank her down again, making her legs dangle off the edge in preparation for my entrance.

"Fuck, Bas. Please. God, please, just do it." She bucked her hips in need, her body so on edge from all my petting.

"Not yet, baby. Not yet. I want to be sure you're really listening to me."

"I am. I am! You, me, future. I want that too. I do. More than anything. Please, please!"

"I love you, Abbigail. I will do anything to keep you safe." I slid my fingers through the wetness that slicked her pussy. Her scent was so heady. Calling to me. Teasing me. I opened my slacks and pulled them down around my hips. Quickly, I did the same with my boxer briefs. I lowered everything just far enough to free my shaft, so hard, thick, and ready to celebrate its newfound movement. "I'm going to protect you with every part of my body ... even if it tears my heart out."

On one long surge, I thrust my cock into her. I didn't stop until I was fully buried in her wet, tight cunt.

"Pull your legs back, Abbi," I told her so I could drive deeper into her. She listened immediately, trusting my experience over her lack of, and immediately felt the difference.

"Jesus, Bas. Oh my God. Ooooohhh!" She let out a string of praises, and my cock swelled along with my ego. I thumbed her exposed clit while I pounded into her, time, and time, and time again. I held her in place for my thrusts with an arm banded around her bent leg on the other side. Sweat gathered on my brow as I felt my balls tightening. I desperately needed to come.

"Red. Come, baby. Shatter around me. Let me feel you, love," I encouraged on every exhale.

"So close, Bas," she chanted. "So close!"

I pinched her clit and then held it between my fingers. I continued to apply pressure to the nub while fucking her with long, savoring lunges.

"Fuck. Fuck! I'm coming, Sebastian. Yes ... ooooh fuck, yes!" Abbigail moaned and then finally detonated with her climax. Her pussy clenched and spasmed around my swollen dick, sparking my own orgasm. I thrust deeply into her, rotating my hips against her body when I came up against her skin, repeating the motion a few more times as I milked every drop of semen from my balls and shaft. When she left here today—when she left me—I was determined she'd do so with as much of my essence inside her.

Maybe even my child.

Fuck!

I staggered back from the table. Yanked up my boxers and slacks just as frantically. I jammed my shirt into my pants and tugged my belt into place. I bent to the ground for Abbi's pants and underwear.

"B-Bas?"

"Get dressed, baby," I returned through gritted teeth. I already hated myself for what was coming. "Please," I amended. "I'll . . . get you a shirt."

I strode directly into my office's attached bathroom. My steps wove, direct victims of the whirlwind in my mind.

What the hell was I doing? Thinking? How could I be mooning about getting her pregnant when I could barely protect her from the asshole lunatic who was following her around town and waiting for the creepiest Kodak moments, starring her—for the sole purpose of taunting me with them? But I'd gone there. Not just gone there but rejoiced in the explosion of images from the idea. I loved thinking about her with my child swelling inside her body and giving Vela a sweet baby cousin to play with . . .

Crazy talk. Crazier ideas. I was going goddamned crazy. Plain and simple. That had to be it. Who else but a crazy person would think of bringing a child—an innocent baby—into this dangerous insanity?

"Sebastian." Her voice was louder now but still unsure. "Is everything okay?"

I ignored her. I had a prime excuse, now digging around in the built-in closet in my bathroom. I kept a few clothing items here for emergency situations, but nothing that would suit a woman. Still, I scrounged for something she could use. Because we wouldn't say our goodbyes with her standing half-naked in front of me . . .

Not an option.

At last I found a plain white T-shirt. It'd be entirely too large but would have to do. Abbigail could change when she was reunited with her own belongings.

For the time being, I had to settle down and deal with the way I'd just fucked her like an animal instead of the loving goodbye I'd really envisioned. Was I honestly incapable of not being a barbarian in the bedroom? Well, there was one hell of a personal growth quest to work on—in my spare time from tracking down a demented psycho, of course.

Abbi was standing by the full-length windows when I came out of the bathroom. She'd been the dutiful girl and done what I ordered, so she was only missing a shirt. Her hair was unmistakably freshly fucked, so she attempted a finger combing after getting fully dressed. Didn't take her long to give up and twist it into a messy bun on top of her head.

"I'm just headed home from here, so it doesn't really matter," she said with a shrug. She was already back to being so carefree. No. Beyond that. As soon as she rolled over the word "home," she broke out a joyous smile. Even darted a delighted wink my way, probably anticipating how we'd make up for last night's spat in our bed.

I was going to shatter her.

I knew that with certainty because I was already feeling it myself.

340

I took her hand in mine. Sucked in a deep, fortifying breath.

It was time. I couldn't delay this shit any longer.

Elijah would walk through the door any minute, and she still knew nothing. That was my fault, but I wasn't ashamed of it. If I could delay this confrontation by fucking her again, I would. Then again. And again...

But time was up. I had to level with her. "We need to talk, Abbigail."

"Okaaaay." She drew the word out while angling a newly cautious stare up at me.

"Baby... I've gone over and over this in my head..." I reached for her hands. She let me take them but not without a discernible quiver in her slender fingers.

"Gone over... what?"

"There isn't a way I can word this where I see you not freaking out, so you need to just let me tell you what's going on. After that, you need to trust me to take care of you. Can you do that?"

"Sebastian. You're starting to freak me out." No exaggeration there. Panic blared across every inch of her features like a neon sign. "I'm not going to just blindly agree to something you're simply describing as a 'this.' On top of that, a 'this' you've had to 'go over' a number of times."

I whooshed out a breath that was surely an oxygenated brick. "Abbi—"

"Just tell me what's going on, damn it."

"Fine. But you need to understand that your safety is my number-one priority. I will do what it takes to ensure you remain safe and secure—even if that seems like it isn't the easiest choice at the moment. I will also do it by any means necessary." I met her stare straight on and dropped my voice to my "don't fuck with me" tone. I did it without hesitation, even ready to take it a few octaves lower. "Am I making myself completely clear?"

She shoved back, yanking her hands away. Well, trying. She didn't get far. I maintained our grip like my life depended on the contact. Right now, maybe it did. "Tell. Me. What's. Going. On."

"When all the bullshit started at the house—the dead shark, Tawny showing up, the piranhas in the pool—we thought it might be best to get you out of harm's way for a while. Frankly, we considered the same for Pia and Vela, as well."

"Okay." She didn't extend it this time. The word was clipped, bordering on angry—right on track for the response I'd anticipated. The reaction for which I could no more blame her than sneezing from pollen. Her fire, will, and strength were what made her the woman I loved. What made her my irreplaceable, perfect woman. "And who exactly are 'we'?" she demanded then.

"Elijah, Grant, and me."

"Ah. Of course. But you and I have been through this." She took advantage of my two-second distraction with her twisted pout to get her hands free. She gripped them around opposite shoulders, hugging herself. More accurately, shutting me out.

"Abbigail . . ."

I stepped forward, reaching for her.

She stumbled back, again warding me off.

"You said you'd listen to me."

"Then talk," she gritted out.

I hated this. Every damn second of it. I still forced myself to go on.

"We have a better understanding of the level of danger we're talking about now, Abbigail. But I convinced Elijah to wait. He wanted to move you two weeks ago, and—"

"Move me?" she sputtered. "Move me—where?"

I raised my hand for her to stop. "After Viktor's bullshit at the reception, I was convinced it was time too."

Her mouth popped open as she continued backing away. "Bas. For the love of Christ! Viktor was just trying to get you riled up! Surely you, of all people, can see through his antics by now."

"Not antics." With each step she retreated, I advanced the same. Before she could interrupt again, because she pulled in air to do so, I spat out, "You don't know him like I do, Abbigail. Don't even pretend you do."

She expelled her air on a grating huff. "Oh my God." Plummeted her head into the cradle of her palms and rocked from side to side. "This is all so ridiculous."

"I wish I could say it was, baby."

My resigned mutter filled the time it took to pull out my phone once more. The air was pensive as I opened the text messages screen. Abbigail remained bunched in and stooped over, lifting only her head to glare at me. Skepticism still claimed her whole face—until I shoved the screen in front of her and started swiping through the mysterious messages— and disturbing images—from this morning.

Her glower flared. Became a stunned gawk. She lifted a hand and scrolled back through each photo of herself, the impact of them finally seeming to set in.

The violation of them.

All the implications from that.

"Wh-Who sent these to you?" Her voice fell to a rasp as

she lifted her wide, tear-filled eyes to meet mine.

"I don't know," I answered. "Elijah's trying to track the number, but so far it looks like a burner phone."

She nodded, but the motion was a collection of unsteady motions. She handed my phone back to me and slid down to the floor with her back against the window. The gravity of the situation was clearly, finally sinking in for her. While I was relieved, another section of my soul fissured. She was terrified and rightfully so. And being with me was the reason.

A sharp knock on the door had us both startling.

"That's probably Elijah."

Her eyes turned into huge liquid lagoons. "Elijah?" She skittered up the wall, gaining her feet but staying pinned. She balled her fists. "Why? What's he doing here?"

I jammed my hands through my hair, grabbing on to the strands for leverage. "I need you to go with him, Abbigail."

"Go?" She flattened herself tighter to the wall. "Go . . . where?"

"There's a house that will be safe . . ."

"No."

"Please don't give me a hard time about this. I'm begging you, Abbigail."

"Are you even serious?" she yelled. "Do you even know what you're threatening to do right now?"

"And you wouldn't have?" I rebutted. "If you'd considered everything that's already happened? If that shark had been left on the front stoop of your condo? Or Sean and Rio's house? If it were her, or any of your brothers, in photos like that?"

The thick pools in her eyes broke open. Her tears spilled down her taut cheeks. "Please! Please don't send me away like this."

"Bas?" Elijah called from the far side of my office door. "Hey, I'm here. Open the door!"

"In a minute!" I bellowed.

I turned back to her. Walked over to her. Gently gathered her back toward me, gulping hard as she spilled full sobs into my chest. "It's not forever, okay?"

"It will be if they finally kill you."

And she'd gone there. Not that I hadn't, at least a thousand times already, in my darkest moments. But I couldn't validate that by even addressing it. Instead, I husked into her hair, "You can come back as soon as we know who is doing this. And as soon as we catch them and make them pay for this nightmare."

She leaned tighter into me. Circled her arms around my neck and twisted her fingers into my hair until my scalp hurt. I welcomed the misery. Outward pain, commiserating with my inner agony.

"What about my family?" she rasped. "What about Abstract? My business? Bas, I—I can't just leave Rio and my clients. We have events coming up and goals to—"

"I have it all handled." I added a gentle kiss to her forehead with my firm assurance. "Grant is going to help Rio. That way he can keep an eye on her. That'll free up a couple of men to join Elijah's main task force."

"A couple of men?" She drew back far enough to scrutinize my whole face. "Have you had my family watched this whole time too?"

"Yes." The time for tactful evasion had well passed. "It was necessary. I think you can see why."

Finally I saw the reluctant agreement that led to her bow.

"The good news is no one seems interested in any of them at this point. Elijah will be with you most of the time. He has specific orders not to touch you. And of course, I will come whenever I can. As much as I can."

Her chin wobbled. Emerald tears continued to well in her eyes and tumble down her cheeks. "Sure," she grated. "Whenever you can."

"Abbigail." I pressed my lips to her forehead again. "I'm sorry, baby."

She jerked away from my touch. "Elijah will take me back to the house, then? So I can get clothes and toiletries? I'll also need some time to handle things. I need to call Sean. My dad. And I'll need to meet with Rio—"

"No," I emphasized. "Everything is taken care of. It's done. This is happening right now."

A harsher sob burst from her. But she said nothing. Did even less. Other than back farther away from me.

She'd accepted her fate.

Another victory that felt nowhere like a win.

I wheeled away and crossed to the door. My shoes felt filled with lead. As I let my friend in, the door felt even heavier.

I stopped Elijah near the door. I kept my eyes fixed on Abbi while addressing him. She looked small and lost against the huge glass plates of my office windows.

"I think she's ready," I murmured.

"The hell she is," she called.

Elijah scowled. "I know it sucks, okay? But I'm sure Bas has explained—"

"Fuck off," she snapped at Elijah.

"Baby." I walked back over. Once more pulled her into my arms. I was more forceful about the embrace this time. "Jesus... Please don't do this." But she didn't reciprocate a thing. She stood as stiffly as the pillars holding up the window, refusing to return my affection. "Abbigail." I buried my face in her hair while whispering the desperate plea.

"Damn it!" A matching entreaty broke through her defenses. She dropped her head to the center of my chest, drenched my shirt with her racking sobs.

"I hate this more than you do, Red," I whispered into her hair.

"Then don't do this! Please!" She curled her hands into the fabric beneath her face. "Please don't send me away. There has to be another way. We can think of something together. Don't give up on us." She raised her face, compelling me to meet her harrowed gaze with the matching sorrow in mine. "I'll—I'll be better. I promise, Bas. I'll be a better girlfriend. If this is about last night, I swear, I'm—"

I stopped her rambling with a plunging, passionate kiss. I swept my tongue so deep into her mouth, she moaned. That didn't stop her from answering my need with her own exigent hunger... her tearful, lustful rage.

We devoured each other like that for extended minutes. I yearned to make it hours, even days, but Elijah gave us a fresh stab of reality by pointedly clearing his throat.

Reluctantly, mournfully, I dragged my lips up from hers. But with a hand still at her cheek and my gaze still penetrating her as deep as my kiss, I vowed, "No more apologizing. You didn't do anything wrong. And now, I just need you to be my good girl and go with Elijah. I will try to see you soon. I promise."

She coiled her fingers tighter into my shirt. Shook her head hard enough to make her tears fly out, their depths glistening in the sunlight before splashing to the floor. "Why?" she rasped. "Why are you doing this to me? To us, Bas?"

"Because I love you with all my heart, Abbigail," I whispered. "Know that every single day, okay?"

I pulled back to a full arm's length. Forced myself to stare more deeply into her eyes, despite how her tears gutted me. Destroyed me. But I reached up anyway, swiping the tiny puddles beneath them away with my thumbs. Another excuse to touch her, if only in this small way, for one more moment.

"Be brave for me, baby. Remember I'm protecting you."

"But that's not what it feels like."

"I know."

"Do you?" she flung between heavier sobs. "Because you know what it really feels like? That you're giving up on us."

"Never!" I grabbed the other side of her face, forcing her to listen to me. To see me. All of me. Every ounce of torture this already was for me. "Are you listening to me, damn it? Never. I love you, Abbigail. I would die for you."

Right words, wrong time. My declaration doubled the intensity of her sobs. Knowing I'd only make things worse from this point on, I pushed her into Elijah's arms. Might as well have handed the guy my arms, legs, and intestines. It would have been less painful.

Elijah all but carried Abbi out of my office. I already knew he had the back elevator waiting and then the town car at the loading dock. Joel would drive them straight to the safe house. Elijah would call later to let me know she was settled in. He had a prescription for a mild sedative if she needed it.

As soon as they were gone, I shut the door.

Actually, I slammed it. Hard enough to make the windows shiver and pens roll across my desk. I didn't give a shit. I wasn't returning to that desk today. The plan for the rest of the afternoon? A whiskey stupor. A deep, dark, heavy one.

One moment.

Changing everything.

Bringing karma's ultimate payback to the great Sebastian Shark.

I had no idea living through heartbreak, like all the ones I'd already caused in my life, would hurt so damn badly.

And the nameless bastards who were causing it? They wouldn't be nameless for much longer. And when I knew those names, they were going to wish they'd never—ever—come across mine.

CONTINUE READING
THE SHARK'S EDGE SERIES

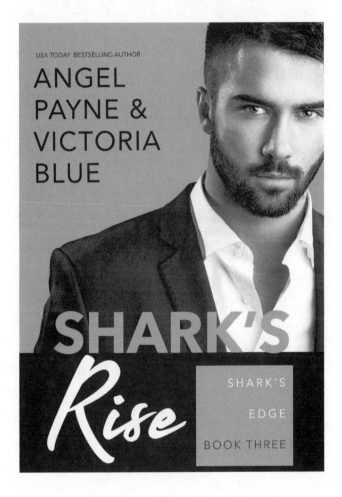

USA TODAY BESTSELLING AUTHOR

ANGEL
PAYNE &
VICTORIA
BLUE

SHARK'S

Rise

SHARK'S

EDGE

BOOK THREE

Keep reading for an excerpt!

EXCERPT FROM *SHARK'S RISE*

BOOK THREE IN THE SHARK'S EDGE SERIES

The mind has a way of protecting itself in desperate times. Never was that better evidenced than in the dream I was having.

"Finally," my dream-self rasped. "Oh God, yes! Finally!"

Sebastian was here with me. Here in this house. In my sanctuary.

In my bed.

He moved his skillful lips away from mine. Trailed them tenderly down my neck—at first. But clearly he'd missed me as much as I had him, and his touch got more demanding. He might have missed me even more, if the steely erection stabbing into my belly was any indication. I wasn't sure I'd ever felt him—no, anything—so hard in my life. His incessant rubs were almost painful. His arousal felt more like a fireplace poker than an excited penis.

"Mmmm, yes, baby," I moaned to my dream lover.

"Open your eyes, Abbigail," he crooned. "Let me see you, love."

I writhed against him while squeezing my eyes closed tighter. "No. I don't want to wake up," I mumbled against soft lips. "I hate it here, Sebastian. I don't want you to disappear again."

"Look at me, baby." He brushed a reverent kiss to my forehead. "You're not dreaming." To each eyelid. "I'm here." Then the tip of my nose. "I've come to visit you. I'm here . . ."

Dream Sebastian covered my mouth with his. Ohhh damn, his kiss was as good as my real man's—especially when he coaxed my lips apart with his own, thrust his tongue inside, and hungrily swallowed my needy cry of passion.

"Don't be cruel," I snarled once he released me. "I can't take it anymore! Not today."

"Little Red," he growled into my ear, just before nibbling the lobe. "Open your beautiful green eyes for me. Silly, silly, girl."

I chanced a peek—but just a quick one. If I were dreaming, I'd be able to sink right back into all the euphoria of him. All the sensual, beautiful glory of him . . .

Yet there he was. Smiling down on me with the full force of his dazzling grin. Kissing me on one cheek, then up and over my nose to the other. Holy shit. It was really him. He was actually in my room at the safe house—in Godforsaken Twentynine Palms!

He leaned up only far enough to frame my temples with his elegant fingers. He mellowed the grin to a smirk before whispering one word.

"Hi."

One word—that was more than enough for me.

Within seconds, sobs burst from every corner of my body and soul. I wrapped my entire body around him. I held on so tightly, neither one of us could inflate our lungs. The emotional breakdown wasn't just because I missed him, although that was a large part of it. There were so many things represented by each tear from my eyes, each shudder down my body, each desperate inhalation and exhalation.

"Hey. Heeeey. Baby, ssshhh." He hitched up a little higher and looked at me thoroughly. "What's all this?"

I shook my head, hopefully communicating that I needed a second. Maybe more than one. All in all, it took several minutes to expunge all my pent-up emotions, but the purge was past necessary. So much shit had built up inside me over the past week. With Elijah being so terse with me, I couldn't very well open up to him about all the scenarios I'd been creating in my mind. All the feelings that had been eating at my confidence, slowly eroding the foundation Bas and I had worked so hard to build.

Finally, I sniffled—fine, it was more of a deep snot suction—causing Sebastian to let me go and dig into his pocket.

"No," I blurted when he offered me a handkerchief. "I'll ruin it," I croaked pathetically.

"Goddammit. Take it, Abbigail. I want you to ruin it." He thrust the linen square toward me again, inserting a gruff laugh. "I see your stubbornness is still in full force. Elijah wasn't joking."

"Fuck Elijah!" I shouted. And meant it completely.

"Wait. Tell me how you really feel." He chuckled again.

"I'm really beginning to hate him, you know?"

Bas heaved out a sigh. "You don't 'hate' him, baby."

"No; I'm pretty sure I hate him. When he's not treating me like a child, he's barking at me like a prisoner. He goes back and forth between the two, and I abhor them both. I've done nothing to deserve this!"

Seemingly in one movement, he rolled over, pushed his back against the headboard, and pulled me onto his lap. His grinning lips disappeared into the loose hair around my shoulders. "God damn I've missed the smell of you," Sebastian growled lowly and nuzzled through my tresses to the skin of my neck. "The taste of you..."

This story continues in
Shark's Rise: *Shark's Edge Book Three!*

ALSO BY
ANGEL PAYNE & VICTORIA BLUE

Shark's Edge Series:
Shark's Edge
Shark's Pride
Shark's Rise

Secrets of Stone Series:
No Prince Charming
No More Masquerade
No Perfect Princess
No Magic Moment
No Lucky Number
No Simple Sacrifice
No Broken Bond
No White Knight
No Longer Lost

ALSO BY ANGEL PAYNE

The Bolt Saga:
Bolt
Ignite
Pulse
Fuse
Surge
Light

Misadventures:
Misadventures with a Time Traveler

Honor Bound:
Saved
Cuffed
Seduced
Wild
Wet
Hot
Masked
Mastered
Conquered
Ruled

Cimarron Series:
Into His Dark
Into His Command
Into Her Fantasies

Temptation Court:
Naughty Little Gift
Pretty Perfect Toy
Bold Beautiful Love

Suited for Sin:
Sing
Sigh
Submit

Lords of Sin:
Trade Winds
Promised Touch
Redemption
A Fire in Heaven
Surrender to the Dawn

ALSO BY VICTORIA BLUE

Misadventures:
Misadventures with a Book Boyfriend
Misadventures at City Hall

**For a full list of Angel's & Victoria's other titles,
visit them at AngelPayne.com & VictoriaBlue.com**

ACKNOWLEDGMENTS

The Shark's Edge series would not be happening without the amazing team at Waterhouse Press, who have believed in this series so steadfastly. Thank you to everyone on this incredible team for your time, passion, belief, and dedication to our tale: Meredith Wild, Jon McInerney, Robyn Lee, Haley Byrd, Keli Jo Nida, Jennifer Becker, Yvonne Ellis, Kurt Vachon, Jesse Kench, Amber Maxwell, and Dana Bridges.

A very special and amazing shout-out to our editorial team, spearheaded by the man with the patience of a god, Scott Saunders. Dude, where would we be without you? We're also grateful to the Waterhouse proofing, copyediting, and formatting teams. Thank you for making it all sparkle!

Gratitude, more than either of us can express, to Martha Frantz for keeping it all real and organized on our social media pages. And to every single member of Victoria's Book Secrets and Payne Passion: We see you! We love you! *Always!*

So many thanks to the beta readers who helped us sort through this one: Amy Bourne and Martha Frantz.

ABOUT ANGEL PAYNE

USA Today bestselling romance author Angel Payne loves to focus on high-heat romance starring memorable alpha men and the women who love them. She has numerous book series to her credit, including the action-packed Bolt Saga and Honor Bound series, Secrets of Stone series (with Victoria Blue), the intertwined Cimarron and Temptation Court series, the Suited for Sin series, and the Lords of Sin historicals, as well as several standalone titles.

Angel is a native Southern Californian, leading to her love of being in the outdoors, where she often reads and writes. She still lives in Southern California with her soul-mate husband and beautiful daughter, to whom she is a proud cosplay/culture con mom. Her passions also include whisky tasting, shoe shopping, and travel.

Visit her at AngelPayne.com

ABOUT VICTORIA BLUE

International bestselling author Victoria Blue lives in her own portion of the galaxy known as Southern California. There, she finds the love and life-sustaining power of one amazing sun, two unique and awe-inspiring planets, and four indifferent yet comforting moons. Life is fantastic and challenging and every day brings new adventures to be discovered. She looks forward to seeing what's next!

Visit her at VictoriaBlue.com